BAD BOY BILLY

A Novel by

LEONARD D. HODERA

ISBN 978-1-0980-9024-1 (paperback)
ISBN 978-1-0980-9025-8 (digital)

Christian Faith Publishing, Inc.
832 Park Avenue
Meadville, PA 16335
www.christianfaithpublishing.com

Printed in the United States of America

SIGNPOSTS

When I first started telling stories about my life, my listeners invariably asked how I remembered the episodes with such clarity. At best, my answer was a blank stare accompanied by a shrug and a few dribbled words. The question, however, took root, and after a while it became clear to me that the significant signposts of my life—anyone's, for that matter—are staked in the heart, not the brain. And that once branded there by intense feelings will remain there as lucid as yesterday. I further formed the opinion that these scars shape a person's personality and that the process is continuous. The premise then: this piece of God's clay was first sculpted into good and bad by a passionate experience and so clarifies and justifies my "Jekyll and Hyde" existence at the time. If this sounds ominous, it need not be, for the underlying gift in my telling is humorous. So hopefully, in this coming-of-age story, *The Adventures of Bad Boy Billy*, you will laugh at my misfortune, credit its innocence, and forgive my darkness. And above all, recognize that although we are all made of the same clay, its form is continuously forged by chance and circumstance. So then, one may ask, are we to blame for what we have become? And if so, to what degree? I leave that for you to contemplate.

—L. D. Hodera

1

Facing Baloney

I'm twelve years old and the folks are kicking me out! Can you believe? They're shipping me up to Wisconsin to live on a farm with Old Lady Ga-raaab, who I met once—which was enough. She doesn't even speak English. In fact, they don't even have electricity. Dick says she's got it, but won't let anybody use it. *And,* that the bathroom is a board with a hole in it...outside, down the hill somewhere. Unbelievable! "Yeah, you heard 'em, huh girl?" Queenie's got her snoot on my leg and I'm rubbing the soft furry hair on the top of her head. She's so smart. She's way smarter than my sister. "Yeah, girl." She just gave my hand a couple'a licks. We've been sitting out here in the dugout, in the prairie out back my house, trying to figure out why they want to get rid of me. I mean like, *what did I do?* Boy, they're just lucky I'm not the type to go jump off a bridge. Anyway. That's stupid. Besides that, I'm Catholic. You go to hell for that: burn, burn, burn. Not me, bub.

So now I'm thinkin' there was that night when I was getting ready for bed, *that* could'a done it. "Stella look," said my dad. "Da boy skin an' bones." And there were tears leaking into his voice when he said it. And *that,* the tears, *that's* the clue. Oh yeah, sneaky, sneaky. You can't trust parents, you know. And like my dad, he's triple sneaky. Oh yeah! My uncles don't call him 'Slick' for nothin'.

Not that I'm not on the puny side and sickly, I am. I catch every germ that exists. Everything that crawls, flies, or glows in the dark.

5

Uh-huh. So tell me, why are they sending me up to a wilderness with horseflies, cholera, typhoid, and the black plague? I'll tell you why. Because they want to break up my gang, that's why. That's gotta be it. Yeah. Just because we got into a little trouble at Montgomery Ward's—stole some hand tools, for Pete's sake. We just wanted to see if we could get away with it. Oh, and then, of course, there was that little episode when Dick and I got caught with Eleanor. But hey, it was her said: "I'll show you mine, you show me yours." Not that there was all that much to see. Heck, I had more fun playing 'Doctor' when I was seven. Boy, I tellya', I had a lotta nerve back then. With girls, I mean. Not now I don't. I don't know why. "Yeah, girl." I rubbed Queenie's ears. She likes that.

"Billy, we're sending you up to Wisconsin to live on the farm with my grandmother." That's what she said, my mom—she's the talker. That's what she said; throwing it out there like it was garbage. My dad just stood there, waiting to see how I'd take it. Like a kick in the pants, that's how I took it. And then she says, "You want to go, don't you?" I shot back, "'Sure! Great! When?" Didn't they know I was just kidding? Just acting tough? I expected her to go on, say something like, "You don't really want to go, do you?" And I would've answered, "Noooo, not really." And then words would be bouncin' off the walls and that would be that. And then probably before I went to bed my mom would get out the graham crackers and milk and we'd sit there and dunk them and smile at each other like we just robbed a bank.

Geez, school lets out next week and it's baseball, and swimming, and…and everything! And I'm going to be up in some dinky little Lublin town, a speck so small it's not even on the map. The train doesn't even stop there, stops eight miles up the track at a dot called Thorpe. That's where my dad's from, Thorpe, Wisconsin. Uncle Tom and Aunt Rose still live there on a farm that's best for growing rocks—thanks to Grandpa Andrew…bought it *sight unseen* when he came over from Poland. But enough of that. I tellya' there's gotta be more to this than meets the eye. I mean, heck, I could get fat right here in Chicago if it means that much to them. Anyway. I *like* being skinny. I can slip through crowds like you wouldn't believe. And I don't hardly take up any room. I don't even leave a shadow. And skinny or not, nobody picks a fight with me because they know it means blood—even if it's all mine. So, here's the thing: *I just don't like to eat.* Stopping to eat when I could be outside playing is just plain dumb. It's stupid! It's Idiotic It's a *complete* waste of time!

Oh, I could've told them all that. All that and more. I could've told them that my stomach was probably the size of a walnut because, way back when, the babysitters shrunk it with their slimy, lumpy oatmeal that I'd spoon into my knee-socks and feed to the wind when it dried. And I could've told them that my Uncle Leo spent more time with my babysitters than I did. He'd pull up in his yellow roadster, give me a nickel, and boot me out the door. No lunch, no snacks, just that wonderful brown slab of Holloway Sucker from the basement candy store around the corner. Ohhh yeah, I could've told them all that. But what's the use. Folks don't much listen to kids—especially when there's a war on. Yeah, World War II is raging. But hey, it's on the other side of the world.

The only good news is that Dick's coming up just as soon as he gets out of Montefiore, which isn't exactly a reform school but you have to be bad to get in. Richard being my uncle is kind'a weird if you ask me, since he's only a year older than me. Anyway, I never-ever call him *Uncle Richard*, except when he twists my arm into a pretzel.

Actually, what gets me, what really hurts—if you really want to think about it—is how they could even consider sending me away. I couldn't send Queenie away for the whole summer. You know how long that is? That's like *forever.* After all, it's not like I'm a piece of old furniture, you know. I'm their own flesh and blood, for chrissake! So what it all boils down to is just this: *they don't want me.* That's it! That's the whole tamale...

The church bell starts ringing out six o'clock. Queenie starts barking. We climb out of the dugout and take off. We run like we always do, fast, like the wind.

2

The Kiss Off

School let out two days ago and already they got me packin' my bag. Geez, you'd think they'd let me lay around a while, get used to the idea. I mean, hey-hey, what's the rush? I've never been away from home before and I'm supposed to act like I'm dying to go? Just because they got this new bulletproof idea that that's what boys do: go away and make their mark in the world. Pray tell, what kind of a dent is a skinny little runt like me going to make? Uh-uh. I just don't think I'm ready for this. What I mean is: I don't feel the urge. Oh, I admit a small part of me does—a very small part, like my little finger.

"Billy, we're going! Come on!" That's brat sister at the bottom of the stairs. You can bet they're not going to send brat-face out into the world when she gets older, out to a faraway destination that's not even on the map. Oh, nooo. She's too cute, too nice, too talented. And on top of that, she's not skinny, or sickly, or whatever. Don't you just hate people like that? Perfect little dumplings with dark eyes, and dark hair—like Cleopatra—and two of the cutest little dimples you ever did see. A living doll, she is. And on top of that the kid tap dances, sings, all that crap. Yuk!

Actually, I'd like to take tap dance lessons. I really would. I'm great on my feet. But I don't dare mention it. If I did they'd probably send me off to a farm in Poland, for chrissake. As for dark hair, I got loads of it. Grows in all directions like a wild plant, and hangs down in front of my eyes no matter how much Wave Set my mom uses.

She wants to try bobby pins but I told her, '*over my dead body*'. My eyes, by the way, are unique: gray-green like my dad's. So, there. Not bad, huh?

So anyway, to be truthful—scout's honor and all that crap—I have to admit stumble-foot is quite good. The only problem is she never looks like she's enjoying it. The kid never smiles. She's got this frozen-doll expression. Yet, I can get her laughing like an idiot just by beaning her with a pillow. Strange kid. I can't figure her out. When I was eight, Ha! I ran wild and the wind played wonderful tunes on my ribs. I swam oceans, climbed mountains, all that stuff. Anyway, forget about twinkle toes. All I'm trying to say is this: *I'm not ready for this trip!* Nope. Sorry.

Down in the kitchen, I joined my dad looking out the screen door... Summer never looked better. Everything green was greener and taller... Even the air smelled green. Dad turned to me and stuck out his hand. We shook, and I kissed his hand—which I didn't have to do unless I was bad, but I did it anyway. He pulled me to his chest and cupped my head with his hand. I could hear his heart beating.

"Be good boy," he said. "And eat!" Then he held me out at arm's length and looked me in the eye. "You need eat, William," he said, his voice growing thick. "Da haying...hard work." He looked out the screen door, his eyes blinking.

"Do I have to go today, Dad? I could go when Richard goes. It be better, Dad!"

"Errrrrrm," growled my dad. "Who knows Richard goes. You got ticket, you go now... It be good." He dug his wallet out of his back pocket. "Open da hand." I did, and he made a big production out of counting five one-dollar bills into it.

"Wooow! Thanks, Dad." I shuffled them together and wondered how much I'd get for coming back.

"Put in back pocket. Don't lose."

I did, figuring that later I'd pin them inside the pocket like my Aunt Minnie showed me the first time she gave me a dollar bill—which she always did.

"Nick! What about Leo?" my mother called out.

"I give 'im already! Agh!" Dad slapped another dollar bill into my hand. "Give Leo. Don't lose." Then in a jerky move, he again held me out by my shoulders. "You eat. You grow big and strong."

And then his mouth kept working, but nothing came out. He stood tall, swallowed hard, and called out, "Stella! We be late!" Again he stuck out his hand...gave me one hard shake. "Stella!" And out the door he went. His long strides carried him down the walkway. He took the stepping-stones left, ducked into the garage, and was gone.

I stared out at the blurry green summer and wondered how I was supposed to grow big and strong when he was not big and strong. My whole family was though. They were all giants. I kid you not! Dad's sister, my Aunt Minnie on the South side, her kids were like unbelievable. They got fingers like sausages and...and shoes like boats. Really. They were like something out of a comic book. 'Course none of that seemed to bother my dad any. He just tapped his temple with a finger and smiled.

I watched my mom at the dining room table address an envelope. She worked now at the new Zenith factory on Austin Avenue. She wound radio coils for walkie-talkies. It was hard on her eyes, but she wasn't about to give it up. She liked the paycheck.

"Dad's waitin', Mom."

"You have your train ticket?" Mom licked a stamp and stuck it on the envelope.

"Yep. It's right here." I pat my shirt pocket.

She slipped the envelope into her purse, popped to her feet, and gave me a face full of troubles.

"Dad's waitin', Mom. You—"

She covered my mouth with her hand and shook her head. "You're too small." I tapped my temple with a finger.

She wrapped her beautiful arms around me, and we swayed from side to side. My mom was a beautiful woman; everybody said so. "Don't lift anything heavy, you hear? Don't try to be like Richard." Mom shot me out by my shoulders. "Promise me."

"I promise, Mom."

She started fishing in her purse.

"Make Dad come up for the Fourth of July, okay?" My voice started to flood. "You gotta come, Mom."

"Here," she said, slapping two dollars into my hand. "For Old Lady Garaaab. Don't lose it." She slapped me another buck. "For Leo." Then came some change: a quarter, a couple of nickels, some pennies...

"That's enough, Mom. I don't need any more."

"Give me some." It was the money-smeller, brat sister, with her hand out. She'd been waiting to be dropped off at the babysitter's.

"Say goodbye to your brother."

"Goodbye, brother." Her hand was still out. I dropped three cents into it. She gave me her sourpuss look. I added a nickel. She clamped her hand shut. "You're going on the faaaarm." Brat face ran out of the room. "Mommy, come on! Daddy's waiting!" The screen door slammed.

Two short notes from our Plymouth cut through the air.

Mom grabbed me, hugged me close, and I felt her shudder. "You have to make the best of it," she whispered. And with a kiss on my forehead, she was off and running. "Don't forget to lock the doors!"

"I won't, Mom!" I yelled after her as she took the steps and flew down the walkway. "Don't forget to write!"

Thinking she might not have heard that last part, I dashed out to the porch railing, but she was already out the gate. I was about to shout again when I heard the car door slam and the roar of the engine. A moment later, the black Plymouth shot left from behind our two-car garage, and with smoke trailing and cinders flying, it barreled past the Lewandowskis', past the empty lot, and then swinging a right onto Altgeldt, the chrome bumper flashed in the sun, and they were gone.

I sat on the porch swing and pushed off the railing. The chains screeched and groaned just like my guts were screeching and groaning, "How can they do this to me?" I pushed off with both feet as

hard as I could. The swing jumped and jerked, the chains shuddering, screaming at me, telling me they were going to snap and send
me flying over the railing…which wouldn't be the worst thing, really.
Through the Lewandowskis' back porch and across Altgeldt, I could
see our school, Saint James. It was a three-story brick with the church
at the bottom—which was kind of depressing, if you ask me, because
once you were inside, you had to go down five wide marble steps,
and then five more, and to me going down was like for hell, going up
was for heaven. Oh well, I guess nobody else gives a shit.

Little old ladies shuffled in for the seven o'clock mass, their
heads covered with babushkas. The church bell started ringing out
a seven count. Smitty and Gene were serving mass; they were altar
boys. I wasn't. I tried out, recited some Latin; that was that. Then
I tried out for patrol boy. I stood on my tiptoes, but I was still the
shortest. That ended that. 'Course if they had tryouts for the bravest,
the smartest, the best-looking guy in school, that one I'd win. Ha!
Who am I kidding?

I kept the swing going with a little push. The cool air cooled my
sweat, and the chains settled down to a soft groan. The prairie out
back of our garage stretched all the way down to the other end of the
block, and in some places it was as thick as a jungle. It was ours, the
guys' and mine. It was our turf. And at this end was our dugout. And
at the other end we'd cleared enough land so we could play baseball
and football… It was ours, all right. We fought for it, bled on it, every
day of our lives. It was our Indian cowboy and Tarzan land. It was
where we play cops and robbers, hide-and-seek, horse and war. It was
where we killed Germans, blew up Japs, and shot the bad guys: John
Dillinger, Pretty-Boy Floyd, Baby-Face Nelson—you name 'em. It
was where we flew kites and played marbles and knocked each other
down. Where we roasted potatoes in a fire till they were black as
coal, salted them, and gobbled them up. It was where I snuck out at
night to stare at the moon and wonder about the stars. It was where I
thought about the oceans I would swim and the mountains I would
climb. It was where I ran through the deep snow with Queenie till
we fell down, then lay still and puffed steam until the cold began

to sting. It was ours, I tell ya! Every lump of dirt! Every rock! Every weed! All of it! A place nobody could take away from us.

Nobody ever!

In the living room I popped out the unique turntable on our new Philco Radio and played my favorite record, "To Each His Own." It was Mom's favorite too. Eddie Howard spun the words:

"A roooose must remain…with the suuuun and the rain…"

Not the greatest voice, but I liked it. He sounded real, like just a regular guy singing a song. "To eeeach his own… I foooound my own… One and only yooou…"

I sprawled out on our Oriental rug and let the music carry me away.

"Two liiips must insist…on to mooore to be kissed. Or its lovely promise wooon't come truuue…"

Funny how a song could grab you and not let go. How the words fit the music so perfectly. Like they were made for each other.

"To eeeach his own… I foooound my own… One and only yooooou…"

I let it play again…and again and agaaaaaain… I woke up, shut down the Philco, and went upstairs to my folks' bedroom. In the bottom drawer of their dresser, I dug out the Chez Pa'ris program. In it were pictures of showgirls in skimpy outfits. I was in and out of the bathroom in a matter of minutes—practice makes perfect, you know. My South-side cousin, Ray Obrycki, told me how the priest caught some altar boys doing the "bad thing" and blistered their hands with a yardstick. Then he pumped his fist in the air and asked me if I knew what that meant. I said I did, but I didn't, really.

But it got me thinking, and it didn't take me long to figure it out. Not a bad thing at all. Terrific, in fact. He also said that if you did it more than once a day, you could go blind. So anyway, I was done for the day, and it was always hard to wait for tomorrow, but it was something to look forward to.

I let the water in the kitchen sink run until it got good and cold then filled a glass and gulped it down. Delicious. The brass alarm clock on top of the oven ticked away 8:51. I had hours to kill.

Uncle Leo wouldn't be picking me up until eleven o'clock. I went out front and sat on the concrete steps to wait for Smitty and Gene. Big black ants scurried about and peeked into cracks. Early morning, and already the sun was blazing hot. Hot enough to fry ants with a magnifying glass. But that was for kids, little squirts. Those days were long gone... Yeah. Bucktown... Rats the size of cats used to barrel down the gangway and knock me over like a bowling ball. Then under the porch their red beady eyes would follow me down the steps to our basement flat. At night they'd be runnin' around inside the walls... I used to think everybody had rats. Huh! Then the attic flat way out west on Luna Avenue. The only good thing about it was the flat roof outside the back window. Dad nailed some boards around it, and we slept out there the whole summer... had the stars and the moon for a ceiling. One night I woke up, and I heard a baby crying. I went into the kitchen, and this big lady dressed in white said to me, "Look what I pulled out of a hat, a sweet little baby sister." I asked her if she could put her back in and pull me out a brother. I was five. What did I know?

Then we moved over a few blocks to Drummond Avenue, into a second-story flat with that mean landlord. This yo-yo drove some nails halfway into his cheery tree so I wouldn't climb it. So the tree bloomed, and I hammered in the nails and got a bunch of flowers for my mom. Yo-yo rapped on the door, and I went three rounds with my mom. I was going to poison, the old fart, but I never got around to it. Dick came over one time. I told him not to cut through the park. He did, and a gang'a girls jumped him and painted his you-know-what with lipstick. I called it the red dart. Dick twisted my arm into a pretzel, but it was worth it. Yeeeeah, that was one tough neighborhood.

During the BB gun wars, I got nailed five times: three times in the back, once in the chest, and once in the leg. Stung like hell...

Then we moved out here, into the sticks, out past the end of the Fullerton Avenue streetcar line, 2510 North Mango Avenue. A brick bungalow with six rooms. And I liked it. I liked it a lot. I even liked the name: Maanggooooo. Got a mysterious ring to it. The streets weren't paved, but who needed it? They were gravel, topped with tar down the middle that bubbled in the hot sun and popped a tune when a car ran over them. You could get a few notes with a bicycle too. Hey, I was even startin' to talk to girls. "Hi ya," I yelled out when I zipped by them on my bike... And there was this girl, down the block, driving me nuts. Arlene Kieta. Every time she looked at me, I about ran my bike into a tree. I was gonna kiss her one of these days. Knock her for a loop. She couldn't wait. I could tell by the way she rolled her eyes at me. Oh yeah, one of these days. *Pow*! Right on the kisser...one of these days.

Boy, oh boy, oh boy, look at all these houses. All lined up shoulder-to-shoulder tryin' to look different. But they were all the same. Except each house was built with a different vomit-like colored brick—breakfast being the lightest, and so on. We lived in a lunch-type.

I guess you could call this a Polish neighborhood because most of the ring tags on my route had names like Kurzawski, Wade (used to be Wadelewski), Neimerowicz, Klescz, Prokopowicz, Borowski, Porkomowski, Kubiak, Kieta, Spitek, Dombek, Benecki (our house), Kalinowski, Kaminski, and more *ski*. Maybe that was why it was such a good neighborhood, because Polish people trusted in God and were honest and hardworking—that was what Sister Sponsa said, my sixth-grade teacher. She said even though Poland was being chopped into pie, the people stood strong and proud and bore their grief with dignity and grace. I didn't quite get it all, but it sounded good.

Right now I had fifty-eight dailies and thirty-seven Sunday papers, but my route was growing because of the war. They said the war would be over by the time I grew up. I hoped not. I'd like to serve my country, get a medal or two or three. My mom would be proud. Dad would say I was a fool, that I could get killed, but deep down, I was sure he'd be proud. There'd be a blue star hanging in our living room window, just like the ones I saw on my route. Some had two or three even, and Mr. and Mrs. Borowski, they had four…two of them gold. A lot of them were gold. When I made the Friday collection at a house with a gold star, you could feel the sadness as soon as the door opened. The lady looked like she'd never smile again. And the inside of the house, you could see looked dark and cold, and even if it was summer, you knew the sun would not find its way in. I didn't ever want to be a gold star in a window and have anyone see my mom or my dad's face. But if the war was still on when I got old enough, I would go to it. And I would pray, like I bet everybody else did, that God would let me live.

Smitty and Gene were crossing Altgeldt. Now there was a name not only looked like a mistake, but sounded like one. Gene was a shirt-and-tie guy. There was like three of them in the whole school, and he was one of them. Smitty was in a T-shirt and blue jeans, our usual garb. Smitty waved a stick in the air, then swung it like a baseball bat. I waved back and head down to the shade of the maple tree out by the street. Queenie started barking; she could see me through the basement windows.

"Queenie, quiet!"

She stopped barking. She was so smart. I jumped up, grabbed a branch, and counted off some chin-ups.

"Three, four—"

"What time you leavin', Billy?" yelled Smitty.

"Eleven o'clock! Seven, eight, nine, ten." I dropped down, grabbed the stick from Smitty, and took a couple of swings. "So what's with the big meeting?" I fished a pebble out of the grass, tossed it up, and smacked a line drive.

"Same old stuff—extra carnival passes for extra masses." Gene leaned over, and with one finger he very carefully swiped the sweat from his brow. "Hey, my dad's going to sponsor our team."

"Yeah! Told ya, Billy!" said Smitty, his white teeth flashing. "Mr. Wade's gettin' us uniforms! Everything! The whole works! And he's going to be our coach! We're going to be the Wrens. That's a bird."

I smacked a high-flyer. "What happened to 'Polski Boys'?"

The three of us looked at each other and cracked up. I tossed the stick back to Smitty.

Gene pulled his tie loose, snapped it like a whip. "League play starts the Fourth of July. We need you, buddy." Gene finished tucking his tie into his shirt pocket. "All you got to do is say the word, and I'll have my dad talk to your dad."

"Mr. Wade's gotten me off plenty of times."

I shook my head. "It won't work."

"What'a ya got to lose?"

"It's too late! I'm leavin'!"

Smitty smacked a hot grounder up the middle.

Queenie was barking now and wouldn't quit. "Queenie, stop it!" She wound it down and stopped. I started kicking at the base of the maple tree. "It'd just be a waste of time, Gene."

"O...kay! It's your funeral." Gene swept the sweat from his brow with all four fingers this time—again, very neatly. Gene was a big-time sweater and wiper.

Smitty swung and missed. The pebble bounced in the grass.

"Norb's splittin' my route with you, right?"

"Yeah, he wants to lose weight." Smit swung again...the pebble climbed the sky. "What do ya think he weighs?"

I shrugged. "I don't know."

"Two hundred, I bet." Smitty tossed me the stick. I tossed it to Gene.

Gene whipped it up and back, making the air hum. "We got to meet the guys, Smit."

"Yeah! Swimmin' lessons start today, Billy!"

"So? Big deal. Dick says we got swimmin' holes all over the place."

"You got girls?"

"Yeeeah, we got girls. Two of 'em. Beauties, Dick says."

"Billy, I gotta tell you, something," Gene put a hand on my shoulder, gave me a big smile. "I got my eye on Arlene."

"So?" I shrugged the hand off. "What's it to me?"

"Oookaaay. Don't say I didn't warn you." Gene tossed the stick to Smitty.

"Let's go, Smit." Smitty stared at me. "See ya, Billy." He knocked me an easy one on the arm and turned to go.

"Wait!" I bit my lip. "I'm gonna come back right after the 4th, right after the hayin'."

"You mean it?" said Smitty.

I looked over to Gene, gave him a nod. "I'll be back, hook or crook." Smitty thrust the stick like a toreador killing a bull. "Mooahhh!"

"Put her there, buddy." Gene stuck out his hand, and we shook. Smitty and I exchanged hard smacks on the arm.

And then just like that, they were gone…off to a great summer.

Gene was a great handshaker. He put it out there with a smile, gave you a strong grip, and added just the right number of pumps, like all great con artists; only Gene was sincere. It was the way he was brought up, on the straight and narrow. So I could never let his dad talk to my dad. They didn't speak the same language.

The ticking clock read 9:45. I opened the door next to the stove, and Queenie came charging up the basement stairs. Out the screen door we went, racing for the gate. I opened it, and in a flash we were running on the path through the jungle of giant sunflower stalks that led to our dugout, an eightfoot square about four feet deep. We'd tried putting a plywood roof over a part of it, but the older guys kept caving it in. I dodged around the dugout and slapped Queenie on the snoot playfully.

"I'm going to miss you, girl."

She yapped and snapped at my hands in return.

We got Queenie as a pup from the Novak's over on Major Avenue. Mr. Novak told us that Queenie was mostly collie and part stranger. When I told people that, they laughed, but they wouldn't tell me why. Finally, I figured it out. I don't see that it's anything to laugh about. Queenie's still the smartest and best-looking collie I ever saw. And like I said, she understands everything I say. And if she does something bad, she puts her head down right away. I'm really going to miss her. Not my sister. Not a drop. She's a pain…you know where. She sneezes and I get blamed.

"C'mon, girl!"

We raced back to the house, our feet barely touching…flying now. We broke out into the cinder alley. I slammed into the gate. Queenie barked her head off, wanting to run some more.

"Go, girl!" I waved down the alley. "Go! I don't want to get all sweated up. Go!"

I slapped my hands together, and Queenie took off. I stepped through the gate, closed it, and hung my arms over the top.

The sunflower stalks had already grown so high I could hardly see the cars parked on Menard, Grandma Helen's street…used to be. Boy, nothing beat Friday nights at Grandma's house. Hmmm, cinnamon babka—the smell alone could make your mouth water. I should've bottled it. I would've made a fortune. It was more cinnamon than cake, and the cinnamon just ooozed out. Ohhh, so good. But it wasn't just the eating part that got me. It was about all of us just sitting around the big round table in the basement talking, shouting, laughing…laughing till the tears came.

Now Grandma Helen was up there with the angels. All because of Ed Moritz. That madman. But I didn't want to think about him. Uh-uh. So anyway, Aunt Jean made the babka after that. That was, until the bank sold the house. I'm going to rob me a bank someday, you'll see. Aunt Jean just got married to this ex-boxer/wrestler guy, George Bauer. He's Hungarian. He told me that was just like Polish, only better. Aunt Jean hit him on the head with a pot when he said that. Uncle George just laughed and said, "My little firecracker. Hit me again, sweetheart." I'm telling you he's a card. I like him almost as much as I like my Uncle Leo.

Damn that Ed Moritz! I couldn't stop thinking about him. His white hair slicked back, that pink face, eyes that burned holes in you. Him and his whips! Three leather strands with a wooden handle, wrapped up like a peppermint stick. He passed them out to the mothers on Christmas Eve to use on their kids. Everybody laughed, thought it was a joke. It was no joke.

A real Dr. Jekyll and Mr. Hyde he was, flashing his good side just long enough for Grandma Helen to marry him. Then Mr. Hyde took over, and Grandma died of a stomach ailment. Uncle Leo found out that Moritz's first two wives died of the same ailment. The family didn't take him to court, but what they did do was take him for a long ride. Then they ripped off all his clothes and warned him about ever returning. And to make sure he understood, they changed his face a bit—like put his nose over by his ear. Nobody has seen or heard of him since.

Queenie came trotting out of the field.

"Have a good run, girl?" I opened the gate, and we ran through the yard, up on the porch, and into the kitchen. It was 10:40! My heart raced. I closed the door, turned the bolt, and latched the chain.

"Come on, girl." We scrambled down the basement stairs.

Without stopping, I snatched up Queenie's water bowl, and we went over to the laundry sink, where I let the water run, let it get nice and cold. Queenie jumped her front paws up onto the sink and started licking my face.

"You know, don't you, girl?" Oh, she knew, all right. You could tell by the way she was nuzzling me and whimpering. I stroked her face. "I wish you could come with me, but you can't. Uh-uh. No! No, Queenie!" I held her by her ears. "You can't! I'm sorry. You have to stay here and take care of the house. That's your job."

I took the bowl back over to the stairway, set it down, and sat on the steps. Queenie took a couple of half-hearted licks at the water then moved up and started nuzzling my hands. "Too bad you can't go with me, girl." I ran a finger along the white stripe on the top of her head. "All that land up there. We could run forever. Milking time we'd run and get the cows, and you could chase rabbits and squirrels, chipmunks…everything that moves. Yeah, too bad." I leaned back on the stairs, and Queenie settled her head on my chest. I rubbed her ears. She likes that.

Two toots from a car horn and I was up on my feet. A barking Queenie beat me to the basement windows. Uncle Leo and his sidekick Dice were out front in his baby-blue Cadillac convertible, whitewall tires, and chrome aplenty. Two longer toots rang out.

"I gotta go!" I headed for the stairs. Queenie barked liked crazy. "I gotta go, girl! I can't help it!" I dropped to a knee and hugged her. She squirmed and squelled and licked my face. I held her head still. Her dark eyes were killing me. "You be good, okay? I have to go and do the haying. But I'll be back, okay?"

Queenie broke my hold, jumped and squealed and barked and cried.

"Queenie, stop it!" I grabbed her tight around the neck. "Easy, girl, easy... No! Now stop it!" I gripped her long hair and held her head still. "You have to make the best of it, see?" Queenie squealed. "You do! You have to!" I tossed Queenie aside and bolted up the stairs. Queenie was on my heels. I leaped into the kitchen and slammed the door in her face. "I'm sorry! I'm sorry, Queenie! I'm sooooorrrry!" I hung there with the doorknob in my hand. I couldn't let go. From the Caddy came a long blaring note that wouldn't quit. Queenie barked and pawed at the door. I let go, grabbed my suitcase, dashed out of the kitchen, stopped, dashed back in, opened the fridge, grabbed the brown bag with my lunch, closed it, and took off though the dining room and the living room. I opened the front door. The Caddy's long noisy note stopped. I pushed the button in on the lock, closed the door, ran to the car, tossed my suitcase and lunch bag into the back seat, jumped in, and we were spitting gravel before my pants hit the seat.

3

The Last Goodbye

Tar bubbles popped as we zipped down Mango. We passed the school building...the reception hall...the rectory...the apple orchard... then skidded to a stop at Fullerton Avenue, the loose gravel pinging the Caddie's underside. Two nuns waiting to cross the intersection spun around to give us a look.

"We're headed downtown, sisters," shouted Uncle Leo. "Need a lift?"

The black hooded nuns poked their heads about like a couple of nervous crows. Dice and I slid down in our seats.

Uncle Leo tooted two short notes and wheeled a left onto Fullerton Avenue.

Everybody envied Uncle Leo's devil-may-care attitude. That was what Uncle George said, and that he was a man's man. And of course, he was also a ladies' man. After all, he was six feet four, and his brown wavy hair gave him at least another inch. You could always spot him in a crowd because he stood so tall and proud. His face used to be a little too cute, but then somebody broke his nose, and that fixed it. But he was not a ladies' man anymore because my Aunt Sophie put a ring on his finger and one in his nose.

My dad always said, "How dat man got woman like dat." He liked the way Aunt Sophie always stuck up for her man. Like even when their ship was sinking, she said not to worry because Leo could walk on water. Truth was, he couldn't even swim. But he was still my favorite.

They worked the graveyard shift at Tropic-Aire. Unc was a foreman, and he was only twenty-three. Dice had a caved-in chest and a honker like Dick Tracy. His real name was Florry, but Unc called him Dice because he was great at palming the cubes. All summer long they beat the carnivals for prizes that they sold at a nice profit. My uncle's part of the deal was to keep Dice from getting killed whenever he was caught cheating, or thought to be—which was pretty much the same thing.

We crossed Central Avenue, and the smooth concrete street changed to bumpy redbrick. This was where the streetcar line started and ran straight as an arrow out to Lincoln Park on the shores of Lake Michigan. Uncle Leo wasn't about to bounce the Caddy's bolts loose, so we slowed to a crawl. He turned the radio on. Perry Como was crooning "Till the End of Time." He was good, but he was no Sinatra.

We glided along, the radio playing one hit after another: "Gooonna Taaake a Sentimental Journey…" Doris Day, oh yeah. "I'm Gonna Buy a Papper Doooll That I Can Caaall My Ooown." The Mills Brothers, smooth as glass. "I'lll Never Smiiile Agaain, Until I Smiile at Yoooou."

Frankie, the swoon king, laid them in the aisles. And get this, he was skinnier than me! Just ahead was Saint Stanislaus. It was huge with a lot of stained glass and a bunch of steeples. I went to first grade there when we lived on Drummond. The first day nun cracked me across the puss, and everybody laughed. And that was all I remember about first grade. Except for this girl with freckles and a cute upturned nose…and big brown eyes. Actually, all I wanted to do was count her freckles. Actually, that was a lie. I wanted to kiss her.

We catch a red light at Cicero Avenue. It was a wide street with a streetcar line that runs on, like, forever. I didn't think anybody knew where it ended. South Cicero was gangster land. Al Capone used to own it. Those were the days. *Rat-tat-tat-tat*…and *rat-tat-tat*, in case they were still blinking.

Crawford Avenue was coming up. It was also called Pulaski Road—don't ask me why. The Embassy Theatre is just off the corner on the left. It's got a domed ceiling with a lotta little lights that blink like stars. You could make out the constellations like Aries, Cancer, Eagle, and of course, Bird of Paradise. It was really neat. And on a small balcony on the left was an organ with huge golden pipes and red velvet all around. When this old man with gray hair played it, it went right through you. It did. Really. We used to go there a lot when we lived on Drummond. We used to walk to save streetcar fare. It took like an hour, with my baby sister in a buggy. On the way back, I'd climb into the buggy and curl myself around sweetie-poo and go off to dreamland—unless, of course, we saw a Frankenstein movie, which in that case I'd be peeking out watching to see if anyone was walking around with their arms stretched out. I'm not kidding!

Dice twisted around in his seat. "Hey! Why so quiet?"

I gave Dice a disgusted look.

Uncle Leo eyed me in the rearview mirror. "He's leavin' home, leave 'im alone."

"Hell, when I was a kid, I couldn't wait to get outta the house. My old man used to beat the shit out of me."

"Tell 'im. Go on, tell 'im."

"Agh!" said Dice, with a toss of his head.

"Go ooon. Tell him."

Dice looked back at me. "It was my birthday, see. I was fifteen. So my mom gets me this birthday cake…candles and all…they're burnin'…and she's singin' 'Happy Biiirthday.' My old man spits on the cake. Yeah. Soooo I got out my Louisville Slugger, and I whacked him. Played a little tune on him."

I caught Uncle Leo in the mirror nodding at me.

"Then my mom picks up the bat, and she plays a few notes." Dice roared crazy like then stopped dead. "The bottle got 'em. Got 'em both."

We weaved through the light traffic; people's heads were turning, staring at us in our classy Caddy.

"Look, the Liberty Theatre." I pointed right and stood up.

"Give me Liberty, or give me death!"

"Sit down," yelled Dice.

"You're gonna fall outta the car! Jee-zus!"

24

Uncle Leo tooted the horn. We laughed. I told them that during the winter, me and Dad and Uncle George used to go there every Friday night. And that Aunt Jean and my mom stayed home because they didn't like cowboy movies. They used to do their hair.

"They got the best popcorn," said Dice.

"Yeah." I licked my lips.

A block down, the Avon Theatre came up. Uncle Leo blared the horn. "Wake up, bums!"

"Triple features round the clock!" yelled Dice, his arms in the air.

"We went there one time," I told them. "Bums were sprawled out all over the place. And when we got home, Mom and Aunt Jean made us take a bath!" Dice threw me a glance. "They did, Dice! I'm not kidding! They did, Unc!"

Uncle Leo beeped the horn at least a half a dozen times.

I thought my Uncle Leo was a little horn-crazy. But hey, nobody's perfect.

Doris Day was cranking out: "A Guy Is a Guy..." Goofy song, but I'd marry her tomorrow.

We reached downtown early, so we zigzagged slowly through the streets and took in the classy girls in their summer dresses. Uncle Leo tooted at the "lookers." On LaSalle Street, the traffic noise drowned out the horn, so I took to waving and yelling out, "Hi!" A girl in a red dress waved back.

"She waved at me, Unc! Did you see her? The girl in the red dress! She waved at me!"

"Kid's a killer! Right, Dice?"

"Kid's a killer!"

We turned under the elevated train tracks at Wells and followed the loop that it made around downtown. I spotted the Chicago Theatre on State Street. That was the stop Mom, Connie, and I got off to meet Dad to celebrate one of our birthdays. We ate Chinese food, then caught a movie and a stage show at either the Chicago or the Oriental Theatre around the corner. Boy, that was what I called a treat.

Under the tracks on Van Buren, everything got pretty quiet. It was like we were going to a hanging. Mine. After a ways, Uncle Leo pulled up to a dark, dingy building with big shiny brass letters over the entrance: "LaSalle Street Station."

"This is it, kid," said my uncle, turning in his seat. "Dice. Go with 'im."

Dice climbed out, grabbed my suitcase, and headed for the entrance. I jumped out with my crumpled lunch bag in hand.

"Got your ticket?"

I patted my shirt pocket. "Yep."

"Don't go screwing any sheep."

I gave my uncle a puzzled look. "They don't have sheep, do they?" Unc flicked a finger at me. "Go."

I quickly laid two dollars down on the front seat and took off. "Bye, Unc!" I caught up to Dice waiting at the entrance.

"Dice!" yelled Uncle Leo.

Dice scooted back to the car with my suitcase still in hand. They exchanged some words, and Dice started back. I led the way through the revolving doors and stopped dead in my tracks. The place was like a huge golden cave, and I mean huge. Hundreds, no, thousands of lights gave the place a golden glow. Even the marble floor shined like gold.

"Wooow. You could play baseball in here."

"Big Muther." Dice ran his eyes around the station, drew on his cigarette. "I can take it from here, Dice."

"You sure?"

"Yeah, yeah. Sure."

Dice set down my suitcase. "You ask for the Soo Line."

"To Lublin, Wisconsin, yeah."

"Thorpe, Wisconsin!"

"Yeah, yeah, Thorpe. The train doesn't stop in Lublin."

Dice took a last drag on his cigarette, dropped the butt on the polished marble, gave it some footwork, then reached over and stuffed something into my shirt pocket. "From Big Lee." Dice pointed his hand at me gun-like: "Pow!" He spun around and went out the revolving door.

I fished my shirt pocket and pulled out a five-dollar bill.

4

Steel Wheels to Paradise

Clickety-clack... Clickety-clack... Clickety-clack... Clickety... The Soo
Line in my dreams went a hundred miles an hour, had a screaming
whistle, and streaked the sky with a white cloud. The clunker I was
on wobbles along on square wheels, had two passenger cars, a zillion
boxcars, and one caboose...and a puffing engine...up in the next
county. My car, which was next to the caboose, was empty except
for a man up front who was slouched in his seat and never moved. I
figure he was dead drunk or just plain dead. Out my window there
was absolutely nothing to see, except a lot of back alleys with a lot of
weeds growing around a lotta junk. The scenic route, this was not.

Clickety-clack... Clickety-clack... Clickety-clack... Clickety-clack...

The conductor showed up, and I was shocked by a face that
looked like it'd been chiseled out of stone. When I asked him about
the man up front, he answered in a low, gravelly voice, "He has a
ticket. Where's yours?"

I handed him my cardboard ticket.

He smoothened it out. "Thorpe, Wisconsin," he announced.

"Yes, sir. I'm supposed to go to Lublin, but the train doesn't stop
there."

"Trains only fart in Lublin." He punched my ticket.

Red-faced, I stammered, "My...my great-grandma's got a farm
there in that...that fart town."

Without so much as a blink, Stony Face clipped my ticket to the seat rail. "Not much excitement there for a city boy."

"Yeah, I was thinkin' about robbin' me a bank."

His dark eyes nailed me. "Got a new one in Thorpe. It's a biggie."

"Oh yeah? What time do we get there?"

"Depends. Tomorrow afternoon, sometime."

"Tomorrow afternoon? That's a whole day!"

"This is a milk train, sonny. Stops every time it sees a cow."

Clickety-clack… Clickety-clack… Clickety-clack…

Five—six—seven—I'm counting the telephone poles and thinking my dad probably counted these same poles when he—*eight*—when he left the farm. He was eighteen…—*nine*—Funny, how I could hear his heart when I left. Clickety-Clack… Clickety-Clack… Clickety-Clack.—*ten*—The shop. *Always the Shop.* But it's okay. I understand. The shop's important. It's… It's just—Ohhhh, I don't know. —*eleven*—He never really taught me anything. How to throw a curve, or kick a football, fly a kite. Not even marbles…—*twelve*—Mom says he never did any of those things, so that's why. He just worked on the farm all the time… And then in the city.—*thirteen*—We've never ever been to Wrigley Field to see the Cubs play. Smitty and his dad go like once a week. Gene, too. Gene—*fourteen*—Gene and his dad go to Comiskey Park, way over on the Southside, to watch the White Sox play… They go to everything.—*fifteen*—They even go to the Ice Capades. Ha-Ha! *Ice Capades*!…—*sixteen*—Frank's dad, he's a fireman, a Captain! He gets football tickets to the Bear games sometimes. And one time—*seventeen*—one time last year he took us guys to see the Bear/Packer game! Booooy, that was somethin'. Reeeally somethin'.—*eighteen*—That's when I knew I was going to be a football player. Nobody can catch me… I'm fast. Yeah…—*nineteen*—I wonder what makes one person faster than another? I wonder if my dad's fast. He walks fast. Takes—*twenty*—Takes those big steps. And he runs fast when the cops are chasing us at the crap games. Oh yeah… Anyway, like I said, he's not interested in sports.—*twenty-one*—It doesn't bother me... Well, in a way it does... And in a way it doesn't... I don't really know my dad, you know?... And he doesn't really know me, either... And that doesn't seem right... I mean, not when you think about it... I mean, after all, I'm his son. He *should* know me... It's not, right! No! It's not!... It's not!......... Sometimes, when I feel bad... real bad... I think I hate him!... And then I hate myself for feelin' like that... I mean... he's my dad.........

One—two—three—four—One time my dad and his little brother were being chased by a pack of wolves on their way home from school and they climbed a tree. And grandpa came—*five*—Grandpa blasted 'im with a shotgun. Blasted 'im......—*six*—Dad says he finished seventh grade, but mom told me it was more like four years altogether, but not to say anything...—*seven*—She had two years of high school, my Mom, and then she had to go to work. That's what they did back then. Uncle Leo started working when he was fifteen because—*eight*—because he was so big... She can read and write and figure the money, mom can. Dad can do the money part, too. But he's not—*nine*—he's not too good a reader. Pretty bad, in fact. Mom tried to help him one time and he started cursing, throwing things. Boy, he was mad—*ten*—I'm a terrific reader. Jaworski's Drugstore put in a bookcase full of books the summer I finished third grade, and I read them all, the whole bookcase. You could check them out like in a library see, and...*eleven*...and it didn't cost you a red cent, unless you were late, which I never was. *Twelve*... *The Count of Monte Cristo, Robin Hood, Tarzan.* The easy stuff was on the bottom shelves, and it got harder going up. *Thirteen... The Man in the Iron Mask.* His own brother put an iron mask on his face. Ugh! Can you imagine? When I...*fourteen*...started reading a book, I couldn't stop until I finished it. Books were...books were like...like magic...like another world... *Fifteen*... In fourth grade, Father George got us playing baseball at lunchtime, and that was another new world. I could play baseball every day, all day, forever. Mr. Wade said I was a natural. *Sixteen*... I still read most of the new books that came into Jaworski's. I guess that was why I was practically a genius. 'Course it ran in the family. Dad's side, the Obrycki's. They were...*seventeen*...they were unbelievable.

Uncle Leo said you could put them on a deserted island with a box of tools, and in six months, it'd be a paradise. *Eighteen, nineteen...*

One thing my dad and I did do together was, when we lived on Drummond, we went to church together. Just the two of us. Mom... *twenty*... Mom went with my baby sister to early mass. Men went to late mass. Late mass was ten thirty. There was a twelve o'clock mass, but that was for big-time sinners.

You didn't want to go then; you'd be a marked man. Old ladies would spit on ya. So when Mom got home, we'd take off. But we never really made it to church, unless it rained, because of the crap game in the alley. My Uncle Leo was always there—with Dice, of course. And sometimes Cousin Bruno would show up. He was a big-time gambler. He went to Vegas and stuff. Yeah, us guys, we'd huddle around in a circle, just like the men, and play marbles. Big-time marbles, all pearlies! No nicks! And sometimes the police would come barreling down the alley, and everybody would be running through yards, jumping fences. Ahhh, it was great! Dad and me never got caught. We were fast. And Dad would always give me some change so I wouldn't tell Mom. And I never did. And I never felt guilty about not telling her because this was my dad trusting me... No, sir, not on my life would I say a word. They could drag me behind a team of wild horses, and I lost count of the poles... There's an old rusty car with flowers growing out of it. Ha! Ha!

There was one other thing we did together: go to the movies. We used to go a lot. Especially when we lived in that sweatbox on Luna. And after that on Drummond when my sister was born. We were really poor then, so Dad came up with some tricks to get us in. Like he'd hang back while my mom bought one ticket with me scrunching down to get in free—which was no problem since I was short anyway. Then we'd park the buggy inside the door, and my mom would give the ticket-taker the ticket, and we'd go in and get two-nickel bags of popcorn. Then about that time Dad would show up and tell the ticket-taker that he was parking the car and that his wife bought the tickets and, "Look-look," he would say, "there's wife with baby and da boy, by candy counter," and he'd wave. Mom would smile, and my job would be to jump up and down and yell out, "C'mon, Dad!"

It worked like a charm, but once in a while, the ticket-taker would ask to see both ticket stubs. Never fear, we had that covered too. Going in I would search the carpeted floor for a discarded stub for dad, just in case. Then, if duty called, I'd run up, give the man the two ticket stubs, and we'd waltz in beaming at my mother, who would give us a look that would wilt flowers. She wasn't too fond of cheating, you see. But it didn't bother Dad any. Me neither, not one bit.

Then I started school, and the nuns taught me right from wrong with a ruler on my knuckles and a yardstick on my pants. So then I refused to scrunch down. In fact, I now stood on my toes, and Mom had to buy me a children's ticket. And so now, if Dad was questioned by the ticket-taker, Mom and I would just turn our backs on him, and he'd have to buy himself a ticket. Then when Dad came up with smoke coming out of his ears, we'd duck into the theatre. Times like that, Dad wouldn't sit with us until the second feature.

This new wrinkle, of course, was costing Dad a good piece of change, so just like that, he came up with a new trick using my little sister. He'd put an old stub—being careful to match the right color from his collection—into Connie's mouth, tell her not to swallow it, and then when they went up to the ticket-taker, he'd say, "Connie, give Daddy ticket." Connie would then spit the gooey stub into his hand, and he'd exclaim, "Connie, what you do?" The ticket-taker would wave them right in.

My dad's tricky, all right. A real con artist. When I grow up, I'm going to be just like him.

Well, maybe not quite. I didn't know yet.

Clickety-clack… Clickety-clack… Clickety-clack…

I opened my lunch bag and found a note inside from my mom.

Dear son,

I made you two sandwiches. Eat the egg salad one first. You can buy some milk on the train, like your father said. And don't talk to anyone! And don't forget to say your prayers.

Love,
Your mother

PS. The summer will go fast, and you will be home soon.

Clickety-clack... Clicketyclack... Clickety-clack... Clickety-clack...

I was eating the egg salad sandwich and thinking about the time I was at the supper table trying to figure a way out of finishing the food on my plate—which I had to do, or I couldn't leave. So to stall for time, I said, "Mom, where did you meet Dad?"

"Hmmmm," she said from the sink, where she was doing the dishes. "At our house, I think."

"Milford Ballroom," came the voice of authority from behind the newspaper.

"Ohhh, that's right. Aunt Delores was dancin' with him, and I snapped him up." My dad ruffled the newspaper but kept his nose buried.

"He was always showing up at our house. I couldn't get away from him," said my mom, clearing the table. "Most times I didn't even talk to him. Didn't even bother to look."

"You was lookin'," said a voice that could cut through steel.

"I was lookin' to see if you were gone."

Dad rattled the newspaper into confetti, got up, and just before he left for the living room—where he would lie on the couch to do his thinking—he said, "She was always lookin'. Didn't talk much till we got married."

I laughed, but I could tell by the way my mom handled the dishes in the sink that she didn't think it was all that funny. Finally, she said, "I remember the first time your father asked me to dance."

I asked her if he was a good dancer.

"No! He was terrible! But that didn't stop him." She chuckled, then dried her hands on her apron, and sat at the table. "Hmmmmm," she said, shaking her head, a smile on her lips. "Those green eyes of his flashin'. Pitch-black hair slicked back." She passed a hand over her head. Then after a glance at the doorway, she leaned over to me and said, "He looked like Tyrone Power, the movie star." Her smile was so big it made me smile. "He was a sharp dresser, your father. White shirt, flashy tie, shoes shining, uh-huh." She nodded. "He was always having his picture taken. Head to toe. Always giving me pictures of himself."

"How come?" I asked.

She shrugged and said, "I guess when he lived on the farm, he didn't know what he looked like. So when he found out, he couldn't get enough of himself." Then she laughed so hard she doubled over. And me right along with her.

Laughing comes easy to my mom, and she has a beautiful smile. Dad never really laughs. A smile is his limit. But he can be funny, like when he impersonates his boss, Howard. He'd screw up his face, chomp his jaws, and say in a high squeaky voice, "George, vat da hell yu dewing!" And if he gets a laugh, which he always does, he'd go on about the time Uncle George chopped Howard's little finger off in a punch press. Oh, funny, funny!

"Aunt Delores said your father was always after her," said my mom, dabbing away tears with her apron as she got up and went back to the sink. "She said she let me have him because she had too many men chasing her."

"What!" I shouted. "She's not even good-looking, Mom! You're the one that's good-looking."

"Well," said my mom, doing the dishes, "she's put on some weight. She never was a raving beauty. And she is older than me...

eight years." She said that last part more to herself than to me. Then, over her shoulder, she shot, "Billy, are you finished?"

"I'm eating! I'm eating!" I yelled back as I went on playing hockey with the peas on my plate. Then, because I'm a genius, I popped, "What's a swayback?"

"Sway—" My mom spun around. She looked like she'd been hit on the head. "Where...where did you hear that?"

"The men," I told her. "They say Aunt Delores used to be a sway-back. And then they laugh like crazy. What's that mean, swayback?"

"Well, it's...it's..." She still looked dazed. "It's her behind. It used to stick out to...to here." My mom held a hand out about a foot away from her backside, then she clapped it over her mouth to keep from laughing. "Men used to say they could park a stein of beer on it!" She let out a hoot, then stopped dead. "Don't tell your father I said that." She went back to roaring, and I joined in. "Ahhhhh, Billy," she sighed. "Go! Go outside. And not a word to your father!"

That was one of the best talks my mom and I ever had. My mom talked to me a lot, my dad hardly ever. But the way I saw it, men only talked to men. So that's okay, because someday I'd be a man, and then we could talk our heads off.

Clickety-clack... Clickety-clack... Clickety-clack...

The train bucked and bucked again. My eyes flew open. The sun was broiling me through the window. We slowed...shuddered... then took the knockout punch. "Guuumee, Illinooois," rang Old Stony, as he came waltzing through the car.

"We're still in Illinois?" I looked up at Stoney. "Geez, if I took this train all around the world, I'd probably be an old man by the time I got back."

Stony's face cracked and a smile leaked out. "Get out and stretch. Be here for a spell."

I checked on the man up front. He was fine, just boozed up like my Uncle John. Some of the passengers in the other car were standing around talking, some were still getting off. I helped an old lady dressed in a classy black outfit take the big steps down to the platform.

"Thank you, young man," she said, her smile warm. Grandma Helen flicked across my mind.

There seemed to be no end to the line of boxcars stretching ahead of me. I wondered how the engine could pull so many and found myself walking up the track, anxious to get a look at this Chugging beast. On the way, I stopped and watched two young guys load and unload milk cans.

Their muscles flashed and bulged from under their shredded blue shirts as they rolled cans of milk into a boxcar and slung empty ones off two at a time. I figured I couldn't even budge a full can. An empty one, I could. Probably even sling it off the train. Yeah. Maybe.

The engine was unbelievably big scary, too, because it was alive. It was resting now, but you could hear the fire licking its belly... smell the hot iron...see the hissing steam feel the power of its beating heart. No wonder the Indians called it the "Iron Horse." A monster in your worst nightmare. But boy, oh boy, what I wouldn't give to ride this demon full throttle: my head out the window, the wind whipping my hair, watching it eat up track and whistle for more.

The boozed man was gone when I got back on the train, but across the aisle, by the window, sat a soldier. His left arm was in a huge white cast. His tanned face had a lot of deep lines in it.

"Hi!" I said, moving slowly past him with a little wave. He gave me a lazy two-finger salute in return.

I sat down in my seat and thought about the medals on his chest. I had to talk to him. Had to ask him about shooting guys, sticking them with a bayonet, about his medals. I waited until the train started up. He wasn't facing me, so I hummed some goofy notes to let him know I was coming up.

His blond hair flashed like a sheet of gold in the sunlight. I went right past him, because... I don't know why. I stopped at the door and stared at nothing out the small round window. With my heart pounding, I turned around, marched back, stopped by his seat... I was stuck for words.

"Take a load off," said the soldier with a nod. His high, squeaky voice wasn't what I expected. I sat opposite him. "Where you headin'?" he asked, in that high, hurtin' voice.

"Lublin, but I'm getting off at Thorpe. Trains don't stop in Lublin, they only fart there." I waited for a smile, something... Nothing. "Where you headin'?" I asked.

"Green Bay."

"The Green Bay Packers! Vince Lombardi! They're terrific! So are the Chicago Bears! I saw them play at Wrigley Field last year. Boy, what a game! But we got beat. I'm from Chicago."

"City of the Big Shoulders," came the squeaky voice. "Husky, Brawling-Hog butcher for the world... Your paaainted wooomen..." His eyes closed, his head fell back, and his mouth opened.

"Soldier!" I put a hand out to shake him but stopped short. "Soldier, are you okay?"

His head came up his eyes, blinking machine gun bullets. "Got me a—" he coughed, "million-dollar wound...millllllion dollll-laaar..." His eyes closed, and his head fell back, again...and again, his mouth opened.

I sat back and waited...

Clickety-clack... Clickety-clack... Clickety-clack... Clickety...

My gluey eyes opened. We weren't moving. The soldier was gone. I was the only one in the car. Night was falling, but out the window I could make out tree lines and a plowed field. I took the steel steps down to the ground. We seemed to be parked in the middle of a field, in the middle of nowhere. The half-moon helped enough to make out a man standing by the passenger car up front. He was looking up ahead. I could smell cigarette smoke as I approached him.

"Excuse me, sir!"

The man jumped as he spun around. He was tall and well dressed. "Why did we stop? Do you know?"

"We seem to have hit some cows." Smoke came out with his words.

I pictured white bones sticking out of red meat. Old Stony-Face came plowing through the night with his chiseled chin leading the way. He told us they were clearing the tracks and for us to get back on the train and to stay there. I asked him about the soldier.

"No soldier on my train. Now go on, get up there." He went off into the falling darkness.

I asked the tall man as we climbed aboard his passenger car if he'd seen a soldier with a white cast on his arm. He said he hadn't. And among the passengers, I saw no soldier. I considered staying in this car, but I thought Old Stony-Face might have a heart attack if he found my car empty, so I went back to my car, sat down, and wondered about the soldier. Maybe he got off and fell down somewhere. I jumped up, went to the back of the car, slid the door open, took the steel steps down to the gravel, and started moving back, past the caboose. The air was heavy and still, and the night darker now with the moon covered by clouds, but I still thought the white cast would stand out.

I followed the tracks…nothing…not left, not right, and not straight ahead. I balanced on one of the rails and started putting one foot in front of the other…one foot in front of the other…one foot.

The cold banging sound of the steel cars froze me on the rails. I could feel it all in my feet: the jerking, the shuddering, the stopping, the starting. I got back to my footwork: one foot after another, one foot after… The banging stopped. I whirled around. A stab of fear shot through me. The train was a good distance away! I took after it like a shot. It was barely moving, but it was moving… I pumped my arms and legs like pistons. I was gaining…but the ground wasn't always good, and I would slip, and then I wasn't gaining. I got real scared and shifted gears. I was flying! Up to the caboose and gaining…past the caboose…up to my car…almost up to the steps…and then I wasn't gaining. I locked my eyes on the handrail, pumped like a demon, and lunged. Got it! I swung aboard and collapsed on the cold steel steps. Nothin' to it…

Clickety-clack… Clickety-clack… Clickety-clack… Clickety-clack… Clickety-clack… Clickety-clack…

It was dark when we crawled into Milwaukee. "For a spell." I wanted to talk to Stony Face about the soldier, but he was busier than heck answering all kinds of goofy questions. I spotted the tall man talking to a young lady. He gave me a little nod. I gave him a little wave. I was standing at one end of the platform, staring out at the moonlit night, when something hit my backside. I whirled around. It was Stony Face. He had smacked me with his clipboard.

"What happened to the soldier?" I blurted.

"Don't give me no more talk about some soldier. I've got—"

"But where is he?" I shouted. "He was on the train. I was sitting right across from him."

Taken aback, Stony straightened up, licked his lips, and said, "There's no soldier. And if there was, he'd be taken care of just fine."

I spun around, but before I could take a step, Stony's hand on my shoulder stopped me.

"Here now, worried traveler." Stony dug a train ticket out of his hat and stuffed it into my shirt pocket. "Now don't bother me till morning." That said, he went off up toward the boxcars.

I crossed to the city side of the platform. Far off, the colored lights from a carnival caught my eye. I watched the Ferris wheel do its slow turn… Best damn carnival in the whole city. The whole world! Ask anybody. People come from all over. All over! We got everything. Nobody can outdo Father Przybilski. Nobody. Got a Beer Garden with girls dancing in Polish costumes, their skirts flying high. Got games—throwing at milk bottles, at dolls, darts at balloons. Even got a shooting range for prize money. My dad could shoot the number 8 out with three shots almost every time. But they only let you win once. Got gambling too. Dice games. Like "26" for prizes. And "Under & Over Seven" for money—which Uncle Leo said has lousy odds and was for suckers.

Gambling, by the way, was okay as long as it was for the church. Father Przybilski said so. He was tricky, all right. He knew how to make everybody happy—even the long-faced mommas that were sour about the gambling. He got them smiling from ear to ear by giving them a special blessing at mass every day for cooking the kielbasa and the sauerkraut, and the potatoes for the Beer Garden. They came floatin' out of church; their feet didn't touch the ground, looked down at everybody, especially the men.

And the rides! The best! The Swings. You could grab your buddy's swing and shoot him out of orbit with your legs. The Tilt-A-Whirl was good too. You could really goose the curves if you shift your weight at just the right time. And rocking your seat on the Ferris wheel on the way down would make you squeeze your nuts every time. And getting stopped at the top, looking out at the world, could get you dreaming... Best damn carnival in the whole wide world. Everybody said so.

I opened my eyes and caught the sun peeking at me from the horizon. I turned my back to the window, closed my eyes, and let the cool morning air carry me back to dreamland. But I didn't get there. I remembered that Stony had stuffed a train ticket into my shirt pocket. I dug it out and on the back of it, printed clearly in pencil, was a math problem:

> Distance around equator: 131,480,184 feet. Train averages 25 miles/hour for 12 hours, and 10 mi/hour for remaining 12 hours. How many days will it take to travel around the world?

Well, hell's-bells, thanks to the nuns and their fast hands, especially Sister Biata—we call her Sister B&B, for *black and blue*—this was a snap. Heck, by eighth grade, we'd be doing calculus with Sister Modesta—she was straight from Poland, got a knockout punch. Yeah, by the time you graduated from St. James, you were either a genius or punchy. Some of us, in fact, would test high enough for junior college. But nobody back home went to college; they went to work.

I took out my notebook and pencil and started figuring.

1) I knew there was 5,280 feet in a mile, so I divided that number into the equator's feet and came up with 24,901.55 as the distance in miles around the equator.

2) The train travels 25 × 12 = 300 miles for half a day, plus 10 × 12 = 120 miles for a half a day, or 300 + 120 = 420 mi/day.

3) The answer then is 420 mi/day divided into 24,901.55 miles...which came to 59.2891 days, rounded off to 59.29 days, or roughly, two months.

A snap, like I said.

We rolled past a big faded frame building with a sign on it that read "GENERAL STORE OF LUBLIN." The train gave a long blast and three toots, and Lublin disappeared. Eight miles more. I could hardly wait. Who was going to meet me? What would they say when they saw me? What should I say?

What about the two girls? Maybe they wouldn't like me. They were older than me. Richard said they were good-looking, especially Vickie. I was glad they didn't look like cows. What if they looked like the pictures in the Chez Paree magazine? I fought the urge to go to the toilet and get the bad thing over with for the day. Actually, I was three days ahead, so now I had to also worry about going blind.

Oh, I almost forgot about Earl. That was Stony Face. Yeah, Earl Weiskoff. Isn't that a great name for him? It really is. Anyway, Earl was real impressed with my answer and how I figured it out. He was so impressed, in fact, I thought he was going to give me a hug.

No kidding. He even brought me a bottle of milk and a doughnut. And he wouldn't take a penny for it. I told him he had a great face, all those angles, and that he ought to be in the movies. And when I said that, his face cracked into about a million happy pieces. For a moment then, I thought about asking him again about the soldier, but I let it go. So anyway, we had a great talk. He asked me all about school and stuff, and he answered all my questions about trains. Like how they kept from running into each other and stuff… I think I'm going to miss Old Earl Weiskoff… A face carved out of stone.

5

No Trumpets in Thorpe

We slowed to a crawl, then went through the "jerk, shudder, bump, and stop" routine. I grabed my bag, waved goodbye to Earl, and jumped into Thorpe. So where was the band? The crowd? The family?

Anyone? Not a soooooul. Not for me anyway. For the milk? Yes, a wagon. For the mailbag? Yes, the stationmaster. For me? Nothing, no one, nowhere. Mmmmmm, let's see now: Earl said they'd know about the train being late, so no mistake about that. So what's going on?

"Hey! Anybody here? Hel-loooow!" Nothing, nowhere, no way.

I was wondering when the next train back to Chicago was due when the stationmaster came up, his white hair poking out in all directions from under his black railroad hat.

"Sir? I'm supposed to meet somebody. Somebody's supposed to meet me. Here! Today!"

"Is thaat sooooo?" drawled the dried-up stationmaster in a voice deep as a well.

"Yes, sir. Did you see anyone? The train was three hours late, so maybe they—"

"Hold on! Hoooold oooon," said the stationmaster with a raised hand, his bulging eyes giving me the once-over as he began digging a finger into his vest pocket—which was over some shirts. (God, I thought, who makes these people?) Finally, he came up with a folded piece of brown bag paper. He unfolded it, held it out at arm's length. "Billy Benec—"

"Billy Benecki! That's me! I'm Billy Benecki!" Saved. Thank you, Lord. "Somebody is supposed to meet me and take me out to my great-grandma's farm. The Popko farm. It's in Lublin. It used to be called the Grabowski farm, and... Do you know it?"

"Yeaaaaah..." said the nodding stationmaster. "Well, boy, I got bad news for ya. Helen Grabowski, she passed on."

Everything stopped, even my heart. Then it started pounding so hard I put my hands over it to keep it from breaking out of my chest.

The old geezer leaned forward, his bulging eyes ready to pop. "Bingo!" He went nuts laughing and jumping up and down! "No, no," he finally sputtered, coughing and stamping his feet. "No, no, boy! Just, just jokin' ya!" He chuckled. "Man's gotta have some fun!" He threw it in my face, cranked his arm at me, and moved off.

I gave my suitcase a good hard kick, then picked it up and followed God's gift to humanity.

Just before ducking into the station, the old fart hung an arm out right and shouted, "Go to the barbershop. Ask for Jake!" The door slammed shut.

Five buildings stand in a row on the left side of a paved street, and that was it. Nothing on the right side except a sidewalk and a lot of grass—which always seemed a little odd to me, and still did. Some dusty cars and a few muddy old pickups were angled at the curb in front of the buildings. The nearest building had a big "General Store of Thorpe" sign above the entrance and all kinds of farm stuff in the windows. The next sported "Saloon" painted on the front glass. And the middle building has a good-sized post painted like a peppermint stick out at the curb, so it must be the barbershop. The building next to it looked to have a couple'a spittoons out by the door, so it was probably another saloon. And the farthest building was a towering three-story red-brick building that stuck out like a sore thumb. Atop it a huge sign read, "Thorpe Bank."

"Uh-huh, 'the biggie.'"

This lopsided town belonged in a movie, if you ask me. A gangster ran out of the bank with a machine gun, and just as he was about to jump into the getaway car, a tall stranger stepped out of the saloon and gunned him down with his six-shooter. *Bang*! *Bang*! *Bang*! And *bang*—for good measure. Actually, the only thing moving in this town was a mangy dog crossing the street, heading to the grassy side. I gave him a whistle. He gave me a lazy glance and moved on, his tail draggin'.

I smelled stale beer as I passed the open door of the first saloon. It was empty, except for a heavyset lady with big arms slopped on the bar. She kept her eyes on me as I went by. The barbershop had a fan inserted above the door, strips of red cloth dance to the hum of the motor. Through the screen door I noticed that, for some reason, everybody was huddled at the other end of the long, narrow room. I passed in quietly, making sure to keep the spring-loaded screen door from slamming. Two empty barber chairs were anchored on the right with the wall behind them mirrored about halfway down to a long shelf that was lined with colored bottles. The rest of the room was painted in two shades of gray, the darker on the bottom. The men, I now see, were mostly gathered around the two men playing checkers. The player on the right was a big roly-poly type, bigger than the potbellied stove that sat behind them.

The barber—had to be—came forward: black hair slicked back, thin mustache, striped shirt, and red garters on his arms, which I thought were really neat. "What'll it be, son? A haircut and a shave?"

I erupted with a giggle. "No, sir. I'm looking for Jake. Is he here?"

"Well, I don't know." Over his shoulder, the barber called out, "Jake, are you here?"

"Not yet, I'm not," answered the big butterball of a man with flaming-red hair. He jumped some checkers on the checkerboard. "I will be in a couple more moves."

There was some chuckling from the group who all looked to be farmers. "Plenty of time for a trim, son. Hop up."

"How much is it?"

"Jake's treatin'. Right, Jake?"

"Joseph's treatin'. Soon's I beat him."

"You couldn't beat a blind man," said the straw-hatted player, opposite.

"True, Joseph, true. But you ain't blind."

6

Jake the Mailman

Riding in a Ford pickup with "US MAIL" painted on the doors made me feel kind of special. You could tell Jake felt that way just by the way he moved, the way he strutted—not like a fat man, not like Norb. No, Jake was important. Jake was a mailman. And today I was his helper. Also, today—the way Jake put it—he had a special delivery: me. Jake was big, like I said, maybe three hundred pounds, but most of him was filled with laughter that spilled out along the way as we flew over hilltops and skidded around turns, making dust our trademark.

Jake said before my great-grandma's farm was the Popkow farm, it was the Szymanski farm, and before that it was the Ostrowski farm, but that everybody around here called it the Grabowski farm, from way back. He said that my great-grandma owned it all now, all 360 acres.

"She married 'em and buried 'em," he said, roaring with laughter. Jake laughed so much he made me laugh.

It was fun jumping in and out of the truck with the mail and putting them in the boxes. I told Jake about my paper route and how most of my customers had Polish names, just like out here.

"All Polish," he said. "'Cept some married different. Jolm Schroeder's, German. And two brothers, Sveedes from Minnesooo-ta, they married the Nowicki girls," said Jake, and he laughed, naturally.

We were riding along, the wind whipping in, smelling fresh, smelling sweet, smelling... "Phew! What's that? Uggggh!"

"Skunk!" Jake took in a big whiff. "Kind'a like it myself." Jake drew in another big whiff. I followed suit and decided Jake was right. Not bad at all.

"Skunk'll spray a dog, he'll smell for weeks. Dog'll rub himself on the grass, in the dirt, won't do no good. But it won't hurt him any. Porcupine. That's different. Porcupine slap him a snoot full, dog'll look like a pincushion. Gotta take pliers to him and pull 'em out one at a time. That poor dog'll whine and cry, his big eyes lookin' at ya, but he won't move. Knows you're helpin' him. 'Course he gets it in the eyes you gotta shoot 'im."

"What about people? What happens?"

"What? You gonna chase porcupine?"

"Not me."

"Better not. But you can grab snakes, if you like. Four, five footers, thick as your arm." Jake glanced at my arm. "Thicker."

"I don't like snakes."

"Well then, you can chase skunk!"

"Yeah! I like skunk."

"Good!" Jake laughed long and loud. And so did I. Oh, we were having a fine time, and I was thinking Jake liked me, and I liked him, too...a lot.

Along a flat stretch, we started to slow down. Jake stuck his tree trunk of an arm out the window and pointed to a house a good ways from the road.

"That's it. The Filas farm." Earlier I had mentioned that I had cousins out here. "Bogart, Cagney, Jean Harlow... Betty Grable!" They named their kids after movie stars." Jake chuckled. "Oh yeah, Pete was quite a character till he started looking at the bottom of a bottle... Land's not the worst. Some flatland."

I'd seen it before with my folks when we stayed at my Uncle Tom's. We brought them a big box of Babe Ruth candy bars one time, and I remembered how the kids peeked out from the doorways but wouldn't enter the room. So my mom put some bars over by the doors, and they snatched them up. It was sad. Driving back to Uncle

Tom's, nobody said a word. Back home the family always said, "Pete's a broken man, living with a broken woman, on a broken farm."

We were well past the Filas' place but still crawling along. I could see Jake was deep into thinking about something. I turned to my open window and watched the forest slide by.

"You can clear the wood out, but not the rock," said Jake in a soft, easy way, no chuckle in his voice now, something different in there now, something that grabbed your ears and held on to them. "Land's no good. Not for farming. Never was. Never will be."

"What's it good for then?"

"Good for breakin' a man's back." Jake kept his eyes on the road. "You can clear the trees and the rock, then put the plow to it and up comes a new crop of rock." Jake shook his head and gave me a glance. "You know what I'm sayin', Billy? Came here from the old country and got taken. Bought land from a map they never set eyes on."

"Why'd they do that?"

"Ahhhh, well…they were buyin' a dream." Jake regripped the wheel. We were hardly moving; I could walk faster. "Come over on a steamship, packed like sardines. Steerage class means below the waterline, the bottom. Came sailing past the Statue of Liberty, came through Ellis Island, kissed the Promised Land and got taken." Jake spat out the window. "Con men, city slickers, sellin' a quarter section, a 160 acres in God's country. Virgin land in Wisconsin, they tol 'em. Deer and rabbit aplenty. Where streams were loaded with fish, jumped right into your frying pan. Oh, they were good. They knew how to paint a pretty picture—160 acres of America right under your own two feet. Oh suuure. My grandfather was one of 'em."

"So was mine. Grandpa Ignatz."

Jake gave me a look. "Yeah, most old folks here got that story in 'em. How they worked in serfdom for years just to earn passage." Jake let out a long sigh and relaxed his grip on the wheel.

"What's serfdom, Jake?"

"Serfdom, you work for a big landowner, ten, twenty years, depends."

"Like a job, you mean."

"Noooo. No, boy, more like a slave. Your folks sign a contract, and you're gone. You're twelve, thirteen, and lock-stock-and-barrel you belong to the landowner. You live in the barn with the rest of the poor buggers. Get beat up regular too. Yeah, get a little wage. Buy tobacco, trade for an old shirt, somethin'. And save for liberation day!" Jake chuckled and shook his head. "Wasn't much to write home about."

"Who'd want to? They sell you off like that."

"Well now, a farm can only feed so many, Billy. Like for you maybe, your folks could get fifty dollars. Or two pigs and some chickens maybe. Maybe a cow if you were bigger, had some meat on you." Jake shook his head. "Hard times, hard times." Jake stared at the road ahead.

"So what happened after they bought the land?"

"What happened! They came out here with their shit-ass map and found out they'd been taken, that's what! Their 160 acres ain't no paradise. It's not even hell. It's worse than hell. It's a 160-acre rock pile, grows boulders the size of pumpkins and watermelons and plenty of cantaloupes and tomatoes, a fine harvest you pile up all over your fields…break your back. And trees! Virgin pine, high and mighty! But no good to a farmer. You chop 'em down and drag 'em out and chop 'em up some more. Then the hard part. The stumps. Chop 'em, burn 'em, blast 'em with dynamite. Rip 'em out with a team of horses pullin' and foamin take years… And what do ya end up with? Land that'll always be more rock than dirt." Jake stomped the gas pedal, and we shot forward and kicked dust.

The face I looked at without trying to turn my head too much was the face I saw on my dad sometimes, a twisted face, twisted tight to keep the hurting inside. I saw that face a lot, even in a mirror. I guess we all did.

After a ways, Jake started to hum a polka. "Um-pa, um-pa, um-pa… Um-pa, um-pa, um-pa…" Jake's eyes started to flutter, and he started to chuckle. "Now the Grabowski farm, your great-grand-ma's place, that's a farm. Rich delta. You piss on it, flowers shoot up, you have to jump back so they don't knock you over." Jake laughed. Jake was back. I laughed along with Jake.

We went on delivering the mail and talked some about fishing. Jake knew a lot about fishing.

He told me how farmers dynamite holes in their creek for fishing and swimming, even though it was illegal. And we talked about the coming Fourth of July, how everybody would be back for the haying. And about the big dance at the Mile-A-Way afterward. I told Jake about Richard coming up and that he might have to drive him out, but that he would probably come up with the relatives for the Fourth. I didn't mention that my folks might not make the trip, but I did tell him that they sent me up here to get fat. Jake exploded with laughter at that one, like I thought he would.

We pulled up to a crossroad with five mailboxes where I was to get out and walk. Jake was running late and hadn't yet delivered the two big boxes in the bed of the truck. He wouldn't do that until after milking time, which was what he was anxious to head back home for. Jake offered to take me with him and to drop me off later, but I didn't want to put him out any more than I already had, so I jumped out, got my suitcase from out back, and went around to his window.

"How much do I owe you, Jake?" I dug out my wad of bills.

"I'd say you earned your way."

I peeled off a dollar and held it out. "This okay?"

"Put that away 'fore I get mad. I'm a little bigger than you."

I wrinkled up my nose, tough-like. "Yeah, but I'm faster."

Jake laughed so hard he rocked the truck. He put his big lump of a hand out, and we shook; it felt hard and heavy...and dead.

"Popkow's place." Jake pointed a thick finger. "Straight up County Road there, 'bout a mile or so. It's a redbrick house. The only brick house around." Jake gave me a nod put her in gear and took off.

"Thanks, Jake!" I yelled and waved.

Jake's big hammy arm waved out the window as he rumbled away kicking dust.

PART II

THE FARM

7

Cracked Face and Crooked Finger

I took hill after hill with the suitcase gaining weight and me losing some to the sweat. Frogs were jumping, grasshoppers were hopping, and me? I was stumbling along on the red sandy road, wondering how far yet to the redbrick house. I passed another farmhouse. That made three so far, but they weren't red, and they weren't brick. I passed a farmer working in a field with a team of horses, and I thought of doing some asking, but he wasn't all that close, and now I was too far, so I kicked myself in the pants and fell over. I counted to eight and got up. It was a trick my Uncle George taught me: "Take the count then get up and hammer him."

At a bridge over a creek, I stopped to watch the dark water rush over boulders the size of watermelons and pumpkins and plenty of cantaloupes and apples too, as it cut a jagged line through the land. I went down the bank took off my shoes and socks and waded into the swirling cool water. It felt delicious, tasted that way too. I filled up and splashed myself silly.

I sat in the sun and wondered about a big broken oak that looked to have been snapped like a twig—could be something mighty big passed through here—King Kong maybe. I quick switched my mind to a dragonfly glued in the air over a flower and wondered how it could do that, hang there like that, wings buzzing… After it zoomed off, I mulled over my chances for survival: could wait on the bridge until a car came by—which might take a week; could follow the creek back to civilization—which might be a hundred miles; could wait for King Kong to waltz by—but not being a girl, he'd probably tear my arms off. Soooo, I decided I would just keep walking until I came to the next farmhouse or the next sign of life and simply ask, "Where's the Grabowski farm? The Popko farm? The redbrick house, damn it!"

I quickly put on my socks and shoes, grabbed my suitcase, ran up to the road, and kept right on running. When my blistered hands burned as much as my lungs, I dropped to my knees, leaned on my suitcase, and gasped for air.

"Could I have missed the house?" I wondered. "No, devil! No! Go away!"

With my hankie wrapped around my right hand, I picked up my suitcase and set a brisk pace. "God," I mumbled, "help me find that red house…please."

The hills melted down until the land was almost flat. At eleven o'clock, I spotted a house; it looked to be red…a dark red, but red. My heart started pounding. I picked up the pace. The house, it looked to be brick. I started humming; no song, just some crazy notes. Closer… Yeees. Closer…

Yeeeeees! A redbrick house! Ha! Nothin' to it.

When I reached the road that zigzagged up to the house, I put my suitcase down and gave it the once-over. It didn't look like a farmhouse at all. Looked, in fact, a lot like our house in Chicago, only bigger. I swiped my brow, grabbed my suitcase, and started in. After snaking through some tall pine trees and around a huge Christmas tree, I came upon a gigantic oak. Oak trees always scared me some because they looked like something out of a bad dream. Always twisted, battered, and broken, with thick limbs jutting out at crazy angles, standing there tall, daring you to look at them until they hypnotized you—at least me, they did.

The winding road straightened out, ran past part of a vegetable garden on the left, then curved right before sweeping left and running up alongside the side of the house. I turned off before that and angled across the front lawn toward the front entrance, passing, on the way, some small bushes and some not so small. The brick porch was overgrown with vines and a tangle of thorny rosebushes.

Sunken stepping-stones ran straightaway from the cement steps and disappeared under a long wooden archway that was also covered with a tangle of growth. The last time this entrance was used had to be before I was born.

I started around to the back of the house. Across the yard on the left was a white painted garage with its doors wide open and empty. To the left of it was the gate to the fenced in vegetable garden, and on the right side of it was an apple orchard. At the end of the yard was a picnic table. When I got there, I was shocked to see that the house was perched on a plateau that ran left and right for as far as the eye could see. The land rolled down from there, flattened out, and ran all the way out to the horizon. It was quite a sight. So was the big gray barn at the bottom of the hill. And the tall silo left of it—which, right away, I knew I had to climb. And then squeezed in between the two, like with a shoehorn, was the chicken coop.

I took note of the large milk can set outside the Dutch doors with the big funnel stuck in the top, which I knew was draped with cheesecloth, so that when you poured your pail of milk into it, it would drain through and leave a heap of foam that looked like ice cream. Yep, I knew a bit about farming, knew it was milking time, knew everybody was in the barn. I'd been at my Uncle Tom's farm enough times to know that everything was geared to the milk, because it was the farmer's paycheck. My Aunt Rose would always say, "Sunup and sundown nothing stops the milking." And then she'd always add, "Ain't that right, Tom?" And then Uncle Tom would give his little smile and say, "No King, or Queen, not even the Pope!"

Another one they had, Aunt Rose would lead in with, "Some mine the earth for silver and gold."

And Uncle Tom would chime back, "The fanner does it the way God intended." They had a number of routines like that. I guess when you don't have any kids you have time to dream up stuff like that.

The back of the brick house had a white wooden porch wrapped around with windows. I went up the wide steps set over right and peered through the screen door. "Hello! Anybody home?" I didn't expect a reply, of course, but you didn't just walk into somebody's house without a warning. I opened the screen door and stepped inside. Part of the kitchen could be seen through a doorway over right that led into the house itself. I tucked my suitcase next to the clothes tree on right and took in the rest of the porch. Over left a bit was a large, round table with four chairs. A rocking chair was next to it but back by the brick wall. And at the far end was a couch with a small table and an easy chair.

"Well, no more stalling," I told myself. "Time for the showdown."

At the bottom of the steps, to the right, large concrete slabs led to a water pump at the end of the porch. Next to it was a chair with a yellow pan and a towel set on it.

"Get a drink," I said to myself, "then go down there and shoot 'em up." My heart started knocking on my ribs at the thought.

And then, as I was drinking the ice-cold water from my cupped hand, a man dressed like a farmer came out of the barn carrying a pail of milk, and not for a second—as he did his pouring—did he take his eyes off of me. And I didn't take my eyes off of him either, not for one second, while I did my sipping. He even gave me a last look before he ducked back into the barn. So then, I stood there waiting because I expected everybody to come running out of the barn shouting my name and do some, "Ha! Ha! Ho! Ho!" But no, not a soul. So finally, I slicked my hair back with my wet hand, hitched my pants, and started down the hill—my right hand hanging loose, ready to draw.

About halfway down, a lady in a red babushka and a long pink dress came out of the barn. I froze. She caught sight of me and froze…only the milk pail dangling from her left arm swayed slightly. Very slowly, I started down again. The closer I got, the more certain I was that it was her, my great-grandmother, Old Lady Gaa-raaab. Had to be because like Uncle Leo said, "Got a face like a prune, more lines on it than a map."

"William!" She opened her free arm to me.

"Grandma!" I rushed in to hug her, and my head smacked into her breast because she was so tall. She hugged me back with one arm—I preferred two, but she had the milk pail in the other and probably couldn't decide which of us was more important.

"William!" And she followed up with a stream of Polish—which was like Greek to me, but I kept throwing in some Ja-Ja's, anyway. She didn't smile, and that was good. With all those cracks in her face, it might fall off. Also, I noticed the tip of her first finger was bent sideways toward her thumb, which I figured had to be great for picking her nose.

An old man sporting a beat-up brown fedora came out, toting a pail of milk filled to the brim. He poured some of it into the funnel, and an iceberg of foam formed as he watched us. He wore a dark vest over a plaid green shirt with dark pants. Grandma and this old man—who I figured must be Great-Grandfather number 4 kicked up a storm in Polish. My ears caught one *William* and a half a dozen *Eddie*'s. Grandpa emptied his pail and joined Grandma staring up the hill at the house. I did the same. All I saw was the house and some white puffy clouds. The old man gave Grandma his empty pail, took hers, and emptied it into the funnel. She looked up the hill again, gave me a quick glance, and went back into the barn. The old man and I watched the foam build like an ice cream cone.

"How was the train ride?" said the old man without any trace of an accent.

I was so surprised he spoke English I had trouble replying. "Ooo-okay."

"Eddie there?" He pointed at the house with his chin.

Puzzled by his question, I stared at him. He poured the last drops from his pail into the foam. "Eddie there?" He did the chin thing again.

I looked up the hill. "Where?"

"The house! How'd you get here?"

"The mailman brought me. Jake! The mailman."

The old man put his pail down, took off his fedora, swiped a sleeve across his brow, and exhaled. "We get any mail?"

I shook my head.

The old man rubbed his shiny chin with his fingers while staring up at the house. That done, he put his fedora back on, picked up his pail, and started for the barn.

"Uhhh," he tossed me, "we eat after milking, Billy."

"It's William!" He stopped. Looked puzzled. "My name is William."

"S'what I said." He gave the house a last glance and entered the barn.

I gave the house a glance—like it was the thing you did before you moved—and went into the barn.

8

Girls, Cows, and Piggy Eyes

There they were—cows, Guernsey cows—all lined up on both sides of the aisle, all greeting me with their swishing tails—which in cow language meant, "Stop staring at our asses and start milking." I wasn't about to tell them that my hands were too weak, that I was building them up by doing the bad thing, that soon I would squeeze their teats with hands of steel, squirt their milk right out the door, and into the milk can. Just then, the cow next to me—having read my mind—raised its tail and deposited a splattering cow pie that would have gotten me good had I not known the danger of "a raised tail" and skipped away.

Giggling came from across the aisle. A dark-haired girl stared at me as she went on milking.

My face did its turning-red trick as I watched her pull on the cow's teats. I moved on.

I spotted Grandpa sandwiched between some cows, milking away, the spurts drilling the pail, the sounds deep and strong. Back home they said Grandpa number 1 went back to Poland because he had brains. And that number 2 died a mysterious death, found frozen in a cornfield with his neck broken. And number 3, they whispered, was in the nuthouse. So shiny face here was lucky number 4. He glanced at me and cracked a little smile. I' was tempted to hold up four fingers and mouth the word *four*, then point at him, but thought better of it; the way he milked, he might aim a spurt at me, put a hole through me. Boy, could he milk.

Grandma moved out from between some cowhide with her bucket and stool, crossed the aisle, then moved back in between a couple of more cows, saying something to the one she was tapping with her three-legged stool to make it move over. She went on talking to the animal as she set up. It must've understood Polish, because it kept blinking its big flirty eyes at her and wiggling its ears.

And then I saw her. She was coming up the aisle, pail in hand, blond bouncy hair—everything bouncy—and a face alive with "goodies." She went by me with hardly a glance, her pail—swinging, as was the rest of her—her backside looking every bit as good as her front side, maybe even better. This one could well send me home with a seeing-eye dog. This one was Vickie, bet the house on it. When the men back home talked about Vickie, they had a tough time trying not to smile.

I sat on the hayloft steps and played with a couple of cats that were hanging around their milk bowl. A third one, a big black-and-white kept his distance. But these two, both brown and white, let me mess with them, especially the smaller one. I didn't know anything about cats, other than that they drank milk and had sharp claws. None of my friends or family had any. But that stinking landlord on Drummond Avenue had one, a scary big dark thing that roamed around the edges of the yard, which was quite all right with me. But I was getting to like these two guys, or girls—whatever they were—licking at my hands with their rough little tongues.

I was tickling the smaller one under the neck when I spotted the man I first saw come out of the barn when I was up by the house. He was heading toward me with his pail and stool in hand. His face was twisted mean, and he had piggy eyes, and that was all I can tell you because you didn't look mean in the eye more than once without feeling fear come alive.

He set up by the cow right next to me by the stairway. I watched him milk: his tempo was quick, swinging the whole bag as he yanked and squeezed in a rough manner. I didn't think he'd like to be squeezed and yanked like that. I didn't think cow liked it either the way she half kicked at his hands until he barked at her. He sounded as mean as he looked…and smelled worse. I didn't ask anyone his name; it just came out of the dirt at some point: Ah-lex (for Alex).

As the milking went on and on, I faded out until I was invisible. Nobody paid any attention to me whatsoever. To the little cat asleep in my lap, I was just a resting place. I could've dried up and blown away, and nobody would have cared. I guess the way they saw it, I was just a kid, couldn't even milk a cow—which, by the way, I was willing to try. I did last year at my Uncle Tom's, but they said I might spoil the milk because I was taking too long—had to rest my hands, you know. But this year I was bigger. And besides, last year I wasn't working on my grip. 'Course I didn't know about my left hand. That could be a problem… Damn! I always seemed to have a problem. I was always too small or too young or too something. Richard never had a problem: he was big enough, old enough, strong enough. But me! I was never enough! Shit! I was only good at one thing: running. I won all the races at the picnics we went to, like at Gages Lake, which was probably where my folks were going this Sunday.

The whole family would be there. Richard too, probably—they let him out on some weekends. God, I wished I were home. Gone one day and I was going bananas. Hope the folks come up for the Fourth, take me home with them. Please, Lord. If you did that, I would sacrifice doing the "bad thing" for a whooole week. Uh, make that threeee, no four days. Okay? Okay, Lord? Okay, it's a deal.

Oh, oh, Vickie's coming back…swinging her tail, I meant *pail*. That yellow dress with the little red flowers sure knew how to hug her curves. If I were a dress, I'd hug her curves…pick her flowers too. Ohhh yeah. Boy, I talked big, but did I do anything? Naaaw. Oh, oh, she's looking right at me! She was…she was coming over! The cat sprang out of my lap just as she reached me. My eyes were looking into her deep blues…and then she quickly bent down and poured milk into the cat bowl. She looked up at me like I was a germ. And then she licked some milk from her fingers and spun away, leaving me to watch her backside shift gears. Gad! She could've at least given me a smile, or better yet let me lick her fingers. Geeez, she was beautiful. Everything on her face was in all the right places and big enough and small enough and…just absolutely perfect. She could be a movie star, easy.

Oh well, the other one, Dorothy, looked okay, got two nice apples. Who knew, maybe I'd get a bite. Ha-ha-ha! Ahhh, who was I kidding. These broads were fourteen, fifteen, sixteen, seventeen—I didn't know. Richard might have a chance. But he was so girl-shy. I was shy outside, but inside I got the devil in me. That was what the nuns always said to me:

"On your knees, William!" *Whack* with the pointer. "Pray! Pray that devil out of you!" *Whack! Whack!* "Don't slouch! Back straight!" *Whack!* "Up, up!" *Whack! Whack!* Boy, I got knees of iron. All of us guys do.

A commotion broke out down the aisle. I jumped off the steps. Ah-lex was beating a cow with his milking stool. He cursed the poor animal in Polish as he clubbed it again and again. Why he did this, I had no idea. Poor cow was tramping back and forth in her stall, her head banging in the iron rectangle that held her as she strained to look back at her attacker, her big eyes filled with fear.

Suddenly, Ah-lex stopped, sat down, and started milking the cow…as if nothing happened. I glanced around; everybody else was back to milking…as if nothing happened. I was shaking like a leaf… because nothing happened.

Dorothy appeared with a shovel and started shoveling the splatter. "I'll do it." I took the shovel. She smiled. It was a nice smile, but she had the saddest eyes I've ever seen. I shoveled the mess down the trough with the rest of the manure, past the row of cows, past the empty stalls in back, and out into a wheelbarrow. Then I wheeled the load on some boards that were laid end to end in the, muck, out to the manure pile and dump it. My suitcase blisters burned, but I ignored them. By the time I shoveled out the trough on the other side of the aisle, I was no longer invisible. But I didn't care. I was mad. I was mad at the meanness that nobody did anything about, that I did nothing about. Mad at my folks for sending me up here to live with strangers. And mad because I felt so afraid and alone.

I ended up outside sitting on a crate with my back against the right half of the wide-open barn doors. My eyes were closed to the warm sun that was working its way down and still had a ways to go. I just wanted to sit here until I melted away. Until God carried me home...or killed me.

The cows startled me as they came spilling out of the barn. Ah-lex popped out after them, and I froze against the barn door, my heart pounding so hard it was sure to bust out of my chest.

"Whoo-waaah! Whoo-waaah!" barked Ah-lex as he herded the cows out to pasture. He hadn't seen me. I started to breathe again.

"Whoo-waaah! Whoo-waaah!" Ah-lex barked well—no need for a dog with him around. Some cows were already on the pathlike road that led up a rise and alongside a hayfield on the right. The open land on the left had a swampy look and was dotted with rotting stumps. Ah-lex moved over to a fence post, fished his pants, let out a stream, and farted a long note. The whole time I didn't move an eyelash, didn't breathe.

Turned the way he was, I felt he was sure to spot me, maybe even hear my heart pounding. He shook his twig, moved off, and went back to his barking routine. I watched until the cows and Ah-lex melted over the rise before I closed my eyes again and gave myself back over to the sun.

"William!"

My eyes snapped open! It was Grandpa leaning out of the barn. "Suppertime. Come." He ducked back in.

9

Water without Wind
and Six Shots

I watched Lucky Number 4 slosh water from the yellow pan onto his arms, face, and neck, then go at them with a bar of brown soap. Farmers, it seemed, had two-tone skin: hands and face brown as a grocery bag, the rest baby white. This Great-Grandpa was not short, not tall, and not bent—not like Grandpa Andrew. No, this one was ramrod straight and on the slim side. Overall, you might say he was delicate-looking—a phrase floated in the air when I appeared at family gatherings and which I thought stank but fit him to a tee. I liked his eyes best. They got a smile in them.

"Next," said Grandpa number 4, as he slicked his surprisingly dark hair back with his wet hands. I filled the pan from the pump, moved it back to the seat of the chair, and started in with the brown soap. This strong-smelling soap was what my mother used to scrub our floors with and my head when I got the lice. If you get some in your eyes, it'd sting like heck and burn them blood red. I ended up drinking from the pump out of my cupped hand and wondered how the water could be so cold. I was about to ask Grandpa number 4, but he was sitting on the steps now and gazing out over the land—like farmers seemed to do.

I joined him on the steps, and as we waited for supper he pulled out "the makings" for a cigarette. I glued my eyes and watched him shake out just enough tobacco from a cloth pouch into a square of white tissue, then with the help of his teeth, he tugged the pouch strings shut and tucked it away. Next, he carefully rolled the tissue with fingers and thumbed until it was round; then pinching it closed, he licked the edge, sealed it, twisted the ends shut, and lit up. Wow! I could hardly wait to try it!

Gramps drew deep on the cigarette and went back to his gazing routine. I looked out, but I didn't see that it'd changed any since I first saw it this afternoon—except that the air had a delicious freshness to it now and the sun felt warm not hot, the fire in it gone now, as it came at us at a good slant and cast a giant shadow of the barn halfway up the hill. It was quiet, farm quiet. A whippoorwill sang its looping notes, a frog croaked, crickets chirped, pigs snorted, a horse whinnied, and surprisingly you could hear his hooves stomping the ground. And far off, a cow did its mooooing and the sound hung in the air for a long time. Soothing sounds that settled you down…like water without wind.

Gramps was now drawing on a butt so short I didn't see how it didn't burn him, the way he had it pinched between thumb and forefinger. Somehow he managed to get another drag out of it before he flicked the glowing dot away and went back to his land-gazing. I stared at his brown cheeked face, so shiny and smooth with nary a wrinkle—those he'd saved for his neck.

Feeling my stare, I guess, he startled me with, "Folks doin' all right, are they?"

"I… Yeah, I guess so. They're both workin'."

"Hmmm." Gramps rocked his head a little—if you weren't watching close, you'd have missed it. "Father's got a tool-and-die shop, I hear."

"Uh-huh He's got a partner, Melvin. He's smart as a whip."

"Doin' good, are they?"

"Yeah, pretty good. They moved outta the garage. Workin' all the time now."

"Good." Gramps got it rockin' better this time. "Workin's good."

"Melvin can talk for hours without stoppin'."

"Must be smart."

"He is. He can recite Shakespeare. Poetry too."

"Poetry! Hmmmm."

"My dad's smart. He's a genius! No kidding. He made a transfer die for hose clamps for the military. They thought it would take three dies, and he made it all in one: a transfer die. It works great. But then the government, they said they weren't big enough. But then another man, Mister Mantel, he got 'em the contract. They're goin' 'round the clock now. Rooound the clock."

"Gotta make do when the sun shines." Gramps had it rockin' good now.

"They take turns fixin' the dies when they break. They sleep on a couch."

"Gotta make do…" Gramps stopped rockin'. He looked up at the sky. His mouth hung open.

"So how you doin', Grandpa?"

Gramps looked at me and chuckled. "How'm I doin'? That's a good one." Gramps chuckled again. "I'm gettin' old. That's how I'm doin'." Gramps took out his makings again and went about rolling another beaut. "It's up to the Lord, how the farmer does…" He tapped tobacco onto the tissue. "The weather…the weather and the market. The milk price." He rolled the tobacco… "Wartime the price is good." He finished by licking the tissue and sealing it. "Now we need the weather to hold for the hayin'." He struck a wooden match across a step and lit up.

"That hard to do? Make a cigarette?"

"Not if you wanna smoke, it ain't." Gramps looked at me. "You smoke?"

"No!" I shouted in surprise.

"You sure?"

"I'm too young, Grandpa!" I was still shouting. I was so thrilled, even though I know he was just kidding me along.

Gramps chuckled, dragged on his cigarette. "Eddie didn't show up at the train station, eh?"

"Uh-uh. I told you. Jake brought me out."

"That you did."

"Eddie's going into the service, huh? That's what my folks said."

"The Navy. Leaves Monday."

"Where's he at now, you think?"

"Probably—" Gramps gagged on his smoke and coughed. "Probably over by the Filas' farm. Your cousins." Gramps coughed some more and spit over left of the steps. "Pete and Joanne got ten kids. All girls, 'cept three. Youngest is named Mickey Rooney!" He laughed, and his eyes twinkled. "House full of movie stars."

"Jake said the Filas' farm is in bad shape. We passed it comin' out."

"Jake's a big talker."

"He's big all over."

"Big enough for two," cracked Gramps. We laughed. Gramps took a deep drag, tilted his head back, and let the smoke float out.

"Jake said this is the best farm around. The best land."

"Three hundred and sixty acres of black delta. Drop a seed in the ground, you have to jump back so it don't sprout up and knock you over."

"My Uncle Tom's got a farm over in Thorpe."

"That's a rock pile, not a farm." Gramps kicked left, toward the woods. "Got enough timber out there. Got water, creek runs through. Got enough pasture for forty cows. More!" He stared out at the land.

I gave it another look, but I still didn't think watching grass grow was all that interesting. The creeping shadow from the barn was almost up the hill now. "You really like farming, huh, Grandpa?"

"I don't. Never did."

I didn't know what to say to that.

"I'm a farmer because I'm not a sheriff anymore."

"A sheriff. You were a sheriff?" I didn't think he was big enough to smack guys around, throw 'em in a paddy wagon.

"Fourteen years in Chippewa Falls."

"Why did you stop?"

"Shot a man."

"Did you have to shoot him?"

"I shot him."

"Why?"

Gramps turned to me. "I got scared." He cracked a smile, his pale eyes twinkled, and he went back to the land. I stared at his smooth face and his wrinkled neck, and I got to thinking that I liked this old man, this fourth husband, this great-grandpa of mine. I liked talking to him. I mean, he really talked to me. And besides that, he shot a man.

Gramps and I were still sitting on the steps watching grass grow, but thoughts were bouncing around in my head like a Ping-Pong ball. I couldn't stop thinking about him shooting a man. How he shot the guy was what I wanted to know. But I didn't want to push my luck and maybe spoil our talk, so I pictured it all in my mind: how he outdrew the guy and drilled him. *Bang, Bang, Bang*...and *Bang, Bang, Bang*, because he was still moving. And then he turned in his badge and his gun and married Great-Grandma? I sneaked a look at Gramps. He was still locked into his staring thing. It just didn't figure. 'Course Grandma was irresistible: got that cracked puss and that hourglass figure with all the sand in the bottom. 'Course who knew what she looked like when they got married.

Might'a been a queen. But I doubted it. I wouldn't bet on it.

The girls stomping around inside the porch slowed. I figured that meant supper was about ready. Ho-hum. I leaned back on my elbows and looked up at the sky. The half-moon was just a wispy speck of a cloud...funny how it filled up so solid and bright when the darkness snuck in.

"Bam!" The barn door echoed like a shot, and there at the bottom of the hill stood Ah-lex. I shuddered like I'd been hit with a cold blast of air. He moved to the trough—now filled with water to cool the milk cans—rolled up his sleeves and splashed water on his face like he was afraid of it.

"Why did he hit that cow?" I mumbled, hoping Gramps would answer. He didn't. "Is he a relative?"

"Who? That's Ah-lex. Hired hand." Gramps shot his chin at him. Then he added softly, like he'd got a bead on him with a rifle. "That's who he is."

"Where's he from?"

Gramps chewed on the words before they came out. "Think your grandma found him on the doorstep." He spit over the side of the steps and chuckled.

I mumbled. "Should a left 'im."

"Hmpt?"

"Nothin'."

"Hard worker."

We watched Ah-lex dry himself off with a rag and start up the hill—which was almost all in shadow now. Right off, you could tell Ah-lex was different than other men and not in a good way. I mean, who or what wouldn't run from just his bark, or his look, or even his smell. And it wasn't just that; the worst thing was you could feel the meaness in him. I felt it as soon as I laid eyes on him, even before I saw him beat that poor cow. Some people were just scary: like Ed Moritz, like the landlord on Drummond Avenue, like the nun in first grade at Saint Stanislaus.

Ah-lex sat down a step below us. He didn't say anything, just got out his makings, and with his big brown hands and long fingers he rolled a perfect cigarette, and he did it faster and better than Grandpa. He wasn't much bigger than Grandpa, not much meat on him, but his bones looked big—made him look lean and hard as a rock. He struck a match on the step and lit up. He had those pig eyes that I first noticed in the barn. I couldn't say what the rest of his face looked like because I didn't want to look too close and have his ugly eyes catch me looking at him.

So we sat there, looking out—as was the custom—and nobody said a word. There were only the soothing country sounds and the buzz of Polish from the kitchen. Finally, I couldn't help stealing glances at Ah-lex as he smoked, and I could tell he knew I was eyeing him. And just like that, I knew that, somehow, I was going to have a big problem with this man. Some things you just knew, and there was nothing you could do about it. I shuddered at the thought, moved my right hand up slowly, and pointed:

Bang! Bang! Bang! And… *Bang! Bang! Bang!* Because he was still moving.

10

Flashing Knives and
an Angelic Smile

"Eat!" yelled Dorothy through the screen door, loud enough to carry the three miles into Lublin. I mean, after all, we were sitting right there under her nose. At least, I was. Gramps and Ahlex had already scrambled up the steps and entered the porch. *Eat!* The word beat on me wherever I went, drove me absolutely insane! They were probably going to put a plate in front of me with enough food on it to choke a horse. I was going to have to sit there until midnight before I could get it all down. Ugh! Just thinking about it was making my stomach do flip-flops. Oh well, better go on in and *eat!*

I sat facing the brick wall. Gramps was on my right, and I could smell Ah-lex on my left. The place across from me—with the best view—figured to be Grandma's. Vickie came out of the kitchen with her hands clamped on the handle of an enormous cast iron frying pan. She set the steaming giant down in the center of the table and jumped back. And just in time too, because without warning Gramps and Ah-lex attacked the sizzling pork chops atop the rice as if they were alive.

What a battle! Sparks flew from their flashing knives as they stabbed, cut, and forked mouthfuls into their chewing jaws. I managed a few jabs in between their swallows and in no time—two minutes tops—the pan was empty, followed by burps of victory.

Hooraaay, for the warriors of Lublin! This was how vittles should be downed, with no quarter given. And of course, you only ate as much as you killed, which for me was like two burps' worth. Wonderful! Terrific! Now all I had to do was to learn how to fence better so my fingers wouldn't be added to the meal.

Grandma brought out a square pan filled with a type of cheese-cake farmers make from sour milk. She shoveled a square on my plate, muttered some Polish, and settled into the empty chair opposite me. A big blue cone-shaped coffee pot was brought out by Dorothy. Grandpa filled my cup as well as his own—Grandma already had hers from the kitchen, and Ah-lex poured his own.

Everybody used sugar, lots of it, and drank it black. Back home I always drank milk. Here only the cats did. So now I was drinking coffee loaded with sugar, had steam going up my nose, and was polishing off the flat cake with my fellow warriors. Now that's what I call, *eat*!

To heck with that stupid saying that you had to eat big to be big. Uncle Leo ate like a bird, and he was six feet four inches. So how did that figure? Could be I was born to be a skinny little runt, no? After all, I was healthy. Except for the cold I carried through the winter to go along with my sore throat. And the fevers I threw in so I could see free movies on the wall: me digging away at the muck that kept pouring in, trying to bury me, until finally I threw up. And then, of course, the folks added the finishing touch with the red-bag sticking the hose you-know-where. And Dad yelling, "Hold it, hold it…" until he counted to ten—talk about a long count! So if I was to remain skin and bones, so what? After all, you didn't have to be big unless you wanted to be a football player or a movie star, right? Trouble was, I wanted to be both.

Grandma went on, filling the air with Polish, and I went on daydreaming, letting the words run in one ear and out the other as usual. As to why I never understood hardly a word of that weird language, I had no idea, never gave it a second thought. No, that was not true. I knew exactly when it started, this deafness to Polish. It was stamped on my brain in indelible ink: first day of school. Yeah, the "coup de grace"!

That was not to say the day didn't start well. It did. It started gloriously: sun shining, birds singing, Billy eating his mother's creamy oatmeal—not the slimy, lumpy, babysitter's special—and Dad standing tall and proud. Ah yes, there I sat sparkling like a diamond, everything I had on was new, top to bottom, inside and out. And so off I went, schoolbag in hand, skipping away to la-la land, and then it hit me: This was the routine I'd be tied to for the next eight years? Are you kidding? When was I going to have time to play? By the time I got home from school, it'd be almost suppertime. Hey, hey, this was not so good. Not good at all." But of course, the buildup had been so big—you had no idea.

The relatives (bless them) said, "Oh, Billy's going to get a girlfriend! Aren't you, Billy? Hee-hee-hee!"

Another said, "Ohhh, Billy's a big boy now! Tee-tee-tee!"

Billy was not a big boy and might possibly never get to be a big boy because just then Billy was thinking about running across Long Avenue with his eyes closed and becoming a smashed little boy. Oh, but not really. Even back then, I wasn't that stupid. I'd figure out something better than being flattened like a pancake. So I came up with, like I could break a leg, then an arm, stuff like that. So anyway, finally, I told myself: "I'll just go in there and size up the joint. What the heck."

Sister Nieroska had the body of a fullback and a face to match. It was hairy and sported a nose plastered to the right. And of course, this face that only God could love—hopefully—was encased in stiff white material and hooded in black from top to bottom. Anyway, to get on with it, Sister was calling us up to her desk one at a time to read from a book of Polish. Yes, Polish! I wasn't paying much attention; nobody was. We were all too busy sizing each other up. There were a lot of us, about forty, about half girls and half boys, and everybody was dressed pretty neat, the girls especially, like it was their birthday.

My row was called up, and we marched to the aisle by the blackboard and stood there in a line waiting our turn. Sister would open a first- or second-grade Polish reader—depending on how Polish you looked, I guess. Like this kid before me must've looked like a Polish genius, because she started him off with a second-grade reader, then quickly pulled out a third-grade one, and finally a fourth, and he got through some of that one too. This little squirt had the whole room watching him as he rattled off sentences like Father Pastor from the pulpit. He was so good, in fact, one might think he was Pastor's son—uh, make that nephew. Sister Nieroska beamed proud, like a mother might, patted his pointed head, and gave him a holy picture. I was next. Now, not everybody could read Polish, and those that couldn't wound up standing in the back of the room. So I already knew my fate—or so I thought.

Sister Nieroska gave me the once-over and decided I had the look of a genius—naturally. So she cracked open the second-grade reader. It had words in it longer than worms. Sooo, not to disappoint, I started rattling off my Polish prayers, which was the only Polish I knew—beside some choice swear words, of course. Sister snapped the book shut, almost catching my nose in it. She cracked open another book and stuck it in my face. I shook my head, and she showed me her teeth. She then picked up this thin book and opened it to about the middle. Lo and behold, a picture of a boat with a cute Polish word printed below. Sister pointed to the word and tapped her finger. I gave her a little smile and wagged my head. Sister's eyebrows arched, and she flipped a few pages toward the front and did the finger tapping again. I gave her a quick shake of my head. Sister straightened up, and her dark eyes narrowed. Slowly, she flipped to the very first page. I can still see it: a big needle with a piece of black thread running through the eye set against a light-blue square. And all around it was the letter *I*, in uppercase, lowercase, printed, and in longhand.

I gave Sister my best trick, an angelic smile, then jabbing a finger at each letter I read, "I-i-i-i." Read all four of them, I did.

Sister hit the page with a fist.

"Needle!" I shouted.

Smoke came out of her nose, and her black wings fluttered.

Quickly I added, "Needle and thread? Black thread?"

Sister's eyes bulged as she gave birth to a right hand that I never saw coming. I was stretching my angelic smile to the limit when it hit. *Crack!* A slap heard around the world—at least the classroom. My face flew to the right, and I stumbled after it until I fell. Stars sparkled in my eyes, my ears rang gloriously, and my face burned like fire. And that's all I remember about first grade. Plus the fact I cried right there in front of everybody.

Polish words were now bouncing between Grandma and Ah-lex like in a Ping-Pong match. Grandpa was sitting back, watching, puffing up clouds of smoke… The kitchen was dark now. A candle flickered at the far end of the porch. The girls were there… Polish was still flying up and back, rumbling through my ears…disappearing in the smoke…

There was one other thing I remembered about first grade. It was about this kid, Charles, who peed his pants every day. He'd be sitting at his desk, and all of a sudden water would be running off the seat and puddling the floor. He'd end up standing in the corner until recess time. The funny thing was, it didn't seem to bother him at all; he'd be making faces at us the whole time. I don't know why I talked to him. I guess because nobody else did. I liked his hair; it grew all around his head in waves and was the color of sand. Charles was the only kid in class that wore glasses. He let me try them on once. It was scary, like being in a cage. Most days I gave Charles half of my sandwich in exchange for the delicious cookies his mom made. Our moms had the same name, Stella. I was glad that was all we had in common.

Okay, listen, that was not really what I wanted to tell you. In fact, I don't know how that goofy thing popped out. I guess, maybe, because it was hard to tell you about this…this secret thing, this good thing. Rather, it could have been good, except I loused it up. Actually, it was about this girl. She sat across the aisle from me, this girl, and—you won't believe me—she had eyes that talked. She did! I kid you not. And when I looked at her, I hoped mine did too. And she had a nice nose, a little turned-up thing. Her lips, they were just okay, but boooy, did I wanna kiss them. And she was loaded with freckles—which made her look extra special, if you ask me. In fact, I hoped someday I could just stare at her and count them all. Another crazy thing was that I liked her shoulders. They were straight and wide, and not too round and not too square. I just liked them for some reason. And she had light brown hair that was pulled back and tied with a ribbon, and I liked that too. She was six, and I was seven—a small seven. She was the only good thing that happened to me in first grade.

Of course, I don't know if you could measure how good it was since I never even talked to her. But I almost did kiss her once by accident. Came so close, just about an inch apart. I was outside the classroom running down the corridor to the door, and she was inside the classroom making for the same door, and we both ran into each other and bumped apart. She stared into my eyes like no one had ever done before. "Kiss me," said her dark eyes. And I wanted to, but by the time I figured out which way to tilt my head and all, she slid past me. Right then and there, I wanted to kick myself in the pants. And I still doooo!

We even walked home together—more or less. She was on one side of the street; I was on the other. But when she stopped, I stopped, and if I stopped, she stopped; and when one of us started up again, the other one did too. Boy, that was something! I wanted to cross the street, but I never did. Then one day she walked home a different way. Why? I wondered. Why would she do that? So from then on I never walked home that way again. I guess I felt the next time she went our way and saw I wasn't there, she'd find out what it felt like. But deep down, I was pretty sure she really didn't care. Why should she? I wouldn't even walk across the street to talk to her. But I couldn't. What would I say? "I wanna count your freckles." Besides, I didn't really want to talk to her; I wanted to kiss her. Boy, did I ever! I would be soooo happy! Geez, I can still see her face...so clear it's scary.

And now this part you're not going to believe at all. Not one drop. You ready? That was Arlene. Yep, Arlene Kieta. They moved in down the block about a month ago, 2546 Mango; they were on my route. And boy, did she look good. Her freckles were gone, but her eyes still talked...and I think mine did too. But the really screwy thing was that she still went to St. Stanislaus. I mean, like hey, that was a lot of walking. 'Course, she could take the Central Avenue bus for three blocks and then the Fullerton Avenue streetcar for about six blocks, but she liked walking. That was what she told me. No kidding! And here's the best part: on her way home she had to walk past my house, and she did it reeeal slow like. And last Friday, after I did the collection, I took her for a ride on my bike. How about that! Oh man, it was sooo great! The cool air was blowing in our face, and her hair kept whipping around…smelled like flowers. It really did. So I showed her my whole paper route. And then, when I pulled up to her house, she jumped off and gave me those eyes…and then she ran into the house. Oh man, if I didn't kiss that girl soon, I was going to go crazy.

11

Scary Dream and Crazy Eddie

My sleepy eyes opened. Gray light seeped in from the window. I panicked! Where was I? Then in a blink, it all came back: the farm! Great-Grandma's farm! The land so grand that when you pissed on it, flowers sprang up. Where cigarettes were rolled and where eating time was a two-minute ritual. But how did I get here? In this room? In this bed? My clothes on that chair? And whose bed was that against the wall across from me? Vickie's maybe? William, get real.

Let's see now: I was sipping coffee, they were smoking, the kerosene lamp was hissing, Grandma started in with the Polish. I started daydreaming about Arlene... I must've fallen asleep. So naturally, Vickie carried me upstairs, undressed me, tucked me in, and gave me a pat you know where. Well, it's possible. Although now it came to me. It was Dorothy. She led me up by candlelight, waited for me to undress, then pushed me into bed, and left. Well, she had her chance.

God, it's quiet. Not that it's that noisy at home. It's not. But not like here. Here it's dead quiet... Everybody's probably in the barn milking, already. What was that sound? My head came off the pillow before I realized it was my stomach groaning as usual. I snuggled back into the foot-high comforter, feathers that were as light as snow. For the record, I was not the type woke up in the morning and shifted into high gear. Oh no. I was the type that opened an eye and shut it quickly, hoping to get in a few more winks. The trick, of course, was to drift back into a dream, like in this case, I was already consider-

77

ing one of my repeater dreams, the one where I was real scared, but everything worked out anyway. It's my Christmas dream. I know, I know, it's summertime, but dreams are pretty screwy anyway, right?

By the way, I'm a big-time dreamer. Dream every night, I do. Also, if I don't finish a dream one night I can go to bed the next night and say, "Continue my dream," and it picks up right where it left off I think that's pretty neat, but when I tell someone that they look at me like I'm crazy. But I like the fact that I dream every night; it's like watching free movies-but not as good, of course. Richard never dreams. Only when he has a fever; which is like twice in his whole life. He's so healthy it's disgusting. Anyway, my Christmas dream comes from a true incident. It's not really a bad dream, but it's kind of a scary one and I'm always glad when it's over. In fact, I always hope I won't have to use it again. But I do.

It starts off we're at the Cukla's—my dad's farmer friends from Wisconsin. I mentioned them earlier: playing 'Doctor'? Patsy and Carol? Boy, those were the days. I haven't had any luck since. Except for Eleanor, who doesn't count, was a complete disaster, which I'll tell you about later, *maybe*—if I want to punish myself. Anyway, I'm like six years old, and it's Christmas Eve, and we're in the living room when Santa Claus comes in carrying two big white bags loaded with presents, naturally. He sits down by the Christmas tree, shivers, rubs his hands together, and tells us how it's colder than a reindeer's ass up at the North Pole, and how he needs something to warm him up before he can get started with the presents. So, Mrs. Cukla asks him if he would like some hot cocoa and everybody laughs. So then she brings him a shot of whiskey and Santa sings out, "Merry Christmas!" and slugs it down.

"Merry Christmas, Santa," everybody yells back.

"Have all you kids been good this year?" roars Santa.

"Yeeeess!" we all shout back.

So then Santa starts pulling presents out of a bag and calling out names. One by one kids go up and get their presents. Name after name is called and many times the same name is called again and again, sometimes four times even, and mine not even once. Pretty soon every time Santa calls out a name I feel myself growing smaller and smaller. One white bag is empty and Santa starts digging into the second one. More names are called and I'm hoping to shrink away to nothing before he's done. Why doesn't Santa have something for me? What am I going to do? How am I going to face everybody? "Oh God," I pray, "please God, make me disappear. Please, God. Pleeeease!"

"Billy!" calls Santa, holding up a present.

"That's me! He called my name! I have a present. I have a present!" I say this all to myself, but I don't move.

"Go, Billy," says my mom, giving me a little push.

So I go up to Santa by the Christmas tree and I can tell everybody is watching me. The present is about the size of a shoebox and it's all wrapped in white paper with a red ribbon around it. I can't take my eyes off of it.

"Have you been a good boy this year, Billy?"

I nod.

"Are you sure?" says Santa, leaning forward, the present now under my nose.

I nod and grab the box, but Santa won't let go. We pull up and back, up and back. Everybody is laughing. Up and back, and I won't let him have it. Finally, I give it a big yank and he lets go. I run back to my folks with the box. Everybody is still laughing.

"I got a present!" I show them. "I got a present!"

"Open it," says my mom.

I tear the wrapping off, open the box, and inside is a Red Truck. It's the best Red Truck you ever saw. And it's *mine*. And it's perfect, with perfect rubber wheels that roll smooth and quiet.

I rolled that truck all over the house for years; traveled thousands of miles with it; stopped at every secret place in the world. It's the best present I ever got. And the very best thing about it is that— even though it's long gone—I can still see my Red Truck anytime I want to, because it's parked right inside my head, way in back, lower left side. It shines, I tell you. Shines bright, night and day, it does. And the motor puuuuuuuuuuuuurrrss.

So that was the dream I dreamed when I was scared, like now, and everything worked out. But it was not working today. Probably because I was way past being scared. I couldn't even do the "bad thing." But that's good, in a way, because I was way ahead of schedule anyway. Damn! Yesterday, when I woke up on the train, I panicked because I couldn't see anything out of my left eye, and then I realized it was glued together. I took that as a warning.

I peeked out over my thick red comforter and gave the room the once-over. The other bed was probably for Richard. The door was on that side of the room. The window was on my side. And across the room was a dresser with a cracked mirror. And that was it. No carpets, not even a curtain on the window, just a rolled-up shade with a finger-hole thing dangling from a string.

I crawled out of bed, tucked my hands under my armpits, and moved over the cold floor to the opened window. The slanting sunlight from over right made long shadows out of everything. The yard on this side of the house had a clothesline running through it, left to right, up and back, up and back. And on the other side of it, there was a field of ankle-high corn, which, if it was knee-high by the Fourth of July, would be right on schedule. One odd thing was that there was a couple of chairs across the yard facing the cornfield. Hmm, don't tell me they sat out there and watched the corn grow—which on second thought might not be so ridiculous, because my dad used to always say, "At night, after a rain, you could hear the corn grow."

So I guess you could see it grow too. That is, if you were that wacky about corn—which, if I was ever that far gone, just shoot me and bury me deep.

Bam!

The sound of the screen door slamming shut was followed by someone stomping around down there. I quickly put on my jeans, T-shirt, and sandals, and moved out into the hallway. At the far end on my left was another door. There was also another door on my side of the hallway and one almost directly across from me. The stairway was to my right. As I tiptoed over to it, the floorboards creaked and squeaked, and the steps also played a tune. The passageway leading to the kitchen was where the bass notes came in. The whole house was like a music box. I found the kitchen empty, but out on the porch, I spotted a blond head of hair sitting at the round table looking out.

"Hey, kid, you got here!" boomed the head without turning. I jumped like a scared rabbit. "What?"

"Get some coffee, si' dooown," drawled the guy I figured to be Eddie, who was tilted back in his chair with a leg up on the table and an arm dangling down from where smoke was curling up from a cigarette. "Hey, fill this up, huh?" He held a coffee cup out left, still without looking at me. I grabbed it, but he held on and pulled me into view. "Jesus, look what the cat dragged in."

I couldn't take my eyes off the guy. Eddie wasn't something the cat dragged in; that was for sure.

Eddie had bright green eyes that flashed like a neon sign and wavy hair that rolled around his head like a crown. And as if that wasn't enough, the guy had a great jaw, chiseled square, with a perfect line of dazzling white teeth. Damn! What a puss. I liked him right off the bat. But right off the bat, I also sensed that he was not the type you turned your back on.

"What're you lookin' at?" said Eddie, exhaling a cloud of smoke.

"Nothin'. You're Eddie."

"I'm Eddie."

"You were supposed to pick me up at the train station."

"So? You got here, didn't ya? Eddie blew cigarette smoke at me while fingering a pack of Lucky Strikes on the table.

I went back into the kitchen with Eddie's cup. The black iron stove on the left took up most of the wall and was alive—kind of like the Iron Horse. I had to use both hands to lift the big blue coffee pot off the hot end of the stove. I filled Eddie's cup and one for myself and took the steaming cups out to the porch. I sat across from Eddie, spooned sugar into my cup, and stirred it with a spoon. I did it all very carefully and felt Eddie's eyes on me the whole time.

"Have a smoke, kid." Eddie shot the pack of Lucky Strikes over to me.

I gave Eddie a glance and fumbled with the tightly filled pack, trying to fish out a cigarette.

Eddie blew a cloud of smoke at the ceiling. "Going into the Navy!" *Bam!* He slammed his fist down on the table. I jumped, as did the salt and pepper shakers. "No more farming!" *Bam!* Eddie snuffed his cigarette out in the tin ashtray and swung his leg off the table. *Bam! Bam!* A left and a right. *Bam! Bam!* "Go ahead."

"What?" I was still fishing for the cigarette. The *bam's* didn't help any.

Bam!

"*Psia krew cholera!*"

Bam! Bam!

The ripples in my cup became waves. "Say, ahhhh, where's everybody?"

Bam! "*Psia krew cholera!* Do it!"

I was thinking, "This guy's cracked!"

"Do it, kid! C'mon!"

I hit the table with my fist. *Bam.* "*Psia krew cholera.*"

"Harder!"

Bam!

The saltshaker toppled over.

"Harder!" *Bam!*

Bam! I smashed the table with my mighty fist; a few grains of salt moved.

"*Psia krew cholera!*" shouted crazy Eddie. *Bam! Bam! Bam! Bam!* Everything on the table danced, and coffee slopped from the cups.

Then I followed Eddie's lead. Crazy Eddie and Skinny Billy!

Bam! Bam! Ba-bam! Bam!

"*PSIA KREW CHOLERA! PSIA KREW CHOLERA!*"

Bam-ba-bam-bam, ba-bam-bambam! Bam-bam!

"STOP!" Eddie's hand shot out. "They'll hear us."

Now he thinks of that? We looked down at the barn, nothing out there but a milk can with foam on the top. Eddie grabbed a smoke from his pack, saw that mine was coffee-soaked, tossed me a fresh one. "Light up, kid."

I did. I struck a wooden match against the bottom of the table like Eddie and puffed up a cloud.

"Don't suck on it like a tit. Inhale. Like this." Eddie drew deep on the cigarette; the tip turned a bright red.

I drew, gagged, and almost puked. "Burns," I croaked, my left hand squeezing my throat.

"Drink some coffee."

I drank some coffee.

"You gotta break it in easy. Like a woman."

I felt blood rush to my face. Eddie didn't notice. He was busy blowing perfect smoke rings.

"My Uncle Leo can do that. He blows them so big I can put my fist through them."

"Oh yeah? He must blow 'em out of his ass," Eddie roared.

I sucked on my cigarette until Eddie calmed down. "Going into the Navy, huh?"

"Fuckin'a."

"You a good swimmer?"

"Fuckin'a." Eddie blew a cloud of smoke at me. "Why?"

"Boats sink." I puffed up a cloud.

"I'm not gonna be on no boat! I'm gonna be on a ship! A hundred times bigger than that barn, kid!" fired Eddie. "They don't sink! Gonna sleep high and dry!"

"*Titanic.*" I slid it in like a knife.

"You're full of shit, kid."

"Billy!"

"Well, Billy, you're still full of shit!" Eddie roared, tossed his cigarette into his sloshed coffee cup, and disappeared into the house.

12

Work Baloney

Everybody was in the barn milking, except Eddie. I didn't know what he was doing—probably practicing his swimming. I started shoveling cow pies down the trough: got a nod from Grandpa...a little wave from Dorothy...to Vickie I was invisible.

Grandma croaked, "Williaaaam!"

I echoed back, "Grandmaaaa!"

And of course, there was Ah-lex, but I didn't look at him, just gave him the corner of my eye until I got out of range.

There were twenty-seven cows, so the milking took a long time, about two and a half hours. I played with Daisy, the cat, and shoveled cow pies, but that left me with a lot of time, so I got to thinking about this milking thing: how it went on every day, twice a day, like forever. Oh, I suppose you could get a couple days off for a heart attack, or pneumonia, but other than that, it didn't end until you were in the ground. Amen. And then, of course, there was all the work in between: plowing, planting, cultivating, harvesting—the backbreaking haying—and almost all of it done under a broiling hot sun. And there was livestock, besides the cows, that had to be taken care of: horses, pigs, chickens, ducks, geese, whatever. Oh, and the vegetable garden along with the canning, and not to forget the wood-chopping. And to top it all off, if you didn't make the right deal with God on the rain thing—not too much, not too little—a year's work could go down the drain. Frightening!

And hey! Even if it all worked out, with God and everything, what was the payoff? You could eat like a horse and fart like one? Why, you couldn't even do the wife thing every day because you'd be too darn tired. And she'd have a headache anyway. Then again, if you did get lucky, you wouldn't even be able to see each other because there was no electricity; this, however, could be a blessing. But wait! The thing you would have: You would be your own boss. Yes! And that made sense because there couldn't possibly be a boss in the whole wide world that would be stupid enough to think that you would be dumb enough to do all those things. God Almighty!

No wonder my dad left the farm for greener pastures. But was working fifty hours a week in a tool-and-die shop any better? Stinking oily air, under oily light bulbs? Not to feel the rain, see snowflakes fall, except during the dark of night, or on a Sunday. Cutting, shaping, grinding steel to within a thousandth of an inch, over and over, day after day, until you dropped dead... Yet he never complained.

I didn't get it. I really didn't. It seemed to me that was what hell must be like—with the heat turned up to whatever degree you were bad. So who needed it? Money? Well, hell's bells, knocking off a bank might just be worth the risk—and a lot more fun, that's for sure. I swear, if somebody asked me again what I was going to be when I grew up, I was going to spit in their eye.

13

Two Wet Globes

I was sitting on my favorite crate outside the barn when the cows started spilling out. I quickly flattened myself against the door expecting Ah-lex to follow, but out popped Dorothy.

"Hey!" she said, cranking an arm at me, then strutting off bare-foot through the barnyard muck as if she were walking on flowers. Actually, I hadn't seen Dorothy or Vicki in shoes since I arrived. Was that yesterday? Boy, these farm days sure are long.

I placed my sandals inside the barn door and started hopping through the oozing muck as best I could. Once I got to the pathlike road, the pebbles hurt my poor feet, but I hobbled on. Dorothy, with her farm feet, was still moving smartly, herding the cows out over the rise. The dry swampland on my left—with its cracked mud, rotting tree stumps, and weird camel-like humps looked like something out of a creepy movie. All it needed was a full moon and some fog.

"Come on!" Dorothy gave me a snappy wrist wave and started leaping from hump to hump after some stray cows in hump-land.

I followed after her, the green mossy-topped humps soft as velvet on the feet.

"Shoo, Bossy! Shoo! Shoo!" Dorothy yelled and clapped her hands at the strays and got them moving in line back to the road. "Get those two!" She pointed to a couple of cows, out a ways, licking a salt block that was stuck on a pole.

I zigzagged the hump tops out to the salt block. "Shoo, Bossy. Shoo! Shoo!" I yelled and clapped my hands, but all I got was a lazy look as they continued to lick away at the salt like it was ice cream—which to them it probably was. I moved closer, repeated the routine, but all they did was swish their tails at me. They didn't move until I got right on top of them, but then, as I raced ahead, they swung around and went back to the salt.

Dorothy, watching from the rise, was laughing her head off. I flew at the two cows again: leaping humps, waving arms, and barking like Ah-lex. "Whoowaah! Whoo-waah! It worked. I chased them all the way back to the road and over the rise.

Dorothy was bent over with laughter. "You can't..." she caught her breath. "You can't run them like that. Their milk will go bad." She stared at me as I shifted my weight from foot to foot to ease my aching feet. "You gotta go?"

Heat shot to my face. "No! My feet burn."

"Do like this," she said, stepping into a cow pie with both feet and crooning like the bad thing was happening to her. "Ohhh, it feels so gooood." I thought sure, the blood pumping in my head was going to squirt out of my ears. "Try it." She pointed to a cow pie to my right.

The greenish brown thing was oozing like a pie just out of the oven. "Are you crazy? It's still alive!"

"Don't be such a baby." Dorothy mushed around in the icky pie...her behind dancing nicely. "C'mon! Try it!"

It was still moving. Ugly things would feast on my feet. Worms would crawl between my toes. "I'm not puttin' my foot in that shit."

"Oh-ho! City boy! City boy!"

I poked the damn thing with my big toe, and it came out all diseased. "Ugggghh!"

"Oh, for Pete's sake!" Dorothy kicked out and peppered me with cow shit.

I teed off at my slimy special and didn't stop until she was spotted from head to toe. She took one look at herself and went screaming down the road toward the creek. I ran after her.

"Dorothy, I'm sorry! I'm sorry!" I wasn't really, but what the heck? Hey, she was the one crazy for cow shit, right? I followed her knee-deep into the creek. The cows had already crossed and were heading out to pasture. "Geez, Dorothy. I'm really sorry."

And now, since she was rubbing at the stuff, smearing it, I actually did feel a little sorry for her. I mean, what the heck, even her face looked bad. I mean whose wouldn't, smeared with shit?

"Hey, Dorothy, guess what? My feet don't burn anymore."

"*Psia krew cholera!*" She kicked a spray of water at me and kept at the rubbing. I sure didn't want to be that dress. Well, maybe I did…hugging all those curves. I crouched down and started splashing around, cleaning myself off, and then she did the same, and pretty soon we were splashing each other, and finally, she started giggling. I was glad of that.

"Wait, stop!" She stood up and turned around. "Is my back okay?"

Her dress was like a second skin—especially the way it curved over those two wet cheeks with the crease in the middle. She started to turn back around.

"Wait! There's a little spot." I cupped some water and rubbed at a perfectly clean spot by her shoulder because I just had to touch her. I stopped rubbing and let my fingers ride down her back…and real quick-like I brushed her moons. "Oops, sorry."

Dorothy spun around, her eyes drilling me, her two wet globes almost touching me. "You have some on your ear." She started brushing my ear. One of her things touched my chest. And stayed there. "How old are you?"

"Uhh, thirteen…and a half." I turned my head away because I couldn't keep looking at her with that lie on my face.

"Thirteen and a half?

"Yeah, I'm small for my age. So's my dad."

"Hmmm." She dipped to one side, so she could look me in the eyes. "Are you educated?" She covered her mouth, quickly, like she had bad breath or something.

"Yeah, sure. Pretty much. I'm going to be in…seventh grade, I lied."

Dorothy giggled and squatted back down into the water.

"Why? What do you mean?" I dropped down opposite her. "Are you educated?"

She giggled low and deep. I wanted to kiss her. She played a hand through the water up and back…up and back…

"So, city billy, what are you going to be when you grow up?"

"What? I can't believe you said that! Why did you say that? Why?"

"Heeey! Don't get mad."

"I'm not mad. I'm just… What are you going to be?"

Dorothy started waving both her hands in the water. "I'm going to get married and have babies. About a half a dozen." Up and back… "Maybe more, God willing."

Again, blood shot to my face. I splashed water on it.

"You could be a doctor. You're smart. That's what they say."

"Who says?" I slicked my hair back.

Dorothy shrugged. "I heard it."

She looked so cute…even with her sad-cow eyes. I leaned in close. "I'm gonna rob banks."

"Billy!" She pushed me away and sent a splash after me. "Don't talk like that."

"You want to be my moll?"

"Moll?"

"My gun moll. My partner. You know."

I gave her shaking head and shocked-look a little splash. She gave me one back.

"You should be a doctor. Doctors save lives."

"Uh-uh, not always. Mostly, they chop bodies open, take a glance inside, and sew them back up—that is, if they're still alive. That's what they did to my grandma. And get this, it's like, dead or alive, give me the money. They get paid either way. Get it?"

"You…you shouldn't talk like that. Doctors help people. That's terrible, what you said."

"It's still either way. Just like lawyers."

"Lawyers? Lawyers are important, Billy!"

"Are you nuts?"

"Stop saying that!" Dorothy started splashing me big time with her foot. "That's not funny!"

"Okay, okay. Sorry. But a lawyer's just a mouthpiece. They twist things around so they sound good. That's what my Uncle George says. And the better the twist, the more you pay them. How about that? Pretty rotten, eh?"

"Aunt Jean's husband said that?"

"Yeah, Uncle George. Ask him when they get here. Ask him, you don't believe me." We moved into deeper water and waved our arms, slowly, up and back...up and back...

"Well... I don't think you'd make a good farmer anyway. Do you?"

"Are you cra? Listen, sweetheart, I'm from Chicago. I like action."

"I know! You could be a policeman!"

"A cop? Are you kidding? You can get killed!"

"How about a... Uhhh, no, I don't think so."

"What?"

"An electrician?"

"Oh, sure. Go up like a roman candle, smoke coming out of my ears."

"A carpenter?"

"Swollen thumbs, black-and-blue fingernails. Hey, Christ was a carpenter. Look what they did to him... What? What're you shaking your head for?"

"The things you say."

"Oh yeah? Listen, robbing banks ain't that bad."

"Oh, I know! You could be the man on the flying trapeze!"

"Now you're cookin'. I could do that. Yeah. Sure... I want to go, go, go. All the way to the moon."

"You're the one's crazy."

"Don't you want to see things?"

"I want... I want what's here. What's human. You're... The way you talk. That's drifting." Dorothy started, kicking her legs at me like she was trying to drown me.

I dove toward the middle of the creek and swam underwater for as long as I could. When I surfaced, Dorothy was gone. I spotted her on the road heading back to the house. I got out and followed the creek downstream, toward the bridge off in the distance.

The creek zigzagged, and I found three quiet pools of water side by side. The biggest one, the middle one, looked like a good swimming hole. That is, if you were brave enough, the water so dark and scary, looking like black ice, hard and smooth. Who could tell what was underneath just waiting for a little kid like me? I wouldn't want to even fish in it. Probably hook a monster, pull you right in.

My dad told me once about when he was a kid swimming with some guys, in a pool like this, they dared a little kid that couldn't swim worth a dang to swim across, and in the middle he went down, and they never saw him again. Dad said the current must've taken him downstream somewhere and that some animal probably ate him up, a bear...or some wolves, most likely. A rustling sound turned me around quick. Ha-ha, just a couple of squirrels running up and down a tree.

I sat on the grassy bank and let the already-hot sun dry me out. Being Saturday, the folks would probably go see a movie tonight. Get some popcorn loaded with butter. My mouth's watering just thinking about it. Tomorrow the whole family would probably go to Gages Lake—like I said. Or maybe even Lake Geneva. That was the best. It was the farthest, but it had got everything: a big beach, all kinds of games, and shops, and a dance floor with an orchestra not some dinky little band. They played Glenn Miller stuff with saxes, trombones, trumpets, drums, the works! Made you swing around even if you have two left feet. A dragonfly hovered over a yellow flower. How the heck did they do that, hang there like that? A cricket lands on the black ice, swims, and cuts a perfect 'V' that grows wider and wider. I heaved a boulder into the middle. *Ka-plunk.* The bull's-eye rolled out, hit land, and the water again became a mirror. I stared into it, but all I could see were the things back home.

14

Dorothy Is Nuts About Me

Breakfast was baloney and eggs and a stack of fried bread. With Eddie added to the table, I had to do some fancy stabbing before the frying pan was empty. I tell you, these people were the greatest eaters in the world. 'Course, not having a lot of teeth in the way helped—you could just shovel it in and swallow. Eddie brought out his store-bought cigarettes, shook one out, and shot the pack across the table, hitting me in the forearm. He gave me a wink, but I let them lie there like I hadn't noticed anything.

Gramps picked them up. "Don't mind if I do." He got one out and slid the pack over to Ahlex, who followed suit. Eddie snatched the pack back and gave me a look that would wilt flowers. I had to freeze my face to keep from laughing.

Grandma came out of the kitchen with a cup of coffee, sat in her rocking chair, and cut loose with the Polish. When she paused, everybody sipped or took another drag, but no one said a word. Grandma fired away again and again. Finally, getting no response, she gave up—or ran out of ammunition, which wasn't exactly the same thing.

I thought it was all over, but then Grandpa broke the silence with a "Ja." followed by some nodding. Ah-lex did the same, and so did Eddie. So naturally, I threw out a big "Jaaaah!" and did some head flopping. It got me a surprised look, but no laugh. Hey, for all I knew, they were deciding where to bury me. Anyway, whatever it was, you could tell the talking was over by the way they now blew their smoke and sipped their coffee, kind of like they were let out of jail.

Dorothy brought out a plate stacked with squares of flat cake, and as she cleared a place for them, her hip pressed against my arm and stayed there. This girl was going to have me twisted around her little finger in no time.

After the cake disappeared, Eddie did a little Polish, and everybody got excited and started gabbing. What I got out of Dorothy was this: Saturday was shopping day, and you could go to town with Grandma and Grandpa if, say, it was your birthday, or you had to have your tooth pulled, or you were going off to the war. Or if you were the new kid on the block (I added that one).

"So when do we go?"

"We're not going," said Dorothy. "It's fifty miles! Eddie's taking them to Marshfield."

"So why can't we go?"

"We have to do the chores. It's just Vickie and the folks. It's her turn. But Eddie can bring you back something."

"Tell him to bring me back an ice cream cone."

Dorothy was doing the laundry; Ah-lex was out cutting hay with Jim, the stallion, farting in his face, I hoped; and I was in the vegetable garden picking strawberries. And after that, I was supposed to do something with the potato bugs. And after that, I figured they were probably going to have me pull out some stumps just to work up a sweat.

The trick with picking strawberries was not to get eaten alive by the mosquitoes. That they loved my city blood was evident by the dance I was doing. I just hoped to get my quart bucket filled before I needed a transfusion. Boy, these buggers really loved me. My blood type must be D for *delicious*. Well, at least it was nice to know somebody loved me, even if was costing me my precious blood in exchange. It also made me wonder what I'd get for one of my bones, all white and shiny—great to chew on. And how about my heart! It ran well...but it also broke a lot, so I guess nobody wanted that. Besides, I was saving it for later because somewhere along the way, I got the idea that when you grew up, you could give it to the one you loved and she would give you hers in return; and then you'd be happy, have kids, all that kind of stuff... God willing.

The sun was frying me like a piece of bacon, and I was getting dizzy—loss of blood, you know—so I gave up the hunt. I didn't see it made any sense to stagger around till I got sucked dry and cooked on top of it. I closed the garden gate, cut across the yard, and spotted Dorothy at the pump.

"You done?" She went on pumping water into a bucket. I told her I was and showed her the pail.

"It's not full."

"I ran out of strawberries. You said just to pick the ripe ones."

She kept pumping. "There's a lot of wild blackberries and rasp-berries along the back fence. You can fill the pail with some of those."

Water started running over the rim of the bucket. She stopped pumping, flicked her pigtail out of the way, and put her lips to the surface and drank. "Hmmmmm..." She patted some water onto her face. "Drink." She pointed.

I put my lips to the surface, filled up...then let my head sink slowly into the bucket. Bubble, bubble, bubble, bubble.

"Billy!" Dorothy pulled me out by my hair. "Are you all right?"

"Sure. I'm part fish."

Dorothy shook her head and grabbed the handle of the pail. "Watch out," she said, hoisting the bucket with one hand while using the other arm for balance. I followed her on the cement slabs, up the stairs, and into the house. In the stove-hot kitchen, she switched her cold pail of water for the hot one on the stove. She used two hands to do it and her apron on the hot handle to boot. I jumped ahead and opened the screen door for her. She took the steps one at a time with the steaming bucket held out in front. At the bottom she regripped with one hand and started walking up the slabs, her right arm out for balance. I followed her out past the pump and around the corner of the house to where a huge galvanized washtub lay on the ground. Long rows of laundry hung dead up and down the yard.

"Pull the washboard out," said Dorothy. I did, and she poured the steaming water into the big washtub. It came alive with bubbles and foam. "You got any dirty clothes?" she asked as she poked at the laundry in the tub with a sawed off broom handle.

"No." I shook my head. I was glad I did my hankie in the creek—my Jockey's too.

"Go get Ah-lex's laundry. It's in his room at the end of the hallway."

I didn't much care to do that, so I didn't move.

Dorothy continued to poke and stir the stew. "Go on! Go!"

Ah-lex's bedroom had a window in all three walls, but the room still stank. The barn smelled better. There was a pile of clothes on the floor by the bed and a pair of yellow-stained long johns stretched out over a chair. When I picked them up, they stayed bent in the shape of the chair. I sat them on top of the pile, pushed the pile over to the window that was above the yard with the clothesline, and threw the whole shebang out the window.

On my way out, I peeked into the bedroom next to mine. It was no doubt Eddie's, with his change of clothes on the bed and half-packed boxes scattered around. But the bedroom across from mine surprised me. It was big and bright and had a huge bed centered between two windows. The windows had lace curtains, and against the left wall was a green velvet couch. Opposite the bed was a gigantic dresser topped with a mirror. Going past it, all I could see was my head; it was that tall. At the other end of the room a low, narrow archway opened into an odd little room that was all angles.

Nothing about it looked right. Not the two narrow windows or its slanting roof, and certainly not all the stuff in it: an Army cot with a doll on the pillow, its big dark eyes looking at you, and across from it, dresses hung on a rod and a bunch of hats stuck on some pegs. Hmmm, even though the girls slept in the nook downstairs, this big bedroom had to be theirs, but what was with this tiny room?

I went back outside and found Dorothy on her knees, scrubbing away on the washboard. I snuck up and tapped her on the shoulder.

She jumped and gave me a disgusted look. "Where's Ah-lex's clothes?"

"Over yonder." I pointed to the scattered batch of clothes lying in the front part of the yard. Dorothy looked puzzled. "Well…bring them over here."

"Yes, my lady." I bowed, galloped on, and dragged Mr. Longjohn back by one leg with the rest of his clothes piled on top of him.

Dorothy stood up and pointed to the tub. "Put'em in." I threw the pile in and sat Mr. Longjohn on top. Dorothy melted him down with the broom handle, did some stirring and poking, then offered me the broom handle. "Here, give them a good going over."

I stepped back. "Oh noooo, my fair lady. You said I had to fight the potato bugs, remember? We were going to march into potato land, and you were going to show me how to slay them."

"You don't wanna do a little sword fighting for me first? Hmmm?" Dorothy wiggled her hips as she stirred the mix. Fair maidens knew how to do these things—but farm girls did them better.

"Noooooo."

Dorothy stabbed the broom handle into the tub over and over, killing everything afloat. Then, in a huff, she took off around the corner of the house. I went after her, and we ended up in the garage. She grabbed a shiny open-topped five-gallon can out of a corner and set it down by the workbench. From a low shelf by the workbench, she pulled out a smaller red can marked "Kerosene." She unscrewed the cap and started pouring its clear liquid into the big can.

"Hey, you're not going to burn me alive over a little scrubbing, are you?"

She stopped pouring, screwed the cap back on the can, and put it back. Grabbing the big can by the handle, she marched over to the garden gate with me bringing up the rear.

"What're you so mad about? What'd I do?"

"Shut up!"

"Okay, okay! Geeez."

We had a victory garden back home, so I recognized the growing rows of lettuce, carrots, radishes, onions, and string beans that we passed. We stopped by the potato plants, which were new to me, and

Dorothy went right at it: slapping and shaking the little brown bee-
tle—like bugs off the leafy plants and into the big shiny can—where
they at least died drunk, I figured.

The potato plants ran the length of the garden, and there were
a good many rows. There were also rows of tomato plants. I didn't
know what had to be done to them, and I was hoping I wouldn't find
out—but I had a feeling I would. I had a feeling that this was just
the beginning, just the thing to pile on a little kid from Chicago just
because he couldn't do the milking. And of course, there would be
more, much more: watermelons and pumpkins and sweet corn that
ran in rows all the way up to the back fence. And not to forget, the
strawberry patch next to the garage—guarded by mosquitoes that
loved type D blood. Ah yes, I must say, I felt like I was about to be
shackled to a ball and chain and made an inmate of this vegetable
prison. At least until I figured out how to escape.

"Billy, come here!" called Dorothy from down the row.

"Yes, Warden." I hustled over.

"Here." She passed me the can.

The bottom was swimming with potato bugs. "Wow, Dorothy,
you got 'em! You gooood. You big-time hunter. Big-big. Yep-yep."

"Okay, get to it." Dorothy nudged my shoulder.

"Awriiiiight, awriiiight. Just don't be so mad, huh?"

"I'm not mad."

"Ho-ho-ho!"

"After you finish," she said, moving off, "I'll show you what to
do with the bugs."

"I'll show you what to do," I mumbled.

"Oh yeah." Dorothy stopped and turned. "What did you say?"

"I said...ahhh, nothin'. Don't you ever have any fun?"

Dorothy marched back over to me. "Put the can down." I put
the can down.

Lightning fast, this fair maiden grabbed me and kissed me! And
I mean kissed! Mashing her soft lips on mine. I couldn't breathe.
Stars came out. I was on my way to heaven. And then she vanished.
I mean, she didn't go up in a puff of smoke or anything, but she
was gone, out the gate and gone! I traced my lips with my fingers.

Woooowwweee! I smacked kisses on my fingertips and on the back of my hand—don't ask me why.

"Get those bugs, Billy! Get 'em! Get 'em! Get 'em!"

I finished all the rows, had drunken bugs in the bottom of the can crawling all over each other. Time to get Dorothy, do some kissin'. Boy, could that girl kiss. Not that I knew a lot about kissin'. Not the kind she handed out. So soft and wet...and juicy. Hmmm. Couldn't wait to get more.

I went around to the side of the house with my prize. Clothes were soaking in the tub, and more were hanging on the line, but no Dorothy. I called out to her, but nothing, not a sound, nothing but the blazing-hot sun beating down. I went back around and pumped myself a cold drink, splashed water on my face, then went over to the steps, left the bug pail there, and went into the house.

A pail of water was boiling away on the stove. The blue coffee pot was on the cooler end. I moved up the hallway, past the dining room on the right, past the stairway on my left and the grandfolks' room that guarded the girl's nook next to it. The tiny bedroom was empty. I moved through the archway and into the large living room. The first thing that caught my eye was the polished wooden floor, the way it shone. The rug that covered it was rolled up against the far wall, the door wall. Over left was a red couch with two matching easy chairs and a coffee table. Way over right was an inside wall that left a long, narrow room closed off at the front with a set of brass-handled doors.

"Dorothy?" I called out, and the sound filled the room. Where was she? I wondered. Upstairs? Too hot. I went up anyway and checked the bedrooms, even the little weird room. No Dorothy.

Where the heck was she?

On the kitchen table was some sliced bread and a jar of dark jelly and a used spoon. I grabbed a cup, poured some coffee into it, tossed in some sugar, and went out to the porch. I gazed out the windows as I sipped away and wondered where else Dorothy might be—

the barn? The chicken coop? Feeding the pigs, maybe? The last made me think of Ah-lex-took a sandwich out to him? Naaaaw. Geez, I hope not. Let him starve… Maybe she went swimming, washing up for tonight? Did they even go out on Saturday night? Richard said Ah-lex got drunk every Saturday, walked to Thorpe—that was about six miles through the fields, he said—and that sometimes on his way back he passed out and slept right where he fell. But that he was always back in time for the milking. He was bad, somehow. I just knew it. Like I knew Moritz was bad the first time I saw him.

Bang! It was the sound of the barn door slamming shut. Dorothy came running up the hill. I went out on the steps. *Bang!* Ah-lex came running out of the barn. He started up the hill, spotted me, and stopped. Dorothy came up, rushed right past me, and went into the house.

"Dorothy?" I followed her into the house. "Dorothy, are you all right? I've been looking all over for ya." She went barreling through the house. "Dor, you okay?" She went into her bedroom nook and slammed the door. "Dorothy?" I knocked. "Dorothy, are you all right?"

"Go away!"

"What's wrong?" I rapped one knuckle, easy-like. "Dorothy?"

"Leave me alone!"

I stared at the door…the varnish was cracked into perfect tiny rectangles, thousands of them. "Dorothy! Open!" I rapped a little harder and took in the fascinating rectangles. I knocked four knuckles, hard. "Dorothhhhhhy! You want me to do something?" A scared feeling started crawling around in my gut. I smacked the door with my fist! "DOROTHY! ANSWER ME!"

"GO AWAY! LEAVE ME ALONE!"

I stared at rectangles, started counting them, got dizzy, and went out to the porch. Down by the barn, nothing—just chickens poking around, clucking, scratching dirt. Then I saw him, Ahlex… coming over a rise, cutting hay Jim farting in his face.

I hustled back to Dorothy's room, raised my fist to knock, and stopped. The door cracked open. A naked slice from head to toe… one eye, one shoulder, one…one of everything. And then, like lightning, Dorothy yanked me into her room and told me how crazy she was about me, kissing my ears and nose and everything. Telling me how we should get married and have all those kids—God willing.

Okay, so she didn't open the door. So what? So hang me on a cross. Big deal! Could I help it if I had an extraordinary imagination? Which was not the same thing as lying, you know. That, anyone could do. The other was a gift. You see, most times telling exactly what happened wasn't interesting enough; it needed to be dressed up a little: a flashy tiiiie, a new haaaat, shiny shooooes. Also, it saved ass. That was what Uncle George said. And he was right, because the truth could hurt. Like when she looked terrible—you say *adorable*. Ugly—you say *interesting*. The door won't open, you say… Well, I don't use that word.

I looked off into the living room. Sunlight was bouncing off the brass handles, turning them into gleaming gold.

15

The Ghost Room

The upper panels in the door were glass, etched with trees. I gripped the shiny brass handles and pushed down. To my surprise, there was a click, and the doors opened wide. A gasp escaped me. Across the long narrow room was a wall adorned with swords set like ribs, and in the middle a mighty sword grasped with a battered white glove, its gleaming blade pointing: Chaaarge!

Magnificent! Below it all was a long table topped with framed photographs of all sizes. Then set off to the left and right were flags of all sorts, standing at attention. The rest of the room, the windows, chairs, almost everything else was draped in red velvet. To think that earlier I had passed this room off as just a large closet of some sort.

I entered, closed the doors, and moved across the oriental rug—much like the reddish one we had at home only this one had more black dancing through it. Suddenly, I felt eyes watching me. I spun around—nothing. But instantly I knew—don't ask me how—that ghostly spirits were about. It was like when you go into an empty church, and it was still and quiet, and you felt spirits slipping around, breathing on your neck, making your heart pound.

I turned back to the table, and instantly a framed photo flashed over right. It was a shot of a round-faced lady with silver-black hair piled neatly on her head. A fancy white collar topped her dark dress. Her warm eyes matched her smile. I grabbed the picture and looked at the back: "Helen Filas" was written in ink on the gray cardboard.

"Hi, Grandma." I kissed the picture and put it back.

I snatched up the picture of a tall skinny man standing next to her. He was posed with one hand on a pillar, the other with a thumb hooked in his vest. I flipped it over; it showed nothing.

A small-framed photograph flashed in the middle of the front row. I picked it up. It was a snapshot of a big-bellied man in a black swimsuit that covered him from elbows to knees; sand, water, and sky lay behind him. He stood tall his chin high, his hands on his hips, his big belly leading the way. Grandfather Bruno passed away when I was three, but I knew—don't ask me how—that it was him. On the backside, there it was: "Bruno Filas," in flowing letters. I studied the intense look on his face.

"Hello, Grandpa."

I eased him back into place and caught sight of a man in the row behind winking at me. It was a studio shot of a dapper-looking fellow in a dark suit, standing with his legs crossed, leaning on a cane, and tipping his straw hat. I picked up the tall narrow frame, turned it over, and sprawled there in fancy ink letters was "Lawrence William Filas." I remembered they talked about a loafer-brother of Grandpa's and figured it to be him. It was said he read books, went to the opera—heaven forbid—and avoided work like the plague. I gave him a wink and put him back.

I went down the line picture by picture trying to spot my mom and dad, or my uncles and aunts, when suddenly I knew—don't ask me how, again—that the people in these photographs were all dead. I knelt down and said a prayer for them, just an Our Father and a Hail Mary, but I did ask God to especially bless my Grandma Helen…and then I threw in Grandpa Bruno and Lawrence.

And then, kneeling there, on that plush oriental rug, an idea came to mind. I jumped up, grabbed the framed photographs of my grandparents and Lawrence, dropped to my knees, and lined them up on the carpet. Suddenly, I bounced back up and grabbed the framed photograph of a shot that my eyes kept going back to—probably because it was of two young guys and a white horse. One had bulging arms and a jaw that hung out like a shelf. He was standing next to the horse with his thumbs hooked in his belt. On the other side of the horse was a short, tough-looking guy. He stood with his arms crossed while leaning against the horse like it was a lamppost. What a picture! I set it over right a bit, then flopped down on my belly, and checked the set up. Terrific!

"You know," I said, "we got a rug somethin' like this in our living room. Same design and all. We got ours at the Olson Rug Company over on Diversey and Pulaski. If you want an oriental rug, that's where you go. They got all kinds. They make them there. You've probably been there. But you wouldn't recognize it now, I bet. It's been completely rebuilt. It's huge, about a block long and three stories high. But outside's the best. Out by the corner intersection they've got a giant waterfall. And there's this bridge over a lagoon that you can stand on and watch the water coming down. It's beautiful! And at night, it lights up with lights that change color because they got colored filters set in front of them that rotate around real slow-like. It really looks great! And up left of the waterfall, there's a big orange tepee, with Indian markings on it. And smoke comes out the top. And then a rock garden winds down with all kinds of flowers. It's really neat. People come from all over just to sit and look at it. It's all set up like in a park, with benches and all. I could watch it forever. And out by the street, there's this Italian man sells hotdogs from a pushcart. And he's got a kerosene lamp on it just like the ones out here, only it's smaller. He sells hot tamales too. I'm crazy about hot tamales. You guys ever have one? I guess you don't eat, huh? Lucky you. But you should try one. Just once. I bet you'd like it. Uh-huh. Betcha… One time I heard a man there say: 'In the Midwest there are no waterfalls except Little Niagara at the one-and-only Olsen Rug Company.' Dad thinks they pay him to say that. But not Mom. You think they do? Pay him?"

I don't know why, but I half expected them to answer me some-how—maybe flash at me like before, like maybe once for yes and twice for no—but they didn't. Didn't do anything.

"Are you still there? I guess I'm just wasting my breath."

I rolled over and gazed at the dark cracks in the white ceiling. There were lots of them. One was pretty wide and ran a crazy line across the width of the room—which wasn't really that narrow, but looked that way, I guess, because the room was so long. I arched my back and looked at the photographs upside down… All at once I felt their presence, like being touched in the middle of the night by your mother. Is there any doubt whose fingers glide on your cheek, kiss your forehead? Not a chance.

I spun around, flopped on my stomach, and started talking.

"I used to lie like this back home and listen to the radio. At five o'clock Jack Armstrong comes on: 'Jack Aaaarmstrong, the All-American Boy!' And at five fifteen, 'The Looone Ranger. Hi-Hoooo Silver, awaaaay!' Then at five thirty, *The Shadow*: 'Who knows what evil lurks in the hearts of men. Only the Shadow knows. Heh-heh-heh-heh.' And then at five forty-five, 'Captaaaaain Midnight.' And at the end they give you a coded message in numbers that you write down and then decode with a decoder that you can get by sending in for. You have to mail them a Wheaties box top, a quarter, and a dime. I listen every night during the winter the whole hour. Queenie, my dog, listens with me. Queenie's not allowed in the living room, but she sneaks in from her place under the buffet when my mom's not looking."

"When I was young," I went on, afraid to stop talking, thinking they might go away again, "my mom and I used to listen to Grand Central Station every Saturday morning. You could hear the train puffing into the station, the bell ringing, steam hissing, and the conductor calling out, 'Graaand Central Station.' They had terrific stories! We lived on Drummond then. And just before that, at 10:00 AM was *Let's Pretend*. It was good too. 'Dom-da-da-da-da. Dum-da-da-da-da.' It's more like fairy tales. More for like little kids." But it knocked me out anyway. It was so unreal it was real.

I eased my chin down onto my hands. "I wish you guys could talk. There's a lot we could talk about. Things I'd like to know, like what do you do when you're dead? I mean, well, you know, a whole bunch of stuff. Like, can you walk through walls? And what's heaven like? Never mind hell. And I could tell you guys things too, that maybe you don't know, like…oh, I don't know. Like everything is rationed now on account of the war. You need stamps to buy food. And gas stamps, to buy gas, naturally. Gas is twenty-three cents a gallon. Milk costs ninety-seven cents a gallon. Bread is sixteen cents. Oh, and Uncle Leo's not going to the war because he's deferred, he's a foreman at Tropic-Air. So that's good, huh? And your other son, Richard, he's coming up here, but I don't know when exactly. Pretty soon, I hope. My mom's fine, she's working now. They're not coming up. Dad can't get away. He's real busy since he started the shop. He's got a partner, Mel. They're making 'hose clamps' for the military now. So they're real busy… Sooooo listen, there is one thing I have to tell you. I hope you don't mind, but, well, I'm really lonesome up here. I mean two days and I'm like dyin'. And…well, I don't know what to do about it." I turned over and sat up. I didn't want them to see my face.

Through my tears I noticed a Victrola set back by the doors, in the right corner. I jumped up and went over to it. The top was open, and I could see the round head poised like a snake. The label on the record was upside down, so I spun it around: "NA POZEGNANIE" ("Farewell to the Old Year"). It was one of my favorite songs, a slow waltz with a lilting melody. It was the last number played at every wedding, every party, everything. But just because it was the last dance didn't mean the dancing was over. It just meant it was time to slip the band some extra bucks so they'd go on playing. They played it a lot in the Beer Garden at our carnival. Night after night it danced its way through my bedroom window and lulled me to sleep.

I cranked the handle till tight, flicked the switch, lowered the needle, and voilà! The melody squeezed its way through the curved horn and came out scratchy and tinny, but it couldn't stop the magic. I spun around the room, and when I got to the photographs, I snatched them up and whirled us around and around. The song could melt a statue into a smile. Lawrence was even twirling his cane. I even started singing in Polish—learned before first grade, of course.

Jak szyb—ko mi—ja—ja chwi—le, Jak szyb—ko
   ply—nie czas,
Za rok, za dzien, za chwi—le, *
NA POZEGNANIE

How quickly flies every moment, How fleet is
    time so dear,
A month, a daaay, a whiiiile spent, *

Ra zem nie be—dzie nas. *
And we may not, be here.*
(*There are many verses, and they all end with
    these last four lines.)

I flopped down on the rug, closed my eyes, and remembered weddings past as men danced the whole night through, dance after dance, shirts soaked, grabbing partner after partner, holding them daintily, a soaked hankie at the ladies back fluttering like a flag, as they stamped away the night to the beat of the polka.

And finally, when daylight turned the dark to gray, coffee was poured, chairs were pulled into tight circles, and words poured out from the heart because they could blame it on the whiskey. There were hugs and tears and kisses. And handshakes and slaps on the back. And fist swinging and cursing too, that would give way to shouting, then rumble down to a whisper, and end with a handshake. Then, finally, here and there, they stood up, stretched, gathered us sleeping children from folding chairs, all covered with coats, and with a last round of hugging, kissing, and handshaking, they would drag us into the brightening new day, boost us into the car, and drive us home.

The honking horn of a car far off drove me out of my dream and opened my eyes... Louder it grew. I jumped to my feet and looked out a velvet-draped window. The black Packard zipped past blaring a screaming note that faded away and finally stopped.

Quickly, I put the photographs back, dashed over to the Victrola, plucked the needle, ran back to the frosted doors, knelt, made the sign of the cross, and clicked the brass-handled doors shut.

Dorothy's door was open. The room was empty. I hustled out to the porch and out the screen door.

16

Wild Eddie

The Packard was down by the barn in a cloud of smoke. Dorothy was standing there like a post. I jumped off the steps and ran downhill.

"What happened?" I said to Dorothy, who was feeding her apron into her mouth.

She pointed like a little girl. "The car came down."

The car was turned sideways, and the four bodies in the big sedan were all seated and looked frozen stiff. The motor started kicking over but wouldn't start.

I turned back to Dorothy and yelled, "Did you see it roll down the hill?"

Dorothy nodded.

"Damn!" I pictured Eddie barreling the big black sedan through the yard and over the embankment. Over the embankment! Kiii-rist! Bouncing down the hill in a cloud of dust probably just missed the outhouse. Then turning to miss the barn, tilting on two wheels, almost turning over, then plopping down and dying in a cloud of squawking chickens—those that were alive, anyway.

The motor turned over again, coughed, and started. Then it ground into gear, bucked a couple of times, and moved off. We watched the Packard make its way along the pathlike road to the long, curving turn behind the cornfield that led up to the county road. It was the route the milk truck took every morning. We raced back up the hill to wait for the sedan.

"Ohhh, I hope they're all right," said Dorothy, chewing on what was left of her apron.

"They're okay. They were sittin' there, right?"

Dorothy's head started shaking. "Ohhhhh, I don't knooow," she moaned.

I wanted to put my arm around her, but she was taller than me, so I just hung a hand on her shoulder. The dust-dirty sedan came along the county road, turned off, and snaked its way back to the yard, then crawled alongside of the house and quit—like it should have in the first place.

Grandma came bounding out of the car like it was on fire, while cursing Eddie at the top of her lungs. She added banging on the hood, then switched to shaking her bent finger at him as she moved up to his open window where she threw a punch at him. And then she spit on him—which I thought was terrific. Vickie and Dorothy tried to lead her into to the house, but she slapped their hands away, her Polish still splitting the air as she made her way by herself with the girls following. Boy, that's what I call mad. Grandpa never said a word, just looked the car over from every angle, including the underside, then went into the house.

I went over to Eddie's window and watched him light up. Without giving me a look, he tossed the pack out to me. "Oh, thanks." I dug out a Lucky. Eddie held his cigarette out the window so I could light on it. I noticed his hand was shaking.

I gagged, coughed, and squeaked, "What happened? The brakes go bad?"

Eddie stared straight ahead, exhaled, and said, "Somethin' I always wanted to do."

"You—" I coughed and squeaked, "You did it on purpose? Wow! On purpose. Woooow!"

"I think I scared them." Eddie chuckled.

"You scared the shit out of us. Dorothy and me." I coughed some more. "Were you scared?"

"Not until I opened my eyes." Eddie roared, and so did I.

The screen door slammed. It was the girls. Vickie's hips came rolling down the steps as she headed for the trunk. I gave Eddie a shit-eatin' grin, but he missed it. Dorothy came around to where I stood by Eddie's window.

"Eddie, why did you do that?"

"Vickie dared me," shouted Eddie, throwing it to the back of the car.

Vickie popped her head out of the trunk. "I did not! He's crazy."

"You could'a got hurt, Eddie."

"Hurt? I'm going off to the war. I could get killed."

"Don't say that."

"You never know, Dor. You never know what's gonna happen." Eddie tossed to me, "Go help Vickie."

I moved to the back of the car.

"Take that box," said Vickie, motioning with her head as she went around to Eddie's window, a grocery bag in each arm.

I watched her put a leg up on the running board and join in the talking. Right now, with her leg up like that, her dress tight, and the way she was shaking the hair out of her face, she looked just like a movie star. Boy! She was the kind fell out of bed in the morning and looked perfect—heard that line in a movie once. I hoisted the box of canned goods out of the trunk and headed for the house.

"Hey, kid!" It was Eddie.

I stopped on the steps.

"Hey!" Eddie waved me over.

I put the box down, caught sight of the potato bug can, grabbed it, and trotted back to the car.

Dorothy was now digging in the trunk.

I heard Vickie say as I came up. "And then what, Eddie?" She hefted the bags for a better grip. "What? Say it! Say something, damn you! Say it!"

"Say it, Eddie!" I said to myself. "Say it! Whatever it is! I would. I'd tell her the world was flat, if that's what she wanted to hear. Tell her I'd get her the moon, if she wanted it. Anything!"

Eddie moved his head like it was caught in a noose. "Jeezus!"

Vickie shoved off, her hips rolling. Dorothy, loaded with brown bags, plodded after her.

Eddie flipped his cigarette butt out the window without looking. It bounced off my chest. I brushed the ashes off my T-shirt.

"Yo, Eddie?" He didn't answer.

We watched the girls go into the house.

"Eddie."

"What?"

"You called me over."

Eddie dug out another cigarette, didn't say anything.

"Say, uh…do you know what I'm supposed to do with these potato bugs?"

Eddie got out of the car, took the can from me, and set it down a few feet away. Then he lit his cigarette and threw the match into the can. *Woooosh!* A ball of fire.

"Holy shit!" I leaned back.

The ball of flame quickly died down. I peeked into the can. A blue glow at the bottom was frying the bugs. "Snap, crackle, and pop," just like a bowl of Rice Krispies.

17

Beauty Hurts

Eddie's favorite pork chop supper went on as planned—in spite of the car thing—and was served with entertainment by Grandma. Every time she came out on the porch, she bopped Eddie on the head with whatever she had in her hand: a plate, a pot, a cup, and she did wonders with a serving spoon. What finally saved Eddie was a money argument between Grandpa and Ah-lex. They went into the kitchen, and Grandma followed. "Women always follow the money." That's what Uncle George said, and I knew he was right because my mom was really good at it. So was my sister. She had a nose for it like a bloodhound.

Eddie sure looked sharp in his dark-blue shirt. He wore it with the collar spread wide open—the blond curls on his chest glistening—and the sleeves rolled up showing his popped-up veins. And on his right wrist was a wide piece of leather fastened with two straps and two tiny buckles—a real eye-catcher. Eddie's wavy hair didn't hurt him any either, not to mention his perfectly straight nose and flashy blue eyes. In fact, I'd trade my looks for his anytime. Not that I thought mine were all that bad, but if you put them next to Eddie's, you probably wouldn't even notice mine. Ahhh, but I had a brain. 'Course, nobody sees your brain. Still, it's supposed to be worth a couple of points. It better be.

The girls brought out some farmers cheesecake for dessert. I tell ya, I'd never been so close—for so long—to girls in dresses that made their globes wave at you so friendly-like. They practically talked to you: "Hi! I'm Squeezy, and she's Squashy. Aren't we cute? Round and firm and ready for pickin!" Right under my nose they were saying it. "Yummy, Yummy," I'd say. That is, if they could really talk, I'd say.

Geez, I had to stop these sinful thoughts because it was hard sitting here with this stick in my pants. I didn't know why they didn't make a separate pocket for a guy's thing. All day long one little-bitty bad thought and bingo! One bent stick. That's why guys walk bent over, you know. And their folks were yellin', "Stand straight!" You'd think they'd know better. And it couldn't be healthy for you either. Might even get warped—like my buddy, Frank's.

Oh yeah, you could tell I was feeling good, right? Why not? Eddie was taking me along to the Street Dance in Chippewa Falls, because I helped him wash the car. Actually, I practically washed it by myself because Eddie became invisible.

Eddie speared the last square of cheesecake. "What's that leather thing on your wrist for?" Eddie snapped a punch into his left hand.

"It's so he doesn't break his wrist when he falls down drunk," said Vickie.

We all laughed, and Eddie the most and the loudest.

"Is the new movie house open yet, Eddie?" asked Dorothy, sitting in Ah-lex's chair but turned toward Eddie. I think she was sitting that way because I was talking to her globes too much.

"Ummgh," grunted Eddie, nodding, stuffing cheesecake into his mouth.

"They got a big sign with a lot of lights. *SUNSET* it says," said Vickie, sipping coffee, her elbows on the table—which made me notice her globes were different than Dorothy's, more up and at 'em. Uh-huh.

"Sign. Arrgh…" Eddie gagged on the cheesecake, sipped some coffee. "Sign goes way up.

"High as a barn." Eddie swigged some more coffee."

"Ohhhh, I wish I could've seen it," said Dorothy, chewing her thumbnail.

"Bulbs. Hundreds of 'em," said Eddie, "flashin' up and down."

I asked Eddie what was playin'.

"I don't know, some war movie. And Tarzan, somethin'."

"Tarzan and the Apes?"

"Noooo. Tarzan *in the Apes.*"

"There's no Tarzan *in the Apes.*"

Eddie broke out laughing and couldn't stop, started pounding the table. Vickie kicked him under the table, and then she too started laughing.

"What's so funny?" said Dorothy.

"Yeah, what's so—" And then it hit me. I could feel my red cheeks flashing like a neon sign.

"What's so funny?" repeated Dorothy in a panic.

"Nothing! Nothing!" said Vickie. "We're laughing at dumb Eddie."

"What's dumb about it?" said Eddie. "Guys do sheep, don't they?"

"Oh, for Pete's sake!" Vickie stood up and started clearing the table. Dorothy pitched in.

"You goin' with me or not?" said Eddie, eyeing Vickie… "Last time I'm askin'?"

Vickie ignored him, didn't give him a drop of sweat. Then, arms stacked with dishes, she headed for the kitchen. Dorothy followed, but stopped in the doorway and gave Eddie a long, empty look before she ducked in. Eddie pulled out his Lucky's and offered me one. I shook my head. The Polish in the kitchen started heating up.

"When we leavin', Eddie?"

"Soon as Ah-lex gets paid." Eddie lit up.

Ah-lex came out the doorway with a shout of disgust. Eddie held up his pack of Lucky's. Ah-lex grabbed it and went about digging out a smoke. Ah-lex looked better than usual due to his clean clothes—thanks to Dorothy and me, mostly to Dorothy. But there wasn't much you could do with his face. It was shaved, but it didn't look like the soap got any higher than his nose. He really looked better unshaved, if you ask me. Not that anyone would want to give that face more than a glance anyway, not with those pig-eyes that could send chills through you. I suppose the best you could say about Ah-lex's head was that it had plenty of hair on it—even though it was the ugliest tangle of red string you ever did see. Alex lit up and went out the screen door. And that's enough about Ah-lex. Too much, in fact.

Vickie came out with a washrag, started doing the table. Eddie blew smoke in my face. "Go change your shirt."

"I did change my shirt."

Eddie jerked his head to the side.

"I'll be right back."

I dodged through the Polish in the kitchen, took the stairway, and shot into my bedroom. Off with my white shirt, on with the blue one. Out the room, down the stairs, pass the girls in the kitchen, and out to the porch. Eddie was not there. I heard the Packard roar. Out the screen door, jumped the steps. The car was moving…crawling…teasing me. Eddie was nothing but tricks. I ran and cut them off where the road started to wind. Boy, I was fast. I waved my arms, hopped up and down, laughed like an idiot. Eddie didn't slow down. I jumped out of the way. The black sedan barreled on, took a sharp right onto the County Road, and zoomed off…nothing but dust.

I ended up on the couch at the end of the porch with a pencil and paper in hand. The girls were still in the kitchen, doing the cleanup. Grandma and Grandpa had disappeared. I thought of them in bed and wondered if they did anything—besides snore, I mean. I wondered if they, at least, held hands… I didn't want to ever get that old.

Saturday night, June 20, 1944

Dear Mom and Dad,

I was supposed to go to a Streel Dance tonight with Eddie in Chippewa Falls, but I changed my mind. We start haying Monday, so I figured I better write you a letter now. Eddie leaves Monday for the Navy-rowboats, I think. How is Queenie? She'd like it up here. They don't have a dog here.

I'm sure you will be happy to hear that I am now eating like a horse. Also, working like one. I chase the cows out after milking. I also shovel the barn out. And I have to pick strawberries every morning too. And tell Dad I know how to do the potato bugs. And that we fry them in kerosene. But of course, we don't eat them. Ha-ha!

The two girls up here are okay. They're older than me. Grandpa's nice. He talks to me a lot. Grandma hollers all the time. All in Polish, so I don't know what she's saying. But she smiles at me a lot when I'm working.

Hey, Mom, I have a great idea! If Dad has to work the Fourth of July week, why don't you come up with Uncle Leo and the rest of the family? And then you could stay longer to make sure I get fat! And then take the train back. And if you're afraid to go alone, I could go with you. It would be a lot of fun, Mom! Really! Think about it. Please give it a lot of thought. Okay?

I reread the last paragraph, and it made my heart race. Boy, would that be great... Out the window, pink and blue clouds were hanging low at the end of the world... I could hear the girls doing dishes...

It was getting too dark to write. No electricity here. Ha-ha! I'll finish tomorrow. Oh!

Is Smitty and Norb doing my paper route? Tell them I said hi!

I watched the pink fade away...the blue sky darken... Eddie was probably in Chippewa falls by now. Unless he stopped off in Thorpe to say goodbye to some friends. Probably not. Probably everybody was at the dance. Not Ah-lex, of course. Ah-lex was going to get stinkin' drunk, fall down in some field and, hopefully, get bitten by a rattlesnake. Or get chewed up by some wolves, or a bear... make mincemeat out of him. Sorry, Lord, I just can't help it. The man scares the daylights out of me. He's just bad. Bad through and through. Eddie's not bad; he's just crazy. Pulled a dirty trick on me... But I still kinda like him.

Night was spreading out over everything now. I heard the hissing sound of a kerosene lamp, and suddenly a shaft of light cut through the kitchen doorway. It drove out the darkness, locked it outside, and turned the windows black. I moved up quietly and sat at the round table. The world was now only as big as the kitchen and the porch. The girls in the kitchen weren't talking much—hardly at all, in fact. I heard water being poured and giggling.

"What the heck was going on?" I wondered. I got up and took a peek.

"Ohhhh my god!" Vickie was washing her armpit: arm in the air, her breast curved up, slanted ribs below... So perfect in the yellow light and the dark shadows. But it was the nipple that nailed me... so pointed and long. My mom's didn't look like that. I snuck back to my chair. My heart pounding, my breath short, my mind stuck on a nipple. I crept back for another look: Dorothy was washing Vickie's back. How could a back look so good? And I was only seeing part of it: a wet shoulder glistening in the lamplight and the long wet curve going down...like a question mark.

Vickie stepped through the doorway with a hissing kerosene lamp. "Billy!" she said, with a little jump. "What are you doing out here in the dark?"

"I was writing a letter back there by the couch." I pointed my thumb. Vickie placed the lamp in the center of the table and sat at my left. "Then it got too dark to write. So I watched it get dark... from back there." I pumped my thumb toward the far end of the porch. Vickie adjusted the flame to a soft hissing glow. "I just sat there and watched the pink clouds fade out. Uh-huh." I started rocking in my chair. "I just moved over here." I rocked my head. "Just now..." I added.

Dorothy came out and sat down on my right, a deck of red cards in her hands. "You know how to play War?" she asked, shuffling.

"I know how to play strip poker." I giggled like an idiot.

Dorothy gave me a puzzled look. "We're playing War." She concentrated on dealing out the cards.

"You can play the winner," said Vickie.

They picked up their cards. "You start. I dealt," said Dorothy.

Vickie laid down a ten of clubs. Dorothy smacked a jack of diamonds over it, squealed, and picked up the win. On and on they played, slamming the table, laughing, having fun.

When I'd glance at Vickie, it almost hurt; she was so beautiful. If God said to me, "Don't look at Vickie or you'll turn to salt," I'd be salt. And happy to be. Dorothy was nice. Dorothy, I liked. Vickie, I'd die for. Go to hell and burn for. If only she *only* looked, *only* said, *only* anything! Once! Just one time! But it could never be. I knew that. And it hurt. And somehow I knew it would always hurt. Burning in hell was nothing. This was pain. Pain inside that nobody could see. Pain that would always be there. Always. Whenever I looked at beauty.

18

Sunday Church

We were in church, packed in like sardines. Ten o'clock mass at Saint Peters, just outside of Thorpe. The sun was blazing through the colored glass windows, cooking people, cooking them yellow, blue, green, red, depending. I was sure I was green no matter what the glass because I was sick. It was the air. It wasn't moving. You couldn't budge it with a truck, couldn't suck it in if you had lungs like a vacuum cleaner—not that you would want to, because it smelled like rotting fish mixed with rose petals. Ugh! The only thing really moving was my stomach, running up and down like waves on a beach. And pretty soon, it was going to run—no, pour right out of my mouth. Yep, pretty soon I was going to decorate someone, or at least the aisle, that was for sure. There was no way I was going to make it out of the pew, up the long aisle, and out the door in time. No. No way. I knew my stomach. Too bad Ah-lex didn't come with us, I could have baptized him, and nobody would have known the difference—not even him, probably. But Eddie was here, fighting hard to keep awake. If I sprayed him, he'd probably wake up thinking he was shot in the war, guts all over the place.

The priest was still into his sermon, not even shaking his fist yet, so he had a ways to go. I was about to give up the fight, duck down to the floor and explode, when Grandpa grabbed my hand and pulled me out of the pew and over to a side door that appeared, miraculously. And just like that, we were outside, and I was under a tree spewing scrambled eggs and baloney. Food and I just didn't get along. Uh-uh. But of course, you already know that.

Grandpa stood in the shade of a huge oak tree, smoking a cigarette. I breathed heavy and felt a whole lot better, but I was so ashamed of myself I couldn't approach him. Finally, he crossed over to me.

"Feel better?"

"Uh-huh. I couldn't breathe in there."

"Yeah. Stuffy." Grandpa took a long drag on the cigarette and exhaled.

"We start haying tomorrow, huh?"

Grandpa gave a nod and added, "The weather stays good." He looked out past the graveyard at the clear blue sky hanging over a field of ankle-high corn, then back at me. "You okay to go back in?"

"Yeah, I think so."

Grandpa pinched off the glowing part of the cigarette and crumbled the remains away. "We can stand in back."

We started up the path that ran alongside the building toward the front entrance. I was totally amazed that he wasn't mad at me for being sick. Outside the entrance, under another big oak, a lady was dabbing at the dress of a little girl with a hankie. She was about the size of my sister. In the dirt was her breakfast. It had a lot of colors in it—much prettier than mine. Grandpa gave the matter a quick glance and started up the steps that led into the church. At least he saw I wasn't the only one to get sick—'course, she was just a little girl.

19

I'll Show You Mine, You Show Me Yours

It being Sunday, nobody was exactly straining themselves, although Gramps and Ah-lex did finally go off to cut and rake more hay for tomorrow's first day of "the haying." Eddie was in his room taking a snooze, and the girls were in the cellar with Grandma doing what, I don't know, and could care less. I decided to disappear before I got nailed for some chores. I ended up watching the men work the hay-fields down by the creek. Molle, the gray mare, was pulling the mowing rig along with Gramps in the driver's seat, its shark-toothed blade clicking, toppling the mixture of timothy and clover and leaving it there for the sun to turn to gold. On a stretch cut the day before, Ah-lex was raking the golden green hay into rows, and the rows into piles, with Jim, the black stallion. The rake itself was just a giant comb with curved teeth set on a couple of very big, skinny steel-rimmed wheels. The sun would do more work on the mounds, and by tomorrow the golden hay would be loaded onto the wagon with pitchforks. That was the hard part. Gramps and Ah-lex would do that part. My job would be to trample down every fork load so that more could be added. I'd done some "trampling" on my Uncle Tom's farm. It wasn't anything to look forward to. I didn't think anybody really looked forward to "the haying"—not even Molle and Jim. It was just something that had to be done. Of course, a lot of things had to be done, but not under a blazing hot sun, in air filled with itching dust, from morning till night, for a two-to-three week stretch—if the weather held. Still, in spite of those drawbacks, I was excited. I'd be working with the men. I'd be doing "the haying."

After a while, I followed the creek downstream, toward the bridge, to where the water split off into a little channel, and there I decided to build me a dam and make me a little bathtub. Only problem was, every time I plopped in a boulder, Eleanor plopped into my mind. Scrawny, straight as a stick, rollen-toothed Eleanor. Gad! I'd squeeze her out of my brain, plop in another boulder, and she'd snap back like a rubber band. It was just a lousy experience was why I kept pushing it out of my mind. Well, it wasn't all bad. Not the first part anyway. I added the final boulder. The pocket of water started building up just fine. I stretched out on the grassy bank to let the hot sun fry me a little…make me gorgeous…make me irresistible. Richard was always ripping off his shirt, looking like chiseled toast. With me, it was more like barbecued ribs.

"I'll show you mine, you show me yours." That's what she said. Can you believe! From out of nowhere! Richard and I were like totally shocked. Unbelievable!

She was a year younger than me, this Eleanor, from the old D& D neighborhood. Came over with her mother, Myrtle the elephant, and her caved-in-chest father, Pete, who worked at the Babe Ruth Company, shoveling coal all day long into the big furnaces. They were originally from Wisconsin, naturally. So she said the "I'll show you" bit, and Dick said, "Okay."

I didn't really think anything was going to happen, and I didn't think Dick did either, but just like that, the three of us jumped into the back seat of her daddy's shiny, new Buick, and without a moment's hesitation, rotten-teeth upped her dress and pulled down her panties and there it was: "God's gift to man," so to speak. I actually found her belly button more interesting, because—unlike mine—it bulged out like a mushroom. I liked mine better.

"Turn around," I said.

She did. Rear globes I knew something about from my earlier "doctor" days—operating with bobby pins, you know where. Oh, naughty, naughty.

"Bend over," I said.

"No! Turn back around," said Richard.

She turned. Richard stared. At what, I don't know. Looked to me like somebody tried to split her in half with an ax and stopped too soon.

"Turn around, again," I said.

"No, wait," said Richard, leaning in for a closer look.

"Your turn," said Eleanor, pulling up her panties and lowering her dress. Dick looked at me with big eyes.

"Go ahead, Dick. You're older." I scooted back into the seat. Dick sat there like stone.

"It's your turn! C'mooon," squealed rotten-teeth.

"You go," said Dick, backhanding me in the chest with his fist.

"You go!" I said, backhanding him back.

"C'mooon!" said Eleanor, stamping her foot. "I showed you mine!"

"Biiilly!"

"Diiiick!"

"I'm gonna go tell my mom!" Eleanor went for the door.

"Wait a minute!" I yelled, sticking my face in hers. "You wanna get killed, Eleanor?"

"Yiiiiiaaahh!" Eleanor opened her door, jumped out, and ran toward the house.

Dick opened his door. I grabbed his left arm. "Wait, Dick! Wait a minute!" I was yelling, pulling on his arm. "What's she gonna say? She's the one pulled her pants down!" Dick stopped. "We didn't do anything, Dick! We didn't pull our pants down! Right?"

Dick looked at me, his wheels spinning.

"She's the one who did!"

Dick bolted for the door again.

"Stooooop! We didn't do anything!" Dick stopped, but he got his door open. "What's she gonna say? They wouldn't pull their pants down?" I let go of Dick's arm. Dick dropped his arm from the door, his wheels turning again.

"Let's get outta here anyway."

"Why? We didn't do anything."

Dick made a move for the door. "I'm goin'."

"Chicken, Dick! Chicken, chicken. Dick's chi—"

Dick slammed me on the arm. "Shut up!"

I slammed him back. He slammed me in the chest. I pulled my feet up and started kicking him as hard as I could. The car door flew open.

"Hey, you guys! What's going on here?"

It was Uncle George, the Hungarian. "Whaa-ut?" I asked, innocently.

"Whaa-ut?" said Richard, a couple of notes higher.

"Jesus!" The air went out of Uncle George. "What the hell did you guys do to Eleanor?"

"Who's Eleanor?" I inquired.

"You pulled her panties down! That's who's Eleanor!"

"No, we didn't!" I yelled. "She's the one pulled her pants down! Honest, Uncle George!"

"Yeah, George. Honest to God. She pulled her pants down."

"That's not what she said. She said you guys got her in the car and pulled her pants down."

"We didn't! She's lying!" she said. "'I'll show you mine, you show me yours.' And then she upped her dress and pulled her panties down. And there was nothin' to see."

Uncle George was fighting to keep from laughing.

"Dick stuck his nose in it," I tacked on.

"Billy made her bend over!"

"Jeee-zus Chiii-rist!" Uncle George started chuckling. "You guys." He shook his head. "Listen, dummies, your ass is cooked. It's her word against yours."

"But we're not lying."

"We're not, George. She's the one."

"It doesn't matter. Come on. I gotta take you guys into the house."

Richard bolted for his favorite door.

"Richard!" yelled Uncle George. Richard stopped. "Don't make me drag your sorry ass in there. Now, come on. You gotta face the music."

Music, shit! The death march! They wanted to strap us in the electric chair. You could see it in their eyes. I honestly think Uncle George thought we were going to get a fair shake, but he wasn't Polish, didn't know much about religion, and sure as heck didn't know much about my mom. She came at us swinging, slapping, crying out, "How could you! How could you! How could you!"

We kept yelling we didn't do anything, but it was no use.

"Nick!" she finally cried out. Then she put her hands together like she was going to pray for us while they strung us up. My dad just stood there with his arms down, his fists clenching and unclenching, his mouth chewing and twitching as if he was working on something to spit out. He just wasn't good at this sort of thing.

Myrtle, her hands on her hulking hips, snorted at us like an elephant about to attack. Husband Pete—sweated to skin and bone from stoking the furnaces—stood beside Hulking Hips, ready to charge, with his snuff-filled lower lip leading the way. And all the while, rotten-toothed Eleanor huddled in front of them and made faces at us.

"See!" Dad finally spit out. "See what you do?" Then directly to Richard, "You! You older! You should know better!"

"Dad, we didn't do anything. It was Eleanor, she—"

"Quiet!" My dad raised his hand to shut me up, not to hit me—I didn't think. He never hit me, never in his whole life, not even once. "Pete comes here…he comes all da way…all da way with Myrtle…and…and Eleanor. And…and you do dis sin?"

"She started the whole thing, Nick. We—"

"Quiet!" Dad yelled, his fist vibrating by his chest. "You!" Dad poked a finger at Richard.

"You older!" Dad always found it easy to pick on Richard. "You always bring trouble! You—"

"Nick, stop it!" cried my mom.

"I don't want you come and…and—"

"Hey, hey, Nick!" said Uncle George, stepping in. "Whoaaa! Easy. Eeeeasy, Nick." Uncle George put his arm around my dad's shoulders. "Come on, sit down. Jean! Jean, babe, get Nick some water. Pete and Myrtle too. Get a pitcher out here."

"Don't want water. Punishment!" said Pete, in his croaked voice, fried from the furnace heat, digging clinkers out of the giant boilers year round. Dad always said no man worked harder than Pete Gratowski.

"We didn't do anything," I pleaded.

"Yes, you did! You did!" Eleanor cried out. "Both of you!"

"Pete," said Mrytle, elbowing Pete's ribs, "give Nick your belt."

"My little girl, she don't lie!" said Pete, choking and gasping, taking off his belt.

"Now, wait a minute! Waaait a minute!" said Uncle George, stepping into the middle of things with his hands raised like a traffic cop. "Look. I'll tell ya what. Let me take these wise guys out to the garage. I'll give them a lesson in manners. Hey, Nick? What do you say?" Uncle George gave dad a big wink. The way he was turned, I was sure nobody else saw it—except me and Richard.

"Pete? How about it? Give me your belt." Uncle George snuck a wink at Dick and me, and we groaned, on cue. I even shook my knees a bit.

"Nick!" said Mom, stepping up, "I don't want—"

"No, Stella! George do right." Dad huddled with my mom.

Uncle George snapped the looped belt. *Crack! Crack!* "Let's go boys."

"I want to watch," said Eleanor.

"Oh, ha-ha-ha!" Uncle George laughed through his teeth. "Ahhhh, it's not…it's not something for a nice young girl to witness. "Oh no, Eleanor. No, no!"

"I wanna watch!" said Eleanor, stomping her foot.

Elephant Myrtle rapped Eleanor's head with her trunk.

"Move out!" yelled Uncle George.

I was never so happy to see the inside of our garage: scrubby two-by-fours, tar-papered walls, and cinders for a floor—absolutely charming.

"All right now. Bend over, gentlemen," said Uncle George.

Dick and I looked at each other and started laughing.

"No laughing matter, boys. You screwed up. Now let's get this over with."

"But we didn't do anything."

"We didn't, George."

"I know, I believe you. But I can't let you guys get off scot-free, get it? Now bend over and grab the family jewels."

Dick and I bent over and grabbed our jewels. "Now yell out like I'm killing ya!"

Yelling was easy.

20

I'm Too Young for This Stuff

On my way back to the house, I spotted Gramps and Ah-lex now working the hayfields on the other side of the creek. The sun was so hot you could almost see it frying the hay to a golden brown. I entered the empty barn and instantly cool delicious air washed over me. So did the aroma of cow pies—which, strangely enough, I liked, but it didn't compare with gasoline. Of course, cinnamon babka in the oven had them all beat. Passing the stairway that led up to the hayloft I heard voices—squeals actually. The girls? What were they doing up there? I snuck up the stairs on all fours and cracked the door open. Voices came from back in the loft, but my view was blocked by the hay wagon. I crept around it and scooted over to a section of the barn's huge framework. Stepping up on a small barrel, I climbed the support beams, and there they were: Eddie and Vickie, in the hay.

What was going on was one of those scenes where the guy was wrestling with the girl, trying to play her like a guitar. I'd seen that kind of stuff at Riis Park, and it always bothered me. But this was Vickie and Eddie, and I guess that made all the difference in the world, because I was all eyes, and I was hardly seeing anything. And then I did, because Vickie broke loose and stood up.

Oh my gooood. Thank you, Lord. What am I saying? Forgive me, Lord! Forgive me! Please don't turn me into salt!

Eddie reached up from behind and pulled down Vickie's panties partway. Vickie spun around and became a fist-swinging machine. I stared at her backside. What were those? Dimples?

"Let goo. Stop it, Eddie!"

Eddie didn't stop it. "Vickiiiiie..." he croaked.

"Vickiiie..." I croaked soundlessly as I stared at two of the most luscious dancing cheeks I would ever see—with dimples yet. Two big beautiful dimples.

Vickie stopped pounding Eddie, pulled up her panties, and reached for her dress.

Eddie snatched it away and held it behind his back. "I don't see what you're so mad about. I asked you to go, didn't I? Didn't I?"

"Eddie!" demanded Vickie, her hand stuck out under his nose.

Eddie spun away, stood up, and pulled the dress over his head. "Help, I'm stuck!"

There was a laugh, and it wasn't me. It was Dorothy. I quickly pulled back into the framework. Damn! What was she doing here? I peeked out. There she was, sitting on a crate by the other support beam. Good thing she didn't see me. At least, I don't think she did. The angle wasn't that good.

Vickie and Eddie finished dressing. The fight was over, but it was hard to tell who won.

Eddie grabbed Vickie from behind by her hair and pulled her head back. "I saw you at church talking to Esther. That's why you're mad, isn't it? Isn't it?"

Vickie answered softly, "I'm not mad, Eddie."

Eddie, in her ear, whispered hoarsely, "Vickieeee, I'm leaving,"

Vickie tried to shrug free, but Eddie jerked her head back again. "It's our last daaay..."

"Let gooo."

Eddie spun Vickie around by her shoulders. "Esther doesn't matter! Don't you get it? She's nothing to me!"

Vickie locked eyes with Eddie. "She couldn't wait to tell me what a man you are."

Eddie slapped Vickie. Her head turned with the blow, then back to Eddie... Tears rolled out of her eyes. "What a man you are."

Eddie grabbed her. "Vickie, Vickie…" He hugged her, but it was like hugging a ragdoll.

Vickie pulled away and headed out. "Vickieeeeeeee!

Vickie cracked open the huge sliding door and disappeared.

"VICKIEEEEEEEEEE!" Eddie went nuts, kicking and punching at anything and everything, growling like a wounded bear. And I was hiding in the beams. And Dorothy was huddled and peeking through her fingers. Suddenly Eddie stopped, crumbled, and lay there in a heap.

In a flash, Dorothy was all over him. "Eddie? Eddie, are you all right? Ohh, Eddiiiie."

And I was hanging there, too scared to move, too scared to even breathe. Scared they'd see me. Scared they'd hear my heart pounding.

Dorothy's tortured voice went on and on. "You can't go away, Eddie… You can't."

Eddie kept shaking his head and saying, "I gotta, Dor… I gotta… I gotta go."

"Don't say that! No, Eddie! No! Stay here pleeease! I'll never see you again! I know it! Ohh, Eddiiiiie…"

"Heeeeey… Hey, hey, now, I'll be back." Eddie broke their embrace. "I'll be back, Dor. I promise. For real. Yeaaah… Dor, I'm gonna be on a ship ten times bigger than this barn. A hundred times! I'm gonna be safe and sound waaaay out on the ocean. Just blue water and blue skies." Eddie lifted Dorothy's chin with a finger. "Want to come along?"

"Oh, could I? Don't kid me, Eddie. Could I?" Dorothy hugged Eddie. "Ohh, Eddie…"

"Heeeey… I guess you're really gonna miss me, huh?"

"Ohhh, yeeees. Yesss…"

"Well… I'm… I'm gonna miss you too, Dor."

Dorothy pulled back to look at Eddie. "You mean it, Eddie? You're not just saying that."

"Nooo…no, kid." Eddie pulled strands of hay out of Dorothy's hair. "Gonna miss my little Dor." Eddie tapped Dorothy on the nose with a finger.

"I'll write to you, Eddie. If you want me to? You don't have to write back."

"Suuure… Sure, why not?" Eddie traced Dorothy's lips with a finger. "Pretty, pretty lips… You got better lips than Vickie. You know that, kid?" Eddie kissed Dorothy and grabbed a breast at the same time. "Hmmm, soft…sweet lips."

Eddie's hand slid down Dorothy's dress and under it. Dorothy closed her legs.

What was happening now was filling me up with madness, but I didn't know what to do. All I knew was that I had to do something.

"Eddiiiiie."

"Eddie what? 'Stop it some more?' Lift up."

"No, Eddie… Noooo! Stop!" Dorothy rolled over and curled into a ball. "Ohhh, I'm afraid…"

"Nothing to be afraid of, Dor. You're a big girl now…" And now, all of a sudden, Eddie was sweet and tender, and I was hanging there listening to him dish out a line about…not coming back… maybe getting killed…maybe blah, blah, blah… I put my hands over my ears, but I could still hear him. And when he was done, I couldn't move. It was like I was paralyzed.

"Eddiiiiie."

"STOP IT, EDDIE! STOP IT, OR I'LL KILL YOU!" I was saying this all to myself now, and now I could move. And I was thinking somehow, someway, A PITCHFORK! I'd get a pitchfork and run him through. Just like in the movies. Yeaaah. Run him through.

"Ya like that? Hmmm?"

"I… I think so."

"Think so?" Eddie laughed. "Ohhhhhh, Dor baby, you kill me."

I was so mad I couldn't stand it. I bit down on my fist. Do something!

Eddie stood up, started unbuckling his belt… Suddenly, Dorothy scrambled to her feet, and in a flash, she was gone, out the barn door. Eddie was left standing there like a post, his pants down around his ankles. Then, like in slow motion, he pulled them up, stuffed in his shirt, did the buckle, and pulled out a pack of cigarettes. He lit up, looked around the barn, dragged deep on his Lucky Strike, and walked out. And I was left hanging there like a wart on Grandma's nose. And I was feeling bad, rotten through and through. And you think you know why, but you don't. You think you do, but you don't.

Believe me, you don't. And it's not your fault. It's mine. I can tell you, why, but I'm not going to.

And that's all I'm going to say.

Oh, hell! Damn it! THE THING IS, I LIED! It didn't happen in the barn the way I said it did. Not everything. Not the last part. Dorothy didn't exactly leave. Eddie threw her out. Well, he didn't exactly throw her out... Well, he did, but not before...not before he... And I couldn't leave because it happened right below me. And so I saw it all. And I did nothing about it. Absolutely nothing!

Yes, Dorothy made a break, but Eddie caught her and put her over his knee and started spanking her. Spanking her, for chrissake! And uttering a word with each blow: "You. Are. A. Bad. Bad. Girl. Dorothy!"

And Dorothy was crying out, "Stop, Eddie. Stop! Pleeease, Eddie! Stooooop!"

"Bad, bad girl running away!"

It was killing me. And I did n-o-t-h-i-n-g.

"Ed-diiiiiiiiee!"

I was going crazy! I wanted to jump down and beat Eddie to a pulp. Stab Eddie, kill him, but I did nothing. Not one thing. Just cringed in fear like a coward. A complete nothing.

And then Eddie stopped. "You won't tell Vickie about this."

Dorothy shook her head.

Crack! "Say it!"

"I won't tell Vickie! I won't! I won't, Eddie!"

Crack.

"S‌top it, E‌ddie!" I yelled, but no sound came out. It was all in my head, and I couldn't move. And then, just like that, Eddie flung Dorothy away. "G‌et outta here!"

Dorothy was on her back looking up at me…

"G‌et outta here!"

I was lying in bed waiting for everybody to fall asleep so I could go downstairs and get a sword out of the ghost room. That was how I figured to do it. Run Eddie through: "Thrust-ho!" Eddie wasn't leaving until early morning, so I had plenty of time to go over the details. And the one thing that kept coming back to me was whether I should wake him up before I drilled 'im… And then later I was thinking that maybe I should just jab him in the ass a couple of times and let the Navy finish him off. Yeeeah, I liked that idea. And then it hit me, what about Dorothy? And Vickie? What would they think? Shit! So I decided to stop my thinking and just wait for it to go dead quiet, go totally black like at the end of the world… And it did! And then, with my heart pounding, I slowly pulled the covers—What was that? Out in the hallway…creaking boards…a light growing brighter…

Someone was coming! Maybe it was Eddie! Maybe he saw me in the barn and was coming to beat the crap out of me. I had to do something. But what? What? Candlelight filled the doorway. It was Dorothy! I sat up, and she vanished. Was I dreaming? I sprang out of bed, rushed to the doorway, and looked out. Dorothy turned into Eddie's room… I stood there a looooong, looooooooong time.

The screen door slammed. My eyes flew open. It was morning. Before sunup, the light a dark, dirty gray. Outside, a motor was purring. I threw off the covers and sat on the edge of my bed. The air was cold. The screen door slammed…then again…and again… and again…and again. Five times. I scooted out the room, down the hall, down the stairs, through the kitchen, and out to the porch, to a side window. There they were, all of them, dark figures huddled around a dark two-door coop, doing the goodbye thing… Then the car door slammed shut, and the dark coop turned around and went out through the yard, its tailpipe smoking. Eddie was gone.

21

Haying Time (Monday)

I knew all about haying. Saw it all on my Uncle Tom's farm, like I said earlier. Only then I was just a kid, going along for the ride. Today was different. Today, I was the trampler, working with the men, not just watching them. Today, I was high-stepping through every fork of hay that was pitched up by Gramps and Ah-lex, packing the load tight so that more could be piled on. Today I was breathing the dusty air that gripped your throat, cut your lungs short, and made your eyes itch—made everything itch.

And tomorrow it would be the same. Out to the fields to do the backbreaking job that had to be done. Today, tomorrow, and the day after, and the day after that, and after…after until all the hay was in the barn. You cut it, let it dry, raked it, loaded it, and unloaded it. Nothing complicated about it. Just brain-dead work done under a blazing-hot sun from morning until night. It was brutal.

Especially if you were twelve, going on thirteen, trying to be fourteen. Trying to be a man.

And so, when the hay on the wagon grew as high as a little house we took her in, Gramps and me. We braced against the top front boards, Gramps with the reins, driving Molle and Jim in a slow, steady pull, heading for the barn.

The tricky part was going up the long runway that led into to the barn. Molle and Jim wanted to get up a full head of steam, and it was up to Gramps to pull hard on the reins, but not too hard, just enough to keep the wagon moving fast enough to take the bump into the barn with the front wheels and the back, then to put on the brakes quick.

"Whoa! Whoa!" shouted Gramps, pulling hard on the reins, Molle and Jim backpedaling, their hooves digging in, pounding the wooden planks like a drum, the sound frightening as we pulled to a halt in the nick of time. Molle and Jim, of course, knew their job. They weren't about to run through the side of the barn and end up in the chicken yard below buried under a wagonload of hay. And I might add, it wouldn't exactly do Gramps and me any good either. So thank God for safe landings and all that, because even though the last bit was exciting, it was very scary.

I wasn't needed for the unloading. Neither was Molle. She snacked on a bridle-pouch filled with oats under a patch of elm trees out past the runway. I wanted to run to the creek and flop into the water, but first I wanted to see if they did the unloading the same way they did at my Uncle Tom's.

At the end of the barn, Gramps got a hold of a trip-line that was attached to a four-pronged apparatus—parked high above on a steel rail that ran the length of the barn—and then he pulled it along the rail until it locked in place right above the load of hay. When he jerked the trip-line, the apparatus released its four three-foot curved prongs, each attached to a chain that made a clicking sound as it came floating down to the wagonload. Ah-lex then sank each steel prong into the hay in the form of about a five-foot square. The apparatus now resembled a four-legged spider.

It was then ready for Jim and Gramps, waiting just outside the huge sliding doors, to power the system. Jim was harnessed to a long, thick rope that passed through two huge wooden pulleys that were attached to the frame structure—one at the bottom and one at the top—then ran back to another huge pulley at the end of the barn, where it then crawled out along the rail and then down to the apparatus.

"Get up!" said Gramps, as he led Jim by his bridle slowly away from the barn, the heavy rope behind coming alive, wiggling out of the dust like an unbelievably long snake, growing taunt, through all the pulleys and then down to the apparatus, which was clicking now as it ate the slack out of the chains. "Easy, Jim. Eeeeasy." Pulling harder now, Jim took shorter steps…the clicking sound slowed… Suddenly the four-curved spider legs bit off an enormous amount of hay from the wagon. Up, up, flew the load, back up to the apparatus where it locked in place, and then the whole shebang sailed down the rail to the far end of the barn.

"Whoa, Jim! Whooooa!" yelled Gramps, and the heavy rope plopped back into the dust.

Ah-lex then yanked the trip line, and the load of hay fell to the floor of the loft. "Whoosh!" Amazing. Just like at my Uncle Tom's. I wanted to watch some more, but my itching body was driving me crazy, so I took off for the creek.

I flopped facedown into the creek, clothes and all, and let the cool rushing water rinse the itch out of my eyes, ears, nose, armpits, you name it—relief beyond words. There was nothing you could do about the pain. It was like going to the dentist. You went to get drilled, and you took it. Only with the haying, you take it day after day, until it was done. When I sensed it was time to go back I got out, shook myself like a dog, picked up my rinsed-out hankie— that I'd spread out on a boulder to dry—and headed back to the barn, the hot sun drying the clothes on me as I walked.

Everybody was settled in under the elm trees having lunch. Nobody was talking—not even Grandma. I had the eerie feeling they were all thinking about Eddie. Three ice-sweaty pitchers and a picnic basket were set up on a wide plank nailed to a couple'a stumps.

"Go on. Take a sandwich," urged Vicki as she got up and filled a pint canning jar from one of the pitchers. "Lemonade," she said, handing it to me.

She refilled another jar, gave it to Grandma, and settled back to her spot next to Dorothy. I gulped the lemonade and eyed Dorothy. She did not give me a look, not even a glance. I took a bite out of the sandwich, chewed, but it was hard swallowing. If she was blind, she could see me better… I didn't blame her one bit.

22

Mysterious Strawberries

I woke up. I was in bed, and I didn't know how I got there. Or how long I'd been there. Moonlight drew a rectangle on the floor and erased some of the night. I remember sitting at the supper table, and then it was lights out. Either they clubbed me, or I fell asleep right then and there.

Dorothy probably tucked me in. No, I guess not. She was still mad at me. Shit! What was I supposed to be, King Kong? I was just a kid, for Pete's sake… And then in the middle of the night she goes. Why? It just didn't figure… I rolled over and dug my face into the pillow, but I still couldn't sleep; my mind was racing around, bouncing off walls. I got out of bed and went to the door. There was enough moonlight spilling in to make my way down Orchestra Hall and the stairs of Tchykowski. I suppose in time one could tell who was coming down—or going up—by the tune one played according to one's weight and whatnot. And so, in this case, I played that cute little ditty:

"Here he comes! That strong! That wonderful! That handsome kid from Chicagoooo, Skinnnny Billlily!"

At the bottom of the stairs, I was surprised to see light coming from the kitchen—nothing the other way, from the girls' nook. I played the low notes that led to the kitchen. It was empty. The only thing alive was the hissing kerosene lamp in the middle of the table. "Must be on the porch," I mumbled as I tiptoed to the doorway and peeked out. "Hmmm, must've gone out." I snapped my head back. My heart thumped. I'd caught something out of the corner of my right eye. I leaned forward: Grandma. She was sitting there in the moonlight, sitting in her rocking chair steady as a rock. I pulled back, exhaled, and relaxed.

A terrible thought crossed my mind: Maybe she was dead? I peeked out again. Sure looked dead.

I backed off again then froze with the thought that I was going to have to check her out, see if she was really dead, might have to pinch her. And if she was only in a coma, she might snap out of it and wallop me! Knock me through a wall! Oh yeah, she was a big one! Stood like a bear, nose up, back straight, paws hanging ready. One, two, *pow!* A bloody mess. The ticking alarm clock on the cupboard read 12:00 on the dot. Ohhh, not a good sign. Uh-huh. I gathered myself together and peeked out again: still sitting there like she's carved out of stone. And then I saw it! She moved! Quick as lightning! Saw her left paw dip into her lap, then go up to her mouth. "She's alive! She's alive!" There! She did it again! And her mouth's moving too. She must be eating something. "Hooraaay!" The old girl was still kicking!

I stepped back, took a deep breath, and without thinking, I stomped noisily out onto the porch.

At first, I pretended not to see her and then acted surprised when I did.

"Grandma! Hi, Grandma!" I stood there in my short pants, waving my arms like an idiot because of our language barrier. I moved closer. She stared at me and looked to be counting my ribs. Probably never saw a kid with a healthy line of ribs before. She shifted her gaze out at the moonlit night. I looked out also, but actually, my eyeballs were straining trying to see what was in her lap: nothing but her hands folded on the apron that she had on over her nightgown.

"Hot! Hot!" I fanned my face with both hands. "*Chepwa.*" The Polish translation just popped into my head. I did know a number of Polish words, you see. It was just that my school-damaged brain wouldn't allow me to string them together.

"*Ja!*" said Grandma. Then she fired off a three-hundred-word composition without moving her hands. And that was the tip-off. Uh-huh. Her hands should've been flying all over the place, as usual. Uh-huh. No doubt she was hiding something in that lap of hers. Had to be, but what?

"*Ja! Ja!*" I threw in here and there and nodded—as if I understood what the heck she was saying. Finally, she quit, and we stared out at the moonlit night. Rather, she did; I faked it. And there! Again, out of the corner of my eye, her hand struck like a cobra into her lap and up to her mouth. "What the heck?" shouted my brain. I didn't dare turn my head, just went on straining my eyeballs…added a little rocking back and forth on my heels…added a little humming. "There! She did it again! *Psia krew cholera!*"

Grabbing a chair from the table, I decided to sit next to her, but for some reason—call it instinct—as I nonchalantly set the chair down, I also scooped up her apron, and there! There in her lap was a bowl of strawberries! Holy tomoli!

"William!" She slapped my hand.

"Ah-ha! Strawberries!" I pointed. "Ah-ha-ha-haaa!" I rubbed it in good.

"Willllliam!" she said, shaking her bent finger at me and laughing at the same time.

"Oh, shame! Shame, Grandma!" I said, not giving any ground, giving her the "for shame" sign—stroking one finger with the other. "Shame, Grandma! Shame! You sneaky thing, you! Sneaky, sneaky! Shame, shame!" I poured it on even though she couldn't understand a word. "Here I am picking strawberries every morning, mosquitoes sucking my blood, injecting it into the strawberries, and you're eating them! You're drinking my blood, Grandma! Like a werewolf. A vampire! Ho-hohoooooo! Oh shame, Grandma! Shame!" I rubbed my fingers fast enough to start a fire.

Grandma was almost falling out of her rocking chair; she was laughing so hard, but not moving her face too much because she couldn't chance it falling off with all those cracks in it, you know. And all the while she was jabbing her bent finger at me; only now she had a strawberry hooked in it, trying to tempt me into taking it. But I was dodging her while keeping up the "Shame! Shame!" bit.

"Sssshhh, Willliarum! Sssssshhh…" She was trying to quiet me now, her strawberry finger up to her lips. She was probably thinking we'd wake up the whole household, and then everybody would eat her precious strawberries. The strawberries I picked out in that jungle out there! Under a blistering-hot sun with man-eating mosquitoes chewing on me! Without thinking, I snatched the strawberry she'd been waving under my nose and popped it into my mouth. She looked shocked, like I'd just sunk a dagger into her. Good! I reached into the bowl, and she swatted my hand away.

"Owwwww!" Her left hook could knock over a cow. Quickly she stuffed a strawberry into my busted mitt, patted me on the arm, and mumbled some hocus-pocus. So finally I sat down and ate the strawberry. And then I had to poke her to get another one. And that was how it went.

LATER, I WAS BACK IN BED THINKING how strange it was that I had to outfox my great-grandmother just to get a strawberry. And that she ended up tickled pink about the whole thing? It just didn't figure. Didn't seem right that you could make points for catching your great-grandmother red-handed for hoarding strawberries, but for knocking yourself out on the hay wagon, you got nothing. I didn't get it.

And then, finally, I did: working hard on a farm was expected. Everybody worked hard. It was nothing special. But having a brain, especially a clever one like mine, that was special! "Ah-haaaaa!"

Yeah. That was it, all right. But having the answer didn't really make me feel any better. It still didn't seem right that you had to trick your own, true-to-life great-grandmother just to get a stinkin' strawberry. I turned over, squeezed my eyes shut, and waited for sleep to carry me away carry me home.

"Ohhh, don't say that word. Don't say that word, Billy. Don't."

23

The Secret of Pain (Tuesday)

I stopped trampling. I was dizzy. I tried blinking it away. It didn't help. I made for the headboards, climbed up, and took some deep breaths. The spinning went away and the scary feeling with it. "Am I getting sick?" I asked myself. "Maybe it was like in church, when it got so stuffy I couldn't breathe." I took more deep breaths.

Gramps and Ah-lex were moving along, swinging their pitchforks like machines. Nothing seemed to bother them—the heat, the itching, the blisters, nothing. How did they do it? The first load of the day, and I couldn't even see straight. I rubbed my eyes as if I was going to rub them right out of their sockets and rubbed my knuckles over my ribs, trying to get at the itch inside them. Even my throat itched, for Pete's sake.

The last time I felt so miserable was the time I got beat up at the carnival. This big jerk kept pushing the back of his hand in my face, wanting me to kiss it like we do Father Pastor's. I ended up with my arms locked around his legs while he beat on me. Finally, he got tired and kicked me aside. I went home, my head and body screaming with pain. How was I going to fool the folks? Don't forget, mum was the word. How was I going to stand straight, sit at the table, turn my head, eat? And then it came to me: I'd have to act as if the pain wasn't there. I'd have to just ignore it. And it worked. I mean, the pain was still there, but I wouldn't let myself think about it. Like at suppertime, I parked my brain up on top of the refrigerator, and somehow I got through it.

"Eureka!" Gramps and Ah-lex weren't there. They had their brains parked somewhere else.

Had to be. That was why they worked like machines, not feeling anything. They were gone. Parked somewhere nice and cool. Somewhere beautiful. Heaven, maybe. Well, not Ah-lex. He was probably parked in some dark saloon drinking beer with the devil— something called, Hell's Brew.

So what I did was I parked my brain and gave myself over to the work. At first I could only do about five minutes. But after a while, I got the hang of it. Worked like a machine, I did. Threw the switch and walked on the hay, around and around. Trampled it, sneezed, blew my nose, but kept moving, because I wasn't there. I was floating in a pool of dark blue water...by a waterfall...white water falling down...cool, cool water... Hmmmm, delicious...

THEY THOUGHT ME A FOOL. I could see it in their eyes. Who, but a fool, would drown themselves in the creek between loads, sneeze like an idiot, blow their nose till it bled, and tramp hay like a soldier marching to the beat of a drum. Who but a fool? But what they didn't know was that once I made up my mind to do something, I did it, no matter what. My mom knew that. That's why she said, "Don't lift anything heavy." I wasn't like my dad. He always stopped. Always played it safe. I don't think that means he's a coward. Probably means he's smart. I don't know. I really don't. Anyway, I guess we are what we are. We don't have a choice. But that doesn't seem right either. Ahh, the hell with it.

And so I never missed a beat on the wagon: made every run, caught hay left and right, and trampled it all down. I did it! But it wasn't good enough. Not good enough because I didn't come back standing tall like a man, like Eddie would have or Richard. I came back with a running nose, itching eyes. And sneezes that would blow a house down. I didn't have what it takes is what they thought. And worse—that I didn't have brains enough to quit. So they thought me a fool. And I guess they were right.

24

Showdown with Dorothy
(Wednesday)

We were about to go out for our first load of the day when a man entered the barn. He was a tall, lanky, farmer-type, and upset about something. Turned out he was a neighbor and that his four-pronged apparatus was stuck with a big bite of hay in its mouth. Ah-lex—can you believe—was pretty funny acting out questions about the situation. So then Ah-lex and Gramps gathered up some tools and went off with him, and I ended up on the porch sipping coffee with a fat grin on my face, but not for long. Grandma came out and announced in her morning sandpaper voice—hands flying, of course—that I was to work in the garden with the girls. I knew I was doomed even before Vickie did the translation. But then I perked up when I realized I'd finally get a chance to talk to Dorothy. I mean, really, a handful of words hadn't passed between us since the barn thing, and it really bothered me; bothered the heck out of me, it did.

A couple of times I worked my way close to Dorothy, but she wouldn't give me a glance. I tried to think of something to say to break the ice, but I couldn't come up with a single word, not one stupid, stinkin' little word. Finally, I got her attention when I blew my nose using Gramp's tricky technique: I pinched one nostril closed and blew a shot of gook out on the ground right in front of her. Stopped her dead in her tracks, it did.

"Billy!" she yelled, jumped back, then crossed over to the carrot patch, a good ways away from me. Well, at least, she remembered my name.

Speaking of tricks, Grandma had a new one: picking up long, slimy worms and putting them into a coffee can. Well, she could salt and pepper them and dip them in chocolate for all I cared. She could sit in her rocking chair, pop them into her mouth, and let them wiggle down her throat for all I cared. Go to it, Grandma. *Naz drovye* (a toast)!

We were all in a rhythm now, hacking away, piling up the weeds, row after row in the hot sun. "Boy," I thought to myself, "these ladies can really work." Finally, Grandma quit in the onion patch, gave a short sermon, and went into the house. Vickie followed on her heels. I went back to hacking away the weeds between the rows of lettuce when Dorothy yelled out from over left: "Billy! Look at these potato plants, they're loaded with bugs! When did you do them last?"

"Saturday," I said, stepping over the rows of lettuce, then beets, to get to her. "Saturday when you showed me how.

"Saturday? You're supposed to do them every day." She fanned through the leafy plants. "Look at them! They're loaded!"

"Do you miss Eddie?"

Her hands froze on the plants. She stared up at me.

"Do ya?"

"Get the can out of the garage and do these bugs."

"Do you miss Eddie?"

Dorothy's eyes burned holes in me.

"Do you or don't you?"

She looked away.

"You do, don't you?"

She didn't answer.

"Does Vickie?"

She looked back at me.

"I do. I miss him."

"You do?"

"Yep. Like a hole in the head."

For an instant there was a smile, then it went the other way. She turned and shot up the long row of potato plants.

"Dorothy, wait!" I scrambled after her. "Dorothy, don't go! Wait!"

Not turning, her arm pointing backward, she said, "Do the bugs like I told you!"

"Dorothy!" I kept after her. She stepped across the rows of onions and beets and carrots and reached the gate. "Dorothy! What about the wolves? DOROTHY, THE WOLVES, DAMN IT!"

She stopped, her hands on the gate, looked back at me. "What wolves?"

"In the orchard, Dorothy! I saw them! I saw them yesterday after supper! It was almost dark, and they were eating something. Over there, on the other side of the garage." I pointed. "In the shadows there. They come in packs, Dorothy. They run you down and eat you. They do! They—"

"There's no wolves!"

"There are, Dorothy! There are! Honest! I saw them, I swear! There's—"

"Stop it! We don't have wolves! Only in the wintertime."

"You...you do? You got wolves in winter?"

"Oh yeah! Big, like elephants!" Dorothy threw her arms in the air and turned back to the gate.

"Well, I'm just telling you!" I shouted. "My dad told me aaaaalll about it! About the snakes too!"

Dorothy stopped dead, and her head whirled around. "Snakes?"

"Yeah, big snakes. They gobble you up headfirst. They got jaws that open up reeeeal wide. They're on a hinge, see. They take out the cotter pin and open up aaall the way, grab you by the head, and just keep working you down, sucking you in."

"Baloney."

"No baloney, Dorothy. You mean you never saw one of those big snakes with the yellow bellies? You never even heard of them? My dad said they come out of the creek, like after a big rain, when the water's way up. No kidding, Dorothy. And the wolves, my dad said, come down from Canada in packs to feed. Come down all the time. Aaaaall the time, Dorothy. So he told me to be reeeal careful. He said they used to chase him and his brother's home from school a lot. Yeah. They had to climb trees to get away. They'd be up there for hours sometimes, he said, waiting for Paul to come with his 30-30. And one time, he said, Uncle Paul only had a club, and he was swinging and grabbing wolves by the tail and knocking their brains out. And one time, Dad said, the wolves got a neighbor's kid, ripped him apart, and ate him up, nothin' flat. Nothin' but bones. But the worst, he said, was when they caught one of those big snakes and the belly was all blown up. He said they sliced it open one time, and a big pig jumped out and ran around like he was crazy. Probably was, if you ask me. What? What're you shaking your head for?"

"You're the biggest liar I ever heard."

"You think I'd lie about something like that? Ohh boy, forget it. You don't want to believe me, forget it. Boy, you're impossible!"

"Cross your heart and spit on your mother's grave, you're not lying."

"I don't spit on my mother's grave for no one."

"Boy, you're impossible!" she mimicked me, then bounced through the gate and headed for the house.

"Hey, Dor! Dor! GET OUTTA HERE!"

Dorothy stopped on a dime, turned, and her face fell off.

THE MEN WERE back in the field haying under the blazing hot sun. I didn't want to join them, but I did. Later, when we were heading out for our second load of the afternoon, Grandpa surprised me by handing me the reins. I was thrilled; I can't tell you how much. All that power, you could just feel it flowing into your hands. Boy, that was something. And then, when we started loading, Grandpa pulled a red bandanna out of his overalls and tied it behind my head. He said it would help me breathe better. I thought, "Gee, he's not even my blood."

AFTER THE MILKING, I WALKED UPSTREAM—which I had never done before—and came upon three dark pools of water, the center one being the biggest.

"Ahhh, the perfect place to drown myself," I mumbled.

The pools were as smooth as black ice. Not a dent, not a ripple, not a clue the water in the middle was moving, sliding left. I stood by the big pool and watched a water bug cut a *V* on the black ice as it headed across. When it reached the center section, the *V* started sliding left. The little bug paddled furiously, and slowly, it got the *V* going again and completed the crossing.

I hung my clothes on a bush and went down the three-foot bank at a spot where there looked to be a sandy ledge in the water. I was knee-deep in the water before I felt the sand. The other side looked farther away than it had from up on the bank. Not only that, the dark sleek surface made me wonder what angry creatures below were waiting to gobble me up.

I dived in and started swimming for the other side. After only a couple of strokes, the water got colder, and the current started pushing me sideways. Then it got angrier and started grabbing at my arms and legs. The harder I paddled and kicked, the more I panicked. Suddenly, the water got warmer, the demons let go, and two, three, four strokes, I was across—just like the little bug.

I made myself do ten laps as punishment for what I said to Dorothy. It got easier as I got used to the feeling of the current, but it was still very scary. When I finished, I recalled the story my dad once told me about a kid drowning in a pool like this, and I realized how easily it could happen. All you had to do was let fear get the best of you, and the monsters would take you down.

25

Richard Arrives (Wednesday)

We were in the barn doing the evening milking when Richard walked in. For him the bands played, the trumpets blared, and everybody jumped up and down—including me. And all he did in return was give us a half-assed grin, grab a pail, and start milking, and everybody's eyes went big. So I quickly got my shovel and started shoveling, and of course nobody even noticed. I shoveled over by Richard and watched him milk. He was good. The milk drilled the pail in long hard spurts.

"Did Jake drive you over? The mailman. Big fat—"

"My cousin, Bogart. We drove all night, straight through," Dick said without stopping the ringing spurts. "Made it in fourteen hours."

"Fourteen hours? Wow! Took me twenty-six hours on the train. The Soo Line. Fourteen hours, wow. That's the best I ever heard."

"We were doin' eighty-five, ninety all the way."

"Woooow."

"He's got a '41 Dodge. We were floorin' it."

"You don't have a license, do you?"

"What a' ya talkin' about?" came with a disgusted glance, but the ringing spurts went on. "I drove half the time."

"We would have made better time, but we hit some cows." And then I laid it on. "Red meat all over the place. Bones stickin' out. Blood all over. The engine looked like it was painted red!"

The spurts never stopped. I scraped the shovel in the trough a couple times.

"Gramps said the Filas got ten kids. Seven girls."

Dick shot me a sneaky grin.

"Oh sure, big make-out artist."

Dick shot another sneaky grin.

The spurts were deeper now, the pail was filling. I banged the shovel in the trough a couple of times and went on my way shoveling pies.

Dick wasn't much of a talker, and even less so, since somebody tagged him, "a man of a few words." But that didn't stop everybody from stopping by with their pale of milk to have their say—even Ah-lex, which surprised me.

AFTER SUPPER I followed Dick outside, and we ended up on the roof of the last outbuilding. Dick pulled out a pack of Camels from inside his shirt.

"Gimme one."

"Since when you smoke?"

"Since Eddie showed me. C'mon."

Dick ripped a cigarette in half, stuck half between his lips, and offered me the other half. "What am I gonna do with that?"

"Take it or leave it."

I took it. "What is this, a Montefiore trick?"

"I'm savin 'em!" Dick struck a match, cupped the flame, and lit us up. "They catch you smokin', you tell them Eddie showed you how, not me."

"Yeah, yeah." I took a deep drag to impress Dick—which I was sure it did. "So how was Monti? They bounce you off the walls?"

"The first day, they line you up and tell ya, 'This is a Reform School. We reform.'"

"Like St. James. They reform your face, right?"

Dick shook his head. "They don't hit ya."

"What? Uncle George said they slap you around big time."

"Uh-uh," said Dick, with another shake. "You stand punishment."

"Like they stand you on your head, huh?"

"You scrub floors. Do kitchen duty. Stuff like that."

"C'mon. St. James is worse than that."

"St. James, at three o'clock you go home." Dick started blinking. "Remember Little Johnny?"

"Little Johnny. Yeah, sure. Great guy. What's he doin'?"

"He's dead."

"Dead?" I froze. "Little Johnny?"

"Yeah. Got drunk, missed a curve, and hit a tree. That was it."

"Geez…" I shook my head. "Ohhhh, God. It ain't fair."

"Everybody said it was because of my sister, Jean. He couldn't get over her… She bawled like a baby at the funeral. George took it hard too."

I dragged deep on the butt and flipped it away. "He taught me how to catch a softball." I cupped my hands and crossed my thumbs. "Geeeezz…"

"Remember in your basement at the wedding, George bet he could hang himself for a minute?"

"Yeah. Little Johnny kept yelling, 'Stop! Stop!' Now he's the one that's dead."

"You never know. Here today and gone tomorrow." Dick did his cigarette trick, passed me half. "Now you get another smoke, see?" We lit up.

Dick exhaled a cloud of smoke. "What did ya think of Eddie?

"Eddie! You won't believe. I—" I was about to tell Dick about what happened in the barn, but stopped. I dragged on the ciggie. "He was gonna take me to a street dance in Chippewa Falls, but he ran out on me." I exhaled. "So we got divorced."

Dick chuckled. "He's a card."

"Yeah, the ace a' spades." I told Dick about Eddie running the car over the embankment and how Grandma used his head for a drum. We had a good laugh on that, smoked our half cigarettes, and stared up at sky that was coming alive with stars. I again thought about telling Dick about what happened in the barn, but decided not to. Not now. Maybe later… Maybe never.

"Eddie'll fuck anything," said Dick. "Even a chicken."

"What kind'a chicken?"

"A chicken! Whatdaya think?"

"You can't do a chicken."

"How do you know? You try it?"

"You?"

"Sure."

"Yeah, sure."

Dick took a deep drag on his half a ciggie and blew it out slowly. "Last year Ah-lex came back from town all beat up."

"Good! Why'd he get beat up?"

"Who knows."

"Probably tried a chicken."

"Probably."

"A dead one. All moldy and diseased."

"Ugh, cut it out," said Dick, shoving me on the shoulder.

I flipped away my butt. "Gimmie a cigarette."

"I just gave you one."

"You only gave me a half. C'mon!"

"You're a smoke fiend. You're gonna get TB."

"You don't get TB from smokin'. You get it from people coughin' on ya." I coughed on Dick, until he slammed me in the chest. "Oww!" Dick passed me a half a cigarette, and we lit up.

"Ever see..." I coughed. "Ever see Eddie with the girls?"

"What da ya mean?"

"With the girls. You know. Fooling around..."

"You crazy? Eddie's their brother, for chrissake."

"No, he's not. I asked Dorothy."

"Half brother. Cousin... He's somethin'."

"Yeaaah..."

The sky was still holding on to some light from where the sun had crawled over the edge.

And now up high in the growing darkness, the moon and the stars were taking over. "What do ya think it's like up there on the moon, Dick?"

"Cold. Colder than a witch's tit."

"Speaking of tits."

26

Haying with Dick (Thursday)

The first thing Richard did when we got on the wagon was to peel off his T-shirt so that the sun could broil him like a hamburger. I didn't think making it easier for the itchy hay to get at me was worth the trade-off. Besides, I was gorgeous enough already with my runny nose and bloodshot eyes; why make me totally irresistible with a tan? But I gave in when I saw that Dick only trampled the hay after Gramps and Ah-lex threw up their fork loads, not meeting the swirling loads head-on and getting drowned like an idiot. But it was still shitty work—especially with the temperature in the nineties and not a cloud in the sky, not a bit of a breeze to cool our sweat.

We plopped into the shallow creek clothes and all and let the cool water revive our tortured bodies. Dick had never gone to the creek between loads before, but he welcomed the idea. I kind of felt that evened the score for the haying wrinkle he taught me.

"What was Ah-lex talkin' to you about?" I said, floating like a dead man.

"I don't know," said Dick, floating beside me.

"He's mean. The first day I was here, he beat the heck out of cow with a stool." I sat up. "He's like Moritz. He ever come after you? Moritz?"

"Noooo." Dick sat up. "Leo told him he'd break him in half if he did." Dick fanned the water. "He did one time."

"He did?" I moved around to face Dick. "What happened?"

"Marcie came home late, like, five minutes, and he locked her out on the porch. It was wintertime, and it was freezin'. So I brought her a blanket, and he saw me and came after me with a whip. 'I'll tell Leo!'" I yelled, and he backed off. Then he beat Marcie with it and left her out there."

"Him and his whips." I kicked up a storm with my legs. 'My mom used one on me once."

"Bull." Dick heaved a coupla' good-sized rocks downstream.

"She did!" I slapped the water. "She did, Dick! Honest to God! One time Connie goes runnin' into the house scream in', sayin' that I tripped her. She had this big bump on her forehead, like an egg. It was a beaut. So mom calls me in and starts hitting me with one of the whips that Moritz made for all the moms at Christmas, remember? It had that long wooden handle with three leather strands on it?"

"C'moooon, she didn't hit you with that." Dick lay back in the water on his elbows and flutter kicked.

"She did, Dick!" I smacked the water with my fist. "I swear to God! She gave me five good licks with it. I kept yelling, 'I didn't do it! I didn't do it!' Boy, did that thing sting. I don't think she realized how much it hurt. It stung even after she was done. Then she made me stand in the corner until I said I was sorry. But I wasn't going to say I was sorry for somethin' I didn't do, you know? Uh-uh. No way. Then later, she caught me smearing snots on the wall, and she sent me up to my room with a couple of slaps.

"I can't believe my sister would hit you with one of those whips." Dick flutter kicked.

"Well, she did… You know what I did about it?"

"What?"

"I got my dad's safety razor and real careful-like I cut each strand partway through." Dick sat up and gave me a surprised look. "I did, Dick. And then the next time she came after me swingin' that whip, bingo! One, two, three, the strands went flying. Ha-ha-ha! I can still see the look on her face." Dick's jaw dropped. "But I wasn't really happy about the whole thing, you know? Then later she came up to my room and asked me if I was all right. I wouldn't look at her. She tried to brush the hair out of my eyes, but I pushed her hand away, and then she started crying. Then we were both crying and hugging and crying… Don't ever tell anyone, you hear? I mean it, Dick. Promise me."

"Yeah, yeah."

"I mean it, Dick! No one, you hear? Uncle Leo. No one!"

"Okay, okay."

"You do and I'll tell about the time you got beat up by some girls in Schubert Park."

"What girls? What're you talkin' about?"

"When we lived on Drummond, remember? You came to visit, and a gang of girls jumped you, remember?"

"You're crazy! I never got beat up by any girls!"

"You did, Dick! I told you not to cut through the park, remember? I told you! I told you that was like wearin' a sign on your back that said, 'Beat Me.'"

"You're full of crap." Dick smacked some water at me.

I smacked some back. "You got to our house, you looked like a truck ran over you. And they painted your—" Dick backhanded me in the chest. "Oooww! I nicknamed it, the red dart."

Dick leaped on top of me and practically drowned me. Finally, I broke away and headed for the bank.

"I'm not going to tell anyone, for crissake! Jee-zus, Dick! Unless you tell about the whips!"

Dick caught up with me. "Wooooop!" Dynamite on the arm. "Ooooh, right on the bone! Geeeeez!"

"You say anything, I'll break your arm."

"Oww, right on the bone… Damn…" We shook ourselves like dogs, then sat on a couple of hot boulders to dry out. Dick blew on his fingers and dug out his cigarettes.

"That was a great park, you know. Schubert. They had those swings and seesaws…and that high bar, remember? You could chin yourself, and that little pool with the water squirting up in the middle? Gimmie one!"

Dick passed me half a cigarette. We lit up and headed back to the barn.

27

Seven Kittens (Thursday—Old '56)

I dumped the wheelbarrow out back of the barn and noticed that the angry streak running across the sky in the north had grown darker and wider. My heart jumped. "Rain?" I went back into the barn and got back to my shoveling when Dorothy popped out from behind the stairway, her face all smiley. She waved me over.

"Uh-oh," I thought, "she's tryin' to trick you, Billy." I stayed with the shoveling.

"Billy!" she called out, still smiling, waving her hand like a windmill. I had no idea what the penalty was in this part of the world for spying on girls in the barn. Hanging you by the thumbs might not be too bad. By your yo-yo would.

What a surprise! The brown-and-white cat had kittens! Seven little colored bundles of fur balls about the size of my fist. Dorothy placed a black-and-white one into my hands, and I was totally amazed. I had never seen a live kitten before. I couldn't believe how perfect it was, how soft, with little perfect eyes, and perfect little ears, and a tiny rough tongue that kept licking at my fingers, and short legs with very sharp claws, and it even had a little tail. It was the cutest thing I ever saw. I held it to my cheek. It was so warm and alive, this little thing. I wondered how God ever thought to make such a perfect little bundle.

A while later, Ah-lex trooped past me with the kittens cradled in his arms. He stopped up front by Grandma, they exchanged some harsh words, and he ducked outside. Grandma kept up with the words as she stopped milking and followed him outside. Dick called to me and cranked an arm for me to follow him. Outside, everybody had their attention turned to Ah-lex standing over by the chicken coop, the kittens at his feet. Grandma, at the foot of the hill, was barking Polish at Ah-lex with both barrels. Ah-lex just stood there like a statue and stared at her. Dorothy was huddled in Vickie's arms and looked to be crying. When I asked Dick what was going on, he shrugged. Grandpa stopped the gasoline engine that pumped water into the large tank that cooled the milk cans, and it was dead quiet. Grandma—out of words, or breath, or both—whirled around disgustedly and headed up the hill toward the house.

Ah-lex picked up a kitten, looked at it for a moment, then a second later it was flying through the air, and a split second later, it was sliding down the flat face of a huge boulder over by the silo. I froze. My heart went crazy. I couldn't believe what I was seeing. I wasn't seeing what I was seeing. Couldn't be. Yet there! There was another ball of fur in the air. Ah-lex was winding up and pitching the balls of fur at the flat-faced boulder one after the other. They would hit, stick there for a split second, then leave a red mark as they slid down the face of the boulder to where their twisted bodies would whimper and their tiny paws would claw at the air. I made a move, but Dick blocked me with his arm, and I made no effort to get past him. Why didn't Dick move? Why didn't Grandpa? Why didn't somebody? How could this be? Ah-lex was smiling, enjoying his pitching, his baseball…kittens flying, kittens smashed…kitten after kitten…

"Richard!" Ah-lex called out.

Richard went over to him. Ah-lex motioned for me to join them. I shook my head. Ah-lex poked Dick and shot his chin at me.

"Billy!" called Dick, with a half wave. I joined them.

Ah-lex snatched up the last two balls of fur, plopped one in Richard's hand and one in mine. He nudged Dick's shoulder, grunted, and flicked a finger at the boulder. In a flash Dick wound up, threw, and another ball of fur slid to the bottom of the boulder.

Dick stepped back so I could take the mound. They were all watching me. Even Grandma, up by the house. Why I did it, how

I did it, I'll never know. Actually, I tried to throw the little brown-and-white ball over the boulder, but I nicked the top of it, and it went squealing and tumbling into the weeds behind it. I ran after it, picked it up, and quick threw it at the back of the boulder. It hit, slid, and lay twisted on the soft grass with its paws jerking, scratching the air, reaching out for help...and dying... I picked it up and threw it again as hard as I could... It didn't move anymore.

After a while, Dick came up with a shovel and said we had to bury the kittens before we ate.

I looked at him. He kept his eyes on the ground. He started to dig a hole over by the silo. "Bring them over here, Billy." I didn't move, couldn't move. A soft misting rain started to swirl around us. Dick came over. "Here," he said, thrusting the shovel at me. "You dig. I'll get the kittens."

I went over and stared at the black hole with the black dirt piled outside of it.

"Make it deep so the chickens can't get at 'em." Dick dropped twisted bodies of fur next to the hole...then did it again...then wiped his hands in the grass. "I gotta go chase the cows out."

"Dick!"

"What?"

We looked at each other for a long moment. Then he turned away and went off. I dug a good size hole, then knelt down, and laid the kittens in side by side, all seven of them. Then I petted them one at a time, the brown-and-white, the black-and-white, the one almost all-white, and the one that was mostly black, and like that, and I asked God if he would bring them back to life so I could hide them. I asked him to do that please. I begged him, please, just this one time to do it. "Please, God. Please..." But the kittens didn't move. And then I asked the kittens to please forgive me, and I told them I was sorry. I told them I was very, very sorry. I told them I was never so sorry in my whole life for something I did... But they didn't move.

Dick came out of the barn. "You done?"

I brushed the misting rain off the little balls of fur.

"You didn't cover them up." Dick picked up the shovel, and just like that the dirt was back in the hole. He finished the job by pounding the lump of earth with the back of the shovel until it was a shiny mound. Then he rammed the shovel into the mound. "Come on," he said. "I'm getting soaked." He went off, stopped, and called back, "Come on, William! Suppertime!"

THE MIST GAVE WAY TO A STEADY RAIN, and by nightfall it beat the roof like a crazy drummer. Lying in bed, all I could think of was how much I hated Ah-lex. My first thought was to kill him. Hours later, I still wanted to kill him. The only question was how. How to make it look like an accident? Happened accidentally—on purpose. Ohhh, poor Ah-lex slipped on the stairs and broke his head open… Smashed! Yes! I would like him to be smashed. Somehow. How to do that? I would think about it, and I would enjoy thinking about it. I felt much better now. I had to tell Dick. I got up and crossed over to his bed, where he lay facing the wall, as usual.

"Dick," I said softly, nudging his shoulder. "Dick, wake up."

"Arrgh," growled Dick, throwing an arm back at me.

"Dick!" I shook him hard. "Wake up!"

"Whaaaaa…?" mumbled Dick, into his pillow.

"You awake?" I shook him some more. "Dick!"

He spun around and got up on his elbows. "What, damnit!" he barked, his eyes locked on mine. "What? Aw for—" He spun back to the wall. "Go to bed!"

I bent close to his head, laid my hand very lightly on his shoulder, and said, "We have to smash Ah-lex."

"Gooooo aaawaaaaay…" He said it soft and easy.

I went back to my bed, lay down, and listened to the rain tell me about smashing Ah-lex.

28

Top of the World (Friday)

The next morning the fireball came up and started to melt the world, and by milking time, it was like living in a steam bath-like the attic flat on Luna Avenue. But they were happy. It was a good rain, they said. Not too much and not too little. Just enough for the other crops, they said, especially the corn. So at night you'd be able to hear the corn grow, that's what I said—or rather, thought. As for the wet hay, the hot sun would do its job with an extra hour or two, and then we'd be back in business.

"Hooo-rah!"

And so they went about doing other farmer things. But I didn't. And I didn't care what they thought.

"Bug off," was what I said to Dick. And he did.

I looked up at the silo so high it lived with the clouds. I had to climb it. Knew it the first time I saw it. Told Dick about it the day he arrived. Told him it would be a great place to look out at the world, see where it fell over the edge, have a smoke. He said, "You crazy? You could get killed!" I studied the clouds up above, watched them float by and by...and by... What I was doing, and I knew it, was stalling. One, two, three, go! I jumped up, grabbed the first rung, pulled myself up—and with sandals pawing the concrete—I reached for the second rung, grabbed it, the third rung, grabbed it, and then I was able to get my feet on the first rung, and the rest was a snap, like going up a ladder.

Hand over hand, step over step I went, and when I got about halfway up, I stopped and looked down. My hands squeezed the rungs; it was a long way down. I went on now one rung at a time: hand, hand, foot, foot. About three quarters of the way up, I stopped again and looked down: "Geez, this is really high!" I squeezed tighter and went slower.

I reached the small dormered window in the dome. A shaft of sunlight lit a rectangle on the curved inside wall. "Helloooo!" I called into the dark hole, and an echo bounced right back. I looked down at the ground: "Oh my god!" My heart beat so hard I felt it in my head… Looking up was just as bad…worse, with the clouds moving, the dizziness. Oh yeah, getting to the top of the dome looked like a very scary deal. There were no grips of any kind to get around the dormered window. After all, it wasn't meant to be a ringside seat.

I had second thoughts about scrambling to the top. "Next time would do, enough for now," I said to myself. And then I surprised myself by pulling myself up into the framed window until I could kneel on the bottom of the wooden frame and then grip the sides of it. From there, I worked my way around the right side of the dormer until I was standing on the flat rim of the dome with my hands plastered on the dome itself. I took a couple of quick breaths.

All I had to do now was scramble up the dormered side of the window to the center of the dome and sit down. And so I did, and I froze. The view was unbelievable. It was nothing like looking out of a high building. It was like sitting on the head of a pin way up in the sky! Almost like flying. Arms out, wind blowing, scary as hell and terrific! Out west, past the lowlands and past the creek, the pastureland ran on forever. South, past the outbuildings, and the pigsty, the stretching hayfields ran out to a line of trees. I spun my bottom on the top of the world and faced north—cornfields and more hayfields rolled on until they melted into the bluff that was topped by another tree line. And to the east, County Road B, ran in front of the house to the left and to the right, up and down hills, dividing the farmland. And sprinkled everywhere were groups of giant oak trees and magnificent elms, with clumps of white birch and maples along the way. And what wasn't green was black delta. "This 'a farm.'" That's what

Gramps said to me that first day. Well, down on the ground it's a farm. But up here, "This 'a magic'!"

And then, when the magic wore off, my mind went back to Ah-lex. How could he do that? How could he be so mean? How could anybody be so mean? Moritz could, of course. But why? Why are some people mean? Does something make them that way? Are mean people made mean by something that happens, or are they born that way?

I was not a mean person. But could I become a mean person? I could be mean to Ah-lex, that's for sure. I could kill him... Well, maybe I couldn't. But yesterday I could've. If he was lying on the ground and I had a boulder high in my hands, I could've dropped it on his head. I think I could. I'm pretty sure. Richard couldn't. I know that. You would think he could, but he couldn't... But just because I could, I don't think that would mean I was a mean person, 'cause I was really not. I know that. I know deep inside me... Hitler was a mean person. He was a devil... And Moritz was mean. But I didn't know why. Maybe, if bad things happened to some good people, they stayed good anyway; and some people, if something bad happened to them, they went bad... Or maybe some were just born bad. Maybe they couldn't be good no matter what. That was frightening... Those poor kittens. So soft. So beautiful. To be born, to be alive, and they knew they were alive. They knew they had a mommy and a daddy. And they were happy. Happy to be alive... And they just got to know that, and then they were dead. Oh, God... Why?

AFTER LUNCH WE GOT IN A LOAD AND A HALF and quit. The day was shortened even more because the hay in the lowlands was too wet. Gramps sent Dick and me back up to the house to see what we could do with the vegetable garden while he and Ah-lex went back out to the fields to rerake the hay. Dick and I gulped ice-cold water from the pump while we watched the girls do the laundry. They were giddy with talk about the arrival of the families due the next day.

"What time you think they'll get here, Dick?" said Vickie, passing us with a loaded basket of dirty clothes.

"Depends on how many flats they get," said Dick, calling after her. "Three cars means—"

"Four!" I cut in. "Four, if my folks come, Dick. You think they'll come? I got a feeling they're comin'."

"I don't know," Dick shrugged. "They didn't show up at the lake Sunday."

"They didn't? Yeah, well…my dad was probably getting things ready at the shop so they could come up."

"Jean said they were going to Detroit."

"Detroit? Detroit, Michigan? Who's in Detroit?"

"Beats me. Com' on, let's get started." Dick headed for the garden.

"Detroit! Why would they go there? Detroit, shit!"

It was hot. Hot without a cloud to stop the burning. Hot without a whisper of a breeze. I went about straightening the strawberry plants pounded by the rain while Dick did the potato bug thing. A tap on my shoulder turned my head. *Eyaaaw!*

Dick was holding a stinkin' snake an inch from my nose. Boy, did I hate snakes. I chased a laughing Dick out of the garden and into the apple orchard. Dick whipped the snake against the trunk of a tree once, and then again, then hung the limp body over a branch. Pulling out a crumpled pack of Camels, Dick passed me a cigarette—a whole one, not a half. My eyes went big.

"That's the last of 'em."

"You're out? You're kidding?"

Dick struck a match with his fingernail, lit up, and held the flame out for mine.

I enjoyed the smoke filling my lungs. "Mmmmm," I exhaled. "You know how to roll 'em? We can get some tobacco from Ah-lex's big jar."

"Can't. Can't even steal his cigarette paper. He counts it."

"He counts the thin sheets? Nobody counts the sheets. Who counts cigarette paper?"

"Ah-lex." Dick exhaled a cloud of smoke.

I exhaled a cloud of smoke. "I saw Eddie and the girls doing it in the barn."

I'd been dying to tell Dick about what I saw in the barn, but couldn't think of how to get into it, but now it just poured out. But I didn't tell him the whole thing. I left out the part about Dorothy. I just told him what happened between Vickie and Eddie. It was enough. Dick didn't move, didn't even blink, not until his cigarette burned his fingers.

"Richaaard! Billllly!" It was Vickie calling out, waving her arm. "Com' on, we're going fishing!"

And just like that, we were pulling bamboo poles out from under the porch and marching down to the creek with the girls and Grandma, and before we could stop giggling, we were plopping our lines into the three dark pools with tasty worms on our hooks—courtesy of Grandma. Sorry, Grandma. How could I have thought she was going to eat them, although that would be one heck of a trick. And there was no doubt Grandma was good with tricks. Like with the strawberries. And like she already caught four husbands with a face that could stop a clock.

But now, I got to tell you, Grandma was into another fantastic trick, a fishing trick, one you're not going to believe. You ready for this? Grandma talked to fish, and they listened. Yep. Take it or leave it. She not only talked to them, she hypnotized them, told which ones to bite on her hook, told the small ones to keep away, and so forth. Some trick, eh?

What she did was swing her fish line out over the water, and no matter where it plopped, as soon as the bobber settled in, she started with the fish talk—which wasn't Polish, by the way, it was some sort of mumbo-jumbo mixed with cooing and exclamation points. And then, when her nose started vibrating, *plunk* went her bobber, and she had a nice bluegill, sunfish, perch, or whatever kind she wanted. She also got a pickerel, which they said was not good eating, too many bones. But Grandma didn't throw him back in because they also said they ate the perch. He was a mean-looking thing with his long, skinny body and a snoot filled with teeth! Hey, I wasn't gonna swim without my Jockey's next time. I didn't want no pickerel think-ing I had a giant perch between my legs.

Vickie hardly had any time to fish for herself because she ended up taking Grandma's fish off the line and rebaiting her hook. She didn't even have time to put the fish into the gunnysack anchored at the bank, just tossed them into the five-gallon can we brought along for stuff.

Dick was catching them too, left and right. He put a worm on a hook in nothing flat, so that after a while, he was helping Vickie with the worms—worming his way in, you might say.

Yours truly caught three nice perch right in a row, right after I shot a nose full of gook into the water. "It knocked them out," I joked to Dorothy. So she moved down to the next pool, sensi-tive-type, you know.

Anyway, it was a lot of fun. We all laughed a lot, except for Grandma. Grandma really only had one expression, which was "no" expression—maybe because of her face thing. Although once in a while, her eyes lit up: like when she talked to the fish or if you caught her red-handed. But mostly, they looked hard and cold. Grandma wasn't easy to figure out, no two ways about it.

My guys and I did some fishing in the lagoon at Riis Park. We didn't catch much. Mostly bullheads, so we threw them back in. I didn't know what it was about watching a bobber for hours on end, but we did it. Relaxing, if nothing else. Lie back and watch the clouds sail by...watch birds fly...spot a red-winged blackbird or a cardinal... See squirrels walk on trees...watch a rabbit hop like crazy. Catch a snake and we stone it to death. And the water, always the water...waving or dead still like glass. And the mystery of the bob-ber, waiting for it to move... Waiting all day without a care in the world... Nice and peaceful. That's about all you get out of it really. Kind of a waste of time, I guess. But a nice way to waste it. Once in a while anyway.

The five-gallon drum got so full of fish they were jumping out and flopping around on the ground, so that's when Grandma and Vickie and Dick quit and headed back up to the house, with Dick and Vickie carrying the drum between them.

I'd been fishing near Dorothy most of the time, but we didn't really talk to each other, just made cracks about the fishing, like, "I got a big one!" or "Look't the colors on this sunfish!" or...or whatever. Crap like that... Actually, I was the one did most of the talking... probably did all of it. But now it was quiet, just the two of us fishing. "Betcha a nickel I catch one before you do!" Not a peep. Then her bobber went down, and she pulled out a small sunfish.

"That one doesn't count. He's too small."

"Don't talk to me." She threw the fish back in and moved down a bit.

"What did I do now?" I plopped my line in next to hers. "So what'd I do? Com' on. What am I, a mind reader?" Just then my bobber went straight down. I pulled out a big perch. "Look! It's the biggest one, yet!" I held it up. "Look, Dor!"

Dorothy gave me a sharp look. Only Eddie called her Dor. I made myself busy rebating my hook with what was left of the worm.

"What you yelled at me in the garden." Dorothy's eyes stayed on her bobber.

"I yelled at you?" I plopped my line back in. "When you left me for the wolves, you mean?"

"You know what I mean." Her eyes never left the water.

"I don't! Honest," I lied through my teeth. "Honest, Dorothy! What?" I laid it on. "Hey, if I yelled at you, I don't remember. Okay?"

"You're lying." Her voice was quiet, but clear as a bell.

"I'm not lying," I said, trying to match her tone. "You got a bite!"

Dorothy yanked her pole back and landed a nice-sized bluegill. I grabbed at the line to take the hook out, but she jerked the pole, and the fish flew back into the weeds. I went after it, and all of a sudden she was standing over me and poking me with the butt end of her fishing pole.

"Oooow! Stop it!" I grabbed the bamboo pole and tried to yank it away from her, but she held on. I got to my feet, and we tried to wrest the pole away from each other. Suddenly, we stopped. We were breathing hard. We stared at each other.

"I saw you go into Eddie's room!" It was not what I intended to say. I don't know what I intended to say. All I know was that I said it.

The fire in Dorothis eyes leaped at me. "So what?" Her hands dropped off the pole. "We're getting married. When Eddie gets back, we're going to get married. He promised." And then she turned around and marched off toward the house.

She never looked back.

29

It's the Family (Saturday)

We were bringing in the last load for the day, turning onto the runway that led into the barn, wondering why the family hadn't arrived yet, when off in the distance the sound of blaring horns caught our attention. Cars were kicking up dust, and the roar of their engines grew louder and louder.

"Whoooooa! Whoa!" said Gramps, pulling hard on the reins, trying to keep Molle and Jim from getting totally spooked. The wagonload of hay rocked from side to side.

"Whoa, Jim! Easy!" Ah-lex caught up to Jim, grabbed his halter and snapped it back hard. "Whoa!" he barked. Jim's head reared back, and the jittery team stomped to a stop.

"That's them," said Dick.

"They're here, Gramps!" I was so happy I can't tell you. They were finally here. Uncle Leo. Aunt Sophie. Uncle George and Aunt Jean. John and Delores. And my folks—I hope, I hope, I hope. Please, God. "How many cars, Dick?"

"Can't tell. Too much dust."

The lead car turned off the County Road in a cloud of dust. "John's DeSoto," Ah-lex called out.

"Looks like," said Gramps.

The next car made the tum. It was a dusty blue. "That's Leo's Cadillac," said Dick.

"It's a convertible, Gramps!" I shouted. And then I stopped breathing. The last car bounced around the turn and sprayed a huge wave of dust. It was dark-looking. Dad's Plymouth was Bla…

"Who's that in the green coupe?" Gramps asked.

"That's George's Cord," said Dick. "It'll do a hundred and ten!"

"Hundred and ten," said Gramps. "Holy smokes."

With their horns blaring, the three cars snaked their way toward the house…twisting through the pines, past the big oak, alongside the garden, then into the yard where they pulled alongside each other and died. The sudden silence seemed strange.

We were halfway there, Richard leading, taking big steps, his hands in his back pockets. I stared at the three cars lined up shoulder-to-shoulder, and the thought hit me.

"Maybe she came with one of them!" I shifted into high gear. Passing Dick, I rang out. "Maybe my mom's here!"

She wasn't… But it was great seeing all of them. I can't tell you how great it was. My Uncle John was probably the strongest man alive. Uncle George's eyes were flashing when he told everyone how John picked up the Cord so they could put a boulder under the axle to change his flat tire. And then he went on to say that John was one of those guys, like Jack Dempsey, that could knock a guy across a room with a six-inch punch. He really liked my Uncle John; everybody did. He had a heart as big as a house. But it wasn't big enough for my Aunt Delores. And that was too bad, because he would have plucked her a star if she wanted it.

And boy, it was good to see my Aunt Sophie. Having Aunt Sophie was like having two mothers; she was always there for me. And she made the best cinnamon crapes ever. But she wasn't so hot with the other garbage, which was fine with me. Oh, and she gave me a letter from my mom that I stuffed into my back pocket to read later. And I already told you about my Uncle Leo. And Uncle George and Aunt Jean were the kookiest pair ever; they fit together like a jigsaw puzzle. Crazy. And Uncle George's mom, Mrs. Bauer, taught Aunt Jean how to make unbelievable Hungarian cookies that melted in your mouth. No two ways about it, I had one heck of a family. I mean, how lucky can a guy get.

Oh, and of course, a lot of other things happened, but I wasn't really there; I mean I was there, in body and soul, but my brain wasn't. It just took off and parked itself up on some cloud so I could watch it all without being bothered...which was kind of weird, I guess, but... Well, that's just the way it was... And I don't know what else to say about it...about the arm pounding with my uncles...and Richard giving a sneaky hard one to Leo, his brother, making his eyes pop... And Aunt Sophie asking me if I had a cold because my eyes were bloody red.

"The haying, you know," I told her...

And Uncle George picking me up and twirling me overhead like a baton, then kneeling down and raising his mitts so I could throw left and rights into them until I missed, landed on my tailbone, and saw stars.

"One...two..." Uncle George was counting me out, "three... four..."

"Ho! Ho! Hooo!" came Uncle John's deep bellow of a laugh.

He snatched me up and put me on his shoulders, which was where I stayed, watching the circus... Watching Grandma, perched like a vulture, watching it all down her broken beak...counting all the heads she was going to have to feed her chickens to, her blinking eyes ringing up the dollars.... The men's eyes on Vickie when she weaved between them...their glance at Dorothy. Aaand the glued eyes of Ah-lex on Dorothy, which not only puzzled me but made me mad. Gramps, of course, was getting the number 4 look—moving from car to car, talking to my uncles about their machines... And then, on the porch, carrying in some stuff, Dick and I ran into Aunt Delores with her spellbinding behinder behind her. Right off, she gave us her Sophie Tucker routine:

"Weeell... Helloooo, boooys!" she said, her behind vibrating. "Seeing much of Eleanooor these daays, hmmmm?" She chucked me under the chin. "Not fooling arooound with any sheeeep, eh, boooys?"

"We don't have sheep," I told her.

"Ha-ha-ha-ha," she roared, and it really vibrated. "Chickens?"

Our eyes popped, Dick and me, and the whole porch shook.

"Weeell, boooys… Come up and seee mee sometiiime.

And as she moved out and took the stairs, Dick and I watched *The Eight Wonder of the World* roll away.

WE WERE ALREADY LATE with the milking, so I ran off to get the cows while Richard helped Uncle Leo and the others get settled. The cows had already crossed the creek and were well on their way to the barn. They were not as dumb as they looked. So after I had chased them into the barnyard, I found myself moving back toward the creek. I wasn't in a hurry, didn't have to be, had all the time in the world, even though the letter in my back pocket was all I had been thinking about, knowing I was going to read it when the time was right…like now. I pulled the letter out, sat on a big boulder, and watched the ankle-deep water swirl around my feet. I didn't unfold the letter, didn't even look at it, just let it hang there in my hand. No rush, plenty of time. I liked this time of day, the sinking sun coming in at a slant now, dulling the fire in it…the cool air rising from the ground…everything still now…the land and the trees…the sky and the water…like in a painting. The kind I'd see in some houses when I did the collection for my paper route. There's one of those dragon-flies again, hovering over the willows, wings a blur… A frog across the creek, croaking getting no answer. I ripped open the letter. Mom's tablet paper, her penciled handwriting filling the page:

Thursday, June 24

Dear Son,

Received your nice letter today. It's quiet here without you around. Your father says you're growing up and that the farm will do you good. I hope so. He says not to worry, but I do. Because you are always getting into trouble! So be careful! We miss you, William.

Your Great-Grandmother Grabowska had a hard life, but she has a good heart with children. Everybody says so. So let us know.

I'm glad Richard is there with you. Don't fight! And don't lift anything heavy. Don't try to be like Richard. And eat! You must eat! But don't get too fat. Ha! Ha!

Queenie wouldn't eat for a couple of days after you left, but she's eating now. Smitty said to tell you the swimming is great. (I know he means the girls.) Norbert and him are doing your paper route, so not to worry. Your sister says hello.

Well, son, that's it for now. Before you know it, the family will be up there—and maybe your dad and Connie and me too. So take care of yourself, and don't forget to say your prayers!

With love, Mom and Dad

I read the letter again. Then I just stared at the writing until it got blurry. I could hear my mom's voice: "We miss you, William... Don't lift anything heavy.... Don't fight with Richard. The family... The family... We miss you. We miss you. We miss you."

"So do I, Mom! I miss you! I miss you so muuuch! I miiiiiiii-isssss yoooooooou! Uggghh."

A longing hit me so hard it doubled me over. With my arms wrapped around my middle, I stumbled to the shore and sank to my knees. A yearning to be home grew in me. "I wanna go hooooooome!" The feeling was so deep, so complete it was filling me up, killing me, just killing me, I can't tell you.

"Oh, God! Oh, God, please take me home. Now! Right now! Please, God! I wanna go home! Now! Now, God! Pleeeeeeaaase!"

The yearning I felt grew out my guts; they were pouring out, pouring out from the bottom of my guts...just pouring, but nothing was there, nothing you could see...but it kept coming...kept hurting...a yearning so hurting, yearning inside pouring out, gagging me...gagging me and hurting...hurting me, the loneliness so hurting, hurting me so deep, going far beyond what I had known as pain. So deep, so deep in me there seemed to be no bottom, just this yearning pulling at me, pulling at me to be home, knowing that only being home could stop it. And that it had to be now! Right now!

"Oh, please, God! Pleeeaase! Take me hoooome! Oh, God! God, I can't stand it anymore. Not another minute! Oh, God! Please, I wanna be home. Pleeeeease, God! Please, I wanna be hooooomme. Now, God! Pleeeeeaaase! Oh, pleeeeeeeeeeeeeeeaaaaaaase!"

I keeled over on my side finally and moaned...moaned for I don't know how long. Until the pulling stopped, until the vacuum swallowed me...until everything in me was gone... And somehow I left my loneliness there...left it buried in the ground...left it there forever... And somehow I knew that was not good...not good because it was part of me...and never would be again...

THE PORCH HUMMED like a beehive with talk and laughter all through a supper of Polish sausage, sauerkraut, and boiled potatoes. But by coffee time, heads were nodding, and by the time the kerosene lamps were lit, only a handful of diehards were left to grumble and puff on their red dotted cigarettes.

Earlier in the day, Dick and I had hauled down wafer-thin mattresses from the attic for the purpose of sleeping on the cement slab out by the water pump, and that was where we ended up. The stars above sparkled like diamonds flung across a sky of black velvet. We didn't have stars like this in Chicago, never like this, not even close, not even on a moonless night like tonight... A blanket of winking velvet to snuggle under and dream... Boooooy, the folks really missed it. Damn them! Damn them! Damn them!

30

Church and the Filas Girls (Sunday)

The church grounds at Saint Peter's was packed with families gathered from all points of the compass. All dressed in their Sunday best, all back to their roots, greeting each other with handshakes and hugs, talking about births and deaths, marriages and jobs, and lastly, the land and the weather—always the weather.

That was what the grown-ups were into. Young people like Dick and I were into eyeballing the girls and commenting without moving our lips. Groups of guys were bolder: they did it by nudging each other, pointing with their chins, and punching each other on the arm. Groups of girls did it by giggling and whispering, tossing their hair around, and messing with their hats.

"Dick, look, those two girls by Aunt Jean and Aunt Sophie. They're lookin' at us," I said it all without moving my lips, naturally.

"That's the Filas family," said Dick, through his teeth.

"The tall one just waved. You know her?"

"Yeah, heh-heh-heh."

"Let's go over there."

"After church."

"After church they might be gone." I gave Dick the elbow. "C'mon, they're smilin' at us."

So we worked our way through the crowd, and when we got there the girls turned their back on us, but the little kid, that the tall girl had by the hand, pulled them back around. They were dressed in plain, faded dresses, but they looked squeaky clean, and they had blue ribbons in their yellow hair.

"Hi ya," said the little guy waving and straining to get free.

"Cooper!" said the tall girl, yanking him back, her eyes on the ground the whole time.

"Hi, Cooper," I said, adding a little wave. Boy, talk about shy, both girls still hadn't looked up at us.

"Hello, Richard," said the tall girl with a glance.

"Hel-yo, Richar," mimicked the little guy. He got another good yank for his greeting.

"Going to church, huh," said Dick

"No, they're going to a ballgame," I cracked.

Richard walloped me on the arm. Cooper squealed, jumped up and down and got yanked in all directions.

"Where's Bogart?" asked Dick.

"He's here…" The girl went up on her toes and scanned the crowd. "He's here somewhere." The shorter girl—about my size—pointed at Dick, and looked at me. "Is he your brother?"

"Naaaw. I don't even know him."

"I'm his uncle!" boasted Dick.

"You're his uncle?" said the taller girl, giving Cooper another jerk.

"Yeah, his mother is my sister."

"Ahhh, my mother doesn't even know him."

Dick backhanded me in the chest.

"Agggggh…" I fell back and made a big show of faking pain.

Cooper started bouncing around, laughing.

"Stop it!" The girl jerked his arm off and put it on a platter. Cooper wrapped himself in her dress and peeked at me through his tiny fingers.

"You going to be here all summer?" said the shorter girl.

"Not me. I'm getting out for good behavior."

"Cut the baloney!" said Dick, flicking a backhand that missed because I twisted away.

"Cut the baloney," I mimicked.

"Cut da bawony," mimicked the little guy peeking out from the dress.

"Coo-peeeer," said the taller girl with a smile this time.

It was a nice smile, showing a lot of teeth, all perfectly even, like Uncle George.

Cooper started kicking at her shins and making strange noises. "Stop it!" Jerk, jerk. "I mean it!" Jerk. "Now stop it!" A super jerk. This kid was going to end up with one arm a foot longer than the other.

"Cooper's a little..." The shorter girl tapped her temple.

"So's Dick!" I did some tapping and scooted over to the side of the shorter girl. The girl put her hand over her mouth to keep from laughing.

We watched Dick kick at a rock sunk in the sandy dirt. He got it free, rubbed it clean, and tried to hand it to Cooper, but the girl pulled him back. "No," she said, "he'll throw it at somebody."

"Oh." Dick rubbed the rock some more.

"Are you going to be at the dance Saturday?"

Dick seemed more interested in rock-rubbing than answering her.

"Yeah, at the Mile-A-Way. Everybody's going. Right, Dick?" I gave the shorter girl a nod.

"Oh, yeah. Sure." Dick was now tossing the rock from one hand to the other.

"Well..." The tall girl went up on her toes. "Bye!" She spun around and dragged Cooper along with her.

"Bye!" The shorter girl did her spin and followed them back to the herd.

Not to be outdone, Dick and I spun away and headed toward the cemetery.

"What's their names, you know?"

"Harlow." Dick ripped the rock high and far into the cornfield.

"Harlow? Mine or yours?"

"Mine."

"What's mine?"

Dick shrugged.

People were swarming around in the cemetery, doing what people do in a cemetery. Dick pulled a cigarette out from out of nowhere. We stopped under a tree, and he lit up.

"Where'd you get the ciggie?"

"Leo." He held the cigarette out, and I took a drag. "I saw her naked," he said.

I gagged and sputtered. "Who?" I coughed.

"Harlow." Dick exhaled a long, smooth stream of smoke.

"Completely naked? The whole—everything?"

Dick stared out at the cemetery. "Uh-huh."

"Oh my god! You're kidding! Down there? Everything?"

Dick dragged on his cigarette, nodded, and exhaled.

"Ohhh my gooood! Gimmie another drag. C'mon, c'mon." I cupped his hand and took a deep drag and coughed. "So…how did it happen? Gimmie the lowdown."

Dick shook his head. "Can't. We're on church grounds. It'd be a mortal sin."

"DICK! Jee-zuz! Okay, never mind. Forget it… I told you about the girls in the barn, you know… So okay, forget it. Just forget it!"

Dick was back to staring out at the cemetery.

"Bet her 'tips' stuck out, right? The tips of her breasts?" I held my thumb and finger about an inch apart, stuck out like that, I bet. Right? And…and blond little curls."

"You're a horny son of a bitch."

"Dicky, Dicky, not on church grounds."

The world stood still. Only blond curly hairs moved…all the way up to the bellybutton.

We went in to hear mass.

BACK FROM CHURCH, change clothes, grab a sandwich, and out to the fields. Working, measuring each other, that was what men do—boys too. I don't know about the fairer sex, not my problem. My problem was big, strong Richard, but I didn't mind. I always took on the bigger guys—had to, everybody was bigger than me. But I beat them all when it came to running. 'Course I was usually running away from them so they wouldn't beat me up. But no, really, at races at picnics, I beat everybody because I was fast. Richard couldn't even catch me, and he was fast. That's what men were all about. Beating the other guy, get it? That's where the word *competition* comes from. I really like it.

Dick and I were moving all over the wagon trampling down the hay, which was coming up on three sides, now that Uncle John and Uncle George were added to our team. I was sneezing, spittin', coughin', and to my surprise, so was Dick, but not as bad as me, of course. After each load, Dick and I ran down to the creek and flopped into the water. I don't see how I could've endured the haying without the creek to take the itch out of me and steal away the heat. I'm sure it helped Dick too, but I'm also sure he could have done without it.

Later, Dick and I were sent to the barn to help Grandma, Dorothy, Vickie, and Aunt Jean, with the milking while the men kept on with the haying. Aunt Sophie and Aunt Delores were busy preparing supper. And where was Uncle Leo this whole time? Only the shadow knows. Needless to say, that didn't go down too well. You could see it in their faces: Hang him by his thumbs; boil him in oil; pluck his eyebrows; make him sleep with Ah-lex (my favorite); kiss Grandma on the lips (alternate)—all these wonderful remedies crossed their minds, I'm sure.

So then, just as everybody was about to pull straws, what happened? Uncle Leo appeared with his sleeves rolled up and a milk pail in hand. A cheer went up! A hero's welcome! Except from wrinkle-faced Grandma, that is. She gave him the shaking bent-finger-in-the-face bit, along with some *rat-tat-tat* machine gun Polish. The stuff bounced off of him like he was Superman, and when she stopped to catch her breath, he hoisted her off the cement—and remember, she was not a small woman—and shook her up and down until her screeching turned to a horsy giggle. And that was the only other time I saw Grandma laugh besides the split-second when I caught her with the strawberries. Boy, I'm telling you, my Uncle Leo could charm a worm onto a hook.

By suppertime everybody looked like a wilted flower. It had been a blazing hot day, and here it was evening, and the air still hung hot and heavy. Talk didn't come bursting out, not tonight; it dribbled out. And it didn't help that everyone knew the routine they would be shackled to for the rest of the week: pitching hay under a blazing sun, or cooking in a kitchen on a wood-fired stove that melted you into a puddle, and of course, the milking—always the milking.

Poor Uncle George was burnt to a fiery red, made his nose look like a strawberry ready for plucking. Uncle John, with his olive skin over layers of lard, had no such problem. Neither did Richard, the All-American tanning freak. Me? I was as golden as the hay. Even my ribs looked good. In fact, if it wasn't for my red eyes and runny nose, one might think I was an exceptionally good-looking young farm boy—although somewhat on the skinny side.

Once the food was down—whatever it was—and the smokes were lit, a bottle of Old Kentucky appeared, as bottles seemed to do, and things picked up. More words were strung together. Laughter didn't fill the air, but it bubbled out now and then. I marveled at the endurance these men and women had and wondered if I would one day be like them. Richard, I knew, would have no problem. But me? I had serious doubts.

31

A Day with Uncle Leo (Monday)

Monday morning, my eyes were glued shut. Aunt Sophie brought some hot water mixed with boric acid out to the porch and soaked them with a cloth until they opened. Then she told me I had to go into town with my Uncle Leo, that he needed me to help him do the shopping.

"But I have to do the haying."

"It'll be here when you get back."

Elbows out the window, hot air blowing cool on the skin, and dust our trademark. "Hey, Unc," I shouted out, over the wind, "you going to do some haying when we get back?" He didn't answer. "Everybody's—"

"I'm on vacation!" He threw it at me and went back to the road. "I did enough haying in my life." He grabbed a pack of Camels from the dashboard. "Take the wheel." I grabbed the wheel and glued my eyes to the road. He lit up with the caddie's cigarette lighter, took back the wheel. "I've got sixteen people to supervise every night. I'm here to relax."

"You like your job?"

He gave me a glance. "Guys would give their left tit for my job." He chuckled. "I got it 'cause I'm tall."

"What?" I asked, not sure I've heard him right.

"I got the job 'cause I'm tall." He gave me a glance, the car slowed, and he dragged on his cigarette. "There's a hundred people

180

standing around waiting. Tropic-Aire was starting a graveyard shift. Finally, a guy in a shirt-and-tie got up on a chair. 'Hey you! Big fella!' I looked around. Everybody was looking at me. 'Yeah, you!' He pointed at me. 'You know how to operate a screw machine?' I yelled back, 'Yeah! Sure!' He yelled out, 'Anybody else?' Nobody said anything. 'Okay, you're my foreman,' he said. 'See me in my office in ten minutes.'"

"He hired you, just like that? Didn't he wanna—"

Unc cut me off with a finger in the air. "So I go into his office, and he's asking me my name and where I live and stuff, and he's looking around for some cigarettes. So I toss him my pack, and we light up. 'Big Lee,' he said, 'how much experience you have with screw machines?'

"Not a drop," I told him. He chokes on his cigarette and almost falls out of his chair. 'You son of a bitch!' he squeaks. 'You got a lot of fuckin' nerve! 'So I tell him, 'So have you, you son of a bitch. You hired me.' His eyes just about fall out of his head. Then he started laughing, and I nailed him. 'How much you payin' me to start, Mr. Burke?'" My uncle burst out laughing, and then I was laughing, and the car was going all over the road.

Finally, we settled down, and he said, "So I go in early a couple days, and he shows me how to run a screw machine." He shrugged. "And I'm the foreman!"

"Woooow, that's somethin', Unc... Wow!"

"Wednesdays we golf at his club, Elmhurst Country Club. Fancy layout. Doesn't cost me a nickel."

"He takes you golfing?"

"I got his handicap down to twelve. He's happy as a lark. We play cards, have dinner... Don's my pal!"

"He'd be mine too, if he took me golfin'!"

"He's a good boss. He knows his stuff... Nick, your dad, he's always shakin' his head."

"Yeah." I chuckled.

"Your dad's a good man. And smart... Works hard too. Too hard."

I looked out at men in the fields doing the haying and said to myself: "Gotta make do when the sun shines."

"I got this one old guy, Dago Joe. He brings in porterhouse steaks from the Black Market. They're like this." My uncle held his finger and thumb an inch and a half apart. "Three o'clock in the morning, we're all eatin' steak. Women bring in pies, cakes, casseroles! I got good people. We get the work out... And Friday morning we play dolly-ball. Fast pitch. Underhand. I gotta broad fires the ball like a bullet. Whooom! They can't hit her!"

"What position you play, Unc? I play shortstop."

"Catcher." Then he added dreamily, "I don't get home sometimes till late afternoon."

IF YOU BLINKED AT THE WRONG TIME, you'd miss Lublin altogether. A big wooden building across from the railroad platform, and that was it; that was the whole town. I'm not sure you could call one building a town, but then again, this was Wisconsin. We pulled into the shade of some big elm trees and got out. The building itself looked like a small barn, except it had two wings: the right one a saloon, the left one a service garage with a gas pump out front. And like every barn around here, it never saw paint—except for the faded white sign above the main entrance with the black lettering that read, "General Store of Lublin." Yep, this was it. This was Lublin—all of it.

We entered the saloon through a screen door. It was empty except for a man at a table at the end of the room. On the right was a long bar lined with bar stools and spittoons. Tables and chairs filled most of what was left of the narrow room. The man at the back table was buried in a magazine and didn't seem to notice us. We moved down the sawdust-covered floor and sat at the bar. While Uncle Leo lit up, I counted the hard-boiled eggs in the big pickle jar. After a couple of drags, my uncle turned to the man at the table and called out, "You the barkeep?"

"I'm everything," said the man, without looking up. "What can I do you for?"

"A cold glass of beer for me, one for you, and a soda for the boy."

The short, heavyset man came rolling over to the bar. He had on a sweaty white shirt with the sleeves buttoned down. His face was puffy looking, and his shiny black hair—what was left of it—was plastered back on his round, sweaty head. We watched him draw the two beers. I liked the way he swiped the foam off of them with a flat stick. "Name's Pete," he said, toasting."

My uncle returned the toast. "Leo. And my nephew, Billy the Kid." They laughed and swigged their beers.

Pete ran the back of his hand across his mouth. "What'll it be, Billy?"

"Ginger ale with ice and a twist of lemon." It came out the side of my mouth, tough-like.

"Oh-hoooo. Okay, kid. Comin' right up."

The glass of ginger ale had four bubbles in it, a chip of ice, and no lemon. I sipped and listened to my uncle, and Pete discuss where you could get a good keg of beer. That settled, Pete named a few farm boys that would never make it back from the war. Uncle Leo seemed to know some of them. I moved down the bar with my soda and carved letters in the sawdust with my toe.

After my uncle finished his beer, we followed Pete through a set of swinging doors into the store itself. It was one big open space with counters, tables, shelves, and barrels—all filled with merchandise. There was canned foods, clothes, shoes, tools, kerosene lamps, container cans, cans of paint and brushes, a couple of counters of fishing and hunting equipment, and all kinds of hardware. This last item—at this time—was our main point of interest, as some cutting teeth on the hay mower needed to be replaced. Pete brought some sharp new cutting teeth over to the cash register, added some rivets, and began wrapping it all up in some old newspapers.

"You got eye drops?" asked my uncle.

"For what?"

"For the eyes," said my uncle.

"Look okay to me," said Pete, glaring at my uncle.

"Not me. The kid."

"Ah! What's wrong with your eyes, Billy?"

"They're all red," my uncle answered.

Pete reached over the counter and tilted my head up with his big fat fingers under my chin. "Yep, they're red, all right."

"They're supposed to be green," I told him.

"Red now."

"So you got eye drops?" said my uncle.

"No drops. Soak 'em with some white bread dipped in milk." Pete put our items into a brown bag. "Anything else?"

"Got some ice?"

"Got melted ice."

"I'll take a quart."

Pete and Uncle Leo locked eyes. Then Pete broke into a roar, and his body bobbed up and down…and, for sure, his belly too, but we couldn't see that part because of the counter, naturally. And then when we left, I got a paper cup filled with ice chips.

WE ROLLED ALONG TOWARD THORPE, the ice on my eyes feeling great, the itch gone.

My uncle tried the radio again, got nothing but static, shut it off, and lit up a cigarette. "Gimmie a drag, Unc."

"You smoke?"

"Eddie showed me how." He passed me the cigarette. I took a deep drag to impress him and passed it back. "Eddie smokes Lucky Strikes."

"He's not so lucky now."

I laughed. "You're deferred like my dad, aren't you, Unc? They can't draft you, right?"

"Better not. I got plans."

"Like what?"

"Going to open up a shop."

"A shop! When?"

My uncle glanced over. "Keep it under your hat. Opportunity is knocking."

"I won't say a word, Unc. Not a word."

"Maybe I'll hire you to do some cleaning up and stuff."

"Oh yeah! Great! I'm ready anytime, Unc. How much you gonna pay me, Mr. Filas?"

THORPE WAS DEAD AHEAD, the five building metropolis where the Soo Line dropped me off eleven days ago—which seemed like months ago really, not days. It was probably the way time passed in purgatory and hell—this last bit was easily understood by Catholics.

We bumped over the tracks at the train station and glide into the one-sided town. People all over the place. Kids running and jumping, mothers jerking arms and hollering, dogs barking; it was almost like in the city. Cars were parked up and down both sides of the street it was so packed. At the end of the block, by the bank, we turned around and headed back, looking for a parking slot. Finally, right in front of the General Store of Thorpe, a car backed out of a slot, and we took it—the Caddy's huge fishtails stuck out into the roadway.

"Want some ice cream?" said my Unc.

"Where they got ice cream?"

He headed for the door right in front of us. "Got a lunch counter too."

The general store was barn-style, like the one in Lublin, only bigger, and it was painted dark red and trimmed in white. The inside was also a surprise, more like a city store: barrels and counters were painted in different colors and fancy penmanship—perfect signs were everywhere, naming everything, which I thought was kind of ridiculous. After all, a broom was a broom. I guess, I liked my country stores to look more "country," like with unpainted wood that could give you slivers and a coat of dust everywhere and some stink in the air—like the one in Lublin.

On the right side of the room, above a set of swinging doors, hung a sign with more fancy letters. It read: "A La Café de Paris." We passed in, and the swinging doors flapped behind us. The long room had a line of tables on the window side, a long counter with stools opposite and knickknacks everywhere. Nice, very cozy, but for me the main attraction was at the middle table. Seated there, with her hands clasped—and looking very grown up about it—was a very pretty little girl in a white dress. A matching ribbon trickles through her dark, dark hair. Chin up, she sat there, listening—or not listening—to her folks dribble on. If I lived to be a hundred, I would never again feel an arrow so deep in my heart. I was ready to die for her. She turned and found me with her doe eyes, and I was ready to kill for her. My uncle and I sat at a corner table, and I forced myself to look at the lady flipping burgers on a sizzling grill. She was tall and had a long blond braid running down her back.

"Want a burger?" asked my Unc, studying the menu.

"No," I answered with a shake of my head. "Just ice cream."

The girl was leaning over to her mother and saying something. Probably telling her to wait out in the car with her father while she gave me a couple of kisses. God, how could anybody look so good, so perfect, just sitting there...her back straight...her chin leading... her hands just so... How was I going to go on living?

The tall lady set two glasses of water on our table and took our order: a double-dip strawberry ice cream cone for me and a single-dip chocolate for my uncle.

I glanced at the girl and caught her staring at me, so I quickly looked up at the ceiling and then strained my eyes downward, so I could look at her without moving my head. She looked so grown-up that for a second I was thinking she just might be a midget. But then I ruled that out because the rest of her was perfect girl size.

"What's up there?" said my uncle, looking at the ceiling.

"Nothing, I'm just stretching my neck." I moved my head around in different directions.

My uncle went up to the counter for the ice cream cones. His was already half bitten away when he returned, and I marveled at the way he could do that. Whenever I bit into ice cream, it hurt my teeth; the pain shot right up into my head, you'd think somebody was trying to scalp me.

"Call me when my burger's ready," said my uncle. He gulped some water and went out the swinging doors.

I chanced a nip at my ice cream and paid the price. Swigging down the water to ease the pain, I then stared through the bottom of the empty glass at the girl. She looked so classy, so elegant, like a queen... I could well be her Prince Valiant, her knight in shining armor—winning battles, bringing her heads on a platter and trunks full of gold, jewelry, and pearls. Stealing kisses from her in the dark until she was breathless, begging me to kiss her more…and some more. A line from one of my mom's romance magazines popped into my mind: "Ah, to kiss those sweet lips…to drown in thy liquid eyes." I looked through the empty glass: "I trail fingers on thy smooth cheek…tears sting my eyes…because she is mine!" I didn't think I read that last part anywhere.

"Burger up and a coffee!" the tall lady called out.

I swept at my nose to make sure nothing was there, then swagger over to the counter, sure that my queen was watching my every move, examining my slim body, her mouth watering. Glancing over as I brought the burger back to our table, I saw that she was again talking to her mother—most likely insisting that she waited out in the car with her father while we dillydallied.

I went into the store and spotted my uncle rummaging by the "Le Ties" sign. My Uncle Leo was a clotheshorse, loved to shop. He could dress in something different every day for a year; that was how much clothes he had.

"Unc! Your burger's ready!"

He held up a tan tie in each hand; one had stripes and the other squares. "Which one?"

"The blue one with circles! C'mon, eat."

The counter table in front of me had a "Le Fishing Tackle" sign on it—which I was, of course, grateful for—otherwise I might think all these hooks, weights, plugs, and things were for landing elephants. What really caught my eye though were the glistening chrome with pearl fishing reels in various colors: green, yellow, white, red. I picked out a white pearled one. It spun and clicked excitingly. The tag read $3. Never in a million years.

My uncle came up empty-handed. We went back into the café. The girl was gone—and the mother, and the father, and the Holy Ghost. Amen. Left, evidently, by a front door that I hadn't noticed earlier.

We're on State Highway 29—a straight shot to Chippewa Falls, thirty-three miles due west. There we would get a keg of beer, said my uncle, and all the ice we wanted. He was also thinking of getting a dress for Aunt Sophie for the dance, he said. And eye drops for me. I was kind of excited. I'd never been to Chippewa Falls, the town where Gramps shot a man when he was a sheriff. I told my uncle that, and he said he knew that old man Popko was a sheriff at one time, but not that he shot anybody. "Shot 'im, hell!" I said. "He killed 'im!" He didn't say anything, so I figured he was impressed, just the way I was when Gramps told me.

The hilly road cut straight through farmland where mounds of boulders, each the size of a small shed, were scattered throughout, piled there over the years so that crops could be grown. And right now, under a broiling sun, in a cloudless sky, men were breaking their backs doing the haying.

"What time you think we'll get back, Unc?"

"Why, you in a hurry?"

"No." I shot him a glance and looked back out at the fields.

"Forget the haying!" My uncle grabbed his pack of cigarettes from the dashboard and pushed in the lighter. "Get it outta your head. You hear?"

"Yeah, Unc." I stared straight ahead, but I could still see men piling hay on wagons as we zipped by.

The lighter popped. The Caddie slowed. Unc lit up.

"You look out for number one, get it? Nobody else gives a shit about you if you don't."

"Uh-huh." I nodded. But the words didn't feel right.

We picked up speed, breezed along, passed more farms, more people working, working under a sun that was breaking records; it was that hot.

WE ZIPPED THROUGH STANLY, a one-horse town, but better than Lublin. The general store was painted, painted green with no trimming. Next was Cadott, then Chippewa Falls.

"Worst farmland in the whole State of Wisconsin," said my uncle, looking out at the fields.

"That's what Jake said. Jake's the mailman."

And then I told him about Jake, about how he said the old folks around here "got taken." It was all true, said my uncle. Then he asked if I knew the story about how my dad's folks came over from the old country.

"I did and I didn't," I told him.

"They were only taking married people on the boat, see. So Paul and Andrew, the hunchback, they meet Anna—"

"He's not a hunchback."

"Whatever. He's hunched. So…" Uncle Leo's eyes fluttered for a couple of seconds, which they sometimes did. "So they're down at the dock, and they get to talking…and just like that, Paul and Anna get married! They don't even know each other. It's just so she can get passage on the ship, get it? Nothin' else, right?"

"Yeah right… I get it, I get it."

"Okay. Soooo they're out at sea, and Paul gets itchy." My uncle chuckled. "Anna's not lettin' him get closer than a ten-foot pole." Unc started laughing so hard he could hardly talk. "So…so he climbs up to the top mast and stays up there! Says he won't come down unless she lets him into paradise!"

We busted a gut!

"The son of a bitch is up there for three days, sicker than a dog. He's dyin'! She won't even look at him!" My uncle's wiping tears from his eyes; he was laughing so hard. "Finally, they bring him down in a basket."

"He's that weak?"

"Weak? He's half dead! And then when nobody was looking, he crawled over to the rail and said he was gonna throw himself overboard! The man was really hard-up.

Finally, Anna's yelling, "Okay! Okay!" But she tells the captain to "tie him down to the bed."

"Tie him down?"

"Ahhhhhh, yeah," he said, giving me a raised eyebrow. "So the son of a bitch chews his way through the rope, and he nails her!"

My jaw dropped. I turned red.

"That's it. That's the story."

"But you said he was half dead."

"So? That half wasn't dead!"

We started laughing so hard my uncle pulled the car off the road. Then we got out and relieved ourselves behind a tree before we got on our way again.

The next thing I knew, my uncle was shaking me by my shoulder. "Wake up. We're here."

"Huh?" I sat up straight and rubbed my eyes. A sign read, "Chippewa Falls."

"What happened to Cadott?" I asked myself.

My uncle turned on the radio, and out came Glenn Miller's "In the Mood," brass horns wailing at each other, grabbing you, rocking you, putting you in the mood until we rolled into town and the static took over. Off with a twist of the dial, and we tuned in the town... It should definitely be a bigger dot on the map. It had stores and shops on both sides of the street and on the side streets too. Cars lined the curbs, and there was people everywhere. We passed a drug store, a shoe store, a dress shop, a men's shop, a tobacco shop, a leather shop, and a fur shop that had a huge brown bear standing outside with its paws up like it was ready to slug you.

"Want to see a movie?" said my Unc.

"Yeah! Where?"

"Up ahead, on the right. Yankee Doodle Dandy."

"James Cagney! Oh, boy! Can we go, Unc?"

"Let's see."

We pulled to the curb by the theatre. The sign in the ticket booth read, "2:00 Matinee." I repeated the time to my Unc with hope in my voice. He checked the clock in the dashboard. "That gives us about an hour." He dug out his wallet. "I'll go see about that keg of beer." He slapped a couple of dollar bills into my hand. "Get your eye drops and meet me back here at two o'clock."

"Okay, Unc. Two-o'clock." I jumped out of the car, and he took off.

Fifteen minutes later, I had eye drops in my eyes and was licking away at an ice cream cone while staring at the big brown bear outside the fur store. My eyes were even with his belly, he was that big. Of course, he was standing on a wooden platform, but still... I bet he could take my head off with one of those big paws...slice me up, down, and sideways with those claws…probably take a good size bite out of me if he felt like it with those big teeth. Ugggh! I'd rather meet up with an elephant. I'd have a better chance. Climb a tree and pee on him, and he'd probably run away. This damn bear'd probably climb right up, gobble me up, and use the branches for a toothpick. Uh-uh. No way, I wanted to meet up with this guy. Not unless I had a cannon or a machine gun…and a lot of bullets.

I finished my ice cream cone and went inside the store. What a fantastic place! Not only were there fur coats in the windows but all over the place, all colors—black, light brown, dark brown, white, and all sizes, for men and women, and kids, kids big and small… fur coats on dummies. And coat racks, they were even hanging from the ceiling on wires high and low. Yeah…the whole store nothing but furs, just furs. Fur skins even. Stacked in piles everywhere. And ho-ho-ho! Bear rugs! Yeah, with heads on them, and big teeth. Hey! This'a fur store! There was only one thing wrong with the place: the smell. It was kind of like when you take a dump.

THE MOVIE WAS GREAT! I told my Uncle that Cagney was my favorite actor, that he could do it all: dance, sing, punch guys, or shoot 'em dead. And to think, he was not big. And not even good-looking. My dad was a lot better-looking. Taller too, probably. But Cagney, he was tough. He even slapped babes around, and they came back for more. Now that was talent. My uncle was for Humphrey Bogart. He said that when he talked without moving his lips, "watch out"; that was when you knew he's gonna drill ya. He said Cagney looked like he got his face caught in a vise.

We drove back at a snail's pace so that the iced-down keg in the washtub—brought along for that purpose—wouldn't slosh all over the trunk. Static scrambled the music now, so my uncle gave the dial a twist, and it was all gone. There wasn't much of a breeze traveling along at this speed, but with the sun behind us, now we're not burning up. Creeping along seemed odd at first, but after a while it felt nice and relaxing. But one thing bothered me, bothered me bad. It was the men out in the fields; they were still at it, still doing the haying. It made me feel rotten; it really did… And I wondered what my uncle's feeling when he glanced out at the fields, which he did a number of times.

Supper was set up outside in the yard: chickens grilled over a fire with mashed potatoes and gravy. And a big kettle of pork and beans, some canned pears, and plenty of homemade bread and butter. And boy, did they eat! And did they talk! And laugh! Of course, the beer had a lot to do with it. It was a big hit. And so, naturally, was my Uncle Leo. The man could do no wrong. In fact, I almost found myself shaking my head like my dad. Uncle Leo just seemed to have it—whatever it was—and everybody wanted a piece of him. Me included.

I called out to Dick several times, but he wouldn't give me a look. He was still mad at me for having the day off and for all the things that I told him we did in the towns we hit. He hammered me a couple of times, and I should have shut up, but I was just too excited by it all. But I did stop short of telling him about the movie; otherwise, they would have been digging me a grave. Of course, seeing it from his side, I could understand it, making him mad and all, but… Oh well, I should've shut up. But then, whom would I tell it all to? Dorothy would have been great, but she didn't have time for me now, not even a glance; she was into all ladies' things now. Bless her big tits!

The sun was a big red spotlight out on the horizon when I grabbed Dick and told him that I had stolen some tobacco from Ah-lex's cookie jar. (Uncle Leo was getting stingy.) Minutes later we were on the roof of the grain shed rolling us some smokes. And since Ah-Lex was counting his sheets, we were using toilet paper from the rolls the ladies brought with them. We tried newspaper and the Sears catalogue, but they burned like a torch. So now our ciggies resembled small cigars, but they worked well enough. That Ah-lex was a real scrooge; or else he just wanted to deprive us of the pleasure of having a smoke. The kind of person he was, it was probably both. And put this in your pipe and smoke it: Ah-lex was now marking the tobacco level on his cookie jar with a crayon. This guy was looking for trouble, biiig trouble, Chicago style.

"You know what we ought'a do, Dick?" I said, puffing away, as we lay on the slanted roof.

"Wha'?"

"We ought'a mix in some horse shit with Ah-lex's tobacco." Dick didn't say anything.

"Dick?"

"Forget it."

"No, listen," I said, leaning up on an elbow. "We take out a big clunk of tobacco, and then we mix in enough horse shit to bring the level back up. See?"

"He'll smell it."

"Maybe not! Besides, horse shit smells pretty good."

"It's still shit."

"So he'll be smoking shit, and we'll be smoking tobacco!" We smoked on. I could tell Dick's rusty wheels were turning.

"Naaaawt," he finally drawled. "Won't work."

"Sure it will. We can doctor it up. Mix in some of Uncle John's chewing tobacco."

"Now you want to steal from Uncle John?" said Dick, rolling up on an elbow to look me square in the eye.

I shrugged. "It's for a good cause."

Dick flopped back down. "It'll still stink."

The light in the sky was fading. The stars were coming out. "We could mix in some aftershave lotion. Maybe some perfu——"

"Forget it!" said Dick, slamming the roof with his foot.

"You got a better idea?" I sat up. "The way things are goin', pretty soon we won't even have matches." I flopped back down. "Boy, do I hate Ah-lex."

"He don't like you either."

"I don't care. He's mean. He's Like Moritz." I got up on an elbow. "Last year, when you were up here, I was over by your house when Moritz went nuts. Teddy did somethin', I don't know what. Moritz was pounding the table and growling like a wild animal. Teddy ran into the back bedroom and dove under the bed. I went in right after him. Moritz got a broom, and he started poking us under the bed. He kept jabbing and jabbing… He hurt Teddy bad. I saw him a couple of days later, he was all black and blue. He said he was pissing blood."

"Didn't you get hurt?"

I shook my head. "Teddy put his body in front of mine… I never thanked him. I should've, but I never did."

"He used to rob houses, you know."

"Yeah, I know."

"I bet you don't know that Moritz turned him in. He turned in his own son… Yeah. The cops came, and Teddy ran up on the roof and jumped and broke both his legs… Moritz was laughin." Dick took a last drag and flipped away the butt.

THE BONFIRE IN THE YARD danced high and bright while the ladies swayed to car music fed from draining batteries. The men slugged down their beer and watched every wiggle and giggle. Then Aunt Delores did a turn around the fire, shaking her behinder, almost blew out the fire. And were the ladies really stripping now, or just roasting some brats. It was hard to tell what was what, with the beer in you—thanks to Uncle John refilling our coffee cups on the sly, Dick and me.

Uncle Leo grabbed Aunt Sophie and started gliding to some big band music. Boy, they were smooth. Dick said that Uncle George told him that dancing was the best way to get into a ladies' pants. I didn't quite get the connection. I don't think Dick did either.

Aunt Jean could really jitterbug, make your eyes wobble, Uncle George throwing her up and down, spinning her in and out, terrific! I fancied myself dancing a slow one with Dorothy…resting my head on her pillows. Oh boy, oh boy, oh boy. Just one more beer and I'll be ready…ready for Freddy. Ohhhh yeah! Talkin' crazy sure comes easy when you got beer goin' down the pipes.

Oh now, there's a waste: Vickie and Dorothy dancing together. I think the men are afraid their ladies will belt 'em one if they break in. Might get away with a little spin with Dorothy, but "Vickie could ruin a man for life," so said Uncle George. And I was sure he knew what he was talking about. Might be worth it, if you ask me. Oh yeah. Just one more beer. Actually, beer tasted terrible. It must be what piss tasted like; it already looked like it, you know. Terrible stuff. But it did make you feel like you didn't have a care in the world—the whole dizzy world. Ohhh yeah.

Now Uncle John, he loved the stuff. Why not? He couldn't love Aunt Delores; she wouldn't let him.

Poor Uncle John, he's got his arm draped around the beer barrel like it's his best friend. My mom said Uncle John was so big because of all the good in him. And that he was the kind of man you could take advantage of, if you were so inclined. She didn't have to tell me that Aunt Delores was so inclined.

Aunt Sophie once told me that Aunt Delores got away with stuff—like when Grandma Helen died, she took all the money; that people like Aunt Delores did things other people would never dream of doing, bad things; and that it didn't bother them one bit. When I told her I didn't understand how that could be, she said I would when I grew up. That's what they always said, of course. It was like when you grow up some kind of door opened in your brain and all of a sudden you're brilliant… I guess.

I could see Uncle John's face in the firelight. His eyes never left Aunt Delores. Such a sad face. A face not trying to look sad; it just is. It's not twisted or creased in pain. It's not anything, just downright, heartbreakingly sad. A wet streak glistened down from the corner of his eye, down past his nose, down to his lips…to where tears were leaking, carving a spot deep in my mind of the saddest face I ever saw.

32

Shop Talk, Bloodsuckers, and Horseshit (Tuesday)

"Billy, get up! It's late!" said Dick, with an elbow.

"Yeah, yeah." I peeked out from under my blanket and saw that the sun hadn't even caught the tip of the barn yet. I snuggled back into my pillow.

"Now!" said Dick, banging my shoulder and whipping the blanket off me.

"Dick!" I yelled, scrambling for the cover. "Five more minutes!" I flopped down and rattled my bones on the wafer thin mattress that, no doubt, was a souvenir from Poland.

"They're milking already," said Dick, rolling up his bedding. "Let's go!"

I rose on an elbow, "So they're milking! They don't need me until they start shitting!" I flopped back down, missed the pillow, and almost knocked myself out.

Dick picked up his bedding, kicked my butt, and headed for the porch. I heard my uncles greet him, heard the buzz, heard them laughing. I got up, pumped some cold water, drank some, and cupped some over my eyes. I got my bedding together and entered the porch. Uncle Leo and Uncle George were at the table, hunched over their coffee and smoking.

"Good morning," I mumbled as I stashed my bedding in a corner with Dick's.

"What's good about it?" said Uncle George. He looked like somebody sat on his face. Uncle Leo looked great, his wavy hair hanging down over his forehead. Richard came shuffling out of the kitchen with a steaming hot cup of coffee.

"Get the coffee pot out here," said Uncle Leo.

"And a cup for the kid," added Uncle George.

"I'll get it." I slid past Dick with a little elbow in the ribs. He nearly spilled his coffee, trying to kick back at me. I filled myself a cup but left it in the kitchen because I needed both hands to carry the big blue coffee pot out to the porch.

"Kid looks like he's been run over by a train," said Uncle George, pouring coffee for himself and Leo.

"Look what's talking," I said on my way back into the kitchen.

I took my coffee out to the porch and sat opposite my Uncle Leo. He shoved the sugar bowl over.

"Yeah, Lee, farming is for the birds," said Uncle George, the words riding out on smoke. "I can't wait to get back to Old Man Howard: 'Jawgh, vhat da hell ya do-ink!' I think I'll chop off his other pinky."

"He should'a fired you," said Uncle Leo, sipping his hot brew.

"Fire me? It was his fault! Ask Nick. I didn't tell him to put his finger in the die. 'Jawgh, let it go!' I told him, 'Are you sure?' 'Dammit da hell Jawgh! Release! Release!' So I released. Next thing, he was eyeballing his pinky, trying to figure out where the tip went to."

"Did he yell?" I asked, blowing on my brew.

"Not a peep. Next day he's walking around, smoking his cigar like nothing happened. Got his finger wrapped up, looked like a banana."

"Should'a fired you!" said Uncle Leo.

"It was just the tip, Lee, for chrissake!" said Uncle George, gripping his little finger, letting the tip stick out just below the nail. "He's proud of it. He sticks it under everybody's nose, like it's a medal of honor."

We chuckled, drank coffee, and the men dragged on their cigarettes.

"Lady at work got scalped last week," said Uncle Leo. "Got her hair caught in a flywheel, ripped her scalp right off. Ugly... Ten minutes before quitting time."

"We had one a couple'a months ago," said Uncle George. "Got caught in a belt on a tapping machine. Pulled out a hunk a hair. Looked like somebody poured red paint over her head. Shit, did she scream..."

"Then they all start screaming..." Uncle Leo ground his cigarette out in an ashtray.

Dick and I peeked at each other over our coffee cups as we sip. Uncle Leo lit up another cigarette, slid the Zippo over to Uncle George.

"My first day at work..." said Uncle George, turning the silver lighter over and over as he went on, "not at Howard's, Federated Tool Works on Lake Street. A kid working next to me caught his sleeve in a punch press. A progressive die. Pulled his arm through station to station. Looked like a jigsaw puzzle." Uncle George shook his head, kept turning the lighter. "Kid never made a sound. Wrapped his arm up in his apron and walked over to the foreman's office, sits down, and asks for a cigarette. Blood is soaking through his apron all over his lap, he's smoking a cigarette." Uncle George left the lighter standing on edge. "I walked out of that place and never looked back."

"Remember Ed Kozin?" said Uncle Leo. "Both thumbs. Right down to the nub. Never said, 'Boo.' You know 'im."

"He was at my wedding. Wasn't he the guy braided that rope with that copper wire?"

"Yeah, he can do everything with his fingers. Gotta hand it to him. Man never missed a beat." The sun had the top half of the barn lit up. I finished my coffee.

"Hey, where's the ladies?" said Uncle George. "Time to eat. Billy, you hungry?"

"Not for fingers and thumbs, I'm not."

WE WERE NINE DAYS INTO A HEAT WAVE, but nobody made anything of it. Just another midninety day on the wagon. You could melt, was okay. Fried into a potato chip, no problem. Rain was the only thing feared. They searched the sky for it and prayed it wouldn't show up. And so far, except for that cloud burst last week, it hadn't. Not a drop, not a dark cloud, not a breath of wind to ride in on. Nothing in that blue sky but a blistering-hot sun rolling lazy like from one side of the world to the other. But we were getting there. Out south, the hay still stood straight and tall and ran on like an endless sea, but now the shoreline was in sight. The tree line was where it would end. Only four more days, and we'd be done with it... And I'd be done with my Indian friends: Itching Eyes, Running Nose, Scratchy Throat, and Burning Chest.

DICK AND I WERE DOWN AT THE CREEK, between loads as usual, when Uncle George showed up. He marched by and called out for us to join him for a swim down by the big hole, but we stayed "put" in the shallows. We knew he'd have us swimming laps until we drowned. Uncle George was a terrific swimmer. His training routine when he boxed was to swim in Lake Michigan every morning out to the pumping station and back. That was miles—I don't know how many—in cold, choppy water. Uncle George kept calling out to us, and we finally relented.

"Dive in! I want to see you guys swim."

"It's time to go back, George," said Dick.

"I want to see your swim stroke. C'mon!" Uncle George slapped the water and stood up.

I pointed and yelled, "You've got something on your chest!"

"Uggggg..." said Uncle George, looking calmly at the ugly, finger-sized, black blobs glued to his body. "Richard, get a cigarette out of my shirt." He climbed up the bank.

"There's one on your right leg! Pull it off, Uncle George!"

"You can't pull off bloodsuckers!" said Dick, dashing back with a lit cigarette.

Uncle George dragged deep on the cigarette and held the hot tip over one of the blobs. It crinkled and dropped off. Dick smashed it with a rock, and two more, and the hard-packed sand turned a bloody red.

Uncle George took a quick drag on his cigarette and handed it to me. "Any on my back?" He turned around.

"There's two of 'em, Uncle George!"

"Well, get 'em off!"

"I'll do it," said Dick, reaching over.

"No! I got it! I got it!" I held the glowing tip close to the rounded head of the bigger of the two blobs, and it snapped into a curl and dropped off. It landed on my foot, and I jumped over the moon.

"Better check my ass," said Uncle George, as he pulled down his Jockey's and bent over. "Anything there?"

Dick and I looked at each other, then back at the pale moons shining at us.

"Hey! Anything?" said Uncle George, waving his ass at us.

"Dick! In the crack! See it?"

"Whaaaaa!" said Uncle George, as he felt up and down the crack of his ass. Dick and I bust out laughing.

"Hey, wise guys!" shouted Uncle George, dressing. "Better check your shorts! They might be nibbling on your dicks." He walked off.

We checked ourselves out and found nothing. And it was a good thing, because we didn't have any cigarettes.

AFTER A SUPPER OF POLISH SAUSAGE AND KRUAT, Ah-lex hauled out his cookie jar, eyeballed his tobacco mark, then took off the cover. Dick and I froze. Earlier that day, we had made the switch to our horseshit concoction. Ah-lex began filling his little tobacco bag, stopped, and sniffed at the jar. We about died. But he finished and tucked the bag into his overalls. Then he took another pinch from the jar, nudged it over to Gramps, and went about rolling a cigarette. Gramps took out a pinch and pushed the jar over to Leo.

"Roll one?" he asked.

"Naturlanie (naturally)," said Uncle Leo.

Gramps tossed him cigarette paper. Uncle Leo dug out a pinch. Dick and I got ready to run.

"Let me try that," said Uncle George.

So there they were rolling cigarettes while Dick and I sat on the edge of our chairs. Uncle George's cigarette looked pathetic, so Gramps did one for him, and they lit up. And there they sat, the four of them, smoking horseshit I must say it smelled pretty good. And it didn't look like anyone was about to drop dead. Not even get rid of their supper. Not the way they were grinning from ear to ear. Looked like they were enjoying it, in fact. Fact is, I could hardly wait to try one myself.

33 & 34

Guns and Bullets (Wednesday)

I woke up Wednesday with a head full of gook. It would take at least three noses to drain it. The night was so hot Dick and I hardly slept a wink. We roasted on our wafer-thin mattresses even though we had cooled the concrete slabs they lay on with cold water from the pump. The only good thing was, we had the stars and piece of the moon. So only three days left after today, but I had my doubts about making it. What if only one day was left and I collapsed? Maybe I should quit now and save myself the agony. The thought terrified me. I prayed some Our Father's and Hail Mary's to get me through the day, and I got up. After breakfast, my prayers were answered.

"Going to Marshfied today," said Uncle Leo, from across the table. "You guys want to go with me?"

"Yeah," said Dick.

"What about the haying?" I asked.

My uncle drummed the tabletop with his fingers. I got out of there fast. Richard was already in the car.

WE SAILED THE HILLS, shot past Lublin, and headed for Thorpe. Music cracked through the static, and there it was: Eddy Howard singing "To Each His Own." Our favorite song, Mom's and mine. I inhaled, held it for as long as I could, then exhaled. I kept that up until the song was over—don't ask me why. Crossing the railroad tracks into Thorpe, I looked down the long stretch of gleaming rails. I'd give a king's ransom to count telegraph poles again.

Our first stop was the General Store of Thorpe. It was empty. We went through the swinging doors, into the "A La Café de Paris." It was also empty, except for the tall lady with the braid. I stared at the middle table until I saw her sitting there, her big dark eyes melting me. We ordered hamburgers and went back into the store.

A big man with a fluffy head of white hair and a beard to match appeared and asked if he could help us. While my uncle started talking about some harness leather we had to buy, I led Dick over to the table with the "Fishing Tackle" sign. He was more excited than me over the smooth, shiny, pearl colored reels: the green, the blue, the yellow, and the white. Boy, how they spun, two little handles around and around. And the clicking sound they made when you cranked them back:

Click, click, click, click, click, click.

"Burgers up!" called the tall lady from the swinging doors. We went back into the café and dug in. They were delicious.

Three steaming mugs of coffee arrived on a tray. The braid on the tall lady swings this way and that as she plopped down each cup.

The tall lady and my uncle locked eyes; they didn't even blink. "Anything else?"

"Not for me," I squeaked.

Dick didn't say anything; he was too busy stuffing his face.

"I'm Leo, from Chicago, and these are my sidekicks," said my uncle, in a voice I've never heard before. "And you're…" he adds, his hand out.

"Marie." She placed her hand in my uncle's.

"Ma-rieeeeee." My uncle held her hand but didn't shake it.

"You want to do some pie now?" said Marie, taking her hand back.

Dick looked up. "Yeah, I'll have—"

"Boys… Go into the store," said Uncle Leo with a little jerk of his head.

On the wall by the "Hunting Supplies" sign were some sleek-looking bows and arrows. The V-shaped arrowheads wouldn't have any trouble sinking into a person, or an animal. *Thump*—and dead. I knew a lot about archery because my cousin Georgie, on the South side, worked for Howard Hill, before he joined the Air Force. Mr. Hill did all the trick shots in movies, like in *Robinhood* and others. Georgie's got arrow-making equipment at home in the basement, so I was explaining the technique to Dick, but he wasn't listening. Dick's not the type for details, so he moved off—which was just fine with me, because in another minute, one of us was going to start smacking the other.

We ended up back in the fishing section, while Uncle—pie, my eye—Leo came back in to close the deal on the leather.

"Is the manager looking?" said Dick, out the side of his mouth.

"No," I answer, doing the side-mouth thing.

Dick blocked the manager's view of me. "Here," he said, holding a fishing reel behind his back. "Put it in your pocket."

I stared at the shiny yellow-pearled reel in his hand.

"Take it!" he said, shaking it.

I grabbed the reel, pulled my shorts and Jockey's away from my stomach, and stuck the reel down by my hose.

"Let's go!" said my Uncle Leo, heading out with several strips of leather slung over his shoulder and a brown paper bag in hand. Outside he looped the leather strips around Dick's shoulders, passed me the small paper bag, and dug out his cigarettes.

"What's in the bag?" I hoisted it. It weighed a ton.

"Bullets." Uncle Leo lit up.

"Bullets?" I gave Dick a look.

Uncle Leo pulled out a gun that was tucked into his belt under his shirt. "Dig out some shells."

I quickly opened the bag and pulled out a small yellow and green box with "22 Long" stamped on the end. Dick grabbed the box out of my hand, opened the end, slid the drawer with the bullets out a little, and started handing the shiny brass-copper tipped bullets to my Uncle Leo, who then slipped them into the eight-shot revolver.

"My Uncle Tom's got a .22 rifle," I told them. "He let me shoot it last year, and I hit everything I aimed at."

"I shot a 30-30," said Dick. "You couldn't shoot it. It'd knock your shoulder off."

"Uncle Tom's got one. Those shells are big." I spread my finger and thumb apart about three inches. "Like this." I turned to my Uncle. "You ever shoot a 30-30, Unc?"

"He shoots everything, he's in the National Guard. Machine guns even. Huh, Lee?"

"Let's go to the bank," said my uncle. He tucked the revolver into his belt under his shirt and walked off. Dick and I gave each other a puzzled look, then hustled after him—me walking like a cowboy because of the crowd in my Jockey's.

The Bank of Thorpe, like I said earlier, was the biggest and best-looking building in town. In fact, it would look good in any town, any city, anywhere. Well, maybe not in New York, but any place else it would, I bet. It was a three-story redbrick structure with fancy iron trim and big glass windows with blinds. We entered through the shiny brass doors and stopped in our tracks. The inside was even more impressive than the outside. Marble everywhere—floors, counters, walls, all in a swirly green-and-white color. Moving on in, we see that the teller cages, four of them, are all trimmed with shiny brass. Another eye catcher was the big curving stairway, the kind you see in movies. It led up to the second floor where a balcony of offices went around like a horseshoe. This made the middle part of the ceiling two stories high, of course, but it looked even higher.

"Wooooow..." was all I could say.

"Dis a bank?" hissed Dick.

The few customers at the tellers' windows peeled away, and we were all that's left. We must look like we're casing the place because big eyes followed our every move, especially those of a well-dressed man seated at a desk behind a low, fenced-off section in back.

"Let's get outta here, Lee," said Dick, ready to take off.

"Yeah, Unc, let's go," I said.

Ignoring us, Uncle Leo headed straight for the well-dressed man at the desk. We followed and stopped at a gate in the polished wooden railing. I watched the seconds tick off the big wall clock behind the seated man—about as many as it took to count a man out—and then there was a buzzing sound, and the gate swung open. Uncle Leo gave us a little head movement, and we passed in.

The well-dressed man—who had a nose longer than my dick—said, "Can I be of some service to you, gentleman?"

"Maybe so, maybe not," said my uncle through his teeth, like Bogart.

We sat in the three chairs in front of the desk, my uncle in the middle. "We just flew in from Chicago, and my boys here wanted to know why this dinky little town has got such a big bank." Uncle Leo chuckled. The man smiled. "I told them, 'because it's got a lot of money.'"

Hose Nose's eyes were now as big as half dollars. He swallowed hard, and his jaw moved, but nothing came out. I myself was sweating puddles while I rolled the top of the brown bag up and down, up and down, over and over. Dick, I don't know—I was afraid to look. He was probably looking for a place to hang himself with the leather straps.

Uncle Leo offered the man a cigarette. The man's head vibrated a, "No." Uncle Leo lit up. The man coughed, cleared his throat, and refolded his hands on the desk.

"How's that?" Uncle Leo glanced at the man's nameplate. "Lionel? You say something, Lionel?"

Lionel's head vibrated so much this time it looked like it might fall off. I was thinking squad cars were surrounding the place, cops were pulling out machine guns, and my uncle was smoking a cigarette. I was looking at the ticking clock on the wall and thinking, "I'll know exactly what time I died. And that I'm going straight to hell because I got my dick stuck in a reel."

"Now, Lionel, let's talk business."

"Yes. Yes, of course. That's why I'm here-ere," Lionel sang out, with an ear-splitting smile and a little wobble. But no one else was smiling.

"That's good, Lionel. Very good." Uncle Leo exhaled a huge cloud of smoke.

Lionel glanced around with blinking eyes—for help, most likely—but the man at the other desk seemed to be paying no heed.

"Now, say I wanted to open a business, Lionel. And say I need, ohhh…$25,000 to get started. You could cover that without any trouble. Right?"

"Weeell, sir, that…that depends on your collateral."

"You're not listening, Lionel," said my uncle, shaking a finger. "That's not what I asked you."

Lionel froze, his moth open. The stupid clock was now ticking louder and louder, and I could tell the well-dressed man was about to have a heart attack, because I was about to have one myself.

Dick, I was sure, was chewing on the leather because I heard faint slurping sounds.

"What is it you want me to do, sir?" said Lionel, mopping his sweaty brow with a hankie.

"Noooow, I see we understand each other."

Uncle Leo ground his cigarette out on a brass plate on the desk, which in no way was an ashtray.

I was squeezing the bag so hard I was afraid the bullets would explode! Dick, I though, had hung himself with the leather, because there was no more slurping, just gagging.

"You're smart, Lionel." Uncle Leo tapped his temple and pointed at Lionel. "You're smart, I can tell. Oh yes, you are, Lionel," teased my Uncle. "So here's the deal. I want you to just think about this, Lionel. I want you to figure out how I can help you so that you can give me say $25,000 for my services. That's it, Lionel. That's all there's to it. Whatever kind of delicate problem you have, or two, I can take care of it for you. Discreetly, of course." Uncle Leo took Lionel's business card from his desk. "Give it some thought, Lionel. I'll be in touch."

Uncle Leo stood up. Dick and I stood up. Lionel stood up. Uncle Leo stuck out his hand.

"Looney's the name. First name is Tunes."

They shook hands. My uncle turned around, the gate buzzer went off, and we walked out the gate, and we kept walking, and it seemed like we were never going to reach the front door, but we did, and we passed through it, and we were outside! We were outside, and there was no burst of bullets!

"Oh, thank you, Lord!"

We headed for the car.

I babbled on, "Let them get shot, Lord! Not me! Not me, Lord, please! Oh, thank you! Thank you, Lord!"

We headed out of town and then turned east on Highway 29; east went to Marshfield, west went to Chippewa Falls. Uncle Leo passed cars like they were standing still even though it looked like nobody was chasing us. After a while, he eased up and lit a cigarette.

"Boy, that was…that was… I don't know what!" I exclaimed.

"Business, boys. Just business," said Uncle Leo through his teeth.

"Nobody even bothered us," said Dick, leaning forward from the back seat.

"Who's gonna bother somebody with kids?" said Uncle Bogart, and just like that, he had the gun out, and he fired three in the air. *Bang! Bang Bang!* It was loud.

"See that sign?" He fired twice.

And twice the metal sign across the road shimmies.

"Woooooww, Unc, you hit it both times!" I turned to Dick. "Did you see that? Two out two!" All of a sudden, there was a gun in my lap.

"Load it," said my Uncle Leo.

Dick made a move for the gun. I grabbed it. "I'll do it! Gimme the bullets."

The gun was heavy and hard and beautiful…and it smelled like my daddy's hands, which I've always liked… Point it, pull the trigger, and *bang*! You were dead. It didn't seem fair. It was too easy… Dick passed me a bullet. I had trouble opening the barrel.

"Gimme," said Dick, again reaching for the gun.

"I'll do it!" I said as we tangled hands. "I'll do it, Dick!"

"Gimme!" said my uncle. I handed it over to him. He snapped the barrel out to the side, steered the car with his knees, and ejected the shells out the window by pumping a rod under the barrel. "Load it." He dumped it back in my lap.

I loaded the gun with the bullets Dick handed me. Uncle Leo snapped the barrel into place, slowed the car, and turned down a dirt road lined with woods. Minutes later, we came upon some open space with some scattered trees. Uncle Leo parked under a big maple, got out, and relieved himself behind one of the trees. Dick raised a leg by another. I did mine behind the car. It was farm quiet, and you could hear peeing in three different notes.

"Get something to shoot at," said Uncle Leo.

Dick and I galloped off. I jabbed a short fat stick into the ground about five paces past the shade of the big maple. Dick piled three rocks on top of each other next to my stick.

Uncle Leo aimed, fired, and nothing moved. The next shot the stick leaned to the right.

"Let me shoot!" said Dick.

Uncle Leo passed the revolver to Dick. Dick held the gun in his left hand—like his brother—aimed, fired, and a puff of dirt kicked up past the rocks.

Just as he was about to fire again, I shouted, "Wait!"

I dashed over to the stick, straightened it, and dashed back.

"Try the stick."

Dick aimed, fired, dust kicked up about three inches to the right of the stick.

"My turn! Gimmie. C'mon!"

"Give it to him," said Uncle Leo.

I put the gun in my right hand and fired four from the hip. *Bang! Bang! Bang! Bang!* It made them duck. I roared with laughter.

"What're ya, crazy?" shouted Dick.

"Billy the Kid! Dance!" I pointed the empty gun at Dick's feet and yelled, "Bang, bang, bang!" Dick danced. Uncle Leo ripped the gun out of my hand. "It's empty, Unc! It's empty!"

"Go sit in the car!"

I climbed into the back seat of the Caddie. They went on shooting. I didn't care one bit. I played with the fishing reel that I hid earlier in a back pocket of the front seat...

Click, click, click, click...

MARSHFIELD WAS PACKED, people everywhere; we couldn't even find a parking place. We passed stores and shops of all kinds...and some fancy-looking restaurants and some banks, which I hoped my uncle was not going to hold up.

"This is a lot bigger than Chippewa Falls, Dick!"

"I know. I been there."

A lot of the cars had out-of-town license plates, mostly from Minnesota and Illinois, but we spotted some from Michigan and Indiana and Iowa too. I spotted a movie house with a big vertical sign and a lot of lights. I thought of Eddie and his Tarzan joke.

"James Cagney!" said Dick.

"Saw it," said Uncle Leo, tossing me a wink.

And then across the street was a bear! And behind it was a big sign: "ARCTIC FURS." Unreal!

"We gotta stop, Unc!" I pounded my uncle's right shoulder. "You gotta stop! We gotta see this place, Unc! Look at that bear! It's just like the one in Chippewa Falls!"

"No place to park." We glided on.

"I bet they got fur coats in there like you won't believe. You gotta see it, Unc."

"Later, on our way back."

We turned off the main street and chugged along. I asked my uncle if we were looking for the place to buy the beer. He said it was too early for that. We turned down a tree-lined street with houses. The trees were big…big elms. It was like driving through a tunnel… and it was cool…and the houses were fantastic…no two were alike… huge, three-story frame structures with big wraparound porches and fancy roofs with curves and peaks and stuff. We pointed and commented about how skilled the carpenters must have been who built these houses. We weaved through blocks and blocks, and after a while, the trees got smaller…and so did the houses…smaller and less interesting. We ended up on some back roads where now, and then a shack popped up…and for some reason, it seemed cats were parked all around them.

"Where we goin', Unc?"

I got no reply. Dick turned to me from the front seat and shrugged. "Where we goin', Lee?"

"Ridin'."

"Ridin'," Dick said to me.

"Ridin'," I repeat.

Then we were by a river in some trees, and we were not ridin'. We were parked. And pretty soon we were asleep.

I woke up. My eyes were all pasty and itchy, and my nose was stuffed, my head a ball of misery. I got out of the car quietly so as not to wake anyone, went down to the riverbank, and gave my head an overhaul: drain the nose, lubricate the eyes, then douse the whole thing in the river until it started working again. It made me angry, this head of mine. Too bad, I couldn't trade it in for a Frankenstein model. Get me one with wavy hair and a crankcase that didn't leak and headlights that didn't itch. And for good measure, I'd have them sew in a brain that didn't keep asking questions all the time.

Dick came out of the thicket and sat next to me on one of the slabs of rock that lined both sides of this angry river.

"Leo up?"

"He's snoring like a horse." Dick shook a pack of Camels until cigarettes stuck out. He offered me one.

"Leo's?"

"Yeah."

We lit up.

"How come you're all wet? You go in?"

"No. Wanna?"

"You crazy? Look at that current."

"Quit calling me crazy, huh?"

"Wha—?"

"You're always calling me nuts and crazy and stuff."

Dick ripped a flat stone sidearm; it skipped on the water a number of times. He did another. I tried a couple. They didn't skip too well. There was a sound behind us. It was Uncle Leo relieving himself behind a bush.

"Where are my cigarettes?"

Dick tossed the pack to Leo, who joined us.

Uncle Leo lit up. "That's a mean river. Got undercurrents. Suck you right down."

"Told ya," said Dick.

We watched part of a tree ride the swirling water, a blackbird hitching a ride on a limb. Uncle Leo went down to the water's edge, rinsed his face off, ran his wet hands through his hair, and he was done and looking terrific. Dick went down to the water, copied the wash-up routine, and he was all set. I was already spic and span, of course, with my ten-minute ritual. We went back to the car and headed for the brewery.

I was excited, thinking we were going to see how they made beer. But it didn't turn out that way. We parked in the loading dock of a big redbrick building. Uncle Leo went inside, and in nothing flat, he came out with a man wheeling a keg of beer and some bags of ice. They put the keg into the washtub in our trunk, added the ice, stuffed a blanket over the ice, then tied down the trunk. And that was it.

"Heck, Unc," I said, as we crawled along so that the melting ice wouldn't slop, "I thought we were going to see how they make beer."

"There's nothin' to see. They throw some hops into a big vat and let it ferment. Then they distill it, and you get beer."

"I'd still like to see how they do it." I hung my arms over the front seat. "Can't be that easy."

My uncle studied me in the rearview mirror. "You ever see the way they make ice cream?"

I shook my head. "No. How?"

"Veeeeeeery complicated."

"So how do they do it?"

"They take cream…and freeze it! You got ice cream." Uncle Leo laughed his butt off.

Dick laughed along and added, "You want chocolate, you mix in chocolate…and freeze it!"

They roared as if they'd just said the funniest thing in the world.

So I said to them, "How about if you mix in some baked beans? What do you get?"

"You can't mix baked beans in with ice cream," said Dick.

"Say you do. Say you mix in baked beans…and freeze it. What do you get?"

Uncle Leo pulled into a space that was across the street from an ice cream parlor. "Okay, wise guy," said Dick. "What do you get?"

"Frozen farts!"

I laughed like crazy, but they didn't laugh. We climbed out of the car and started across the street. "Frozen farts, shit," said Uncle Leo.

"Frozen Farts," said Dick.

We looked at each other, and we started laughing...and we couldn't stop!

BEER WAS STILL BEING POURED when Dick and I snuck into the garage with a flashlight to examine our stolen loot. Dick brought the little bundle down from the rafters and placed it on the large stump in the corner of the garage. Then, very carefully, we peeled away the red work rag, and there it was: the chrome-and-yellow pearl fishing reel. It was beautiful, shining bright under the flashlight that Dick held. I'd been thinking about it on our drive back from Marshfield—I'm sure Dick was too—picturing how I was going to cast it out and reel in the big ones, the kind that just about pulled your arms off. Not here, of course. Not in these dinky fishing holes, but in Lake Michigan! Ride out with my guys on our bikes to the Montrose Avenue rocks and pull in some big-time lake trout! Maybe even get my picture in the newspaper. I could see the headline. "LOCAL BOY LANDS FIFTY-TWO-POUND TROUT AFTER EIGHTEEN-HOUR BATTLE!" Oh boy!

"You can have it," said Dick.

"Huh? You mean it?"

"Yeah. Take it... Go ahead, take it."

I picked up the jewel and spun the reel. *Click, click, click, click, click, click, click.* I placed it back in the middle of the cloth. "You can have it, Dick. You're older."

"Naw, that's all right. You keep it."

I shook my head. "Naaaaw, you. You're the one took it."

"You stuffed it in your pants."

"You handed it to me."

"So what?"

"So take it!"

"I don't want it!"

"I don't want it!"

"TAKE IT, Billy!"

"NOOOO, YOU TAKE IT!"

We stared at the reel: the gleaming chrome, the pieces of yellow pearl that fit so perfectly, the clean clicking sound that it made… Beautiful! Magnificent! A masterpiece! And then—without saying another word—we sledgehammered it to death, smashed it into a million pieces…buried it deep. Later, Dick said we could go to hell for stealing it. I told him purgatory, not hell. And that he would burn longer because he was older. That was the last time we ever talked about it.

35

Another Day of Pain (Thursday)

In the early gray of Thursday morning, the air was cool and delicious. Then the sun came up and ruined it. Came up low out front of the house and in no time started cooking us again. Yet the farmer was happy. Better to be cooked than wet when it came to haying. Wet could wipe you out, kill you. Cooked only burned you. So three cheers for another day in the furnace! But I was cheering for another reason: one day less. And tomorrow would be another day less. And then it'd be Saturday, the last day, and it'd be mostly cutting and raking, and at night there'd be the big dance at the Mile-A-Way. Then Sunday it'd be church and goodbye time. And just maybe, I'd go home with Aunt Sophie and Uncle Leo. It was possible. Aunt Sophie told me I could go back with them if I wanted to. But I mustn't think about that, not too much. Not yet. Just do my time here in purgatory with the others. Endure like the others. No more going to town. See it through to the end. Leave it up to God. Trust in him, yeah. So then I knelt down and asked God to get me through the rest of the week. And then I went out and fried.

36

Moonlight Madness (Friday)

Friday evening, we finished it. Finished the haying. And at dusk, under a sky full of stars and a slice of the moon, we ended up down at the creek. All of us. Not all at once, but in dribbles, until we were all there. There, in the cool soothing water for the day had been the hottest of the week. The red mercury had boiled its way up to the ninety-six-degree mark by lunchtime. Ninety-six degrees, imagine! And that was on the shady side of the barn, where the silo cast its shadow. And just a while ago, when Dick and I came down—we were the first ones; it was still a hair above ninety degrees, and still not a breath of wind. But enough of that. The important thing was that the haying was finally over. Over, mind you. We did it! We finished it! Finished it! Me! Skinny Billy! I did it! Thank you, Lord.

Uncle John bellied out a deep, "Ho! Ho! Ho! Ho! Hooooooooo!"

Down the creek, the echo bounced back, "Ho, HO, HO, HO, HOOOO..."

I howled like a wolf, "Awoooooooooooo!"

Dick topped the dying echo with a lung-bursting howl of his own: "A woooooooooo-oooooooooooo!"

Even Ah-lex joined in, barking like a dog, naturally—and looking like one: "Hoow! Hoow! Hoow! Hoow! Hoow! Somebody bellowed like a cow, "Mooooooooh!" Gramps cut in with the whinny of a horse that was perfect, "Hee-hee-hee-hee-hee-hee-eeeeeey!" Others joined in with the hoot of an owl, the growl of a bear, the

216

roar of a lion…everybody laughing, splashing, going crazy! Then the girls started quacking like a duck, and it spread until everybody was quacking!

"Quack quack! Quaaack! Quack quack! Quack quaaack! Quaaaaaaacckkk!"

It was the craziest thing ever. And I was never going to forget it.

37

The Fourth of July (Saturday)

We gathered in the yard, and everybody was dressed to kill. Men in dark suits and white shirts—except for Uncle Leo. Dark ties for the farmers and big flashy ones for the city slickers—except for Uncle Leo. Uncle Leo sported a fancy gray outfit with a black shirt cut with a *V* down to his belly. It was a stunner. Nobody seemed to know exactly what to say about it, and that included me. Dick and I wore dark pants and white pressed shirts, but no ties. And...ahhhhhh, for the ladies: flowers of the night, with Aunt Sophie blooming like a rose in her red Marshfield special.

Boooooom! The ground shook, and a dusty red cloud of smoke filled the air in the cornfield behind the vegetable garden.

"Lee!" Aunt Sophie clung to Uncle Leo's arm. "Oh my god, Lee! What was that?"

"Dynamite!" Uncle Leo laughed.

Grandpa and Uncle John appeared with smiles flashing. Grandma shook her fist at them.

Grandpa gave her the fist right back. Uncle John bellowed, "Happy Fourth of July!" And we were off to the Mile-A-Way.

Dick and I were in the sky-blue Cadillac with Uncle Leo and Aunt Sophie. The setting sun was in front of us, the green Cord behind us, and behind them the gray De Soto, and last in line was Gramp's black Packard. All off to celebrate before winding back to

Chicago, back to the factories, vacations over for another year. And I was going back with them…or did I dream that? God, let it be real.

At the blacktopped crossroad we turned south, and the big red sun slid around to our right.

Aunt Sophie turned to the sun and her face glowed, her dark curls danced, and her lipstick-red lips burned bright. Uncle Leo looked terrific too—his dark shirt flapping in the breeze. Most men couldn't wear clothes from Smoky Joe's, down on Maxwell Street, without looking ridiculous, but not my Uncle Leo; he looked like Zorro. Dick and I looked pretty sharp too. Especially with the wave that Aunt Jean had glued into our hair with wave set. Dick's wave stuck out like the prow of a ship; mine was starting to fall into my eyes, but I'd have Aunt Jean fix it with some spit when we got there.

The roar of a car engine grew, and suddenly Uncle George was alongside, trying to pass us.

Uncle Leo floored the Caddie, and we raced side by side with the green Cord.

"Don't, Lee… Stop it, Lee! The baby!" screamed Aunt Sophie.

Uncle Leo took his foot off the accelerator, and in a split second the green Cord flashed past. Looking back, I saw Uncle John's De Soto not far behind, but no sign of the black Packard. Ahead of us, Uncle George was flying, and I was wondering if I was the only one thinking about Little Johnny.

Uncle Leo got my ear when he started telling Aunt Sophie how the Mile-A-Way was constructed. He sounded like a schoolteacher the way he started explaining it all step by step, saying that they decided to make it into an octagon so that the sides wouldn't be too heavy to swing open for ventilation. And that the floor had to be double thick crisscrossed oak, with extra beams, so that it would hold the dozens of people hopping to the beat of a polka. And when Aunt Sophie asked him how he knew all that; he said because he helped build it—which got even Dick's attention.

"Boys, did you hear that?" said Aunt Sophie. "Your uncle built the Mile-A-Way."

"He's not my uncle," said Dick.

"He's my uncle... But you're not my uncle. They say you are, but... Owww!" Dick backhanded me one in the chest. I swung a fist, and we went at it.

"Boys, stop it!" cried Aunt Sophie. "You have your good clothes on! Lee!"

"Cut it out!" rumbled Uncle Leo.

We cut it out.

"When did you build it, Lee?" said Aunt Sophie, going right back to it.

"I don't know. I was fourteen, fifteen."

"Oh, Lee, you were just a boy."

I was about to bust a gut, but I caught Uncle Leo, watching me in the rearview mirror.

"The Cukla boys...they were good. They could build anything: houses, barns—I remember, one time, Pete built a car out of scrap parts." Uncle Leo chuckled. "Nothing matched. Every fender was different. One side looked like a Ford, the other side looked like a Chevy...and the back was open like a pickup. He put a Studebaker-six in it... Pete's the one that got the Mile-A-Way going. Got the co-op behind it. He'd pick us up, Bogart and Flynn, and another kid... I forget his name. Took us the whole summer. Girls used to bring us sandwiches, lemonade..." Uncle Leo laughed.

"What, Lee?" said Aunt Sophie. "What so funny?"

"Nothin'..." Uncle Leo went on laughing and couldn't seem to stop.

"What? Tell me!" Aunt Sophie shook Uncle Leo's shoulder play-fully. "What, Lee? Tell me!"

"Nothin'! This... This girl used to bring...lemonade, and I lemonaded her."

Dick and I looked at each other with big eyes.

"Ohhhhh my god!" Aunt Sophie squealed like she'd been stabbed.

"What?" said Uncle Leo. "It was nothin'."

"Oh my gooood! And in front of the boys!"

"What, Aunt? What? I didn't hear anything. Did you, Dick?"

Dick elbowed me in the ribs.

"Soph, it was nothing. Don't be—"

"Don't say another word! Don't you dare! Ohhh, Lee. How could you?"

"You asked me, I told you… You shouldn't have asked me."

Aunt Sophie scooted all the way over to her door and looked out at the sun, a sinking ball of fire out at the edge of the world.

"Soph, it was nothin'! I was fourteen, for chrissake!"

The Mile-A-Way was a pimple out on the horizon dead ahead.

38

The Mile-A-Way

Honking cars raced around the octagon that was the Mile-A-Way and parked every which way. Everybody seemed to have arrived at the same time. Families unloaded and were strung out as they snaked their way between cars to one of the many entrances. We entered the bar section—which was packed with men—and headed straight across to where Aunt Jean had corralled some folding chairs along one of the sidewalls. The band, which was next to the bar section, was already playing, but there weren't many dancers. The place was bigger than it looked from the outside. And the eight-sided idea for ventilation was ingenious. Also, the way the angled roof came together in the middle was very impressive, as were the floorboards. The place was a work of art, if you ask me.

You could see Aunt Sophie was impressed, because she was all over Uncle Leo, and ten minutes ago, you know, he was poison ivy. No doubt, a couple months from now, she'd be telling everybody that her man not only built the place, but that he designed it. I didn't think that's what my dad meant by *loyalty* exactly, but I was sure that was part of it.

Right off the bat, everybody seemed to be having a great time: women were sitting, standing, talking, laughing, sipping their drinks, and pulling their men away from the bar to dance. And those that escaped went on drinking their steins of beer while talking, roaring, and slapping each other on the back. And zigzagging all over the place were the kids. Me? I pretended I had the job of checking the poles that propped open the eight-hinged openings in the eight sides of the octagon. Oh, and by the way, Richard was sitting with his head hanging down. His sister, my Aunt Jean, was talking to him. I was pretty sure it was about him staying on the farm for the whole year. I didn't want any part of that, so I kept moving around, checking poles: grabbing them, shaking them, making sure that they were locked in place, but what I was really doing was giving everybody the once-over, especially the girls, the younger ones—but not too young; they had to have bumps.

"Excuse me, ma'am, I have to check that pole," I'd say, if some ladies were blocking my way, and they would scoot their chairs apart so I could pass. And if they watched me, I would make the job look very important by looking at the pole from every angle, shaking it, scratching my head.

"What are you doing?"

"Huh?"

It was the girl. The one from the Café de Paris! A hot flash shot through me. She was looking up along the pole... She had the straightest nose I ever saw; you could use it for a ruler to underline stuff. And her eyes showed you what the color green could really look like. And lips...little girls weren't supposed to have lips that looked like they were begging you to kiss them.

"What's up there?" she said, still studying the pole.

"Hmmm?"

"What were you looking at? What's up there?"

"A sky with a zillion stars."

"You can't see the sky. The wood is in the way."

"X-ray eyes." I pointed at my eyes. "Yep." I rocked up and back on my heels and toes.

She giggled and turned on her smile. My heart bounced around in my chest. I would kill tigers, rip lions to shreds, smash elephants, just to hold her in my arms and...

"You're the one from the café. Uh-huh." She nodded.

I shook my head. "What café?"

She pointed her finger at me. "You were with that tall man." She poked me in the chest and ran away.

I wanted to run after her, but I didn't. I just touched where she had touched…figuring I'd paint an *X* there later. Somebody slapped me on the back. It was Dick.

"What're you doin'?"

"Bleeding."

"What? Where?"

"What were you talkin' to Aunt Jean about?"

"Nothin'. C'mon, let's get some beer."

We started weaving through the crowd. Dick shouted over his shoulder, "She's going to open a beauty shop! I'm going to live with them!"

"That's good, huh? We can go back home with them!"

"It's not until next year. They have to save up."

This stopped me in my tracks, and by the time I started moving again, I'd lost sight of Dick. The dance floor was suddenly crowded now with people whirling around, doing the polka, so I had to work my way around them to get to the bar. The air was heavy, I was sweating a ton, and my eyes were searching for the girl… She touched me to see if I was real. She couldn't believe I was so big and strong… skin like steel…almost broke her finger. I'll have to kiss it and make it well.

I reached the section where the band was playing. There was six of them, and they were not old, but they were not young—plenty of snow on the roof, as they say—but they sounded good. The guy playing the piano looked to be the youngest; he's got most of the dark hair that's up there. The bass player was wearing overalls—probably came right from the haying. The drummer's hands moved about as much as hands moved when they milked a cow. Now, the guy in front, playing the violin was fun to watch…the way he swayed from side to side, then stood on one foot, and kicked out the other one. Crazy. The sax and trumpet players waved their instruments at each other a lot—I don't know why. Could be some kind of sign language… There was no sign of the girl.

I reached the bar section and joined Dick watching two sharp-looking chicks, a redhead and a brunette, that were cornered by at least a half a dozen guys. We exchanged pokes, our eyes on the girls.

They were smoking, sipping beer, laughing. They were the only girls wearing slacks, the way it looked. The redhead kept throwing her head back, made her hair whip around. Seemed to me, she wanted somebody to grab it. Somehow I got the feeling the guys were a little afraid of them. I know I was.

They seemed dangerous. Hubba, hubba, hubba.

"Hey! Wallflower boys!" called a voice from the crowd at the bar.

It was Uncle George, waving us over. He was looking happy, a stein of beer in his mitt. Uncle John was next to him, talking to two men who had forearms like hams! I didn't know forearms could get that big! They were huge! They gotta be as big as my waist!

"Look at those arms," I whispered to Dick as we moved up.

"Uh-huh."

"Eleanor's looking for you guys," said Uncle George, with that face-splitting grin of his.

"Who?" said Dick.

"You guys were sticking your nose into it, that's who!" Uncle George sipped his beer.

We wagged our heads, embarrassed at the memory.

"Hey, her mother, the fullback—what's her name?"

"Myrtle," I told him.

"Myrtle, yeah! Christ, I have to get her a tryout with the Bears," Uncle George toasted. "I'll be her agent…make a mint!"

"How about a sip, George?"

Uncle George passed Dick the almost full stein of beer. "You guys want to do some sniffin', you better hurry. Pete's heading back to Chicago tonight."

"Tonight? Why tonight?" I took the beer from Dick.

"He likes driving at night. No traffic, he says. They're at the other end of the bar." Uncle George pointed with his chin. "Go over! Say hello! What'a ya got to lose?"

"Thanks for the beer." Dick slapped the empty stein on the bar.
"Yeah, Uncle George."

We moved past Uncle John and gave him a little punch. He gave us a lopsided smile. I got a close look at the forearms of the two men he was talking to…unbelievable.

"See them?" I said over Dick's shoulder as we moved on.

"Yeah, like hams," said Dick. We reached the other end of the bar and stopped. "See Eleanor?"

"I don't want to see her."

"There she is," said Dick, sneaking his little finger at her.

"Oh, yeah," I said, peering over Dick's shoulder. "She's looking this way. Oh, oh, here she comes!" I quickly turned around and weaved my way through the crowd. I glanced over my shoulder; Dick was not following. I pictured Dick in the car telling Eleanor to bend over. It got me laughing so hard I couldn't stop.

"What's so funny?"

It was the girl. My laughing stopped like I'd been unplugged. I stared at that face. That face that if I lived to be a hundred, I would never ever see the likes of again…and it was killing me.

"What were you laughing at?"

"Laughing? I wasn't laughing."

"Yes, you were! Why? Tell me!"

"I was laughing because…becaaaause…" I couldn't think of what to say…and it was killing me! Never again would eyes look so deep into mine and see my bleeding heart…and it was killing me!

"It was you at the A La Café de Paris."

"You speak French. How delightful."

"I know it was you."

"Uh-uh." I shook my head.

"Uh-huh," she said, swinging a foot up and back. "Mother said you were staring so hard at me she thought your eyes were going to fall out."

Who said that? Not the girl. She didn't say that. She said, "Your eyes are as deep as the ocean." Yeah, that's what she said. "Hey, listen, you want some beer?"

"Beer?" Her perfect nose wrinkled up.

"Yeah, beautiful. We get some beer. Walk in the moonlight... How 'bout it?" All I wanted to do was kiss her. And then I didn't care if I died.

Her green...green eyes swallowed me up. "Want to dance?" She smiled.

I've seen smiles, but this was something else. This was a smile that made you glad you were born.

I shrugged. "I don't know how."

"You're Polish, and you don't know how to polka?"

"How do you know I'm Polish?"

"You look Polish."

I snuck a swipe at the snooze, thinking it might be dripping. "So what are you, sweetheart?"

"Come on." She grabbed my hand, and I lit up like 100-watt bulb.

Where she was taking me, I didn't know, and I didn't care. Anywhere with her. All over the world, to heaven or hell, I didn't care. I glanced around, hoping Dick hadn't spotted me. This girl was mine. All mine! Share her with no one! Die first! We went down the steps next to the band, and we were outside. She led me around to the next section of the octagon, and then she stopped and leaned back against the building. I faced her...no night dark enough to erase her eyes, her perfect nose, her red lips. The sweeping waltz of a polka floated above us through an open wing... She put her hand on my shoulder. I could smell her sweat, feel her breath—I was that close.

"What's your name?" I whispered.

"Loretta," she answered, in a voice coming from a place deep inside her.

"Loretta... Loretta... Loretta," I chanted as I moved around to her side. "Look!" I pointed. "The stars. Now you can see them. And a piece of the moon."

"You want to kiss me or look at the moon?" She giggled.

And then there was only the music as I turned to Loretta, pulled her close, looked into her eyes, and...

"Heeeeey, what's goin' on down there?" came a drunkin' voice from above! "Look 'it, guys! We got lovebirds!"

Beer came pouring down on our heads, followed by roars of laughter.

Loretta and I stood there dripping beer in a state of shock. She burst into tears. Without thinking, I grabbed a broom from the wall, swung it up, and knocked the support pole away from the hinged wooden window. It swung down and smacked some heads.

"Loretta." I grabbed her and kissed her. Kissed her beery-wet lips, mixed with salty tears, and beer-stringy hair.

RICHARD FOUND ME out by the pump rinsing beer out of my hair. Unfortunately, four wise guys also found me—one with a bloody head. I had told Dick, more or less, what had happened, but left the girl out of it—which wasn't easy and altogether didn't make much sense. I should probably add that they were bigger than us. So anyway, in a nutshell, after the talkin', which there wasn't too much off—farm boys were doers, not talkers—Bloody Head came at me and was about to wallop me when Richard stepped in and took the blow. They were on the ground goin' at it when Uncle Leo stepped in, picked bloody head off Richard, and threw him away like a sixty-yard pass. In fact, I think he's still flyin'.

The dance floor was loaded. Everybody was dripping sweat, and I was dripping beer… And there was no girl.

"I danced with Eleanor," said Dick. "She's a good dancer."

"You ask her to go steady?"

Dick loaded a fist to slam me but didn't. "Let's get some beer."

We zigzagged through the crowd. I was going nuts trying to spot the girl. And I thought Dorothy could make me feel bad. Heck, that was nothin'. A fart in the wind. We stopped. We could feel the music in our feet. We watched the dancers whirl around, hopping, stamping. Skip, skip. *Bam, bam, ham!*

The night was in full swing, everybody was laughing, having fun, and I felt like shooting myself. Even Uncle John was smiling, spinning around with Aunt Delores, looking so proud. Aunt Delores, you couldn't tell snots, not from that mask she wore for a face. But she sure knew how to shake that behinder of hers.

Dick gave me an elbow. "Leo and Sophie!" he shouted in my ear.

"Yeah!" I shouted back.

He was really something, my Uncle Leo. Looked like a huge tree gliding around out there, so straight and tall. Aunt Sophie looked happy, turning around and around. The red dress was made for her.

"Uncle John and Delores," said Dick.

"Yeah, yeah."

Behind us, Dorothy was still sitting with Grandma. She looked so wide-eyed, so innocent…but she had got those "moods," drive you nuts—I should know. Besides, she was too old for me, going to be fifteen. Just right for Richard. All of a sudden, dancing from out of nowhere came Vickie and Gramps! Holy tamole! Heeey, the ol' boy was pretty gooood. Lot of spring in those sticks. Yeaaah. I started to point them out to Dick, when he said, "I see them." I looked back over at Grandma; she was wearing her usual vulture look. Dorothy was bouncing on her chair, saying things to her, laughing… Boy, for a young girl she sure had big ones—nice, big ones.

Dick dragged me over to the bar area, and there we spotted the two Filas girls from church. They were standing with their clan in the corner of the bar. Something about them—all of them—stood out, and it was not just their clothes; it was in their face, in their eyes. It was hard to look at.

"She's wavin' at me."

"Wave back… Wave back, Dick!"

Dick didn't, so I did. 'They're comin' over. Theresa, right?"

Dick took off.

"Dick, wait! Where're you—Dick!" I chased after him.

Dick stopped. "You see them?"

"Let's talk to them."

"They're coming. C'mon!"

"Dick!" I followed him.

He was really moving now. We stopped in front of the band. The polka music was fast, the dancers flying; you had to yell to be heard.

"Dick! Let's talk to them!"

Dick went off; I didn't move. They came up, dressed pretty much like they were for church, but now they had red ribbons in their hair, which helped a lot. Also, the taller girl had a necklace made out of what looked like flat river stones. And her younger sister had one made of what looked like coffee beans.

"Hi!" said the taller girl.

"Hi, Theresa!" I shouted and gave the other girl a nod. She smiled and gave me a little wave.

"Where's Richard?" said Theresa, peering between people.

I shrugged. "I think he went to the bathroom."

She went on searching the crowd. I moved next to her sister, who was watching the band, and I knocked shoulders with her. She did the same to me. I did it again. She turned and slapped me playfully on the shoulder. I faked pain. She giggled. Suddenly, Theresa grabbed her sister's hand, and they started dancing the polka. They didn't start off too well, but pretty soon, they got the rhythm right and spun off and disappeared.

I SPOTTED RICHARD. No wonder we couldn't see him; he was standing behind a blimp. I circled around them, taking in this corn-fed wonder, this "Eighth Wonder of the World." She saw me and laughed so hard the double-layered floor shook, extra supports and all. When she finally quit, it took a while for everything to stop moving.

Richard danced off with this…this balloon, this floor-shaker. Talk about big. She was way bigger than an elephant; she was like an aircraft carrier! They were knocking people over, squashing them, bouncing them off the walls—and it didn't help any, of course, that Richard had two left feet and that one of them had ten toes. So okay, I was exaggerating a bit. And actually, Dick didn't really look like he wanted to dance, but she pushed him into it, and you couldn't just push back on an aircraft carrier; you could rupture yourself. What he should've done was… WHO AM I KIDDING? Oh god! I'm disgusting! Rotten to the core! The lowest of the low!

You see, she wasn't big and round. She was tiny. One of a kind, in fact. Had the most perfect, straightest nose, the greenest-green eyes, the greatest lips, and…and it was funny, but I couldn't seem to remember her name now. In fact, I bet by tomorrow I wouldn't even remember what she looked like.

And then Dick told me that the whole time they were dancing, all she talked about was me…

She asked him about me? Was he sure? He was. Did she—shut up already!

Loretta… Loretta…

39

Bad, Sad Sunday

No packed church today. No city people. No smell of squashed bodies simmering in the heat, flies buzzin' around. They were gone, all gone—except for a few strays, of course. All headed back home. Home to the big two: Chicago and Minneapolis, and to some smaller places in between. And earlier this morning, before church, I had my chance to go with them...and I chickened out.

"Who wants to come with us?" That was what Aunt Sophie tossed in the air, as Dick, Dorothy, and I helped them pack up their car.

I hopped into the back seat of the Caddie. "All aboooard. Pull up the anchor, Unc."

Dorothy chuckled. Dick growled.

My aunt put her hand on my shoulder. "Do you really want to go, Billy?"

"Soph," said my Uncle Leo.

"He can come with us, can't he, Lee?" She kept her eyes on me. "You want to go home, Billy?"

I stopped chewing my lip. Dick had his eyes on the ground— one of them blackened. I drew a deep breath, exhaled, and said, "I have to stay here for the summer with Dick." And that was that.

Just before they left, I gave Aunt Sophie a letter for my mom that I wrote earlier this morning, during the milking. It was long; it filled both sides of the paper. In it I told my mom what a terrific time I had with my uncles and aunts. That it was like when we used to go to Grandma's house on Friday nights for the babka, everybody having a great time. Told her about eating in the yard, with the big bonfire, and the dancing with the music from the car radios. Told her about going to Chippewa Falls and Marshfield with Uncle Leo and Dick, eating hamburgers in Thorpe, and about the big bears standing in front of the fur stores. Told her about all of us swimming in the creek. And about us fishing. How Grandma could talk to fish. And about the Mile-A-Way, how everybody was there. Told her about the polka music and the dancing. But I didn't tell her about the girl. And then I told them they missed it aaaaaaaalll.

And then I added a "PS," and I got real tricky. I told her to tell dad that I was getting to like living on the farm and that I was thinking of staying the whole year here with Richard. And that they wouldn't miss me. That it was only a year. One little ol' year. Go by in a blink. *But* that if they did miss me, I could catch the next train home. Of course, if they said it was okay to stay, I was going to kill myself.

But now, here in church—ignoring the service the way I always do, because it's in Polish—the more I thought about it, the more I thought that it wasn't such a good idea after all. That it was too big of a gamble. That if I really had to stay on the farm the whole year, I would really have to kill myself. And then the thought came to me, that if I did that, that I might as well kill Ah-lex too… But then, that last part didn't make me feel any better anyway. In fact right after all that thinking, I felt rotten, worse than rotten, because now I was getting that bad feeling, that emptiness, that yearning to be home. So then, I started praying for all I was worth, asking God to stop the sick feeling that was coming on in my stomach. And thank God, he must've heard me, because after I kept swallowing over and over, it went away.

After church, the groups of farmers talked and smoked and kept glancing at the sky in the northwest, past the cornfield. Oh sure, the sun was still giving its all in the clear blue, but way out there in the northwest, low and far away, was a wall of gray. For ten solid days, the sky had been as blue as an ocean, with only a few puffy white clouds daring to sail across, but now it looked like change was in the air, and now was the time for it, because the hay was piled high and dry in the barn. So no one was concerned…but me. Why, I don't know. I just had a feeling.

Heading back to the Packard, I spotted my Uncle Tom standing with a small group of people. He was staring at me, his broken nose leading the way, his Indian-smooth skin shining—skin that needed shaving only a little around the chin. He was tall and lanky with light, curly hair. He was the only one looked like his mother. My dad and his youngest brother, my Uncle Frank, were on the short side, and both had straight dark hair and had to shave daily. My dad's sister, my Aunt Minnie, the saint, didn't look like any of them; she was too beautiful. Uncle Tom nudged Aunt Rose and pointed his beak in my direction. She shielded her eyes from the sun, caught sight of me, and waved. I gave her a little wave-in fact, you could hardly call it a wave, just a limp hand up and down.

After we drove off, I was mad at myself for not going over and saying hello. It's like I'm afraid to talk to people, I don't know why. Maybe it's because I'm afraid I won't be able to think of anything to say. Yet, sometimes I'm a blabbermouth…especially with girls, which is weird.

40

Open Your Petals (Sunday)

There wasn't much to do back at the house. The line of clouds in the northwest hadn't moved much, if at all. We had lunch, and then everybody disappeared. Turned out everybody was taking a little snooze. Dick and I had our room back, so we were upstairs in our beds, lyin' on top of the sheets, shifting around in the heat, trying to sleep. What made it at least bearable was the stiff breeze blowing in through the window.

"Dick. You sleepin'?"

"Yeah."

I went back to sleepin', but it didn't work. "Dick! I can't sleep."

"Close your eyes and shut up."

So I closed my eyes and shut up. It didn't work. "Diiiiick," I said softly.

There was no reply.

"Dick!"

Dick bounced on his mattress until his back was turned to me. "I'm going down to the girls' room. Want to go?"

No answer.

"They're probably lyin' there naked. Probably just waitin' for us."

Dick was either sleepin' or dead.

"Dick! How do you get it open? Know what I mean? What's the combination? Like what do you say, 'Open your petals so I can ram it in, sweetheart'? What?"

Dick rolled over and looked at me like he'd been hit on the head with a hammer. "Open your petals? Where did ya hear that?"

I shrugged. "So what do you do?"

"You just stick it in, goof!" Dick turned back to his favorite friend, the wall.

"Stick it in your ear," I mumbled.

Shit! He didn't know any more than I did. I wanted to know exactly how to do it. I didn't want to poke around like some amateur. Hell, it could go in sideways, for all I know. Shit, I could get lucky and she wanted to do it, then what? Not that I wanted to. I really didn't. I was too young... But I wouldn't mind playing doctor. That'd be okay. Look it over real good, get it mapped out. Heh-heh.

"Hey, Dick," I said, swinging my feet to the floor. "Last chance." I put on my shorts and T-shirt; hummed some notes to let Dick know I was getting ready; then tiptoeing past his bed, I whispered, "If I'm not back in a day or two, don't come lookin' for me."

"Grandma's gonna hang your balls," said Dick without moving.

It took me forever to get down the hall and then the stairs, because I stopped at every creaking sound and counted to thirty, or more, depending on the loudness of the note. Moving up the hallway to their nook, I did the same thing, but it wasn't as bad, only two scary squeaks.

There they were under a sheet, smooth pieces stickin' out, shinin' like some delicious fruit, wild hair all over the pillows. Dorothy was closest and showed the mostest. I could even smell them. Smelled like... I don't know, but I was getting hard. But there was no way I was going to go in there. I wasn't that brave. Put a gun to my head, I wouldn't. Damn! And now I couldn't go back upstairs, not right away. Dick would never let me hear the end of it. I was stuck, glued to the floor, waitin' for Grandma to sniff me out and knock my head off. And then it hit me. Shangri-la!

41

Ghosts à la Carte (Sunday)

I clicked open the brass-handled doors and passed into my magic room, my ghost room, my Shangri-la! Right away I felt good. Not church good—I'd never felt good in church—but a safe kind of good.

"My daughter, marry that atheist?" boomed a voice from the flashing photograph of my grandfather on the long table up front.

"Now, now, Bruno," flashed Grandmother's photograph. I glanced around the room uneasily.

"Come, come, William. Don't be afraid," came a lighthearted voice from the flashing photograph of Lawrence.

"I'm not afraid," I said, moving closer.

"Well then, speak up!" came the deep voice from the flashing photograph of my grandfather, standing there in his long, black bathing suit.

"The news! The news! Tell us the news!" flashed the dapper dressed Lawrence, tapping his cane.

"Lawrence! For goodness sakes, give the boy a chance," flashed Grandmother Helen, her snow-white hair framing her round face. Turning a smile on me, she said, "We missed you, William. Where have you been?"

"I've been… Hey, how come you guys can all talk now?"

"We always talked, you weren't listening," said Grandfather Bruno. "Now tell me. Did our daughter marry that…that atheist? What's his name?" He pulled on his earlobe. "You know, that misfit.

Used to work with your dad. Chopped off his boss's finger. Agh! What's his name?"

"George Bauer," said Lawrence, with a twirl of his cane.

"Bauer, that's it! The atheist! And another toolmaker—a little shrimp—was after Jean."

"Little Johnny," said Grandma. "Such a nice young man. He came up and did the haying last year. Uh-huh," she said nodding.

"Came up for more than the haying," said Lawrence with a wink.

I didn't know how to tell them that little Johnny was dead, didn't know where to begin.

"She can find better," said Grandpa. "My little daughter's a beauty! So is Stella!"

"So are the boys, dear. Big and handsome like their father."

"Well…they are. That's the truth!"

"Any more babies, William?" asked Grandma shyly.

"Speak up, boy," said Grandpa. "Speak up!"

"Uhhh. Well, first off, no more babies, ma'am. Aunt Sophie had one on base, but she didn't get it home. But she's got another one in the oven. So that's good, huh?"

They stared at me, their mouths open.

"Richard lives with them!" I plunged on. "On weekends, that is. Because he goes to Montifiore, you know. But he's up here now. For the whole year he's going to be here. But you know that too, I guess. So since Eddie's gone into the Navy, that's going to be good, huh?"

Their eyes were still locked on me.

"Hey, kid! Who was all here for the Fourth of July?" It was the young guy with the bulging arms and the jaw that hung out like a shelf. The white horse was still the best thing in the whole picture. Forget the other guy, the short, tough-looking guy, leaning on the horse like it was a lamppost. But even with him in there, it was still a heck of a shot.

"So tell us what happened this past week," said Lawrence, doing a dance step and tapping his cane.

"But you know that. You were here."

"We weren't here!" said Grandpa. "We were… Agh! Lawrence, tell him."

"We were at our annual meeting: Ghosts à la carte!"

"Ghosts à la carte!" Grandma chuckled. "Oh, Lawrence!"

"Come, come, William," said Lawrence, tapping that cane of his. "Fill us in."

"Well...everybody came up, 'cept my folks." I mumbled the last part. "Uncle Leo and Aunt Sophie. And Uncle John and Aunt Delores. And—get this—Aunt Jean came up with her husband! Yep! She got married!"

"Not that atheist?" said Grandpa. "Or that little shit?"

"Now, Brunoooo!" said Grandma.

"The atheist, yeah!" I blurted out. "He's a great guy, Grandpa! He's Hungarian! He said it's just like Polish, only better."

They looked puzzled. Again, I plunged on.

"He's a card," I said, throwing in a chuckle. "Oh! And he's a Catholic now! Aunt Jean made him convert."

"Oh! See, Bruno," said Grandma.

"He goes to church on Sunday?" said Grandpa. "Confession? Doesn't eat meat on Friday?"

"Well, I... I think he skips sometimes."

"The man's damned to hell!" shouted Grandpa. "My daughter's living with a devil!"

"Now, now, Bruno," said Grandma, her hands moving about nervously.

"Great news, kid," said Jawbone.

"Where did I hear he was a wrestler?" said Lawrence. "Or a boxer?"

"Oh, Jezus," sighed Grandma, a hand at her heart.

"No, no! Not anymore! He's a toolmaker! Like my dad!"

"Ahhhh, so the man's not a dummmmmy," Lawrence rang out.

"No! He's smart as a whip. And on weekends he makes extra money by hanging himself." One by one, their mouths hit the floor.

"I saw him do it!" Their eyes got bigger. "He did it in our basement on his wedding day!" I was digging myself into a biiiiig hole, but I couldn't stop. "Oh, he's okay. Don't worry. He's fine!"

Now they were chewing air, but no sound came out.

"Aunt Jean calls him her Crazy Hungarian." I laughed. "'Hey, Crazy Hungarian! Go hang yourself!' That's what she says when she gets mad at him." Now I was laughing so hard I couldn't stop.

"Oh, Jezus, Jezus," said Grandma, making the sign of the cross.

"This atheist hangs himself by his neck?" said Grandpa, looking like somebody's just hit him on the head with a two-by-four.

"I thought he had a brain," said Lawrence.

"That's a lot of bull," said Jawbone, waving it away.

"Yeah," said Tough Guy.

"On his…his wedding day?" said Grandpa, his eyes starting to focus. "Wha… Why?"

"Because he couldn't face the bride," said Tough Guy, stamping his foot and laughing.

Jawbone joined in. So did I. But not the others.

I screamed out, "He does it for the monnnnney!" They gave me their big eyes again. "For the money. He bets people. He bets he can do it. Get it?"

"So it's a stunt," said Lawrence. "A trick of some kind."

"No trick! He does it!"

"It's a trick!" said Tough Guy. "You don't hang around and live to talk about it."

"Yeah, it's a trick," said Jawbone. "'Member that guy ate those nails, turned out to be spaghetti? He was—"

Lawrence tapped his cane like a machine gun. "How does this man, Mr. Bauer, go about it? Tell us what you saw step by step. Every detail. Leave nothing out."

"The boy doesn't have to talk about it," said Grandma.

"Oh yes, he does!" shouted Grandpa, who was now back among the living.

"It's okay, Grandma. I don't mind."

And so I started, right from the beginning, and told them how my mom and I fixed up the basement for the reception with crepe paper and stuff, and how everything looked great, and how Dad even hired two men to play the violin and accordion, and how everybody was having a grand old time, and that when everybody was well oiled, Dad yelled out and pointed, "George can hang from dat I-beam! Hang with rope by his neck!"

"Hang himself? With a rope?" somebody said.

"Like hell he can!" somebody else yelled out.

So Dad said, "I bet five dollars, anyone. George hangs by da neck, ten seconds."

But Uncle George, who'd had a few too many, piped up, "For a minute! I'll hang a minute! Siiiiiix-ty secondssss byyy the neeeck," he said drunkenly.

Dad jumped up. "George! Your wedding night. You need strength."

Everybody laughed.

"Ten seconds," Dad said, "who bets for five dollars?"

And then Little Johnny—he's Uncle George's best friend, you know—he stood up and said he would bet twenty-five dollars George couldn't hang for half a minute. And that if he croaked, he got the bride because he knew her first. And then he started laughing like mad. And people joined in because they thought it was a joke, see. But not everybody was laughing, because some people knew Little Johnny was crazy-bananas about Aunt Jean, right? So now Little Johnny was telling Uncle George not to worry, that he'd take good care of Aunt Jean if he croaked. And he was slapping Uncle George on the back and laughing his head off.

Uncle George pointed his finger at Little Johnny. "I don't croak, I'm gonna bust your ass."

"Oh, sorry, Grandma, but that's what he said."

So then everybody started talking, saying stuff like, "Ahhh, he's only joking."

"They're both drunker than a skunk."

"Forget the whole thing."

Uncle George yelled out, "Ooone minute…for ooone huuun-dred dollars! Geeet the rope!" he said to Little Johnny.

"Forget it, you craaazy Hun-gaaarian!" said Little Johnny drunkenly. "I don't waaanna buuury yaaa. Yaaa stuupid jerk."

"Lisssten, runt," said Uncle George, through his teeth. "Get the rooope and shut up."

And everybody went quiet. Uncle George and Little Johnny looked like they were going to tear each other apart.

Uncle Dino—the mad Russian—piped up in his whiskey voice, "I got tweeeenty bucks of that hundred he dooon't do a minute!"

"I got ten!" somebody else called out. "I got two!"

Money was waving in the air. My dad threw his arms up and said he wouldn't do it. Wouldn't take bets for a minute. So then Uncle Leo started taking the bets.

Men were yelling, "I'll take five!"

"I'll take a dollar!"

My dad said later he was really worried because Uncle George had gained a lot of weight since his fighting days. And that even though he had a neck like a bull, he was afraid Uncle George was going to kill himself. In fact, he was willing to bet on it. No, no, I just threw that in.

"Oh, Jezus! Jezus!" said Grandma, clasping her hands together in prayer and holding them to her lips.

"*Cho to robicz*? Huh, Grandma?" (Yeah, I'm learning Polish.)

Jawbone and Tough Guy were slamming each other on the arm; they were laughing so hard.

They were both in front of the white horse now, almost fallin' out of the picture.

"Go on, William! Go on!" urged Grandpa. "What happened?"

"Uhhhhhhhh."

"George said he'd hang for a minute," said Lawrence excitedly as he leaned forward on his cane. "And they started taking bets. And your dad was afraid it might kill him, you said."

Boooy, did I have their eyes glued on me or what.

"Yeah, right! Soooooo then they couldn't find any rope. But then somebody brought in a clothesline."

"A clothesline?" said Tough Guy.

"That's no good," said Jawbone. "You can't—"

"Stanley! Henry! Quiet!" said Lawrence, punching his cane down hard enough to drive it through the floor.

"Soooooo, Uncle George doubles up the clothesline, puts it over the I-beam, pulls on it, and it breaks."

Stanley and Henry whooped it up and exchanged punches.

Real quiet, I said, "So then, somebody finds some coated copper wire and a guy with no thumbs braids it in with the clothesline and makes a noose. And my dad talks them into wrapping a dishrag around the bottom half, but the noose still looks miiiighty scary."

"But George must be all right, isn't he? He's not here with us," said Grandma.

"Here? He's in hell!" yelled Grandpa, laughing hard now.

Tap, tap went the cane. "Go on, William."

"Weeeell... Uncle George gets on an empty beer crate, puts his head in the noose, moves the dishrag around a bit, then grabs the I-beam, kicks away the crate, aaaand..."

"Oh, Jezus!"

"And slooowly he lowers himself. You can see the noose tightening, squeezing his neck. Then he lets go, drops his hands to his sides, and he's hanging there."

"*Psia krew cholera!*" said Grandpa, slapping his knee. "That's a dumb Hungarian for you!"

"Little Johnny is looking at his wristwatch, counting...seven... eight...nine...ten seconds...eleven—" Richard appears, and he's leading Aunt Jean down the stairs, and she's yelling, 'Georgie! Georgie!' And then she sees him and screams, 'Geooorgie! Stooop it! Stop it!' Aunt Sophie and the ladies grab her, hold her back. She's sobbing now, 'Oh my god! Oh my god!' Over and over.

"'Twenty seconds!' shouts Little Johnny. Uncle George is red as a beet. Veins are popping out all over his face. More ladies are coming downstairs, doing the 'Oh my god!' bit. The men are all frozen, the only thing moving is the curling smoke from their cigarettes. 'Thirty seconds!' shouts Little Johnny. "'Come on, George, that's enough!' He stops looking at his wristwatch and starts bouncing around. 'George! For God's sake! Enough!' Uncle George puts up a hand to keep Little Johnny away. His face is going purple. His eyes are slits with tears running out. Snots are coming out of his nose. I'm so scared I don't know what to do. I just want him to stop. 'Nick, stop him,' my mother cries out. 'Leo!' she yells. And she's crying. And the ladies are crying and screaming, 'Stop! Stop!' I'm crying too and screaming, 'Stop! Stop!' Richard is on his knees, yelling, 'Stop it, George! Stop!' But nobody's moving. And Uncle George is hanging there blue-faced now, and his hands are twitching at his sides. It's awful!

"'Forty-five seconds!' yells Uncle Dino, the mad little Russian. He's taken over the timing 'cause Little Johnny is on his hands and knees now, slapping the concrete and yelling, 'Stop it, George! Stop it!' Uncle George looks bad, looks dead. I can hardly look at him. Sweat is dripping off his face, and blood is running out of his nose. He's hanging there like a sack of potatoes. Everybody is dead quiet now, not moving an eyelash.

"'Fifty-eight... Fifty-nine... Sixty! Sixty!' yells Uncle Dino. But nobody moves. Uncle George is still hanging there! 'George!' Little Johnny cries out, jumping up and down. 'Sixty seconds, George!' Nothing happens! Then it hits everybody that just because Uncle George hung himself doesn't mean he's going to unhang himself, and Little Johnny and Uncle Leo quick grab him, hoist him, and get the noose off him and flop him into a chair. Uncle Leo pounds him on the back, and Little Johnny massages his neck, but he looks deader than a doornail."

"Oh, Jezus Christus!" cries Grandma, and she got her hands over her face and rocking and going, "Oh, Jezus, Jezus!"

"But then! But then, Grandma, listen!" I dropped my voice. "Theeeeen...there's a loooong, loooud gasp...and then coughing and more gasps and more coughing, and Uncle George is...his head is vibrating now, and his arms are starting to shake. And all the while Little Johnny is rubbing him like mad. 'Breeeathe!' he's yelling. 'Breathe, George! Breathe, damn it! Breathe deeeeep!' Somebody throws in a wet towel, and Little Johnny starts wiping Uncle George's face, and the dark ugly color is gone now, and Uncle George is looking much, much better, a nice, rosy red. Little Johnny has Uncle George's face in his hands, and he's yelling at him head-to-head, "You son of a bitch! You almost killed yourself! You crazy son of a bitch! You son of a bitch!'

"Uncle George raises his head and says in a croaked voice, 'Where's my hundred bucks?' The men start laughing and shaking their heads and squaring up their bets. And somebody passes a shot of whiskey to Uncle George, and he downs it. Uncle Leo gives him a handful of money. And then Aunt Jean comes flying at him, yelling and slapping. He shows her the money, and the next thing you know, she's sitting on his lap, hugging and kissing and grabbing the money. I see my mother shake a fist at my dad. Dad looks over at me and winks. And I'm just feeling so happy by then I'm jumping up and down like a nut. And...and... So anyway, now we got a crazy Hungarian in the family who's an inch taller since his wedding."

They stared at me...not even a blink. It was like we were posing for a picture.

"Well!" said Lawrence finally. "Well, well, well! That's quite a story, William. And well told. Well told."

"It's just what happened."

"Too bad we missed seeing this guy, George," said Jawbone Stanley.

"Yeah. We got plenty of rope," said Tough Henry.

"Boys! Enough of that talk," said Grandpa. "Now go."

And suddenly Stanley and Henry were frozen flat into the picture, like when I first saw them.

"So what do you do with all your time, William?" said Lawrence.

"What time? I'm so busy I hardly have time to eat... You guys don't eat, do you?"

"Of course not," said Lawrence. "We're ghosts."

"So...what do ghosts do?"

"Work!" said Grandpa, with a glance at Lawrence. "Except those that read books."

Grandma gave Grandpa a disapproving look before turning to me. "We walk the house at night, William, to let our loved ones know that we're watching over them."

"Well, that's...that's good. But what do you do in heaven? What's it like up there?"

The three of them looked from one to another. Finally, Lawrence spoke up, "Like Helen said, we watch over the family, all of them, our children, and our grandchildren, like you William. And when our job—our work—is done, then we go to heaven. Not before."

"Oh… That seems like a long time."

"Nothing comes easy, William," said Grandpa. "Only in heaven with God Almighty. Up there, the work is easy."

"There's no work up there," said Lawrence.

"You'll never know, Lawrence!"

Grandma raised her arms to heaven and spoke, "Oh. Lord, peace within and with each other."

And in a flash, Grandpa and Lawrence were back to being frozen photographs.

"What happened? Why are they gone?"

"Somebody's near." Grandma smiled, and in a flash she was frozen back into her frame.

The brass-handled doors rattled as if somebody was trying to open them… The rattling stopped…

They rattled some more… Then stopped… And just when I thought it was over, there was another try, a short one. Yet I saw no shadow on the frosted glass. I heard no footsteps. I counted to a hundred, went to the door, pressed down on the handles, and they clicked open. They weren't locked! Peeking out, I saw no one.

Turning back to the photographs, I went to one knee, crossed myself, passed through the frosted glass doors, and clicked the brass-handled doors shut.

42

Smashing Ah-lex (Monday)

The line of dark clouds that hadn't moved, moved; and by milking time, the sky was dark, and there were buckets of milk and buckets of rain. Supper was leftovers, coffee, cigarettes, and the storm did all the talking. And all through it, Ah-lex never took his eyes off of Dorothy, and that made me mad… Also, to be honest, it gave me a creepy feeling…and yeah, altogether it scared the hell out of me.

It rained all that night and straight through the next morning—*poured* was more like it—but come high noon, it eased up, and by lunchtime it stopped. All that was left were some empty clouds flying with the wind, going wherever clouds go to get filled up so they could go drown some other place. Faces tight with worry began to loosen up; words started to leak out.

"Lowland's flooded."

"South cornfield is half under."

"Creek's up."

"Be okay, don't rain no more."

And as the sky brightened, so did their mood.

"Land had a good drink."

"Corn needed rain."

"It got it!"

The deep-lined faces curved into smiles. Grandma got her Polish going as we finished eating, and everybody scrambled off to work. Dick and I ended up in the garden. Sunken garden, that is.

Plants stickin' out, tryin' to breathe, except for the strawberries. They were drowned, wavin' goodbye in their watery grave.

"We gotta drain it," said Dick. "C'mon."

We headed for the garage. Dick grabbed a long-handled shovel just inside the swinging doors. I rummaged around and came up with a coal shovel.

"What're you gonna do with that?"

"What? It'll be good for scoopin' water with."

"We gotta dig a canal. Go see if there's a spade in the toolshed."

"How about a McCoye?" (If I haven't mentioned it before, McCoye was the code name we used to go off and have a smoke.) I started back into the garage for the coffee can of tobacco we kept hidden under the workbench.

"Later! Go get the shovel."

"What's the rush?"

"Go on!" Dick took off.

The toolshed was actually a lean-to in back of the chicken coop. The chicken coop was between the barn and the silo. And by the silo, hidden among the boulders and weeds, would be the mound of black dirt with the spade shovel stuck in it—unless somebody had moved it. I hadn't looked at that spot since the family came up. Not from the house, not from the water pump, not from anywhere. I looked past it, around it, everywhere but at it. And now, there it was, right in front of me: a lump of shiny mud stabbed with a spade and surrounded by water, like an island. I didn't want to think about what the seven little kittens looked like under all that muck. But I did. All wet and squishy and twisted and broken and smashed. Oh, God… So soft and furry. So perfect and alive. I swabbed away tears, wiped my running nose on my forearms, and pulled out the spade. Water slowly seeped into the cut.

"Why wasn't I brave? Why was I such a coward? Why, God? Why?"

I smacked the smooth mound with the spade to close the wound. And again…and again.

"Forgive me, my kittens. I'm so sorry." I swallowed hard and looked up. Gray clouds were dancing all over the sky, laughing at me, laughing at this coward.

I looked up at the dizzying height of the silo sailing through the clouds...then down at the ground, the boulders, the grass... then back again at the top...then down again...up and down... And as I did this, an idea burned its way into my mind. I broke into a sweat. As I started back up the hill to the garden, I was shaking with excitement.

I wanted to tell Dick about my plan, but he was so engrossed with channel-digging I decided to wait for the right moment. The soft ground tore open easily, and we hacked out about a twenty-foot canal running from the strawberry patch, around the back of the garage, and down to the apple orchard. The water churned through the waterway and into the orchard. It was time for a McCoye.

We sat in the orchard and rolled a couple of toilet-paper beauties on a flat rock. Dick was getting really good at it—even though they looked more like cigars than cigarettes. Mine usually looked like a banana. Well, not that bad, really. Anyway, we had plenty of "makings," because we socked away stuff from the relatives before they left. We lit up, leaned back against a couple of apple trees, and puffed away.

FIRST OFF, I TOLD DICK about climbing the silo and about the view. Dick started right in with how dumb, how stupid, how ridiculous I was, but he shut up quick when I told him I had a plan on how to get Ah-lex. I reminded him that Ah-lex liked to have a smoke while parked on a boulder by the silo. And that, I told him, was what gave me the idea on how to smash him. That all we had to do was get a boulder up on top of the silo, and...

"I'm not going up there!" said Dick.

"No. I'll go up. We need two boulders. Okay? And we'll need a short board to put on top of the dormer. Then I put the bigger boulder on the back end of the board and the smaller one on the front, see. Then I push the board—"

"Yeah, yeah," said Dick, who was never one for details. "So?"

"So theeen," I said, with a gleam in my eye, "I tie some rope around the back boulder so that when we pull the boulder off from down below, the board tilts and the front boulder drops down and bingo! One smashed Ah-lex!"

"How you know it's gonna hit 'im?"

"We have a practice run. See where it hits. Then we get Ah-lex to stand on that spot."

"Oh sure. 'Hey, Ah-lex! Stand over here, I'm gonna take your picture.'"

"Yeah! Terrific!" I slugged Dick on the arm. "You're a genius, Dick! Great idea! Great idea!"

"You're outta your mind."

"Hey, listen," I said, feigning punches at him. "Who's got a camera? You know?"

"Cut it out!" said Dick, swatting my hands away like he would flies. "It's not gonna work!"

"Why not?"

"Because Dick's gonna be ten miles from here, you try that shit."

"It'll work, Dick! It's our chance! We'll smash 'im good!"

"They'll fry you in the electric chair! You'll look like burnt toast! Your own mother won't recognize ya!" Dick flipped away his butt.

"We got to do somethin', Dick!"

"You wanna kill 'im?"

"Nooo, nooo. Just...hurt 'im, you know." I sat back and tried to think of a way to convince Dick to help me. Finally, all I could come up with was, "I need you to help, Dick."

"Forget it!" said, Dick. "Get it outta your mind!" Dick grabbed the coffee can and got out the makings.

"Did you see the way Ah-lex was looking at Dorothy last night? His eyes never left her."

"You're dreamin'," said Dick, rolling himself another beaut. "What would he be lookin' at her for?"

"What do you think?"

Dick looked at me, then grabbed the banana special I was making.

"Gimme that." He started over with the mess I'd made.

"It's not the first time I caught him." I told Dick about the time I saw him chasing Dorothy out of the barn and how he stopped when he saw me. And that Dorothy was crying, really bawling her eyes out.

We lit up our McCoyes.

"We don't need a camera," said Dick, exhaling. "A whiskey bottle on the spot would do it."

"Yeah!" I exhaled. "Great, Dick! Great!"

IN THE SHED WE FOUND a roll of heavy twine and a perfect plank about four feet long. Out by the silo, we selected two boulders: one a little bigger than a bowling ball, the other a little smaller than a softball.

"Okay, I'm goin' up. You know wha—"

"Yeah, yeah. Go on!"

I jumped up, grabbed the first rung, pulled myself up, grabbed the second, the third, got my feet up on the first rung, and from there I scrambled up quickly to impress Dick—which I was sure it did. About three quarters of the way up, I stopped and looked down.

"Damn! Just as scary as last time. Scarier, because there was a breeze blowin'." I had to concentrate hard just to get a hand loose from the rung to wave at Dick. I started up again, but now, slower and more carefully. Reaching the window at the top, I waved a salute, but didn't look down. I could well do without looking at a head the size of a potato. All right, so I was exaggerating. So what? High is high…and scary. I grabbed the window opening, pulled myself up until…

"Careful, William!" yelled Dick.

Until I got my knees up on the bottom of the dormer, then my feet, took a breath, and got around to the side of the dormer, and from there it was a snap. I crawled to the center of the dome and sat on top of the world for the second time and looked out at my kingdom…at the peasants working the south cornfield. My right foot jerked! My heart jumped, and my hands slammed down on the concrete dome before I realized it was Dick, jerking on the twine tied to my ankle.

"Billy!" came Dick's voice from over left. He was standing on the roof of the chicken coop, waving at me.

I waved back. "Pull up the board! Hurry up! Don't worry, Dick! They're still working out there! Pull it up! C'mon!"

I crawled out on the flat top of the dormered window, straddled it, untied the twine from my ankle, and pulled up the board. I laid it down on top, untied the twine from the board, and tossed that end back down.

"Now tie the big boul—"

"I know, I know!" came Dick's irritated reply.

The sun broke through the clouds. It was a hot, frying sun. I lay back, closed my eyes, and thought of Riis Park, where we'd climb out of the pool and press ourselves flat on the hot cement to warm our numb bodies and take the blue out of our lips... The brightness faded. I opened my eyes and watched the swirling clouds... Suddenly I was moving! I slammed my hands down, looked out at the horizon, and the world stopped spinning...but my heart kept pounding. My left hand started jerking! Again, it took me a split second to realize that it was Dick pulling on the twine that I had wrapped around my hand this time. I peered over the front edge.

"Don't pull so hard! You almost knocked me off'a here! Pull up the boulder!"

That was easier said than done, but the calluses from the haying toughened my hands so that I was able to wrap the twine around one hand and pull up about two feet of it, then rewrap and pull again, over and over, until I could grab the boulder—it was the bigger one—and pull it onto the board.

"I got it, Dick!"

"Are they still workin' on the corn?"

"Yeah. They'll be there all day." I slipped the twine off the boulder and dropped the end back down. "Tie the other..." I shut up.

They were all out there in the south cornfield, bent over, breaking their backs, freeing the knee-high stalks from the muddy puddles, straightening them out. Whoever it was said a farmer needed a strong back wasn't kidding. Anyway, I didn't want to be a farmer.

Didn't have the nose for it, that was for sure. But it was not a bad life if you were the right type—got muscles in you ears.

Actually, I wouldn't mind owning a spread…riding a horse, roping cattle…but no cows. They say cows are so dumb that, sometimes, if they fall down, they can't remember how to stand up again. Now that's pretty dam dumb, if you ask me. Pigs, on the other hand, are supposed to be smart, but I don't believe it. Anything that rolls around in the mud all day can't be all that smart. Horses are smart.

Take Molle and Jim, they knew when to stop and go, lots of stuff. And dogs? They're the smartest. Why, I bet if Queenie had as many tap-dance lessons as my sister, she could tap-dance too.

"Okay, William! Pull it up!"

"Okay." Even though the second boulder was lighter than the first, my hands still took a beating. "Okay, Dick, I got it." I untied the smaller boulder and retied the twine onto the big boulder.

"Hurry it up."

I finished and placed the smaller boulder—the smasher boulder—on the front end of the board. The tied-up big boulder I put on the back end and dropped the rest of the twine down over the back of the silo.

"I've gotta push the board out, Dick! Move back!" Dick backed up to the hill.

I sat down behind the board and pushed it out slowly with my legs, a little at a time, until the front end of the board with the smasher boulder on it was overhanging the top of the silo window by about a foot and a half, and all the while, making sure that it was balanced there solidly by the big boulder on the back end of the board. After checking the set up carefully, I started down.

"C'mon, hurry up."

"Cut it out, Dick!" I was nervous enough at this point with the wind pickin' up and all. I did a lot of baby-steppin' and then one rung at a time until I was able to jump to the ground.

"You're nuts, climbin' up that high."

"It was pretty scary. But the view is great, Dick. You should—"

"Yeah, yeah. So now what?"

"So now we test it. Okay? You go back up the hill. But keep me in sight so you can signal me when Ah-lex is on the spot. Then I'll pull the back boulder off, the board tilts, and the small boulder slides off...and bingo! Okay? Get it?"

Dick growled and walked off. I guess he thought it wasn't going to work. But it was going to work. Going to work just fine. I wrapped the twine around my left hand and crouched down in the weeds behind the silo. Dick lined himself up between the outhouse and me.

"Ready, Dick?"

"Yeah, go ahead!"

"Give me a signal!"

"What signal?"

"That Ah-lex is standing in the right spot! The spot we're going to mark with the bottle!"

"All right. He's there."

"A hand signal! You have to give me a hand signal that Ah-lex—"

"C'mon already! He's there!" said Dick, giving me a quick salute.

Aggghh! I took the slack out of the twine...then pulled slowly and evenly until...

"Bingo!"

It was delicious! It was stupendous! It was spectacular! Except for one small detail. The board. But everything else was, like I said, *spec-tac-cu-lar!* That is, if you liked surprises. And if you weren't Dick, of course. Because the board, you see, somersaulted...and somersaulted...and almost nailed Dick to the hill. In fact, it was a good thing Dick was fast on his feet.

"Dick," I said, running up. "Dick, it worked!"

"Uuuuuh?" said Dick, looking a little pale.

"Dick!" I shook his arm. "Dick, are you all right? Dick, it worked!"

"Oooooooh?"

"Listen Dick, all we gotta do now is mark where the boulder—"

"Boooooard!" said Dick, his eyes frozen wide.

"Yeah, yeah. We tie the board to keep it from shooting out. Anchor it. Get it?"

"Boooard heeeeeere," said Dick, pointing to the board sticking in the ground next to him. You could tell Dick was a little upset by the whole thing. But his color was getting better. "Jezus Christus." I made the sign of the cross over him, jokingly.

"Caaaa…cut it out," said Dick, his eyes blinking, coming alive.

"It worked, Dick," I slammed Dick on the shoulder. "C'mon, let's go see the boulder."

The boulder hit was perfect, right in line with the rungs, and sank about a third of the way into the muck. I tried pulling it out, but couldn't. "Here, you try."

Dick didn't move.

"C'mon, Dick. You can get it out." I grabbed his arm.

Dick pulled away from me like in slow motion. "Get away from me," he said, dark and low.

Something wasn't right. If Dick was really mad at me, he'd yell at me, pound me, maybe even hang me from the silo by my toes. But he didn't. Didn't nothing. Didn't touch me, didn't raise his voice, nothing.

"What's the matter?"

"You want to kill 'im," he said it dead-on without a ripple, and it scared me.

"Nooooo." I pressed the Lie button—the big red one plastered on my forehead. "We'll just scare 'im, Dick. We're not going to put him right where it falls. Nooooo. We'll put him next to the spot. Scare the crap outta him. Get it? He's bad, Dick! Baaaaad!"

Dick squatted down, gripped the grapefruit-sized boulder with his fingers, and pulled it out.

We stared at the dent in the muck… Dick tossed the boulder down. It plopped an inch away from my toes. I watched him walk on, on up the hill. Dick was mad at me all right. Mad in a way I never saw him before, and it made me feel terrible. After all, he was my friend. More than my friend, he was my uncle. More like a brother, actually, if you think about it. A lousy older brother was what he really was, yeah. But I still felt awful, really rotten. Like maybe I was going to bust open again…but I didn't. So then I picked up the boulder and took it over to the shiny mound in the weeds—not too many steps away—and I plopped it down right on top, not too hard, just enough to make it stick. Then I knelt down, crossed myself, wiped my nose, and asked God to forgive me… But this time was different, because the trouble was, I didn't know exactly for what. And that really bothered me.

I found Dick in the garden freeing the drooped strawberries from the mud, but they wouldn't stand up. Of course not; they were my strawberries. I went to work on the cabbage plants. Without warning, Dick jumped me, got me in a headlock, and started choking me. All I could do was pull on his arm locked under my chin and swing punches up at his head. I stopped when everything started to turn black… I found myself on the ground coughing and gasping. Dick gave me a farewell kick and went about freeing the broad cabbage leaves from the mud. I went way over to the other side of the garden and did the tomato plants.

DARK CLOUDS again lined the northwest sky. It was milking time, and everybody's face turned sour. By the time we finished, you could smell the rain—you could even feel it—but you couldn't see it. Not a dimple on the puddles. But it was coming. No doubt about it. Dick and I started the cows out to pasture. We didn't talk about the silo or the choking. We just went on like it never happened. Some cows balked at crossing the swollen creek, but we got them going with some shouting and clapping and some raps with a stick. A big log came floating by, and we started peppering it with stones.

"That thing's really movin'," I said, firing away. "I hit it! I hit the back! Did ya see?"

"Agh!" replied Dick, firing away.

"It's outta range."

Dick ripped one last shot with everything he had… It fell a little short. Dick's got a good arm, but nothing like my buddy, Frank. Frank's got a throwing motion as smooth as silk. Dick's was short and jerky—like mine—but there was still a lot of zip to it.

"C'mon," said Dick. "Time for a McCoye."

We scooted down behind some bushes, got out the makings, and went at it. Dick struck a match to his McCoye, but the wind blew it out. I cupped my hands around his, but again the match went out. And that was when we first noticed how much the northwestern sky behind us had changed. The clouds were now black and blue and high as mountains. These were end of the world clouds. We took off, leaping the camel-like humps that stuck out of the water, cutting across the partially flooded lowlands as we headed for the rise on the dirt road, which wasn't all that close because we had followed the floating tree so far downstream. Bits of everything started blowing past us as the wind kicked into high gear. I ducked behind a giant oak to take in the approaching storm. Dick shot past me, yelling at me to keep going.

Lightning flashed.

Crack-ba-boooom! Ba-boooooom!

The next thing I knew, I was on all fours. There was an odd smell in the air, and my ears were ringing. The oak behind me was split. Part of it was lying right alongside me, close enough to touch. Dick was waving his arms and yelling, but I couldn't make out what he was saying. I got up and fell back down. Tried it again and again fell down. Fear shot through me.

"What's wrong with me?" I asked myself.

Thunder and lightning cracked all around me. *Ba-boooooom! Boom-boom-babooooom, caarack, ba-boooooom!*

I struggled to get to my feet again, and did, but I felt wobbly. Then the cold rain hit me like a wave and almost knocked me over. But suddenly, two black shapes had me, one under each arm, and we were moving toward the barn.

Crack! Ba-ba-boooooom!

The ground shook. We slopped through the barnyard muck, slipping and sliding, before we flopped down inside the doorway.

"You okay, Billy?" It was Dick.

"Lightning...knock me over." I said shivering, my teeth clicking.

"I told ya to keep goin', I told ya. I told ya."

We were moving up the aisle now, the rain beating the barn in waves.

Crack-baboooooom!

The barn shook. My armpits started talking to each other in Polish... My teeth were chattering. I was cold.

Crack-ba-boooom! Ba-boooooom! Boom-boom-caarack-ba-ba-boooooom!

The storm was going crazy, like maybe the sky was falling down!

"One, two, three, go!" Out the door we went. The rain beat on us from every angle, and going uphill didn't make it any easier.

Crack-ba-boooom! Ba-boooooom!

When we plopped through the porch door, we were greeted with Grandma's, "Oh, Jezus Chrisstus! Jezus! Jezus! Oh, Jezus, Jezuuus!"

Dried with towels and wrapped in blankets, I ended up on the couch on the far end of the porch with a cup of hot tea. What burned in my mind the whole time was... It was Ah-lex. Ah-lex and Gramps..." It burned there like a hot iron, and I couldn't get rid of it.

Later we had supper. I don't know what we ate, but it tasted like fear. Nobody said more than they had to. I think most were praying. I know I was. Dick didn't say a peep. Grandma did some groaning in her rocking chair, but no stream of Polish for a change. There was a mumble and a gasp now and then from someone, and that was it. The storm did all the talking, all the cursing and yelling. The storm was boss. You couldn't fight him, couldn't knock him down. All you could do was bite your nails and take it. And pray, like I said.

When the rumbling and flashing finally rode away, it left behind the rain. A heavy, steady pounding rain, the kind it had used on us before. And after a while, I wouldn't say we accepted it; no, we just got used to it, like static on a radio. Finally, we all went to bed. I don't think anybody slept a wink. I know I didn't.

43

Rain, Rain, Rain (Tuesday)

The rain never stopped. The lightning and thunder did, but the rain never even slowed down. And now, as we sat at the table waiting for breakfast, it was pouring. Pouring like you wouldn't believe. Pouring cats and dogs, you say? Pouring buckets, you say? Hey, I'm talking pouring. Pouring pots and pans, barrels, sinks, bathtubs! I'm talking pouring Niagara Falls! Pouring! P-o-u-r-i-n-g! Get it? I hope so, because nobody here ever saw rain like this before. Maybe nobody, nowhere.

And that was not the worst of it. We got a creek that was climbing the banks and was now a river! And that was not the worst of it. We got cow trouble. Cow trouble in a big way! Oh, and I got a sore throat, could hardly swallow, but that ain't nothin'. It was the cows! The cows couldn't get across the water so they could get milked. And if you didn't milk cows... I don't know, I guess they blew up or something. Yes, sir, and that was only half the problem. And what the other half was nobody was saying. Richard said he knew, but he didn't. If he knew, he'd tell me. He likes to brag.

Ideas were tossed around, mostly in Polish, so I didn't know what, exactly, but finally, in the afternoon, it became clear that the plan settled on was this: Ah-lex and Gramps would go by way of the County Road to the bridge, cross over, and then cut through the pasture to the woods. There they would round up the cows and lead them to a good spot to swim across. Then Dick and I were to march them, slowly—lest they rupture their bloated bags or slip and break a leg—back to the barn.

The four of us got dressed in rain gear—mine was on the big side so the girls folded the legs and arms under and secured them with rubber bands. Dick and I were supposed to give the men an hour's head start, but we were too anxious to battle Mother Nature, so after watching the clock drag on for about twenty minutes—in spite of Grandma and the girls yelling at us—we ducked out.

The storm was blinding, blowing, really terrific! It was everything you could imagine, plus cold. But I didn't mind at all! It was too exciting! And so far we had just made it down to the barn! We ran down the aisle to the back of the barn and cracked opened the door. The barnyard was a solid mass of water with the rain hammering big spikes into it.

"Let's go out the side door in the hayloft, Dick."

For once Dick didn't argue. We ran back to the stairway. The higher we climbed, the louder the sound of the pelting rain and the howling wind. When Dick opened the small hayloft door, the wind whistled and roared. It was frightening beyond belief, like the whole barn was about to be ripped apart and blown away. We went over to the big sliding doors, and as soon as we cracked it open, hay started swirling all around us.

"Let's go!" said Dick.

We slipped through the opening, slid the door shut, bent to the wind and the rain, and followed the high ground to the rise. Once there, we were amazed at the sight before us: no creek, no river, but a lake. We scampered down the slope to the water's edge, now about a football field away—it was double that yesterday—and watched everything but the kitchen sink (as the saying goes) get carried downstream by the swift current. Trees, bushes, and logs were expected, but not chairs, barrels, milk cans, boards...you name it.

"Look, the cows!" said Dick, pointing upstream.

"Where?"

"Across, by those birch trees."

We moved upstream counting cows. Three cows, standing knee-deep in the water, seemed to be watching us. Another one, at water's edge, mooed a long note over and over. Dick counted eleven, and so did I.

"Where's the rest of 'em, you think?"

"Must be in the woods. You see Grandpa or Ah-lex?"

"What's that in the water?" I pointed downstream.

"C'mon!" Dick took off, and I followed.

Four cows were swimming, fighting the current, only their heads sticking out of the water. We ran along the water's edge, trying to catch up with them, but the mud-sucking ground was tiring, and we had to stop to catch our breath. We lost sight of them altogether where the water narrowed and made a sweeping bend. When we got to the high ground at the bend, we scanned the water in the downpour with our hands hooded over our eyes.

"Look, down by the bridge!" said Dick pointing. "They're coming out of the water. See them?"

"I see three… Where's the other one?"

We didn't spot any more, so we went down the rise and ran along the water's edge toward the three cows plodding toward us in single file. The first one "mooed," but the sound was different than usual, had more notes to it, sounded the way the cow did that Ah-lex beat in the barn with a stool. You don't forget notes of fear and pain.

"How come he helped me?" flashed in my mind.

We backed away from the water's edge to give the cows plenty of room to pass.

"Look'it the blood, Dick!"

"That's from the barbed wire, I bet."

Their teats were a mess: some were cut badly, a few were hanging by a little skin, and some just weren't there. Their bodies, too, bore bloody gashes. I couldn't take my eyes off their bloated bags. Dick told me to get the cows back to the barn, that he would stay and watch for the men.

I followed the cows at their own pace into the barn and locked them into their stalls and fed them some hay. Thin streams of milk—some mixed with blood—ran from their bloated teats and puddled the floor. Grandma wailed a sickening scream when she saw them. Vickie and Dorothy held hands and had tears. The poor cows rolled their eyes at Grandma as she rubbed their heads and talked to them in a soothing voice. You could see it helped; she was good with cows. After a while, we went back up to the house to wait for the men.

THE RAIN NEVER SLOWED. It whipped the house every which way. Richard came back, but not the men. Supper stayed in the pots. It got dark, and the men still weren't back. Finally, they came staggering up the steps and through the door. Whipping off their raincoats, they plopped into their chairs. We waited for some words while they caught their breath, but none came. Vickie poured them steaming hot cups of coffee, and Dick told them about the cows we'd spotted. Grandpa nodded, cleared his throat, and tried to say something but gave up on it. Grandma crossed an arm over her breasts, turned away, and went into the kitchen. I gave Dick a questioning look. He answered with a shrug. The men got out their "makings" and rolled themselves a smoke.

Gramps leaned toward us, drummed his fingers on the table, and said, "The three in the barn. And the eleven in the patch of birch trees. That's all you saw?"

"We saw four swimming across," said Dick. "Then they went around the bend. And when we got there, we saw three."

I held up three fingers. "Only three came out of the water... I went with them to the barn, and Dick stayed."

"We saw two get swept under the bridge," said Grandpa, staring at the table.

"Bridge is out!" shouted Ah-lex. "Water took it."

The girls went into the kitchen, their voices buzzing. A split second later, Grandma came out with a stack of plates, slammed them down on the table, and got into it with Grandpa. Ah-lex joined in. Then the girls. All in Polish, of course. Dick and I looked from one squawking head to the other. It didn't last long. Dick and I cornered Dorothy in the kitchen and asked her what it was all about. It seemed Grandma just couldn't understand—or didn't want to understand—why the men couldn't get to the cows and milk them, bridge or no bridge. Finally, they got through to her that the current around the bridge was too strong. And that Gramps had, actually, gone out on a rope and that Ah-lex had to pull him back or he might've drowned. I didn't much care to hear anything good about Ah-lex, but there it was. But if you think about it, it wasn't such a big deal, because if Ah-lex had been out on the rope first, Grandpa, naturally, would have pulled him back in. So it was pretty much a two-way thing.

So then the girls served supper, a thick stew—you could've built a house with it.

The wind died down and finally quit, but the rain didn't. It beat a soothing rhythm while we ate and soon sounded like it belonged, like it found a home here in Wisconsin, like maybe it was going to fill up the whole state and make a Great Lake out of it like Lake Michigan. Make it Great Lake Wisconsin! We could go sail on it and explore! Boy, oh boy, wasn't I the clever one. Big-city smart-ass, that's me.

And then I saw the cows again. Saw their blood, the hurt in their eyes, heard their painful mooing, and all at once I hated the rain, what it did to the cows, to Grandpa and Grandma. That the girls were saying: it could ruin them, wipe them out, that they could lose the farm, lose the only life they knew. Lose it all because they couldn't start over...they were too old. That Grandma had said they might as well be dead now, not have it drag out, have it dwindle down to nothing and then die... And not only them, but other farmers would go down as well. And then I watched Ah-lex and Grandpa sew up the ripped teats and udders, watched them use a red-hot iron to cauterize, watched Grandma rub the cow's faces while she talked them through their pain and fear. And then I wasn't such a smart-ass. A smart-ass didn't cry.

LATER THAT NIGHT, I WENT TO BED with my throat so sore it hurt to swallow my own spit. I also had a fever, naturally, but I didn't say anything. Hell, I still had my tits. And when I fell asleep, I had my usual fever dream: me shoveling like mad to keep from getting buried by some stuff that looked like lumpy oatmeal; only it was black. It got higher and higher, and I shoveled faster and faster, and I was getting it down to about my knees when suddenly more got dumped in, and pretty soon it was gaining on me again: up to my waist, up to my chest, and just as it closed over my head, I woke up all sweaty and ready to puke. If I were back home, I'd be getting the black bag by now. My guts would be bursting, and my dad would be saying, "Hold it! I count to twenty!" And then, he'd count like he didn't know all the numbers. I'd be crying out, "I can't hold it anymore!" Ugh, I didn't want to think about it. Now that was back home. What they did out here, I had no idea. Probably kick you down the hill. Throw you to the pigs. Bury you in the silo. Agh! Enough already! I went downstairs and found Grandma sitting in her rocker out on the porch—probably had a bowl of strawberries under her apron.

"Gran—" she jumped, and it made me jump.

I went over to her, knelt down on one knee, and made all kinds of painful faces with my hand at my throat. I even threw in a couple of moans. She put a hand on my forehead and jerked it back like she'd touched a hot stove.

"Jezzus!" she said disgustedly. She got out of her rocking chair, threw her shaggy shawl at me, and pointed to a chair. "*Ujchotz*," she said and went into the kitchen. I sat down, wrapped her shawl around me, and listened to the rain.

She came back with a rag and a bottle that read, "Sloan's Liniment." She had me hold my T-shirt up while she slapped the stuff onto my chest and back and started rubbing it in—I think the last time she did this was to a horse. The stuff smelled good, like peppermint, but it burned so much I thought my skin was going to fall off. Not to mention my eyes—way worse than onions. She worked some on my forehead, my upper lip, and just for the heck of it, I think, drilled some up my nose. I was on fire, inside and out. Then she wrapped this flannel rag around my neck, chest and back, put on my T-shirt, and disappeared into the kitchen. I sat there burning up with my arms hanging out, turning into ashes. She came back with two cups of steaming-hot tea and a pint bottle tucked under her armpit. She poured a shot of Old Kentucky into mine and made hers about half and half. We went at it sip for sip, and then I went upstairs, my burning body lighting the way. I slept like a rock.

44

Rain, Rain, Go Away Already (Wednesday)

I woke up the next day, and I was cured! A miracle! I couldn't believe it. All I felt was a little twinge in the back of my throat when I swallowed. I got dressed real quick while the rain continued to drum its dreary tune. Downstairs on the porch, everybody looked like it was the end of the world. And I guess it was, because even though Ah-lex and Gramps could see the cows, they couldn't get to them. Not with the bridge out. They had tried at first light, but it was hopeless. The current was too strong, they said.

So there we sat with the rain beating on the roof and the ticking clock from the kitchen beating on our brains. After a lot of thought, over cups of coffee, the best idea anyone could come up with was a "boat." But nobody had a boat, not nearby that we could get to. So it looked like the cows weren't going to get milked, not this morning anyway. And if we found a way later, would that be too late? Would they go bad by then? Explode into a million pieces? What? I still didn't have the answers, but now was definitely not the time to ask. Besides, even if the rain stopped, right now, this very minute, there still wouldn't be a way to get to them until the water went down. And who knew how long that would take. Boy, things really looked bad. Totally hopeless, you might say. So hopeless, in fact, that they were all starting to go nuts. They'd start yelling and shouting one minute, and the next minute go dead quiet for I don't know how long—until another wave hit them. So then, finally, Dick and I thought we'd go nuts, so we put on our rain gear and ducked out.

The three wounded cows looked better today. They chewed their cud, and the fear in their eyes was gone. Even their cut teats didn't look all that bad. But the ones that were missing did; they looked like a mistake. I didn't know how they milked them, if they did milk them. I guess they did.

Out back of the barn, Dick and I stuck to the fencing on the right of the dirt road, until we reached the rise. We were surprised to see that the water—which was once a creek, then a river, and now a lake—was only a stone's throw away. Indeed, the last marking stick that we had stuck at the water's edge yesterday was now a good twenty yards out! This lake, I realized, was now bigger than the ones we used to go to with the relatives. But it was a weird, scary-looking lake, more like something in a bad dream: bent trees and burnt, ugly stumps with clumps of bushes popped about; with fence posts and barbed wire running in and out of the water; with the hairy, green-topped camel humps underwater waving goodbye. But out in the middle was the scariest. There, an angry wide ribbon of water churned and twisted and carried everything that would float downstream, while underneath the surface, who knew what else? Cows, for one thing.

We went back to the barn. Vickie and Dorothy were sitting on the hayloft steps in their raincoats petting the brown-and-white cat, the one that had the kittens. It was cuddled up on Dorothy's lap. We stood there fidgeting and telling them about the waterline being up another twenty yards, which now made the widest part of the creek/lake about 150 yards wide since the rain started three days ago.

Stroking the cat, Dorothy said, "God's punishing everybody because of the war. That's what Grandma said. God punishes those that kill. And that everybody is going to—"

"Ohhh, Dorothy, stop it," said Vickie in a bored tone.

"That's what Grandma said. That everybody that sins gets punished!"

"That's right," said Dick. "It's in the Bible. This—"

"You don't read the Bible," I injected. "You're Catholic."

"So? This little guy at Montifiore was always saying things from the Bible. Redheaded guy. It rained for forty days and forty nights. God told Noah to build a big ark. Bigger than this barn. And to load his family and two of everything in it. All the animals. And they were the only ones saved. Everybody else drowned. Noah believed in the Word of God and was saved! Hallelujah!"

I was stunned. And you could see the girls were too. It was mostly, I think, because of the way Dick said it, like a preacher. Unbelievable! Dick hardly ever put more than a half a dozen words together about anything, and never about God. In fact, I think he had it in for him because he took away his parents.

"Yeah, well…" I finally said, "it's not gonna rain here for forty days."

"How do you know?" said Dick.

"Because, for one thing, God's not going to waste that much water on Wisconsin."

The girls giggled.

"Wisconsin's farmers and their families," I added. "He doesn't want to hurt them."

"God only punishes bad people," said Dorothy.

"Billy's bad," said Dick, dotting my chest with a finger.

A hot flash shot through me. I couldn't believe my ears.

Vickie sprang off the stairs. "I've got to pluck some drowned chickens." Vickie grabbed the basket with the eggs from the bottom of the stairs. "Come on Dick, give me a hand!"

Dick moved off and followed Vickie's swinging hips. Heck, an army would. Dorothy stroked the cat in her lap. I sprawled out on the step below.

"You wanna hold her?" said Dorothy, leaning forward, making a move with the cat.

"No, no," I said, begging off. "She likes you." Dorothy sat back, laid the cat on its back in the groove of her legs, and shook its paws like you might a baby's hands. "Pretty kitty-kitty," she cooed. "Pet her. She needs petting."

I reached up and rubbed the white stripe on the cat's head with my finger. She kept blinking at me. I tickled her under the chin, and she licked at my fingers with her rough tongue, then tilted her head up and purred. "She likes that, huh?"

"Sure she does. Don't you, Lilly?" said Dorothy, shaking Lilly's front paws again. "Poor, Lilly. She misses her babies. Huh, Lilly? Pretty, pretty, Lilly."

"Did Dick tell you about the silo?" Lilly went on licking at my hand. "Pretty, pretty Lilly."

"Did he tell ya?"

"No. What? The silo? What about it?"

"Nothin'. Never mind." I folded my arms on my knees.

"He said you're bad."

That hot feeling again. "Well...you may as well know. I am bad."

"Don't be silly. Climbing the silo doesn't make—"

"I wanted to kill Ah-lex!" Dorothy stared at me in disbelief.

I nodded. "I wanted to smash him. I did. I planned it and everything." I shook my head. "I still want to. I can't help it. I—"

"Stop it! Stop it!" Dorothy threw her hands over her ears.

Lilly jumped out of her lap, leaped down the stairs, and ran off. So did Dorothy, right out of the barn.

I felt like an outcast. Nobody seemed to see things the way I did. Was I wrong? Was I really bad? I didn't like Ah-lex right from the start, and I still didn't like him. And then the kittens, and I hated him. I know, I know, he helped me, but I still hated him. Was that wrong? Was it right? Half right?

Oh, God… It didn't seem to bother, Dick. It didn't even seem to bother Dorothy that much, which really surprised me, or maybe it did, but she didn't show it… Oh, God! Where do you get the answers? I know you know, but you're not talking. You never do. Unless a person's a saint or something. Some people say God talked to them, but they were mostly nuts… So, God, listen. Please. I'm asking you to help me because I can't go on like this. I've got to have some answers. Please, God! You have to help me. You just have to. Nobody else can. Right? So c'mon, God, be a sport. Please! And that's the last time I'm gonna ask you. I mean it. And if you don't, I'm gonna do something bad! I know I am! I just know it! I can't help it! Ohh, Gooooood!

BACK UP AT THE HOUSE, things looked bad. Chairs were upset and broken, plates on the table were also broken, a pot was caved in, and the smell of whiskey was heavy. Slouched on his arms at the table was Grandpa. On the floor against the brick wall was Ah-lex. Both were passed out. Both were snoring. Grandma, in her rocking chair, gave me a glance then turned back to the rain tapping on the windows. From the kitchen, the smell of chickens cookin' on the stove filled the air. I crossed in and found Dick and the girls seated at the leaf table with coffee cups in hand, lookin' glum. The only sound was the crackling wood in the hot end of the stove and the drummer on the roof beating his insane tune. I joined them. Dorothy brought me a steaming-hot cup of coffee. They started talking.

There'd been a fight, they said—which was pretty evident. Ah-lex ended up choking Grandpa. Dick and Vickie tried to pull him off but couldn't. Grandma then beaned him with a pot, slugged him four or five times, before he let go and passed out. I asked them what the fight was about. They said they didn't know. But the way the girls looked at each other, I thought they knew. I thought they just didn't want to say, like it was some big secret. I told that to Dick when we went up to our room. He said I was crazy, that it was just the whiskey.

I WOKE FROM MY NAP SWEATING BULLETS, and again, my throat was so sore I could hardly swallow my own spit. The Sloans I'd slapped on before I came up didn't help at all. Geez, I was so sick of being sick. I mean it! And not that I'm trying to pile it on or anything, but if the truth be known, I think I have polio—or something worse, like something you get just before you die. Really! I'm not kidding! And like I said, I was really totally disgusted with everything! Take wonderful Richard there, sleepin' like a rock. He was never sick. And our blood was the same—half of it. So I was loaded with brains. So what? A lot of good it'd do me when they buried me six feet under. My gravestone would read, "Billy never knew the combination." That was a hell of a way to go; you have to admit. Especially for someone who wanted to die in the saddle. Not that I knew what that meant exactly, but Uncle George said it all the time, and it sounded pretty good. Terrific, in fact.

Oh look, there's that pole bustin' through my shorts again. I'd have a go at it, but the Sloan's might burn it off. I could still smell the stuff on my hands. Damn... I wondered what the girls were doin'. Probably dreamin' about me.

"Eay, Dorothy? Dreamin' about baaaad Billy, always lookin' at your globes?" Gee, already I was feeling better. "Dick! Oh, Dicky boy!"

Crap, it's no use. Dick shuts his eyes, and a plane could fly through the room and he wouldn't know it. Me, a pin dropped, I was looking for dragons.

"Dick!" I tried again, "Hey, Dick-shit!"

Dick growled. I knew that growl. It meant "Go away or I'll kill ya!"

So I went downstairs alone, and I didn't have to be careful about the creaking steps because the rain was really pounding. I was kind of hoping Grandma was still out on the porch so that I might get her to give me another rub-a-dub with the Sloan's, but I saw that her bedroom door was closed, so I figured she was probably in there, and Gramps too, I hoped. I didn't want to have to deal with the men, especially you-know-who. The chicken soup smell was heavy in the kitchen, and the big kettle was now simmering on the cooler end of the stove. The ticking clock, now back in the kitchen, surprised me with a read of only a few minutes shy of three o'clock, meaning the day was dragging. I'd only been upstairs a little over an hour.

Grandpa was the only one out on the porch. He was curled up on the couch at the far end of the porch. Ah-lex's rain gear, I noticed, was missing from the clothes tree. Through the rain-streaked windows, I spotted him slopping around by the shed in back of the chicken coop. He was up to something for sure, but I couldn't tell what. I should've left a boulder up on the silo with a rope hanging down. Maybe he would've pulled on it and killed himself. Finally, I saw him drag a couple of big planks into the barn. Hmmm, maybe he was going to nail himself to a cross.

I moved back to the kitchen, checked the kettle, stirred the chicken soup with the big wooden spoon, and voilà, inspiration dawned: the ghost room. I started up the hallway, took a little look-see into the girls' nook, and was instantly turned to salt: creamy smooth skin was peeking out from under a sheet that lay molded to the kind of hills and valleys I'd been dreaming about. Vickie was behind Dorothy, facing the wall, and the sweeping curve of her naked leg from hip to toe made the hair on the back of my neck stand up… among other things. Dorothy's eyes opened. I froze in her headlights. She held the sheet up and beckoned to me. All she had on was her panties. I tiptoed in, closed the door, dropped my pants, and slid in back first. Dorothy's arm wrapped around me, pulled me smack up against her, and just like that, I was in heaven and hell. Listen, if you haven't been there, you don't know. So then what happened I'm not going to tell because you wouldn't believe me anyway. I didn't even tell Dick because I knew he wouldn't believe me. I'm not even sure I believe me. Heh-heh-heh-heh. Only the shadow knows…

OH SHIT! I can't stop thinking about it, so I'm going to tell you exactly what happened. You can believe it or not, I don't care.

Like I said, Dorothy held up the sheet, and I slid in ass first, and right away she wrapped the sheet around us and pulled me smack up against her—like I said—and I felt all of her skin on my skin, except for my Jockey's saying hello to her pink panties. And boooy, that was something: being smothered in skin with two soft globes massaging my back. You should try it sometime if you don't believe me.

And then…a hand trickling down my bare chest to my shorts, my heart pounding faster and harder than the rain, and I was scared stiff—pardon the pun. Then somehow my shorts were down around my knees! I kid you not! And I didn't know the combination!

Moments passed, and nothing happened. I was thinking she was waiting to see if I was going to die of a heart attack—which was one hundred percent fine with me. Anything but this. And then all of a sudden, her hand was wrapped around my hose! I didn't move. I didn't breathe. I didn't blink. I wait. And I waited...and nothing happened. And I mean nothing! It was just there! So I waited some more... And then I figured I should at least breathe a little. So I did, very carefully, three times. And then I went back to the waiting game... And then it hit me! It was probably my move! What! What! What! What was I supposed to do? Dial the combination, maybe? No, can't be. We're not facing each other. What! What! And then I heard a sound... It was like... There it was again...soft and even... Again! I twisted my head around as far as it would go. Oh my god! Dorothy was snoring! She was snoring with my hose in her hand!

And Vickie was looking at me! Her head twisted around like mine, one eye looking at me like she must be dreaming. So she turned back and flopped down. Hey, I was the one that had to be dreaming. I was in bed with two naked broads, covered with a sweaty sheet that's got more hills and valleys on it than the road to Lublin, and what was I doing about it? Nothing! Absolutely nothing! And why was I doing nothing? Because one of the broads had her hand wrapped around my hose, and she was asleep!

I was petrified! All I wanted to do was die! Actually, if you think about it, I must be nuts! Guys would give their eyeteeth to be where I am—probably an arm or a leg, probably both!

So then I was thinking, how could this be? How could Dorothy be snoring with my hose in her hand? How was this possible? Wasn't she excited? Was she so used to holding a sausage that it was nothing? 'Course I smelled like a peppermint stick from the Sloan's, but it was not a bad smell. Not bad at all. So whatsa-whatsa? Maybe my hose wasn't big enough? Maybe it was too big! Maybe it was too fat, or not fat enough. Maybe it was too hard? You could knock down walls with it. She could've at least have said, "Oh my! Do you have a hoist to help you carry it?" Or "How long does it take to fire?" But she didn't say a word. She didn't even ask if I knew the combination—which I was most grateful for, believe me. I was really happy about that. I couldn't tell you how happy I was about that. I mean, really! I mean the whole thing was just too much for me. Way too much. I was just not ready for this stuff. Uh-uh. No way… Of course, next week might be all right. Hey, hey, why rush things? After all, there was plenty more where this came from. Oh yeah! I'd get the combination and…oh-oooh…she was…she was…and she was still snoring! Oh well, enough of that. Why bore you with details. Heh-heh-heh-heh!

I told Dick about it. How I was smothered by mountains and hills. How I had hands all over me. How we played doctor with me doing both of them at once. How I…

That was as far as I got because Dick said he didn't believe a word of it. I'm telling you, you talk to some guys, it's a waste of breath. They got no style. No imagination. Now me? I even knocked off the "bad thing" again. And it was still early! Why, before this day was over, I'll probably go blind!

PART III

45

The Clouds Run Dry

We were finishing an early chicken soup supper when the drumming rain started changing its beat. Softer and higher, it went. I turned in my chair and joined the others staring out the window.

The beat came back heavy like a wave then faded and faded until it was gone. The quiet seemed unnatural and a little scary. Grandma stood up and went outside, and one by one we followed.

The sky had brightened, raindrops were dripping off the roof, and puddles were as smooth as glass. No one jumped up and down, laughed, or cheered; they just stood there like zombies and took in the fields, the fences, the trees, the spooky clouds and the flooded land. Had the clouds finally run dry? Grandma went to her knees, crossed herself, and started a prayer. We went to our knees and joined her.

Then, cutting through the stillness was the whinnying of horses and their stomping hooves. It was Molle and Jim galloping up to the side of the barn. We flew down the hill to greet them. They were in good shape except for some barbed wire nicks and one long gash across Molle's chest.

Questions popped: "Where did they cross?"

"See any cows?" Grandma's Polish, as usual, filled the air.

Moments later everybody split: Grandma back up the hill, the girls off to check on the pigs and chickens, Ah-lex and Dick down to the water to find the crossing tracks and to see if they could spot any cows. And that left Gramps and me to take care of Molle and Jim.

I brought out the bridles, and Gramps slipped one over Molle's head. "Easy, girl," he said softly. He passed me the reins and moved over to Jim, who was tramping nervously. "Easy, Jim!" I rubbed the short hair on Molle's long face, her big eyes looking me over, looking scared.

"Let's take 'em inside," said Gramps.

We entered the barn, and the sound of clippity-clopping hooves on concrete was like no other, as good as rain on the roof except when it didn't know when to stop. We led Molle and Jim into separate stalls in the back part of the barn. Grandpa put feed bags on them while I fetched the rope-handled wooden bucket, the first aid kit for animals. Grandpa dug out some cotton swabs, dipped them into a big bottle of peroxide, and went to work on Molle, digging into her cuts hard, especially the two-footer across her chest. Molle didn't even flinch, just kept munching on her oats.

"Doesn't it hurt her?" I asked.

"They take it better than we do."

Grandpa got a big jar of Vaseline out of the bucket, unscrewed the cover, and scooped out a big glob of the yellow guck with two fingers, plopped it into his other hand, and made a hole in the middle with a gooey finger.

"Okay. Now pop the cork on that Epsom Salt bottle and fill up this hole."

I knelt down, locked the blue bottle between my legs, popped the cork, and with two hands poured in the white crystals. Gramps brushed away the excess and started stirring the glob into a paste with his finger.

"Hold your hand out." I did, and Gramps wiped a glob of the mixture into my palm and stood up. "Now you do like this," he said, swabbing the mixture with a finger into one of Molle's smaller cuts. "That's all there's to it. Go ahead." I went at it while Gramps worked on the two-foot gash on her chest.

"Easy, Molle... Fix you up good. Easy now..."

"Grandpa?" I said, smoothing the mixture into a nasty nick. "Why do you use barbed wire? Can't you use plain wire? You could make like four or five strands even."

"Animals rub the wire with their nose, and when they hit a barb, they back off. They remember that. How're you doin' there?"

"I got 'em all, I think."

Gramps patted Molle as he checked her out. "Uh-huh, that should do it."

"Grandpa?" I said, following him out of Molle's stall.

"Yeah? Hand me that lantern there." I did, and Gramps popped a match with his thumbnail and lit the wick. "Whoa Jim, whoooa." Gramps moved in with me following

Gramps went on talking to Jim as he patted his left flank and slowly worked his way down to his bad hoof. "Hold this." I took the lamp. "Let's get a good look here now, Jim." Gramps hoisted Jim's leg and straddled it like blacksmiths did in the movies. "Easy Jim, easy…" Gramps dug out his pocketknife and thumbed out the smaller blade. I held the light closer and watched Gramps dig mud out of the hoof while he went on talking to Jim, who went on nickering and neighing the whole time.

"Is it bad?"

"Doesn't look to be… There's the cut, see here?"

I leaned in with the lamp and saw blood seeping out of a cut just above the hoof. "Uh-huh."

"It's not bad, but it's in a bad place." Gramps released Jim's hoof. "Move back now, and put the lamp out. And stay back." Gramps patted Jim's flank as he moved up to his head. "What was it you were askin'?"

"Uhhh, I forgot." I turned the wick down, watched it glow red and go out.

Gramps had slipped off Jim's feedbag and was now snapping a strap onto Jim's bridle and securing it to an eyebolt on the right. "Easy, Jim." Gramps moved to the other side of Jim and did the same, with an eyebolt on the left. Jim could hardly move his head now, and he started to act up. "Easy, boy. Easy," said Gramps, stroking Jim's neck. "Give me some of that Vaseline mix. Don't come up behind him."

I circled wide and moved slowly. Gramps swiped the mix from the lip of the bucket with a finger and held it out to where Jim could lick at it.

"See, Jim? Nothin' that's going to hurt you." Gramps patted Jim's flank as we moved back to his injured leg. "Put the bucket down by my foot and back off. Move slow now…"

"You going to cauterize it?" I said, backing away.

"Nooo, the cut's too close to the hoof."

I watched Gramps dip the cotton swabbed sticks into the peroxide and clean out the cut and then pack what was left of the mix into it.

"Does that work good on people? On cuts?"

"You can use it on a back that's been whipped."

I didn't ask any more questions. I didn't want to even think about what Gramps had just said.

I just hoped he wouldn't say any more. He didn't, I guess, because he was too busy talking to Jim while he finished working on him. Overall, I was surprised how little blood there was. Gramps said that horses didn't have a lot of blood vessels in their lower legs, and that was why they didn't heal well, and why you usually ended up shooting them.

We moved out to the doorway and sat on a couple of milking stools while we waited for Jim to settle down. Gramps lit up a smoke. We watched the gray-clouded sky churn wildly, as if it was fighting to keep from sliding off to the east. The barnyard had a rather pleasant sweet-sour smell to it now that it was covered with water.

"How long you think it'll take the water to go down, Grandpa?"

"She feeds in from the north, up there." Gramps waved a finger off to the right. "Once she tops out…well, she goes down pretty fast." Gramps dragged on his cigarette.

"Gramps?"

"Yeah?"

"I remember what I wanted to ask."

"Well, ask, boy. Ask."

"What was the fight with Ah-lex all about?"

Gramps flicked ashes off his cigarette. "That's what men do, William. They fight." He took a quick drag.

I needed a better answer. "But there must've been—"

"Ah-lex!" Gramps snorted. "He wants to marry my girl, Dorothy."

To say I was stunned didn't do it, didn't even come close. It was more like when I almost got hit by lightning. *Whaaaam!* Actually, it was a double *whaaaam*, because first of all, somehow, I didn't really know they were his girls. It was like when you know somethin', but you didn't know how you knew it, and you think, whatever it was, it was probably not true. And *whaaam*—number 2 was that stinkin' son of a gun wanting to marry my girl! My girl...and Eddie's.

Gramps flicked his ashes and gave me a little smile. "So how do you suppose we solve this dilemma?

"Well...you could shoot Ah-lex and get a new hired hand."

Gramps gave me his twinkling-eye look. "Yeah...that's one way."

I pictured Gramps walking down a dusty street with a couple of six-shooters on his hip. "You miss being a sheriff, Grandpa?"

"I'm sixty-seven years old, boy."

"You don't look it."

"Well, my bones do."

"I bet you miss it, huh? Walking around with a gun and all?"

Gramps choked on his smoke, swallowed, and said, "You seen too many movies, boy."

"But you packed a gun, didn't you?"

I got a sneaky eye this time. "A snub-nosed .38. And I used it mostly to club drunks with. And I'm too old for that. Too old for all of it." Gramps dragged on the little nub of his cigarette like he always did. I don't know why his fingers didn't burn off.

"Geez. Your girls, Vickie and Dorothy."

"Who'd you think?"

"I guess I thought they just...got here, like the hay and the corn."

"Just drop a seed in the ground and watch them pop up, eh?"

"Ha-ha! Yeah! Just pop up Where did Eddie pop from?"

"Frank Shyzmanski. Your grandmother's third husband. He's in the asylum in Marshfield. That's where we went that Saturday before Eddie left. Poor man didn't even recognize his own son." Gramp's dragged the butt so tiny I couldn't even see it, then rubbed it to dust and flicked his fingers.

"Let's get at it." Gramps stood up and arched his back with a groan. We gave the gray sky a look. The ragged clouds were still swirling around, looking angry and wasted.

"What do we have to do yet?"

Gramps bent over and picked up his stool. "Wrap the leg with honey. That should do it."

"Honey?" I picked up my stool and followed Gramps back into the barn.

"Bacteria can't live in honey. Way back, olden times, you got slashed with a sword, they wrapped it in honey. Healed up as good as new." Gramps gave me a glance and added, "Good for buckshot wounds too."

"Grandpa?"

"Yah? What now?"

"What's it feel like to kill a man?"

Gramps froze with a hand on the gate to Jim's stall. "Kill a man?" He like said it to himself. Then he looked at me over his shoulder, gave a little shake with his head, and said, "Not good." He opened the gate.

I followed him into the stall. "But what if he's bad? You know, really bad?"

"Who's to say a man's all bad? What about the good in him? You kill that too, you know." Gramps closed the gate, turned, and looked me in the eye. "No. Not good... But that doesn't mean it doesn't have to be done."

46

Ah-Lex the King!

There was electricity in the air. It was like we were all plugged in. And it was all because of Ah-lex. He held all the aces, and he knew it. And it made him bigger than life. And he knew that too. And the worse part was, Gramps knew it, Dorothy knew it, we all knew it. Yes, damn it, he was the whole show. And the very worst part of it all was, he was good at it. Being the whole show, being boss. And what did it all was just one thing: the plan. He had a plan. A damn good one. So good, in fact, it was the spark that set us on fire.

So now we were all snacking on a treat of fried bread and singing "Hail to the King!" But wait! I'm getting ahead of myself. I must first tell you of the hopeless state we were in, how bottom of the barrel low we were feeling before wonderful Ah-lex burst in ten feet tall and presented us with a sketch, a superb sketch, a blueprint actually— kind of like the ones my dad spread out on our dining room table. Yes, yes, there it was, the answer to our prayers. And oh yes, before that blessed moment—make no mistake about it—we were back to being zombies again; that is, dead without hope, dead without feeling. Sitting there on the porch without even breathing. So bad, in fact, I was contemplating on saying something wild, something so far out, something outrageous—just to break the ice, mind you, so I said. "What did the cubs do today?" No, no, I didn't say that, but I wanted to. Wanted to say something so crazy it would stand them on their ear. But no, what I finally said—which I said mostly to Dick—

was, "We fixed up Molle and Jim." Not a ripple, not even a burp. I pushed on with the peroxide, etc. and finished with the honey wrap. Nothing! Absolutely nothing. Not a peep.

And then, all of a sudden, I had the sneaky feeling that everybody was faking it, that they were up to something, that they all knew what it was except me. I kicked Dick. He didn't kick back. Uh-huh! A sure sign! They were going to do something drastic to me, something unspeakable, like boil me in oil just for kicks. No! For being with Dorothy! Yeah! That's it! That's it! Dick must've squealed. I broke out in a cold sweat. The silence was driving me crazy! I thought, just maybe, I should suggest they hang me by my thumbs... not upside down by my ba—But wait! Grandma just bolted into the kitchen. Yikes, she's back! Her eyes glazed as she sailed right past me, in her ramrod-straight way, and docked back into her rocking chair. Now I don't know why, but it seems to me old people just don't look right unless they're bent over a little. After all, this straight-as-a-board posture looked great on Uncle Leo, but on Grandma, it looked like she had a rod rammed up her. And that was when Ah-lex strode in with his bullshit idea and his half-assed sketch. Bless him, and bury him. Quick, before he stank up the place.

So anyway, to get back on track, earlier today Ah-lex was building a raft, but now his proclamation was to convert a winter sled into kind of a raft boat and have Jim and Molle pull-swim him across to the cows. And this idea, along with the sketch he presented—drawn in great detail, mind you, on a large piece of cardboard—was why we were all on our knees, bowing, and chanting: "Hail to Caesar-Ah-lex!"

And so we went at it, inspired by Ah-lex's sketch—which I concluded he must have stolen from the devil; no, made a pack with him was what he did, so that one day he was going to burn in hell! Ha! Ha! Ha! Ha! Ha!

TWO LONG, FAT LOGS were to be lashed to the sides of the sled at the crossing site for buoyancy, which would also add depth, so that inner tubes could be secured in the pocket formed underneath the sled floor. And some small scattered blocks were to be added to the surface for gripping purposes. And trailing behind would be two inner tubes with barrels stuck in them: one for tools and the other for first aid stuff. Oh yes, we were ingenious because we were inspired. Inspired by Ah-lex, a man only a mother could love.

During that night—what was left of it—I woke up and had trouble breathing. There was a gurgling sound in my chest as if I was breathing underwater, and I couldn't draw a full breath. It scared the heck out of me. And when I tried to move, a stabbing pain hit me in the left side of my back just below the shoulder blade. That spot had bothered me some the last couple of nights, but I always felt better after I'd been up for a while. But what was with this gurgling sound? Here I am, having a dream that I'm drowning, and when I wake up, I'm drowning! I tried to call out to Dick but ended up coughing a load of gook into my hand. So in spite of being stabbed in the back, I got up, stuck my head out of the window, and coughed my lungs out. Right then and there, I decided I was going to write a letter home and have it ready for when the water went down. But I'd have to be real tricky about it, like my dad.

So first off, I'd tell them about the flood. And that now that the waters down there was really nothing left for me to do, so I might as well come home. And then I'd give them a little hint about my back, say that it was probably just a slight case of polio. And I'd throw in something about my breathing problem, that I was drowning, that my lungs… Well, I'd better leave that part out. The polio bit should be enough. No need to scare the daylights out of them. But hey, it could be polio. Who knew? It was something. Could be leprosy for all I know… Got that stinging spot there below my left shoulder-blade the size of a fist…probably got a hole rotting there… Probably rot right through and my shoulder would fall off. Hey, hey! Enough of that! No need to exaggerate. Only God, please don't let it be leprosy! Maybe I better say another prayer right now, just in case. Yeah.

The Crossing

"Up! Up! Richard! Billy! Get up! It's time!"

I opened an eye. "Vickie?" She was standing in the doorway with a candle. "Get up! Now!"

"It's still dark out!"

"Richard! Get Richard up. We're going to cross." She put the candleholder down on the floor and left.

Dick hadn't moved. I swung my feet to the floor and coughed a few ugly ones. The pain in my back was still there, but it felt a lot better. Am I a fast healer or what?

"Dick! Get up!"

"Uggggg..."

"C'mon, get up! We're crossing!"

While the men put the finishing touches on the sled-raft—which now didn't look like anything that would possibly float—Dick and I went out to check on the two possible places to cross that Gramps outlined in the dirt with a stick. The sky was a gray cloudy mess from one end to the other. From the back of the barn, just over the rise, we were surprised to see that the water had backed off about five yards, but it was still a lake with an angry river running wild in the middle.

The downstream spot Gramps marked was not a good choice. There the lake narrowed, then rushed between two high bluffs, then widened again, and from there ran on straight for the bridge—which wasn't there anymore, of course. Dick said he wouldn't try crossing here even in a rowboat—unless he had a motor, a big one. And what did we have? A raft powered by two horses with a pig-eyed madman aboard who couldn't swim—but would probably float anyway because he was so greasy. I, without a doubt, would've been a much better choice. Skinny Billy didn't float well, but at least he could swim.

So then I told that to Dick, and he said, "So who's goin' to milk the cows?"

He had me, but I fired back instinctively, "Guess who?"

To which he replied, "Stick it up your nose."

Gramps's other choice was way upstream where the creek used to elbow in from the northwest corner of the property, but was now flooded into a huge curving lake that covered the cornfield on our side and pasture land on the other.

"Better here, huh, Dick? What da ya think? Hardly any current."

"Yeaah, I guess… Boy, that's a lot of water to… Cows! Look!" Dick pointed straight across from us. "Two of 'em. See 'em? Up in the woods?"

"Look! In the water by those birch trees!" I pointed upstream a bit. "See 'em?"

"Yeaaah. And back in the woods." Dick started poking his finger at the cows as he counted, "One, two…three, four, five, six, seven… seven…"

"And the one by the water, and the two in the woods," I tacked on. "That's ten!"

"Stay here. I'll go tell 'em."

"I'll go with ya."

"No, stay here! Watch them! In case they move." Dick trotted off.

I went downstream a bit to get a different angle into the woods, but I didn't spot any more, other than that handful. I glanced farther downstream, and suddenly my heart jumped. There was a dark hump sticking out of the water, moving with the current. A cow! Had to be! I was already running along the water's edge when I spotted another hump! Two cows bobbing along! I ran faster, looked farther downstream for more, when all of a sudden, one of the cows rose out of the water a couple of feet then went straight down and disappeared! I cupped my hands over my eyes to see better, when the other cow did the same thing! Up...and gone! Disappeared, both of them in a blink.

Those weren't cows, William. Couldn't have been. I scanned the water up and down, every which way, nothing. What the heck were they? Couldn't have been cows. Not the way they poked up like that. Too big. Way too big. Devils maybe. Devils could poke up like that. A chill shot through me. Tree stumps could—nooo. Not the way they shot up and then down. Straight down, like a bobber when a big fish hits your line. I knelt down, splashed water on my face, and very slowly this time, I scanned the water...nothing.

As I walked back along the water's edge, the clouds in the sky grew brighter. The sun was up, but it was still hiding. In fact, I hadn't seen it since... I counted on my fingers, Monday, Tuesday, Wednesday, Thursday...four days. Seemed longer, seemed like weeks. When I got back upstream, I checked again across the water: still only the one cow in the birch trees by the water, the others scattered up in the woods...and nothing downstream, thank God.

I sat on some driftwood and stared at the water. Dick came to mind. Things weren't the same between us anymore. Not since the silo... Oh, most of the time we were okay, but once in a while, he gave me that strange look, and I knew he was not completely my friend anymore. And that bothered me. The whole thing bothered me. Bothered me bad. I peeked across the water...nothing.

I peeked back at the barn, "Where are those guys?"

One thing's sure: my folks would rather have Richard as a son than me. I mean it. After all, he was big and strong. And healthy. Healthy? Hell, he didn't know what sick was... But he was... Well, he was kind of a deadhead. But actually, that type suited them better. It really did. Now don't get me wrong; Dick's okay. I'm not trying to put him down or anything. He's just not adventuresome was what I mean. But one good thing is, he doesn't let on when he feels bad. He just takes it. That takes guts. And now he's got to stay up here for a whole year with Old Lady Gaaaa-rab. Poor sucker. She was my great-grandmother, and I wouldn't mind if she was my great-great-great-great-grandmother; the farther down, the better.

Actually, I thought the best thing would've been if Richard was my big brother instead of my uncle. After all, it was too late for me to have a real brother anymore. If my folks popped a kid now, by the time he was old enough to play with, I'd be… Hell, I'll probably be in China by then, or the North Pole. Maybe the South Pole with Shackleton! He's… Ahhh, he'd probably be dead by then. Frozen stiff, all his toes cut off… Maybe I'd be in a war, flying an airplane like my genius cousins, Peter and Georgie. Ray was too young. He'd be sixteen Christmas Day. Being born on Christmas, he got short-changed out of presents, but Aunt Minnie told him he was extremely fortunate to be born on the same day as our Lord. And he bought it. I wouldn't—not unless I got extra presents.

Mr. Sun came slanting in, burning through the clouds, instantly hot on my back. I needed that. Needed it for the ache there… I closed my eyes, hung my head, and let him work on me.

If I could actually pick a big brother, I'd pick one of the South-side cousins I just mentioned. The Obryckis were not only big and strong, they were smart. Peter, in fact, was so smart I couldn't even begin to tell you how smart he was; I didn't have enough brains to tell you how smart he was. He was way above genius-smart; in fact, he was so smart that all those big-time schools in the East that were after him didn't know what to do with him. So he was going to Notre Dame; rather he would have, but he joined the Air Force. Dad didn't think that was too smart. I did. Who wanted to go to college when you could fly an airplane? Georgie, the second oldest, was supposed to be a priest, go to a seminary; that was like prison, only worse—like if you think about girls, they tied a weight to your thing to keep it down, but he outsmarted them and joined the Air Force, like Peter. I told you those guys were smart.

On my mom's side, nobody's ever even graduated from high school, but that was because as soon as they hit sixteen, they had to go to work. Uncle Leo, in fact, started when he was fifteen because he was so big. I was going to graduate, of course. So was Richard. I was even thinking of going to college.

Uncle George said, "It beats working."

Yeah, I was really lucky to have such great uncles and cousins. In fact, I hate to say this—I really do—but I actually liked my Uncle Leo and my Uncle George better than my dad. I mean, in a way I did, and I couldn't help it. And I hope that was not a sin, but that was the way it was. I didn't know what else to say about my folks that I hadn't already said. One thing though, they shouldn't have sent me away. I was too young for this crap. And the worst part was, they didn't seem to even care I was going. And unless they sent a boat for me real soon, I was going to… I jumped up and looked back toward the barn.

"Where the heck are those guys? What are they, building, an ark?"

I ran into the water and swam as fast as I could for about twenty yards, then stood up. The water was up to my chest, and the bottom was icky with corn stalks. The cow across the way looked like she was watching me. I waved my arm and gave her a call, "Moooooo-uh!" She didn't move. "Don't worry! We're going to come and get you!" She just stood there. "You can 'Moooo-uh' me, you know." Nothing. "Dumb cow."

I drifted downstream about ten yards over to a bunch of tree branches and found that they weren't rooted there, just hung up on some old fence posts. I was careful grabbing onto one, but I still managed to prick my left knee on some tangled barbed wire.

Damn, that stuff was sharp. I held onto the post, sank down, and opened my eyes… Things floated by, but the water was too cloudy to make them out. A big slimy, hairy, clump of grass rubbed past me—I think it was grass. Devils flashed in my mind's eye. I got outta there pretty quick.

I was lying on some high ground, letting the sun dry me off, when a big black ant galloped past my nose and headed for my feet. He covered the ground fast. I picked him up and put him back over-head. Seconds later, he was already past my knees. Again, I picked him up, but this time I spun my arm around every which way before I placed him back overhead. It didn't fool him one bit; he was back on track and heading home. I bet I could take this little bugger all the way up to Alaska, and he'd know his way back. Wouldn't have to check any road signs or anything. Just *bang*! Headin' home. I got a brain a million times bigger, and I couldn't do that... My dad could. When we traveled, he always knew exactly where we were at. He could turn off on some dinky road to avoid traffic, or something, and *bang*! Hey, you could drop him in Portugal, the Sahara Desert even, and I bet he could—providing he had enough water...and maybe an umbrella, yeah.

The faint sound of drumming hooves grew in my ears. I jumped up. There they were: Molle and Jim coming at me at a slow trot, with Richard at the reins on the sled raft, and Ah-lex and Gramps bringing up the rear.

"Whoa! Whoa!" shouted Richard, pulling on the reins and looking good doing it. "Whooooa!" Molle and Jim stomped to a stop. They were lookin' even better than Richard.

"What took you so long?"

"We had to reinforce the runners... So...the...where's the cows?" Dick ran down to the water. "Where's the cows!"

We ran down to the water's edge. A bolt of heat shot through me. "They were right there." I pointed straight across. "Right there, Dick! Just like when you left!"

"I told you to watch them!"

"I did! They were right there the whole time." Gramps came up. "They were, Gramps. One was down by those birch trees. And nine were scat—"

"Where did they go? I told you to watch them, Billy!"

"All right, all right, boys, that's enough," said Gramps.

"They were there," I snuck in softly. "The whole time."

"Nine, you say?" said Gramps. "That's all you saw."

"Ten altogether. Nine, and one by the water." I pointed and added softly, "They were there."

"Richard!" called Ah-lex, moving upstream.

Dick waved his hand at me in disgust and hustled after Ah-lex. "Where're they going?"

"Ah-lex wants to look over another spot up there." Gramps waved his hand upstream, crossed his arms back on his chest, and gazed out at the water. "Your Grandma thinks some cows might have gone over to Slotkowskis' on the other side of those woods."

"You think they did?"

Gramps shook his head. "I doubt it." Gramps scratched under his chin. "There's good pasture there, but the land's too low…must be flooded."

"But he could've got to them, maybe. And milked them? You think?"

"Could've." Gramps went on scratching. "But not likely. That land flooded early." Shaking his head a bit now, he added, "Noooo. Those cows got trapped good."

"But it's possible, isn't it?"

"Oh, sure. Some could've got there early on. It's possible. Better than possible." We gazed out across the water, our eyes peeled for cows.

"Yo!" It was Dick on the run. "It's better here!"

GRANDMA AND THE GIRLS joined us, and we got the rig ready for the crossing. You could feel the excitement, the electricity between all of us, but there was little talk—actually, little was all that was needed. After we unloaded everything, the two logs were lashed, one to each side, and the two inner tubes were secured in the pocket underneath. The rig was ready to test. And so ready, set, go!

Ah-lex, standing by the side of the rig, cracked the reins and barked, but he was no John Wayne—more like Gaby Hayes. Slowly Molle and Jim pulled the rig into the water.

Weeell, the rig did float, but the deck only stuck out of the water by about two inches. And that was with nobody on it. Worse yet, the thing was about as stable as a seesaw. Ah-lex almost broke his tailbone trying to board it. His feet went up and "smack-o!" He slid off like a dead fish. Richard crawled on, and when he stood up, the rig tilted and sent him sailing into the water too. I was the only one that could ride it. Ho-hum. Grandpa, of course, didn't try.

"If we nail two barrels on it, Grandpa, Dick, and I could sit and—"

"We could nail two boards out to steady it," said Dick, making wings with his arms."

"Yeaaah! Great idea, Dick. Then we—"

Ah-lex started slinging Polish up and back with Gramps. The outcome was to saw an opening in the rig for Ah-lex's legs. Not a bad idea, I have to admit. Also, that left open the possibility that Ah-lex could fall through and sink like a rock. That'd be nice.

Sorry. Lord, sorry, but I can't help it. He's so bad. You know he is. He beats cows, poked pigs with a pitchfork—I saw him! And he hurt Grandpa, you know. And what about Dorothy? He'd hurt her too. You know he would. He's mean. And the kittens. Aghhh, I hate him! I'm sorry, Lord, but... No! I'm not sorry! I'm not sorry! No! Not one bit!

We beached the rig so the hole could be cut. While Gramps and Ah-lex went at it with a keyhole saw, Dick and I padded the leather strap across Molle's cut chest. That done, Molle and Jim pulled the rig back into the shallow water where Vickie and Dorothy tied the two trailing inner tubes, with the inserted barrels of supplies, to the back corners with about six feet of light rope. Lastly, Gramps attached one end of the huge coil of 5/8-inch rope—knotted every ten feet—to an eyebolt in the middle of the backboard. Again, we were ready to sail. Sail across a lake that had no name, so I named it Wild Lake. And our ship, the *Rig-Go*. Grandma led us in a short prayer, and that was it.

"All aboooooard!" I rang out.

"Hold her steady, boys," said Grandpa, as Ah-lex crawled aboard and settled into the cutout.

Grandpa handed Ah-lex a hunting knife in a leather sheath. It wasn't very big. My dad had a bigger one.

"Hee-yaaaw!" yelled Gaby Hayes, cracking the reins.

Molle and Jim splashed into deeper and deeper water, the *Rig-Go* set so low it made Ah-lex appear to be sitting on the water. Except for Grandma, we all waded into the water holding onto the knotted rope that was slowly uncoiling on shore. The *Rig-Go* sailed on smoothly until Molle and Jim stopped, for some reason, about thirty or so yards out distance is hard to judge on water.

"Yaaaw!" Ah-lex growled and snapped the reins.

Molle and Jim moved forward and were instantly in deep water, swimming with their heads sticking out. We let the knotted rope continue to slide through our hands as we stood strung out in the water from about waist-high for Gramps and less for the rest of us. Every second knot had a makeshift ring of cork added to it; some-body had had a good idea. Grandma was at the water's edge now, her stream of Polish filling the air, while the girls jumped up and down with excitement. Everything was going as planned.

Suddenly, the whole *Rig-Go* started sliding sideways, moving downstream. It was expected, of course, but it scared me—all of us, I guess, because the cheering stopped. The *Rig-Go* would have to fight through the current in the middle section, and then the last part would be easy, and they'd be across. Ah-lex was cursing and smacking the water with the reins.

"Keep going! Keep going," I urged under my breath. On shore the rope was uncoiling like an angry snake, feeling hot in my hands… and then it stopped.

"Move to the right!" yelled Gramps. "Pull everybody! Pull!"

We moved to the right with Gramps, trying to string the *Rig-Go* out into a straighter line. At the same time, of course, the rope was also pulling all of us into deeper water.

"Let gooo!" Gramps shouted, and his arms went up in the air. Dick let go, and his arms went up in the air. The rope went slack, so I knew the girls had let go. I didn't, for some reason. I went past Dick…then Gramps…

"Let gooo!" they called out. "Billlllly! Let goooooo!"

I saw the clump of branches that hid the fence post with the barbed wire coming up, and I was afraid to let go and afraid not to. My hands started slipping down the rope. A cork buoy came up and made holding on easier. I kicked out at the post and slid past it by inches.

"Now I can let go. I'm past—"

The rope jerked to a stop. I looked back and saw that the rope was hung up on the clump of branches. Before I could think of what to do, the whole shebang tore loose and came trailing along behind us.

"Can't let go now…got the whole dam fence!"

The rope stopped pulling, went slack. Everything was now moving downstream in a straight line with the current: the horses, the *Rig-Go*, me, and the barbed wire fence at the end. On shore everybody was running and shouting and waving their arms. I had all I could do to stay afloat.

Hand over hand, I pulled myself along the knotted rope. One buoy…then one more and another… I broke the cork of a buoy and stuffed it into my short pants, and it helped keep me afloat, but my hands were numb, and I was losing my grip.

"Ah-lex!" I yelled, but he went on slapping the reins and shouting at Molle and Jim.

I grabbed rope and more rope, but I kept slipping back to the same knot. The now empty shoreline was slowly sliding by. If I let go and swim hard, the wire should miss me. Take a deep breath… Again. Ready, set. WAIT!

They're turning… How… They're turning around! They're hung up! Oh my god! Jim is trying to climb on top of Molle… Where's Ah-lex?

"Ahhh-leeeex!" I'm getting closer. That's a tree! It's tipped over… "Ah-leeex!" I'm going to go passsssss. Go! I let go the rope and swam all out, kicking and paddling, for all I was worth. I missed the *Rig-Go* but caught the dangling left inner tube. The barrel in it was gone, and it was going flat. I took in the short rope up to the *Rig-Go* and climbed aboard.

"Aaghhhhh," I screamed, shrieked, yelled—whatever you want to call it.

Ah-lex's bloody head was sticking out of the water, staring at me. He was tangled in the reins and tangled in the black circle of roots of the upturned tree.

"Ah-lex! Ah-lex, can you hear me?" Nothing. "Say something! Blink! Blink if you can hear me! Ah-lex!" I wanted to get away from him, but his eyes were open and so alive. "Ah-lex," I pleaded. "Pleeeeease say somethiiiing."

The *Rig-Go* tilted forward and sank a notch. Jim was struggling to keep his head from going under, a ghostly shadow of Molle under him. Ah-lex's head and shoulders, somehow, now cleared the water, his left arm loose, and dangling. The rest of him seemed to be even more tangled up in the reins and the roots of the tipped over tree. I was surprised—and then again, I wasn't surprised—at how calm and alert I was throughout this nightmare. It had happened before: the bus skidding... I was calm, braced myself...sliding sideways...the smell of rubber...tipping over...bumping, bumping...the crash, the crunch, screeching metal. Others were in shock, and helpless, but I wasn't. I eyed the bobbing inner tube off the right corner, the barrel gone. Ah-lex's eyes were locked on me.

"Ah-lex? Ah-lex, you're dead!" I smiled. He didn't.

The *Rig-go* tilted and sank some more. I lunged for the empty tube, hooked it, and popped my head and arms through it. The big black circle of the uprooted tree blocked my view of the shoreline. The sinking *Rig-Go* was sure to pull my tube down if I didn't untie it. I tried, but my hands were stiff and useless. The other end was tied to the *Rig-Go* right under Ah-lex's nose. Even if I could untie it, I'd probably drift back and pop the tube on the barbed wire. The fence has got to be dangling out there, waiting for me. I drop my head on the tube and pray.

"Lord, I don't wanna die. Please, Lord... This can't be the end. Can it? Listen Lord, I'll do anything! Just name it. Name it, Lord! Anything!"

"Billllllly," floated a voice from somewhere.

I raised my head. "Ah-lex? Ah-lex, is that you?" I shaded my eyes with my hands because the sunlight glaring off the water was blinding me. Something was flashing in the water under Ah-lex's nose. I gripped the rope, pulled...grabbed the corner of the deck with my left hand and zinggo! There's a sharp pain in my hand, and there was a knife sticking in it! In my hand! My hand was pinned to the deck with a knife? I couldn't move it! I couldn't move it! I went nuts! You know, fists, feet, teeth, nails the way I did when Dick was suffocating me with a pillow... Blood...blood all over... In the water I was floating away in the inner tube.

Swirling water boiled and churned all around me. Barbed wire burned my right thigh, nicked my right ankle. I pulled up my legs... The current got stronger, meaner...pulling me, pushing me, twirling me, jerking me up and down. Monsters, demons, devils trying to gobble me up. Pulling me doooooown! I popped up coughing and sputtering. Monsters were eating me up... Eating...chewing me up...

God was punishing me... Punishing me for being baaaaaad. Baaad, baaad Billllllllllllly...

48

The Rescue

I was out of it for two days. All I remembered was smelling vinegar, smelling Sloans, my left hand hurting, sweating, burning up, and more sweating, and in between it all seeing pictures on the wall: water swallowing me up, Jim trying to trample me under, Molle swimming like a turtle, Ah-lex's bloody head gliding around on ice skates, his eyes rolling in his head like a slot machine, spears shooting out of them and pinning me to the wall.

I woke up screaming and mistook the sweat rolling down my face for blood. And then we had the second feature: sunlight flashing under Al-lex's nose, the throbbing pain in my left hand, bouncing along with the current, swallowing water, coughing, monsters snapping at my legs, devils poking me with pitchforks, the current strong now…sucking me down… I was choking. I woke up. I caught my breath. I passed out.

And then one night I woke up on the living room couch, and I was cold and scared. The hissing lamp on the cocktail table gave the big room an eerie glow… I spotted the brass-handled doors. Grandma Helen was standing there, smiling at me. I wasn't afraid anymore… I fell asleep, and I didn't see Ah-lex, and I didn't see the devils, and I didn't feel the monsters.

DAYBREAK AND VICKIE APPEARED. I pretended I was asleep. She wiped my face with a wet vinegar-smelling cloth and asked how I felt. My left hand was killing me, but I didn't want to talk, didn't want to open my eyes, so I just coughed and nodded my head. She pushed the hair out of my eyes, patted me on the shoulder, and left. I watched her walk away... It was a good thing my left hand was hurt and not my right. I'm so disgusting.

A LITTLE WHILE LATER, I heard a lot of movement in the kitchen and a buzz of talk. Then approaching footsteps, and it was Dorothy, bringing me a steaming hot cup of coffee. I had questions—especially about Ah-lex—but I didn't really want to know the answers. So I just sipped coffee and "purrrrrrred," like Lilly, and she slobbered all over me. When I asked her if my folks were coming up, she said she didn't know, to ask Dick. Then she said everybody thought I was really going to die. I tell her I did, that I saw monsters and devils. She gave me the, "God this and God that" bit! And then she asked about Ah-lex. I shrugged, shook my head, and bit my lip. Her eyes turn red, and she runs off. I felt rotten.

DICK CAME IN a short time later with a bowl of oatmeal. He asked if I was still sick. My hand throbbed, my throat hurt, and my back burned. Also, my brain was tied in a knot. I told him I felt terrific, never better. He said I looked worse than when they found me—which was on the Kalinowski farm, which was way past the washed-out bridge. That was actually a place nobody ever set foot on because they had a bunch of shotgun-happy kids and three crazy dogs that would track you down and eat you alive. Dick went on to say that Gramps pumped me the same way the lifeguards did the kids at the pool at Riis Park. And that they thought I was dead until I started coughing and mumbling about devils. I told him hundreds of 'em were trying to pull me into hell. I told him everything, except I never mentioned Ah-lex. And then he said Aunt Sophie was going to call my folks, that they were out of town. And then he asked if I was going to eat my oatmeal. When I shook my head, he went at it like he always did, like he was starved.

"My folks are out of town? Where?"

Dick shrugged. "Gramps talked to the sheriff this morning. They came by in a boat."

"A boat?"

"Yeah. Everything's flooded. We still got a lake out there." Dick went on shoveling and swallowing "You done with that coffee?"

I passed my half-full coffee cup to Dick. "What happened to the cows? Did we get 'em?"

"Umm, fifffteen…ann wan calf," bubbled out of Dick's mouth. He swiped at the leakage with the back of his hand, "Com' bac' by 'emseeelves."

"Fifteen? What about the rest?"

Dick shrugged. I tried to think of a way to ask about Ah-lex, when Dick popped. "How come you don't ask about Ah-lex? You asked about the cows."

"So what about 'im?"

"Can't find him." Dick spooned in the last of the oatmeal and put the bowl on the table.

"Can't find him?" That was a shock. I thought they would have found him hung up.

"We found Jim." Dick hooked an arm over the back of his chair. "One eye was poked out. Grandpa shot him. He was all busted up. We didn't find Molle."

"She's dead."

"How do you know?"

"She was under Jim. He was climbing on top of her the whole time."

Dick leaned the chair back on two legs. "How come Ah-lex didn't get in the tube? You got in the tube."

"I don't know… He couldn't swim, right?"

Dick flopped the chair back down. "You want anything?" He stood up.

I thought of what Uncle George might say: "Get me a piece." But all I said was. "No."

Dick left. My head was pounding. I put a pillow over it and squeezed hard.

I SLEPT ON AND OFF the rest of the day. I didn't dream anymore, but every time I woke up, I thought about Ah-lex...saw those eyes staring at me. Grandma had a go at me with her cure-all: Sloan's Liniment and spiked tea, but it didn't do much good. The liniment set my nicks on fire, and the tea made me sick to my stomach. She gave me a little sock on the chin before she left, I had to open and close my mouth about a half dozen times before it would work right.

GRANDPA CAME IN after supper. He didn't ask how I was, just sat down and rolled one of his beauts. When I asked him how long it took before he could make them like that, so perfect, he said, "Oh, I guess I had the knack for it early on." He zipped a match along his thigh, lit up, then leaned his crossed arms on his crossed legs, and added, "Had a knack for shooting too." His eyes twinkled.

"So does my dad." I told him how my dad could shoot the number 8 out with three shots at the carnival, and how after he did it a couple of times, they wouldn't let him shoot anymore.

Grandpa chuckled and flicked ashes into the palm of his hand. "What's your knack?"

"Me? I don't know. Trouble, I guess. My buddies always say that their moms don't want them to hang around with me because they always come home all dirty and banged up."

Grandpa laughed. "Well, I'd say that's because you're adventuresome."

"Adventuresome." I liked the sound of the word. "You really think I am? Adventuresome?"

Grandpa flicked more ashes into his cupped hand. "I'd say you were. But I guess you had enough swimming for a while." He dragged on his cigarette but kept his eyes on me.

A hot flash shot through me. "I couldn't let go the rope... And then it was too late. I thought the barbed wire might get me."

Grandpa sat there, arms crossed, barely nodding, but nodding. "You did the right thing."

I dropped my head. Glancing up, I saw that Gramps was gazing out the front window. "He's dead, Grandpa." I told him all about it. About Ah-lex's bloody head...his arm tangled in the reins and in the tree...him staring at me with his dead eyes...how I kept calling to him, over and over. "He's dead."

"Ummm." Gramps ground the glowing dot of his cigarette into his cupped hand. "Then you untied the tube and went with the current."

"Yeeeah... No! I dunno! I dunno, Grandpa." My head kept shaking. "I couldn't untie it. My hands were too numb." I gasped, and air filled my lungs. "I pulled myself back to the *Rig-Go*...and then a knife was sticking in my hand! And...and I went nuts! Like I do, sometimes. But I always know what. But I didn't... And then... and then there's blood...and the water's all bloody... And the next thing... I was floating in the tube...floating away..."

Grandpa's eyes were locked on me.

"He's dead, Grandpa... He's dead... He is, Grandpa! He's dead!"

"Easy, William! Easy! It's all right!

"He kept staring at me. 'Ah-lex! Ah-lex!' I kept calling out. I did. But he didn't answer. He didn't answer!"

"William!" Grandpa put a hand around my neck and shook me. "It's all right! It's all right... Now listen to me! Listen... Whatever happened, happened. You can't change it. You understand?"

I looked into his eyes.

"It's done, boy. It's over. It's done and buried. You hear? Now you have to put one foot in front of the other and go on. That's all there is now..." He took his hand away from my neck and patted me on the shoulder. "Remember this: there's a big difference between wanting to do something and actually doing it. It's night-and-day difference. Understand?"

I gave him a nod and said, "Okay."

Gramps stood up, walked away, and took his ashes with him.

But it wasn't all that different. I wanted a man dead, and he was dead. I made plans, everything. I couldn't just put one foot in front of the other and forget about it. God wasn't going to forget about it, uh-uh. No. Couldn't forget about it. Couldn't forget about Ah-lex. He wouldn't let me.

I WOKE UP DURING THE NIGHT, and I knew what I had to do. I took the hissing lamp over to the brass-handled doors, set it down, gripped the handles...and I froze.

"What if they won't talk to me? What if they're not there? What if I imagined it all? Stop it, William. Of course they're there. Sure as shootin'... You know they are... But what if they're not?"

My hands dropped. I stared at the handles...handles so shiny and bright.

I WASN'T GETTING ANY BETTER, feeling worse, in fact. The fever was back, off and on, and everything hurt: my ribs, my back, my throat, you name it. I was a mess. But there was no way I thought I was going to die. Although they must have thought so, because the rumor had it I was going to be shipped home like in a box, COD. But no, not really, the word was Aunt Polly was going to pick me up. I didn't know why she, of all people, would be picking me up, but it didn't really matter. Anyway, I didn't want to get my hopes up too high. After all, the whole thing was just a rumor. But just in case, I became a praying machine. Praying for this and that, on the drop of a hat.

Oh, I suppose I should mention that I've also stopped talking. It seemed to me that the best way to stop feeling anything was to stop talking altogether. You just kind of erased yourself. It was not easy to do at first, but like Gramps said, "You do a thing often enough you get good at it." Actually, I didn't think anyone wanted to talk to me anyway. Sooo, I simply started to erase myself. I rubbed me out, you might say. Just rubbed away the lines and the curves until there was nothing left.

They, of course, thought I stopped talking because my throat was too sore. Then they thought it was because I was in shock. That I couldn't hear, couldn't see, couldn't think. Well, naturally, they were wrong. I just wanted to stop feeling, like I said. Besides, it seemed to me that talking was highly overrated. You could talk until you drop; it wouldn't chase the blues away.

To stop thinking, on the other hand, was much harder to do. Not easy, for sure, but I worked at it. After all, no system is perfect.

49

Aunt Polly and Archie

The following day, I think it was the next day—whatever day it was—Aunt Polly came by to pick me up in her big yellow Packard. She came by way of Minneapolis, Minnesota, where she was visiting family—was the way it was put—but the truth was she was visiting her husband who was in jail there, like for life, but nobody ever talked about that, naturally.

Aunt Polly came from the mysterious side of the South-side family, the nutty side, you might say, because she had this idiot thirty-seven-year-old son, Archie, who had the brain of a four-year-old—a very dumb four-year-old. Aunt Polly had carrot-colored straight hair, loads of it. It grew like a weeping willow and would have covered her up completely, head to toe, if she hadn't kept it cut straight across at the shoulders and across the forehead in front, giving her a nice square opening around her face. Archie was also a carrot head, only his was as wavy as the sea, with the sides shaved all the way up, so that it didn't help his face any, being that it was all squished into the middle, which left a lot of room around the edges for pimples, which grew there very nicely, in fact—in nice ripe bunches, ready to be picked.

I didn't really know Aunt Polly. I was pretty sure she wasn't my real aunt, because everybody called her Aunt Polly. I really only saw her a couple of times a year, and that was at Aunt Minnie's and always with Archie, of course, and her parrot. A big green thing, with a multicolored head and a big—and I mean *big*—hooked nose. Aunt Polly could make him say, "Polly wants a cracker," which made everybody chuckle, but she'd keep it up and keep it up, so that pretty soon, everybody wondered what that bird would look like in the oven at about 360 degrees.

Be that as it may—an old English expression, no doubt—the bird's four-word vocabulary was bigger than Archie's. All poor Archie could say was, "Ar-Ar-Ar-Archie, O-o-o-o-okay."

Archie stuttered, you see. Archie also had a big head compared to his body and itty-bitty hands. Poor Archie. I always felt sorry for him, but I had to confess, I wondered if he just might be better off dead. Now I know that sounds terrible, but really, the poor guy was just an empty head with a bunch of carrot-colored waves on top... plus pimples. I don't know. It was really sad.

NOBODY SAID GOODBYE TO ME. Not really, not at the end. Except there was a shot of Polish in the air from Grandma, so the odds were it was for me. And then Richard tagged on that I broke my promise, that I was supposed to stay with him, and that my folks didn't want me. And then he shook my hand and made noodles out of my fingers. And then he helped Grandpa put me on the floor of the Packard's back seat on some brown cardboard. Then Grandpa put a beat-up blanket under my head and patted my shoulder and gave me a little smile...or was it a frown? It was hard to tell when you were looking at somebody upside-down. Nobody else did anything or said anything—you know who I mean—they just stared at the two idiots in the back of the car until the door slammed.

Actually, it shouldn't have bothered me all that much, but it did. And this skinny, coughing, germ-infested lump lying on the floor of the Packard shouldn't have bothered me much, but it did. And I shouldn't have cared about not seeing Dorothy or Richard or Gramps anymore, but I did. And I knew it was bothering me quite a bit because I was crying. But I also knew what I had to do about it. Just had to do more rubbing, really put the elbow to it, get it all out and gone, yeah. Just needed more work—erase, erase, rubba-dub-

dub. Booooy, I bet they thought I was going to beg to stay on their stinking farm. Ha! Ha! Ha! That'll be the day.

ARCHIE KEPT KICKING ME. Stomping me, actually. He'd drum his feet on me real fast, then scoot over into his corner. It didn't hurt much, so I let him have his fun. After a while though, I started to feel like mashed potatoes, so I kicked back at him. Stupid Archie loved it! I guess he thought it was a game. So finally, I gave this nutcase a good one on the shins, and what did he do? He started stomping me with his heels for all he was worth. So then, real quick-like, I sat up and bopped him one on the nose—not hard, but it caught him right on the button. Poor Archie threw his little hands up over his nose and didn't make a peep, not a sniffle. Boy, did I feel rotten. I wanted to tell him I was sorry, that I didn't mean to hit him so hard, but I didn't. But I wanted to. But I guess he wouldn't have understood any-way—him being an idiot. So then I made a big show of punishing myself by biting my fist. Idiot Archie did the same; only he howled like a wolf after he bit down.

"Archie!" Aunt Polly slammed on the breaks, knocking our speeding bullet down to 25. Archie's howling stopped on a dime. "Archie? Archie, okay?"

Archie was back to his hands over his nose.

"Archie, answer me," she said, the back of her head moving, searching for him in the rearview mirror. "Archie?" Aunt Polly hooked a big arm over the seat, turned around, and the next thing you know, we were bouncing along on the shoulder.

"Aaaaaaaaaaaaaaaaaagh!" rang an inhuman note. It was Archie, screeching like a wounded animal, the sound terrifying.

Certain we were headed over a cliff, I braced for the fall, but the big Packard swerved a little, tilted a little, skidded a little, and stopped.

Archie's inhuman note never stopped. It rang out high and clear. Aunt Polly's door popped open. Moments later Archie's door flew open, and Archie sprang screeching into Aunt Polly's arms, where she rocked and baby-talked to four-foot Archie-baby, and pretty soon the screaming changed to gurgling, giggling, and finally cooing. It was real creepy seeing them act like that—his mother holding him, rocking him, talking to him like he wasn't even a little fart, just an itty-bitty tiny baby. Ugh! Creepy-creepy.

"Oh? There's blood on my Archie's nose." Aunt Polly dabbed at squish-face with her hankie-covered finger. "Ohhh, my poor Archie. Tch-tch-tch." She spit-shined Archie's puss with her hankie "William! How did this happen?" The baby-talk now out the window. "William, answer me."

I stared at her, trying to think of some words, but I was out of practice.

"You didn't hit Archie, did you? Tell the truth, William. What happened?" She started going at me nonstop: "Yak, yak, yak," just the way the nuns did before the roof fell in on you, which could be anything from a half a dozen cracks on your butt with the pointer rod, to some rapid-fire face slapping—plus, usually, kneeling at your desk for a couple of hours while writing some dumb sentence over and over a hundred times. Like the one I had to do just before school let out: "I'm sorry I sat by Joan Mindykoska during the movie." (She was the one with bumps on her chest.)

"Answer me, William." I started to slide back down to my cardboard stove. "William! Sit up this minute. I'm talking to you."

I sat up. Aunt Polly was now into the Gestapo routine and about to bust a blood vessel, going on about respecting my elders. Well, that certainly didn't apply to me. I respected my elders. I just didn't respect them as much as I used to.

Aunt Polly was now turning a pretty color purple and foaming at the mouth. I wouldn't have been able to get a word in even if I wanted to, and I didn't want to, because I was passing out, sliding down and down, until I was flat on my back on my hot cardboard bed again. Aunt Polly must've gotten her second wind because she sounded stronger than ever.

So there I was frying on the cardboard like hamburger on a grill, and also baking on my topside from the sun pouring in through the open window—not to mention that all the holes in my head were plugged up with gook so that I could hardly breathe. And as if all that wasn't bad enough, my stomach started doing that thing it did before it came flying out of my mouth, which in legal terms is referred to as *throwing up*.

All of a sudden, the car door slammed shut, and Archie and Aunt Polly were gone. I blew the gook outta my nose into my hankie and smeared some on the cardboard under the folded blanket that was my pillow. I took some deep breaths, but the air was so stinkin' hot it only made me dizzy.

The front car door opened on the passenger side, and I heard Archie scramble in and the door slam shut. Then the driver's side opened, and Aunt Polly climbed in.

"Archie okaaaay?" said Aunt Polly, slamming the door shut.

"A-A-A-A-A-Archie, o-o-o-okay." Guess who.

The motor started, and a moment later the car bumped back onto the highway. I climbed up and lay on the seat. The breeze started to flow in through the open windows as we picked up speed. It felt so good I almost felt alive again.

I woke up to the perfumed smell of gasoline and realized we were parked by a gas station. It was broiling hot, but I just couldn't find it in me to move a finger; that is, not until I heard the scraping sound of devils trying to claw their way in. So biting my lower lip to fight the pain in my back, I sat up. Archie was outside on the hood scrubbing the windshield—about an inch at a time. I opened the car door, leaned out, and blew the yellowest, greenest, gooiest stuff you ever did not want to see come out of a nose. However, the gasoline now smelled better than ever. I took some deep breaths, and my head cleared up some.

"Archieeeee," Aunt Polly's voice carried from a picnic table under a tree.

Archie slid off the hood and zigzagged over to her like a chicken with its head chopped off.

"Willlliiiam, come eat!" Aunt Polly wound her arm at me to join them.

I waved her off and drew my head back in like a turtle. Food, I didn't want. Burning sun, I didn't want. What I wanted, what I needed was for this torture to end, for my head and body to stop itching, and to breathe again without pain, or else I might as well drown myself in some cool water.

What am I saying?

A tapping on my door made me jump. Archie stuck his arm in through the window and held an opened bottle of smoking-cold Coke under my nose. I grabbed the dripping ice-cold bottle, put it to my lips, and gulped.

"Hmmmmm." Nothing would ever taste this good again—not if I lived to be a hundred. I swigged some more. Totally delicious! Better than the bad thing—and that was hard to beat...

"Why can't they find his body?" my mind screamed at me. "Why?" I found it every time I fell asleep, right there in front of me, staring at me. "Stop looking at me!" I yelled. But it didn't do any good. He wouldn't go away.

I woke up. I was stretched out on the back seat, a cool delicious breeze washed over me as we moved along; the sun was almost down. I figured Archie to be curled up on the front seat, Aunt Polly not trusting me anymore, probably afraid I'd bloody him up some more. Geez, I should've slugged him earlier. I wouldn't have roasted on the floor all day.

Wonder what'd happen when I got home, coming in on a slab the way I was? Probably get the black bag. (Okay, so it was red.) I could have a brain disease, and right away I'd get the black bag. Of course, I admit, I did feel better after it. 'Course who wouldn't, after they stick that poker up your ah-ah and blow you up like a balloon, then have the nerve to tell you to hold it while they figured out how to count to twenty. Not to mention, of course, how embarrassing it was to display your ass to the heavens. My mom said she kept her eyes closed, but I was pretty sure she cheated. Ugh, the whole thing was disgusting—absolutely, totally, disgusting... What happened after that, I didn't want to even think about. I was always letting them down. Better to have it end, right here and now. Over and out. End of the line. Six feet down and covered with dirt. Let the worms eat me. God, what a way to go. I had such plans. The whole world to see...oceans to swim, mountains to climb...

Just before dark, Aunt Polly pulled the Packard off the road, parked us under some big trees, and announced that it was time to get some sleep. She told me to get back on the floor, then ushered Archie onto the back seat. By the time I got settled in, Aunt Polly was already snoring. Archie also seemed dead to the world, probably in some dreamland where idiots go, or maybe someplace where four-year-olds could be kings. Wherever he was at, I hoped it was a nice place, a place where he could be happy. Me? I deserved to boil on the floor, and did, but I cheated by cracking the door open. Of course, that made it easy for the buzzing-hungry mosquitoes… So what the heck, I fed 'em a bony arm.

We were rolling before sunup. The air flowing in through the windows was cool enough to raise goose bumps and worth a king's fortune. Archie was still curled up on the seat. I didn't want to move either, just wanted the cool, crisp air to breathe on me till the end of my days.

The sun started peeking in through my window. The radio went on and for once was picking up more than static: a little music and a lot of talk. The guy on the radio was saying that we were in for another hot day. That was enough for me, I tuned out. A good while later we slowed down, which probably meant we were coming to another town. The radio guy was now talking about the war. He stated that General MacArthur had said, "I shall return." Heck, I didn't even know he'd left. This was the first news I'd heard since the relatives left. Geez, that meant altogether I'd only been gone about seven weeks… Wonder how guys in the war did it? They did years. And some came back without arms or legs…or in a box. And I was coming back with one mosquito-eaten arm and a bloody nose.

"Archie? Archie, up, up! Up, William! We're coming into Janesville!" Aunt Polly's voice was filled with happy notes. "Up, boys! Up, up! Time for breakfast!" I struggled to a sitting position on the floor.

Archie was already sitting up in the corner, eyes blank, hands folded in his lap. He looked like a stuffed doll. I wiggled some fingers at him, but he didn't even burp.

"Archie, okaaaay?" sing songed, Aunt Polly.

"Ar-Ar-Archie, o-o-o-okay...okay." It took him so long it hurt to hear it.

"Good boy, Archie," said Aunt Polly, dropping the car to a crawl. "William, okaaay?"

I wasn't okay, so no answer was my answer.

She asked me again and then gave up on it. Next thing, she wheeled us into a Texaco gas station. She got the attendant, an old man—with white hair sticking up like a porcupine—to hose in the gas. I cracked the door to let the gas smell in. Aunt Polly got Archie out and told me that after I got cleaned up, I should meet them at the café across the street for a good hot breakfast.

Food? Hot or cold, boiled or fried, laced with diamonds and pearls...need I say more. But I did want to get cleaned up. I didn't want to go home looking...well, like I looked. I sat up on the back seat. The numbers spun, and the gallons pinged from the gas pump. Slowly, I leaned sideways then flopped back down on the seat.

The car door opened. "Up, William, up! Come on, Wil—You're bleeding! William, what's wrong? Here," she said, handing me her hankie and running off.

Archie was standing there with his finger in his ear, rocking from side to side, sneaking glances at me.

Aunt Polly came back with the old guy, and they got me out of the car, laid me on the grass, and got me cleaned up with a couple of red work rags and some water from a pail. Boy, she sure knew how to make a big thing out of a little blood, even though it was coming out of all the holes in my head. But it didn't hurt, felt good in a way. I stared at Archie, rooted there the whole time, digging his fingers into his ears. Maybe he was thinking I was wounded in the war. Could be. Hey, who knew what a nut might be thinking. Me? I was just trying not to think, not about anything. Not about Ah-lex, especially. Fat chance... Stupid idea sending me up to the farm. They should've known better. They knew I was not Superman. I was not even a small Robin. Why did they do it? What did I do that was so bad? I was just adventuresome. Like Gramps said... Ahhhh, who am I kidding? I'm bad.

"Is that better, dear?"

Nobody ever called me *dear* before. I gave Aunt Polly a big smile, but with tissue up my nose, and in my ears and all, I'm not sure she caught it.

50

The South-Side Detour

All my life when I woke up, I was at home. But not laaately. Lately, I wake up and I was on a train, up on a farm, on a couch, or in a bed plastered to a naked broad holding my—what, you forgot?—and now, this time, I was in a hospital with a plastic tent over half my body, and it scared the heck out of me. I figured I must be so contagious they didn't even want to touch me; or maybe they were piping in cyanide gas so they could send me home in a box. So I screamed bloody murder, and they told me it's oxygen to help me breathe better. So I should trust them? After that tonsil operation I had when I was six? Which, don't worry, I'm not going to go into. I don't want to disturb your sleep. Anyway, figuring they might switch to gas if I give them a hard time, I lay there like I'm dead—which wasn't very hard to do.

And then I started to recall the blur that got me here: the car speeding, horns blaring, people shouting, trucks rumbling, streetcars screeching, the smell of exhaust fumes, all that big-city stuff, and then, Aunt Minnie's upside-down face peeking at me through the window—which struck me as odd—and why was the big house on Hamlin Street behind her, why wasn't that my house out there? And so, just as I was about to panic, my genius brain kicked in and informed me that since Aunt Polly was never at my house; she didn't know the way. Tralaaaaa! And sooooo, my folks would come and get me later. Of course! Right after supper! Wow! Thank you, Lord! Thank you! You're the best!

But I didn't go home. I didn't even get out of the car. Aunt Minnie climbed aboard, and with Archie in the middle, off we went at about a hundred miles an hour. And the whole time, nobody said a word to me; it was all Polish-Polish. And then when we wheeled past a sign that read "Saint Mary's Hospital," my blood ran cold: I was dying! All this rush-rush could only mean one thing: I was dying, and my folks were here with the priest waiting to administer the last sacrament. And then I'd be dead-o, and right away they'd bury me because I was contagious. I'd never even see home again, or Queenie, or my friends. And then I started praying to God like I never prayed before.

"Oh, God," I said, "please, don't let me die. If you let me live, I'll go to church every day for the rest of my life, I promise. Oh please, God, don't let me die!" And then the coup de grâce, I added, "And I won't do the 'bad thing' anymore—until I get well—if that's okay."

And he answered! God did. He said, "You're not going to die, dummy. You're not going to get off that easy."

And I thanked him! Dummy me, I thanked him! And then, they wheeled me in and tore off all my clothes. I guess I looked like something the cat dragged in, the way they went at me. They used every piece of chrome they could get their hands on. Should a knife and fork appear, I was ready to yell, "Stop! If you eat me, you will die of itching, inside and out!" And I would also add, "A horrible way to go, I guarantee you!"

And it was about then that I thought I might be losing it. My marbles, that is. That my genius brain might be getting scrambled from my sickness. That pretty soon, Archie and I would be best of friends. We'd probably even start some sort of club: Sawdust Heads, maybe. For membership you'd have to learn to say four words: "Polly wants a cracker!" And if you said them without stuttering, you'd get a red star stamped on your forehead. So okay, I might be going off the deep end a bit. But! As my Uncle George used to say, "Most doctors don't know their ass from a hole in the ground." Which, if you think about it, is pretty ridiculous but it sounds good.

The one good thing I had going for me was that Aunt Minnie was there. If there was anybody you want in a hospital with you, it was somebody like my Aunt Minnie, because she was going to be a saint when she died; everybody knew that. Her husband, Fred, of course, was going straight to hell; everybody knew that too. So there she stood, Aunt Minnie, at the foot of my bed, watching the whole show like a hawk and praying. And you knew that was worth a whole bunch of points because when Aunt Minnie prayed, God always listened; everybody knew that too.

So after everybody had their fun poking their chrome in places you wouldn't believe, ramming sticks up my nose, painting my throat, and squeezing eye drops into my eyes, they put me back in that bed with the tent, so that now all I had to worry about was the gas thing. But actually that was pretty dumb, because now that I was all perfumed and sterilized and had Aunt Minnie buzzing through the rosary beads, I was a sure bet to see tomorrow, tomorrow, etc.

So now all I had to do was wait for my folks to arrive. Then I could relax and go to sleep. But the big thing was, I still didn't know what to do about them... Oh, deep down I had an idea, but I was afraid to face up to it. Afraid it would hurt too much. Anyway, I just hoped they got here before I fell asleep. I mean, they better. They just better.

Boy, my head was killin' me. So was my back. Funny thing was, now that I could breathe, my back hurt more than ever, hurt every breath. Boy, I was a mess. I didn't even think about the "bad thing" anymore. And when that happened, you knew things are really bad—and I think I'd said that before, that was how bad off. I'm sorry.

I opened my eyes, and I was underwater. I was holding onto a rope, and I was swallowing water, and I couldn't breathe... And Ah-lex's bloody face came floating by, and he was reaching out for me, and I was kicking him away, and he was grabbing my feet, and I was screaming, but there was no sound because I was underwater... I couldn't breathe anymore... I was drowning. DROWNING!

I woke up! I was all wet, and it was dark outside, and I was trapped...trapped in some kind of tent! I started kicking and all at once I remembered where I was...hospital... I was burning up...

cooking…cooking good, like I was on the floor in the car… The bed across from me…somebody in it…in a tent like mine…machines all around it…like my machines… No one else around… Dead quiet… tears…bitter tears… They never came. They never came!

51

I Don't Need Detroit

The folks were in Detroit. That was what Aunt Minnie told me the next day. They were there on business, she said, and she quickly changed the subject.

"Why did my mother go?" I wondered. "Why wasn't she at work?" I was wondering about a lot of things. So much so that I was going to start talking again, asking questions, but the nurses came in.

They were really getting me teed off. Always bothering me. I couldn't even get any sleep. How was I supposed to get well? I swear, they had this master plan that as soon as you dropped off, they were all over you. If they weren't feeding you pills or sticking you with needles, they were washing you, combing you, fixing your bed, or taking your temperature—which they did both ways, mind you. And these were nuns—don't forget; they wore the headgear and all, but the colors were much better, light blue and white. But really, there ought to be a law against that temperature business. Who the heck cared what it read down below? I mean, what's the difference if your ass is freezing or boiling? A lot of goofy stuff going on around here. Believe me. Take that old man who was groaning and moaning in the bed across from me, he was gone! They came in, drew the curtains, and then not a peep—just clean sheets. Yep, just like my Uncle Leo always said about hospitals: "You go in, you come out in a box." So no matter how much my back hurts when I breathe, I didn't make a peep. And I still didn't talk, of course. Didn't really need to. And I did most of my coughing under the covers, where I also spit all my gluey mucus into a tissue. Actually, I was pretty damn sick. I had pleurisy, not pneumonia, like everyone thought, and no doubt some kind of allergy—which was what Aunt Minnie told them right off the bat, the allergy thing—but nobody seemed to be doing anything about it, except they did give me a lot of tissue paper.

Pleurisy, they tell me, was the envelope surrounding your lungs. Mine was leaking like a sieve, so I expected they were going to put in a new one—which I was not looking forward to at all.

AUNT MINNIE WAS AROUND A LOT. About half the time I opened my eyes, she was there. She really was a saint. Aunt Polly's there pretty much too. So was Archie. He brought me flowers, put them on my lap, and stuck a finger in his ear. It made me swallow hard every time. Actually, it was Aunt Polly that first mentioned that my folks were in Detroit. Aunt Minnie nailed her with a look when she said that. Then she told me she was going to call them and talk to them after supper.

"You do that," I said to myself, "'cause I was not. Never! No way! Detroit! What the heck are they doing in Detroit! Business? Detroit, shit!"

THE FOLKS BECAME A DEAD ISSUE. They weren't coming back until the end of the week. Aunt Minnie told me just this evening that Aunt Sophie told her on the telephone that my dad got an interview with an automotive supplier, so they might have to stay an extra day or two.

But here was the thing: they said they couldn't do anything for me anyway since I was still in the hospital.

Couldn't do anything for me? Are they kidding? Didn't they know that all I wanted was to see them coming through that door? Standing by my bed? Have my mom push my hair back, hold my hand. See my dad's worried face? Give him a little nod, crack a little smile, so he'd know I was going to be okay? Didn't they know that much? Didn't they need that? I needed that. I needed it bad. What was wrong with them? What kind of parents were they, they don't know that much. They shouldn't have had me, they don't know that much. They shouldn't be allowed to hurt me like this. I feel so bad right now, I can't tell you. It's like everything inside of me is hurting. And the tears are bloody and they're burning me. And it hurts. Hurts so much, I can hardly stand it. Honest it does. It hurts too much…

52

Bad News from Detroit

I got here Friday. That was... I counted on my fingers: Saturday, Sunday, Monday, Tuesday. That's four days. That's when they took me out of the oxygen tent, put me on a gurney, and wheeled me out of intensive care. Yeah, yeah, I was learning a lot of new words even though I was still not talking. In fact, I didn't think God wanted me to talk—maybe never again. Anyway, I was pretty sure they weren't taking me into the operating room, but just in case, I quickly raised myself up on my elbows and looked around a lot just to show them how alert I was. And it worked because they put me in a nice room all by myself with no machines in it, just three other empty beds. So I guess they figured I was going to live. Well, heck, I knew that. God didn't save me from drowning just so I could die in some stupid hospital. Although I had to admit, up until today, that "go in, come out in a box thing," was flashing in my brain like a neon sign.

I WAS SIPPING APPLE JUICE through a curved glass straw when Aunt Minnie came through the doorway followed by Aunt Polly.

"Ahhh, look, Minnie," said Aunt Polly, gliding around the room. "Look at the nice room William has all to himself."

Aunt Minnie settled into the wooden chair on the right side of my bed; she had bad arthritis and stayed on her feet as little as possible. Smiling, and with a nod, she said, "Well, well, look who looks better today. It's about time." She chuckled and patted my hand.

I smiled back and thought, "This aunt, whom I see so little of throughout the year, has done so much for me. And Aunt Polly, who I hardly even know, she too."

"Your father is doing well too," said Aunt Minnie. "The automotive supplier he saw in Detroit is getting him an interview with the Ford Motor Company." She beamed and gave me a nod.

Aunt Polly, at the foot of my bed, followed up with, "Your mother's supervisor at Zenith arranged it all."

Aunt Minnie turned sharply to look at her. "Mr. Davos... Davos? He's Greek, isn't he, Minnie?"

"I don' know," answered Aunt Minnie quietly. "Polly, tell Will..."

"A self-made man. Isn't that what Stella said, Minnie? Worked himself right up the ladder."

"Polly, tell William the surprise you have for him." Aunt Minnie dabbed perspiration from her face with a hankie. "Polly? Father Thomas?"

"Yes...yes, I haven't forgotten," said Aunt Polly, waltzing up the side of the bed opposite Aunt Minnie. "William," she said, folding her hands up high on her chest, "the Wheelchair Priest is going to pay you a visit this afternoon." A big, warm, smile lit up her face.

I turned my head from one to the other and back again.

They started talking over each other excitedly:

"Father Thomas gained recognition worldwide..." "Known as the Wheelchair Priest..." "Service here at St. Mary's every day..." "For eleven years, William, so..." "Hasn't missed..." "People stricken with sickness..." "Yes, Father Thomas..." "He visits patients, cheering them up..." "Hearing confessions communion and..."

And on and on they went.

"Mayor Daley..." "Key to the city..." "Highly respected in all..."

It ran through my ears on and on...

Finally, I yelled, "When are my folks coming back?"

They stopped dead and stared at me. It was the first time I'd said a word in many a day.

"Your mother said they'd be back Saturday," said Aunt Minnie calmly.

"Minnie, didn't you say Stella said Saturday or Sunday?"

"SATURDAY or SUNDAY!" I screamed. "What happened to TODAY or TOMORROW?" I screamed again… The phrase echoed in my mind, over and over: "Saturday or Sunday! Saturday or Sunday! Satur—" I grabbed the box of tissues and flung it as hard as I could at the opposite wall. It bounced off with a dull sound and fell to the floor.

Aunt Minnie leaned forward and said, "Let us thank God for all his blessings." She grasped my hand, and Aunt Polly the other. "Let us pray."

They prayed aloud in Polish—which I could do but didn't. Aunt Minnie squeezed my hand several times, as if to urge me to pray with them, but I didn't utter a sound. Their praying went on for a good fifteen minutes, because saints probably weren't allowed to pray for less than that. When they finished, they let go my hand, crossed themselves, and leaning close to me, Aunt Minnie whispered, "Pray for forgiveness, William."

Aunt Polly brought the box of tissues back; one corner was smashed in. She put the box back on the table and helped Aunt Minnie to her feet. Then they both turned their sad eyes on me, mumbled a blessing, and left.

I wrapped my arms over my eyes, and crazy as it sounds, I wondered who was taking care of Archie. And Queenie. She must be locked up on the porch with only the Lewandowskis to look after her. Poor girl.

53

Bad Breath and Naked Woman

Later a doctor came in. He had this cute little nurse with him, looked like an angel. She was beautiful and very short—but taller than Archie—and her name, she said, was Sister Celia. And boy, did she have a great smile. I was ready for anything she wanted to do to me; being "bad" allowed such thoughts. I didn't catch the doctor's name, but I did his breath—terrible, and he wasn't even old. He was all smiles though. Hey, who wouldn't be with Sister Celia as a side-kick? He studied my chart and asked me how I felt. I didn't answer, naturally. Besides, I figured if he couldn't tell from my chart that I was now only half dead, he wasn't much of a doctor. He went at me with the stethoscope, all over my back and chest, had me taking deep breaths, which hurt like hell—a pinching kind of hurt—and asked me to do it over and over, again and again. It figured, he didn't like the tune my lungs were playing, or else he would've quit, right? In fact, if it wasn't all that serious, you'd think he'd at least let me listen in a little, but naaaaw. Finally, he unplugged and told Angel Celia to schedule me in for a scratch test. Well, that was good, because I was still pretty itchy.

THE SCRATCH TEST was no big deal. That is, if you didn't mind getting about a fifty scratches on your back with broken pieces of glass. What they did was, first, Angel Celia scrubbed my back…and then my chest…and then I grabbed the sponge and told her it was my turn… So okay, maybe I didn't say that exactly, but I almost did, because she gave me this big sexy smile—I kid you not! Unbelieveble! What a broad! Especially since she was a nun, you know? Anyway, so then this elephant stumbled in with this cart, with the main thing on it being a big square board with about a thousand holes drilled in it, and each one with a skinny glass rod sticking out of it. And that was when I wanted to run because I thought they might want to pin me to the wall. But I didn't budge because Sister Celia was staring deep into my eyes… I swear, the poor girl was nuts about me. And then this Dr. Bennin showed up flashing an ear-to-ear grin, and the fun began.

Simple really. Archie could have done it. Sister Celia passed the doc a glass rod, he broke it in half and put a scratch on my back starting in the upper left-hand corner. He did this over and over, up and down my back, until he ran out of space. And then he said we'd wait for a reaction: If a scratch turned into a blister, that would mean I was allergic to whatever was in that particular rod. Right? Elementary, dear Watson! And of course, the bigger the blister, the more allergic I was to whatever—could be almost anything: cats, dogs, weeds, hay, strawberries, potatoes, bad breath, and naked women. I'm not sure about that last one.

So there they were, staring at my back, waiting to see if I would pop them some blisters, when voilà! Their eyes grew big, and they started to giggle, then drool…their tongues were hanging out. And that was when I suspected I was beginning to look like the Hunchback of Notre Dame. Why? Because I didn't have blisters; I had golf balls—and maybe baseballs! I'm not kidding. The place became a circus. Some of the staff was even betting on how big they'd get before they'd pop. They were taking pictures and everything. I was a celebrity! A big shot! And me just twelve years old. How about that?

Angel Celia even chipped in. She said I had the highest allergic reaction ever recorded, that I was a record-holder. But I liked the way the doc put it best: he said I had the biggest balls. Of course, it wasn't really a laughing matter, although the doc and the staff tried to make it one. So after everything cooled down, Angel Celia gave it to me straight. She said that if I had stayed on the farm, it would have been all downhill. That I was allergic to almost every tree and grass known to man and some foods too—foods, I could've told her, didn't surprise me any, especially lumpy oatmeal—and that my sinuses and ears were badly infected. Oh, and she explained that my back was hurting because pleurisy was like rubbing sandpaper on an open wound. Wow! But not to worry, she said, beaming her great smile, because they could knock all that stuff out with medicine. All but the allergies, she said, bouncing up on the bed and parking her little self right next to me. That it was the allergies, she went on to say, that could "eat you right up." That you had to avoid them like sin, she said, shaking a finger in my face. So I snapped at the delicious little morsel, and she slapped me. And just like that, she flapped her wings and took off... Oh well, nobody ever said fooling around with angels was easy.

It was real quiet. Everybody dies around here as soon as the sun goes down. Me? I was just feeling blue. Not about Angel Celia, not really. Well, maybe a little. But it was more than that. Oh, and Father Thomas didn't show up. Probably got a blowout speedin' around in his wheelchair. But it was more than that too. It was more like, now that I knew I was going to get well, I've stopped flying high and I was falling, falling down and down. Maybe it was because I wasn't scared anymore, I don't know. Sounds odd, I guess, but when I was scared, I was really at my best. I was like King Brave. My mind was going a hundred miles an hour. Wisecracking came easy. Everything came easy. All because I was scared. But now that I'm "over the hump," as they say, now that I know I'm going to get well—and that was good, of course—I was just plain me. And "me" just wanted to be home. And it hurt me terribly that my folks didn't really seem to care about me. I know, business...business, but you would think my mom would at least come. I needed her more than my dad.

54

Confession

Late afternoon of the following day, Sister Celia flew in, stuck a thermometer in my mouth, checked my chart, straightened up a few things, and did it all without a smile, without a glance.

I spit the thermometer out on my chest. She picked it up.

"Open," she said.

I squeezed my lips together.

"We can do this another way." She reached for the covers.

I grabbed them, and my mouth snapped open. She stuck the darn thing back in. God, I couldn't believe she'd do such a thing. Ugh! She's no angel; that's for sure.

"You're having a very special visitor today, Billy," she said, tucking in the sheets at the foot of my bed—which I hated because it bent my toes. "Reverend Thomas is stopping by anytime now. He's an inspiration to us all." She threw in the sign of the cross and went on bending my toes. "What a blessing to have Father Thomas in your family." She moved up, grabbed the thermometer out of my mouth, gave it a read, and beelined it out the door.

We didn't have a priest in the family. What was she talking about? We had gamblers and jailbirds and inventors and geniuses; Dad's even got a cousin that's been divorced, but priests? Naaaw... Well, Georgie Obrycki did study for the priesthood, but they kicked him out. He was too...adventuresome. So he joined the Air Force, just like his brother, Peter, the biggest genius in the family, the one

326

so loaded with brains those eastern colleges didn't know what to do with him. So now he was in a mental hospital because they said his brain snapped. But that was a lot of baloney according to Ray. And Ray ought to know because he was his other brother. So like I said, on my father's side, they were all geniuses. But no priests. Uh-uh. Aunt Minnie was a saint. But no priests. Who could forget a priest? We skipped a priest and got a saint. And a saint was better. It was right up there next to God, like his right hand…or his left, whatever.

And don't you know, just as I was mulling this stuff over, who came wheeling in but Father Thomas.

"Are we related?" I asked him.

And just like that, I was talking. Hey now, I hadn't said a word for—except for that one time—about a week and a half, and all of a sudden I was talking? Hmmmm.

"Oh yeah. Sure. We're related," he said, pulling up to my bed and parking—which I noticed was done by pushing a couple of levers. "Let's see now, Polly, my mother, and Minnie are sisters-in-law. And Minnie is a stepsister to your father. Sure, we're related. Give me your hand."

I plopped my hand in his, my head still spinning about what he had just said.

He covered it with his other hand, bowed his head, and started mumbling. I stared at a head of wavy black locks.

"Join me in a prayer, Billy?" he said without looking up.

I bowed my head and joined him in an Our Father, saying it loud and clear to impress him.

Finished, he looked up and said, "Okay, what'll you have? A beer or a shot of whiskey?" He laughed so hard I was thinking he was going to fall out of his wheelchair.

"I killed a man," I said it flat out, figuring I'd shock him.

Still laughing, he leaned forward. "You did what?"

"I…killed…a man."

He stopped laughing, locked his dark eyes on mine, and said, "I killed five."

We stared at each other for… I don't now how long…and then he grabbed my hand—which was dangling off the bed—grabbed it with both his hands and squeezed it. I squeezed back... When we finally stopped, which seemed to be a heck of a long time, we prayed again. We did a Hail Mary and an Our Father. Finished, Father Thomas grabbed the pitcher of water on the small table and poured us a glass. He handed me mine, took his, and started talking.

"I killed five men." Father Thomas held up his left hand, his fingers spread. "Five," he said. He gulped some water and went on. "We were on our way back to Milwaukee from Chicago. The day before, three of us had been ordained. The happiness in that car was..." He drew a breath and sat up straight. "We were on cloud nine."

Then he dropped his eyes and went to brushing specks of dirt—which were invisible to me—from his lap. Finished, he looked off and said, "I never saw it." He shook his head. "Metal from a muffler. Never saw it." His eyes drifted back to mine. "We blew a tire, went off the shoulder, rolled over, and hit a tree."

He sat back, laced his fingers in his lap, and with his head bowed, he went on.

"They didn't die right away. One by one for weeks it went on. Five men. All with mothers, fathers, brothers and sisters, uncles, aunts, friends..." He looked up, swept a hand in the air. "All suffering because of my incompetence, my..." He put a hand up, stopped speaking, then dropped it. "I was speeding." He drew a deep breath, exhaled, and relaxed. "So God saved me. And at the time, I wished he hadn't. My guilt was insurmountable! I wanted to be dead! Inside I was dead. I was also partially dead from the waist down, but that didn't matter. Nothing mattered!" He pressed back into his wheelchair. "Ohh, I prayed, and I prayed. I prayed for God to cast me into hell, to let me burn for all eternity. But instead he started to heal my broken body. Why? I wondered. Why would he heal me? Why didn't he let me die with the others? Why? Why was I spared? Surely, not to live in anguish, a wasted life, a burden to my brotherhood." His shoulders dropped. "And all the while, in the back of my mind, I knew the answer: God had a reason. It was that simple. But what was it? What could a cripple do? What could a cripple do to make up for the waste of five wonderful men? What? Build a temple? A church that reached the high heavens? Lay the brick, brick upon brick. Ha!

I could barely take care of myself. So I prayed. What else could I do? Night and day I prayed, 'Tell me Lord. Tell me...' And then, miraculously, the very first time I came here, to St. Mary's, I knew the answer. He wanted me to serve the sick and the dying. That's all he asked of me. After all the pain I caused. Can you imagine? How merciful he is? How giving..."

Father Thomas relaxed back into his wheelchair, his fingers laced together.

"So that's what I've been doing ever since... God saves us for a purpose, Billy. He saved you, and..."

"Grandpa saved me."

"Billy, Billy. Ultimately, it's God who saves us. He saved you for a purpose."

"Like what? I'm not going to be a priest! I can't build a church!"

Father Thomas smiled. "In time, you'll know. God has a plan for—"

"No! No, Father! Don't you see? Yours was an accident! Mine was different!"

"How different?"

"Different! I planned it, Father! I planned every detail! Ah-lex was bad! I wanted him dead. I thought about it every day."

Father Thomas leaned forward, his eyes locked on mine. "What plan? What was the plan?"

I told him about the silo—all of it, the boulders on top, every-thing. How I talked Richard into helping me. How I lied to him. How I told him we were just going to scare Ah-lex.

"But I knew it could kill him, Father. I was hoping it would kill him. Don't you see? And when we tested it, it almost worked. And I told Richard I could fix it. And he stopped me. Otherwise, Ah-lex would've been smashed, killed, dead. And me that did it."

"But you still left it to chance. You couldn't be sure the boulder—"

"But I wanted it to. I... What's the difference? He's dead!"

Father Thomas sat back and relaxed, his elbows on the arms of the wheelchair, his fingers laced.

"But why did you hate this man so much? Did he ever hurt you? Or Richard?"

"No. But he hurt the animals." And then I told him about the cows and the kittens.

"Hmpt!" he said, shaking his head, his chin cradled on his laced fingers. And then he spoke, "You say Ah-lex never hit you. Or Richard. But did he ever...touch you? Or Richard?"

"No." I shook my head and stared into his eyes. "No, Father."

Father Thomas brushed invisible specks off his lap with a prayer book, then looked at me.

"You're sure?"

"Uh-huh," I nodded. "He was a hard worker, I'll say that much for him. And he could roll a cigarette better..." My eyes filled with tears.

"Billy? Are you okay?"

I nodded.

"I want to go back to the crossing, Billy. Now as I understand it..."

"I don't like to think about it."

"I know. I know. But I have a reason, trust me."

"What reason?"

Father Thomas smiled. "To put it to rest. A confession. To gain absolution."

"But I didn't do anything wrong, Father. Except the silo thing. And I told you about that."

Father Thomas sat there biting his lower lip. I wanted to run, run as far and as fast as I could. "They found his body, Billy. The official cause—"

"Where did they find him?"

"Three miles downstream from the Popko farm. In Lafayette County... There are some questions about the condition of his body."

"Like what?"

"We'll get to that. It's my understanding you were hanging on a rope behind the raft."

"It was a sled with inner tubes under it. *Rig-Go*, we called it... A raft, yeah."

"Tell me what happened. Don't leave anything out. Tell me every detail."

I didn't want to do it. Didn't want to think about it. But out it came: Hanging on the rope… The barbed wire fence behind me. The *Rig-Go* turning around…got hung up… Jim climbing on top of Molle… Swimming for it, catching the inner tube… Ah-lex! All bloody, tangled in the reins and the roots of an upturned tree… His eyes wide open…bloody head… Me yelling at him, "Ah-lex! Ah-lex!" Nothing… Staring at me… "Blink, Ah-lex! Blink!" I was yelling. "Can you hear me? Ahhh-leeeex!" He was dead. Got to be… The Rig-Go tilted! It was sinking! An inner tube was tied behind on a rope. I leaped! I was in it! But the *Rig-Go* was sinking, pulling the tube down. I tried to unite it, but my hands wouldn't work. I pulled myself back to the rig…and…and that's all I remember.

"And that's all that happened. That's everything you remember?"

"Uh-huh."

"Your left hand, Billy. That's a stab wound. How did you get it?"

I started shaking my head. "I don't know… Something was flashing… The sun was flashing on the water, blinding me. Flashing right under his nose… Oh my god."

"What? What, Billy?"

"His knife."

"What knife?"

"He cut the rope… He cut the rope! Ah-lex cut the rope!"

"So he cut the rope, slashed his throat, stabbed himself seven times, then swam three miles down the creek, and hid himself in some bushes."

"Whaaaa?"

"Aloysius Moritz's death has been recorded as a drowning, Billy. He drowned. Whatever happened after that doesn't matter… Do you understand?"

"Moritz? You said Moritz?"

"Yes. Aloysius Moritz. The man you refer to as Ah-lex."

I was puzzled. "My Grandma Helen married Edward Moritz?"

"Yes. He was Ah-lex's father."

It was too much for me. My mind went blank.

Father Thomas drilled me with his dark eyes. "Asphyxiation, Billy. The official report is death by drowning. He drowned, Billy. The case is closed. Nothing else matters." He bowed his head and laced his fingers. "Come now. Let us pray."

55

A Night in Hell

It was a dull night. The body count was zero. Nobody died... Daylight creeping in gray daylight... Stabbed seven times...the chest...in the back...the heart, right in the heart, the stomach. Geez, seven times... Why? Case closed... Closed... Over... Done...

"Hey, kid, how're doin'?"

"What? Who're you?"

"The boss down below sent me up to have a heart-to-heart. You already met him. Big fellow, hell in his eyes, fire on his breath?"

"What do you want?"

"You got potential, bright eyes. I'm here to see you don't go soft."

"Get outta here!"

"Oh, sure, kid. Sure. You kill me. Ha-ha-ha! Listen, these creeps here are about to make it party time here. They're going to go all out with the goody-good stuff. But you're not going to fall for that crap. You're tough. Right? Right! So keep punching, kid. I got a hunch you're going to run with the 'Red Fork Gang'!"

"What's in it for me?"

"Are you kidding? You get all the goodies. Stuff like that Sister Celia dancing on a table with a couple of Band-Aids here and there, get it? And halitosis with a knife and fork, drooling, ready to dig in, but there's a fire under his ass for penance, so he gets snots, get it? Adios, amigo!"

Boom! Ca-rack! Thunder and lightning split the sky, knocked out the lights, and a cold wind blew in and made me shiver. *Cra-crack!* Lightning flashed, burned away the dark, and gave everything a scary look. Rain started beating the windows and bombing the roof. I pinched myself to see if I was dreaming.

"Owww!"

And then just like that, the storm was over and I was floating in darkness. Then somebody started switching on the lights, brilliant lights, like in an operating room…and guess who was on the table.

Then bursting through the door came a procession of people, all holding hands, skipping and dancing, circling me and chanting: "Repent! Repent! Repent!" Angels came floating down from heaven; devils came up from hell; relatives came crawling out of the woodwork. Everybody showed up except God—and my folks, of course, because they couldn't tear themselves away from Detroit. Even Father Thomas was there, standing at the foot of my bed—no wheelchair in sight. And everybody else was kneeling, and swaying, and praying, and swaying… And all around us thousands of candles were flickering with foot-long tongues, while rainbow-colored smoke danced off the walls. And gathered close by was Saint Aunt Minnie and Part-Time Saint Aunt Polly! Yes, and surprise! Aunt Polly had two daughters that were nuns! Now how was that for holy-holy? But of course, on the other side of the coin, there was Archie—plus a husband in jail, for life. So really, no matter how you flipped it, Aunt Polly still had to be regarded as a "part-time saint." So boy, oh boy, I mean, the walls in the room were glowing! Know what I mean? Celestial music was floating down, and I was the only one foaming at the mouth, because that's what happens when you're the only sinner in the room. I mean, I was totally outclassed and totally terrified. Oh, and behind them were Dorothy and Vickie, with Richard standing in between, digging in his nose.

Suddenly, more lights went on, and set on a table next to me was Ah-lex, holding his guts in. Dr. Bennin marched in with an operating crew—complete with masks and rubber gloves. Angel Celia appeared with a thermometer in each hand—one for the top, one for the bottom. And the rest of the operating room was stuffed with

more doctors and nuns and staff, plus janitors, carpenters, visitors—
even a deliveryman with this round thing everybody here was so
crazy about called "pizza"—which smelled like a disease. And what
was everybody doing in this gigantic tomb of a room?

Praying! Praying and chanting on their knees for little ol' Billy
to repent! Praying that I would cry out: "I'm sorry Ah-lex is dead!"
And if that wasn't the silliest thing you ever heard of, I'll eat that
stinking pizza thing.

Like at one point, I hollered out, "What if Hitler dies! Am I
supposed to be sorry?" Well, right then and there, you'd think they
were going to stone me! No kidding! I mean, you couldn't win with
a mob like this—especially if they were on their knees. Uh-uh. Man,
I can't begin to tell you how scared I was. It was absolutely the worst
nightmare I ever had. It was like the Noble Prize of Nightmares! I
mean it! Really! They were rolling over me in waves, yelling, "REPENT!
REPENT, BILLY! REPENT!"

And so I did. I mean, Ah-lex was hanging over me, holding his
guts in with one hand and flashing his knife at me with the other.
What else was I supposed to do? After all, how much was a little kid
like me supposed to take? Here I am lying on a cold slab, half dead,
with this circus going on and a flashing knife dancing over me. Get
the picture? So finally, with dawn on the horizon, I threw up my
arms and yelled, "I'm sorry! I'm sorry the son of a bitch is dead!" So
okay, I left out the best word. But mind you, the intent was there.

Boy, oh boy, oh boy! You wouldn't believe how happy they all
were. You'd think the war was over. They were jumping around, yelling, hugging, kissing. Ah-lex, on the operating table, was cutting up
his guts and tossing them into the air like confetti. I mean, absolutely
nuts, all of them! And do you think I got any of those hugs and
kisses? Naaaaw. Just bloody confetti.

I was the latest miracle at St. Mary's: the Talking Boy. So now
the boy who wouldn't talk wouldn't shut up. The staff circled with
pride. Sister Celia, if she hadn't been a nun, would probably hop,

skip, and spin on the table, with nary a piece of clothes to hinder her movements, while halitosis circled the table with… Ah-ha! See what hell does to you?

"I wanna go hoooome!" was the rallying theme. I yelled it over and over, in various tones and volume, trying to find one that would work. "I wanna, wanna go hoooooome," was one variation that I sang out in various keys, even tried some Bing Crosby, Eddie Howard, and Doris Day—not that anybody could do Doris, that doll. "Hooooome, I wanna gooooo!" Oh, I gave it my everything, but they were deaf to my pleas. I could've been speaking Hebrew, and it wouldn't have mattered. All that mattered to them was the miracle. So finally, I shut up, and they went away.

Not long after that, the two saints walked in and said they were taking me home—Aunt Minnie's house, you know. I was ready to jump up and down and do somersaults, but first off we had to pray. And that was good. You couldn't go wrong with praying. Except if you prayed for like an hour nonstop—which was what we did because, you know, with two saints, you had to make a double impression. I was absolutely sure we prayed for everybody in the hospital and half the people in the entire world. So okay, I figured I owed them that much. And so, finally, late Monday morning, I was whisked away ceremoniously in the yellow Packard by two saints and an imbecile.

56

The Obryckis

The roar of low flying planes had me peeking out of the Packard's side window as we cruised past Midway Airport. One of the big birds came crawling across our bow, flashed in the sunlight, and floated down like a feather. Wings baloney, it was magic.

Five minutes later, we were there, the Obrycki house. The gray frame wasn't anything special...kind of odd, actually, being that it was plenty long enough and high enough, but not nearly wide enough—looked, in fact, like a good wind might knock it over, a real eyesore to be perfectly frank. The best part was that it stood in the middle of a three-acre corner lot, not squeezed together like the rest of the houses down the block.

But the heck with the house. It was my cousins: Peter, Georgie, and Raymond, and all the things they did that made my blood race. They could and did build anything and everything: motorcycles, race cars, and a motorboat so big they had to knock out a garage wall to get it out. They even tore down a junked Great Lakes Trainer and completely rebuilt it, then learned to fly it. And besides all that, they played football and baseball, shot guns, bows and arrows, threw knives, played guitar—Georgie did, Peter the piano, and Ray the drums. And they played good, not great, but good. But—and this is one heck of a *but*—there was something lacking. Something not quite right, some big black hole that you couldn't see but knew was there, could feel it in your heart. There, in that huge house on Hamlin, eyes never fully filled with joy, and although laughter roared aplenty, it could turn on a dime and go ugly. And how or why, I had no idea.

But besides that, there wasn't any other place in the world that I'd rather be, except for home, of course—which was out of the question because Aunt Minnie said that my dad had a big-time meeting today with someone who might get him a meeting with someone who knew someone high up at the Ford Motor Company.

I stood at the window of Georgie's bedroom in my pajamas and watched my grandparents, Andrew and Anna—who lived in the basement—work their sprawling vegetable garden under the hot afternoon sun. They had clothes piled on them from head to toe and moved like old people moved: slow and unsteady. Grandma wobbled up a row with carrot bunches in each hand, and Grandpa did the same from another row with beets in hand. At the end of the rows, they added their vegetables to a parked wheelbarrow, then shuffled slowly back down the long rows to get more.

I thought about Richard and wondered what he was doing. Wondered if he thought about me when he smoked a McCoye.

"Hey, Dick, how about a McCoye?" I don't know where I picked up that word, but it sure fit the occasion. Had a nice ring to it: "McCoye." Yeah, I'd have to say smoking up on the roof of the shed while the sun sank away was the best part of the day. And then when the relatives came up, boy, that was the very best. And at night, lying under the stars out by the water pump, those sparkling diamonds hypnotizing you into dreamland. Booooy…

Hearing someone coming, I dropped to the floor on my knees by my bed and pretended to be praying just as Aunt Minnie came in cradling a big stein of milk. She gazed down at me with smiling eyes; being caught on your knees in this house was about the best thing that could happen to you. I don't know why I was praying. Hey, I don't know why I did half the things I did. I crossed myself and shot to my feet. I didn't want to chance Aunt Minnie joining me, because saints—as you know by now—put in a half hour at the drop of a hat.

"I brought you some warm milk," she said, setting the thick glass stein down on the night table. "Now drink it before it gets cold."

Warm milk was second to lumpy oatmeal of things that could make me vomit. I peeked into the stein and shuddered at the skim-covered milk.

"Uhh, could I have some coffee instead, Aunt Minnie? That's what I had up on the farm."

"Didn't they give you any milk?" said Aunt Minnie, pulling up the wooden armchair from the wall by the window.

"Oh yeah, sure. But mostly coffee. I really like it."

"Hmmmm." The hum came with a disapproving look. Aunt Minnie picked up the stein. "I'll put some Ovaltine in this. You like Ovaltine, don't you?"

I shrugged. "I don't know. I never had it."

"Never had—hmpt. Get back in bed." She turned to go.

"Is Grandpa a hunchback?"

It stopped her in her tracks. She straightened up and looked back at me.

"He's hunched over, you know," I said, climbing back into bed.

"You would be too, if you piled boulders up all your life." She left the room.

I put a pillow behind my back and folded the sheet down nice and neat. On the green wall, above the leather sofa chair across the room, hung a big picture of Jesus on his knees, his hands clasped in prayer. Rays of light poured down on him. I knew this picture; everybody did—except atheists, naturally, like my Uncle George, who was now working at being a Catholic, thank you. It was of Jesus on Mt. Olive praying to God, his Father, to stop the horrible thing that was coming in a matter of hours: his crucifixion.

"How could God make his Son suffer like that?" I wondered. It didn't make sense. He was God; he could've figured out another way. "And how could those people beat him like that? Beat 'im and beat 'im and hang him on a cross with nails?"

And Jesus said, "Forgive them, Father, for they know not what they do." I shook my head and thought, "The heck they didn't. They knew."

Ray walked in with my Ovaltine. I talked him into drinking it. I marveled at his big-boned frame and head, topped with dark, heavy hair as he gulped the stein empty. He had just finished working at Howard Hill's Archery Barn. Howard Hill was the famous archer that did all the bow-and-arrow shots in the *Robin Hood* movies and others. It was Georgie's job before he left for the Air Force. Boy, what I wouldn't do to work for Mr. Hill. He wouldn't even have to pay me.

From the sofa chair, Ray said with his easy smile, "What do you say, when you're allowed out of bed, I show you how to shoot the bow?"

"Yeaaah, that'd be great, Ray. Yeeeeh…"

Ray stretched his arms out overhead, and his voice went up with it. "I can even show you how to make some arrows, if you want?"

"Really?"

"Sure." Ray brought his arms down, and his voice with it. "By the end of the week, you'll be a regular Robin Hood."

"I'm not going to be here that long."

"That's what your Aunt Sophie said on the phone yesterday. She told my mom that your folks are picking you up on Sunday.

"She did? Sunday?"

"Yep."

I thought to myself, "That's a whole week. Today's Monday." Then to Ray, I said, "Ahhh, I don't care if they ever come, Ray. No kidding. I'd rather stay here, anytime."

"Weeell, we got plenty of room now that the boys are gone." Ray fell into talking like he was all grown-up, which he always did, even though he was only fifteen. "Noooo, on second thought, your folks won't let you. They'll want you home. Yeah."

"Yeah." That's what I said, but Sunday was still blinking at me.

"Well," Ray slammed his hands down on his knees, "I gotta help Grandpa and Grandma."

"Is Grandpa a hunchback?"

Ray cracked his easygoing, lopsided smile. "Hunchback? Naaaw, he's just old." Ray pushed off his knees, stood up, and arched his back. "Uhhhgh." He straightened up, walked over, and grabbed the empty stein. "Grandpa makes a nice buck on those vegetables." Ray tapped me twice on the shoulder with his fist. "See you tomorrow, Billy. I got football practice tonight," he started out.

"Can I watch you practice?" I called after him.

Ray stopped in the doorway. "Yeah, later this week." He rapped the doorframe and left.

I scooted down under the sheet and stared at the white ceiling with no cracks. Sunday...

I OPENED MY EYES. The sun threw a long rectangle on the shiny wooden floor. Aunt Minnie was sitting in the armchair by my bed smiling at me.

"I brought you some spinach soup."

"Ahhh-uh," I sighed and sat up. "Thank you, Aunt Minnie."

A big white bowl on the night table next to me was steaming.

"Eat it while it's hot."

I swung my legs down, picked up the spoon, and fished the green stuff. "There's some white lumps in here." I held up my spoon.

"That's a hard-boiled egg I chopped up in there. Eat it. Eat while it's hot."

I blew on the spoon, sipped, and chewed. "Hmmm, good."

As I spooned in the delicious soup, I noticed that Aunt Minnie was staring into the dresser mirror across the room...turning a bit this way and that way...chin up, chin down...and so on. True, she was a beauty—with dark flashing eyes and a fine chiseled nose with not much lip under it, and a swell jawline—but I found it surprising that a saint would be looking at herself so much in a mirror.

"What did you do when you lived up on the farm, Aunt Minnie?" I said between gulps. "When you were my age."

"I cooked breakfast every morning for half a dozen lumber-jacks." She tossed it off all to the mirror. When I asked her what lumberjacks were doing on our farm, she gave me a surprised look and answered, "Cutting down the trees, William. Pine trees as big around as a kitchen table."

"Did they have to cut them down?"

Now she looked stunned beyond surprise. "They cut them down to save the farm, William. Didn't your Father ever tell you?"

I shook my head. "Nope."

"Hmpt! Finish your soup."

I went at my soup.

Aunt Minnie was looking off, a finger on her lips. I could tell she was thinking. "One night my father was out drinking with the lumberjacks. Hmmm…" Aunt Minnie's nodded. "Pete was a drinking man."

"Who's Pete?"

Aunt Minnie stared at me a moment. "Pete was my father, William. Andrew, downstairs, he's your father's father. Pete married Anna first. Then when Pete died, Andrew married her." Aunt Minnie leaned forward. "Your father's my stepbrother." She settled back. "But he's more than that, because Pete and Andrew were brothers. Understand?"

I nodded, then shook my head, and said, "But you're still my Aunt Minnie, aren't you?"

"Yes, yeees!" Aunt Minnie chuckled. "Now finish your soup." She looked off in thought.

"Anna's father took a liking to Pete, right from the start." Aunt Minnie smiled at me and nodded. "Ohhh yes, Pete was a charmer. And handsome! And full of mischief, my mother said." Aunt Minnie chuckled. "And he had good teeth. He was always smiling from ear to ear, showing them off. Uh-huh." She chuckled and shook her head. "And he was strong. Ask your Father. He could knock a man down with one punch." Aunt Minnie caught sight of herself in the mirror and threw a punch.

We both burst out laughing…

Then wistfully she went on, "Andrew was shy…very shy. But he played the flute beautifully. Long, haunting melodies that he composed just for her." That was what she said. Aunt Minnie smiled sadly. "Ohhh, it's a long story, William."

"They bought the farm from a map, sight unseen!" I exclaimed. Aunt Minnie raised an eyebrow in surprise. "My dad said they bought it because it had a creek running through it."

"Yes," said Aunt Minnie, nodding. "That's true…" I could see her eyes drifting back into the past. "Lilly," she said wistfully. "Isn't that a pretty name? Lilly… They all left New York for the promised land... But then in Chicago, when the train left the station... Oh, it was terrible."

"I know that train. The Soo Line."

"Anna's father fell off the platform, and he died."

"He fell off?"

"He fell off. He just...fell off." Aunt Minnie shrugged.

"Geez."

Aunt Minnie sat there, her head rocking. "Anna's mother and Lily went back to Poland, and Anna never saw them again."

"Geez, she was all alone."

Aunt Minnie leaned forward, grasped my hand, and looked me hard in the eyes. "It made her strong," she said. "With prayer and determination, William, we can get through any hardship." Aunt Minnie put her hands together, bowed her head, and...

"What about the trees, Aunt Minnie?" I cut in quick, because I could see prayer time coming, the half-hour kind. "How did they save the farm? You can't stop now, Aunt Minnie. Please! I have to know."

Aunt Minnie dropped her hands, leaned back, and stared into the mirror...

"That first day on the farm was the happiest day of their lives. She told me that many times. They found a clearing by the creek, and they knew... They dropped to their knees and gave thanks."

Aunt Minnie drew a deep breath, exhaled, looked at me and went on.

"In the morning, they walked their land from boundary to boundary, north to south, east to west. The land was too poor to farm. Too much rock...especially boulders... And too many trees, giant pine trees that would have to be cut, and the roots...impossible." Aunt Minnie shrugged. "It was hopeless. Their dreams were slipping away... But they didn't say a word to each other. Then, that evening at supper, Anna started to say grace, but she couldn't finish. Pete started ranting and raving, kicking and cursing, cursing the heavens... Then Andrew started playing the flute, and it saved them. Saved them from despair, she said. She said the notes came out of his soul and went ringing high and clear through the darkness...carrying away their grief." Aunt Minnie sighed. "They cleared a patch and planted vegetables. Andrew worked hard. He clawed away at the boulders and piled them high. Andrew was a dreamer. He believed in miracles. Not Pete. Pete was a realist. He knew it was hopeless. They would lose the land. The con men in New York would foreclose and sell it to the next poor soul."

"That's what Jake said. The mailman. He told me a lot of farmers 'got taken.'"

Aunt Minnie squirmed in her chair, let out a long breath, and went on. "Pete would go off and drink with the lumberjacks. Andrew kept breaking his back, killing himself, my mother said."

"Why? I mean, if they were going to lose the land, why would he work so hard?"

"Ahhhh, yes. Why?" Aunt Minnie rocked in her seat. "Andrew was a dreamer, yes. But he was no fool. There was more to it."

"What? What, Aunt Minnie?"

"Well…there was Andrew's dream, of course. For twenty years, he pestered my father about going to America, after they served their serfdom. To go there and start a new life. Your father's like that too. Nick gets his teeth into something, he won't let go. Not Pete." Aunt Minnie shook her head. "But there was more to it than that." Aunt Minnie smiled, and the smile wouldn't leave her face.

"So why? Why did he—"

She held up the "Wait" finger. "Andrew went on piling boulders, piling them up as neat as a pin, said they were his adversaries. That they deserved respect. You know what *adversary* means?"

"Enemy?"

"Yes! His enemy. He said he'd beat them and would go on beating them. And he did! Beat them on a patch here and a patch there. And so they deserved respect, he said. Hmpt! Everybody thought he was—" she twirled a finger up by her temple—"but not Anna." Aunt Minnie rocked in her chair. "She knew his secret."

"WHAT? What was it?"

Again with the "Wait" finger. "So that's how it went. Andrew clearing the land, Pete sneaking off to drink. They argued all the time. And when it came to blows, Andrew was no match for Pete.

He would just knock him down and go off to do his drinking. But one time, Anna said, he came back very drunk and wanted to take advantage of her." Aunt Minnie looked down her nose at me and said, "They weren't married, you understand."

"They were married on the boat."

"That was a civil ceremony! My god, William!" said Aunt Minnie, flapping her arms so hard she almost flew out of her chair. "So! So that night they fought, and Andrew tried to stop him, and Pete knocked him down. But Andrew kept getting back up. And Pete kept knocking him down. So Anna got the shotgun out and told Pete to get out or she'd shoot him. Well…he came at her, and she shot him.

"She shot 'im?"

"Well, she aimed at the floor, but she nipped his toes."

"But if she—"

She waved me off and went on, "So two days later, a lumberjack came by with a letter." She put her fingertips to her lips and smiled.

"So what did it say?"

"Shhhh!" She waved me off again. "I'm trying to remember just how he put it." She rubbed her lips. "He said that he wasn't coming back unless they lived as man and wife. That he almost died on the ship waiting for her to make up her mind and that he wasn't waiting any more. Oh! And that she must know he cared for her, because no man would want a woman that shot a man's foot off." She chuckled. "He signed it: 'Your husband, like it or not, Pete.'"

"Oh, wooooow!"

"Anna wrote back, 'You're not my husband! Come back and I'll shoot off your other leg!'"

I laughed.

"Two days later, Pete came back drunk as a skunk. Came back with some lumberjacks, and they started shouting: 'We're going to save the farm! Save the farm!' And then they started dancing around, jumping up and down, going crazy, yelling: 'The hell with the crops! We're going to harvest the trees!'" Aunt Minnie started rocking with laughter.

"They wanted to cut down the trees? But why?"

"Why? To pay the mortgage, William! That's why!"

"Ohhhh! I get it."

Suddenly, Aunt Minnie's face fell off, and she said, "Then he wanted a reward."

"A reward?" I played dumb, but I wasn't that dumb.

"Um-hmmm." Aunt Minnie looked down her nose at me again.

I started nodding like a woodpecker. "So then they got married, right?"

"He didn't want to wait."

"Oooooooh," I leaked under my breath.

"Anna told him she wanted to be married by a priest! And that she wanted a log cabin by the creek. Or nothing doing."

"Holy moly!"

Aunt Minnie chuckled, and a big smile filled her face. "My mother said she never saw anything built so fast in her life. Every time she blinked, the house grew another foot." Aunt Minnie started roaring, and pretty soon we were both practically rolling on the floor.

Wiping tears from her eyes, she went on, "I was firstborn. Paul was born a year later. They named him after Anna's father." Then, just like that, Aunt Minnie's smile turned to a look of pain.

I leaned forward. "What's the matter, Aunt Minnie? Are you okay?"

Aunt Minnie waved a hand in front of her face. "It's getting late. Say your prayers now, and go to sleep." She braced her arms on the chair, pushed, and stood up.

"Wait!" I practically fell out of bed, getting a hand on her arm. "You can't stop now. What about the secret? You have to tell me, Aunt Minnie. I won't be able to sleep."

Aunt Minnie's eyes blinked like a machine gun. She patted my hand. "The secret... Andrew would do anything just to be near Anna...even pile boulders."

The door slammed shut, and The Piper Cub hanging high in the corner behind it swayed...

Nobody built airplane models like Georgie. You couldn't take your eyes off it; it was so perfect, the huge wing tilted, coming in for a landing…the big round motor, covered by a huge cowling, quieting down, its pistons firing easy…the black stripe on the yellow fuselage—so perfect, not a wrinkle anywhere… The landing gear with perfect little balloon tires that rolled perfectly…cellophane windows all around the cockpit and inside—which I had examined many times—the man sitting there in a brown leather jacket with a white scarf, the control wheel in his hands, the instrument panel with all the gauges, so perfect you could see the needle settings. Here it comes…lower and lower… Level now…easy…down…down… touching down, a perfect three-point landing!

THE SUN WAS GONE from my window when I heard someone at the door. Quick as a flash, I knelt on the bed, in case it was Aunt Minnie, and as the door opened, I said, "And please bless Aunt Minnie and Uncle Frank. Amen." And quickly again, I scrambled back under the covers and sat there like an angel. Aunt Minnie came in with a big smile and a plate piled high with slices of red apple. As she settled into the wooden armchair, I gave her the "An apple a day keeps the doctor away" line, and then, between delicious crunchy bites by both of us, she proceeded to tell me why that was so—that the skin was good for digestion and that the pulp was good for almost everything, including anemia, diabetes, heart disease, eye disease, rheumatism, cancer, teeth. And as she went on and on, I quickly asked the Lord if he would fix it so my mom and dad would talk to me more and tell me things like my Aunt Minnie did.

"How come you know so much, Aunt Minnie?"

"I'm old." She chuckled and chewed, put her elbows up on the armchair, laced her fingers, and looked out the window. "It was two days before Christmas." She swallowed, looked back at me, and went on. "Pete and Andrew were hauling logs on a sled, and a chain broke." She curled her lower lip over the top one for a moment, then went on.

"If Pete wasn't so strong, he…uhhh… Andrew wanted to use the horse. But Pete thought they could wrestle it back on." She shook like a chill had hit her. "They got the log back on the sled, but Pete hurt something inside of him," she rubbed her stomach, "in his guts... The next day was Christmas Eve. Pete got up a little late, got dressed, and joined us at the table. We were having a treat: cinnamon babka." Aunt Minnie wrung her hands. "He was sitting there, eating, drinking his coffee... And then he made a little sound and dropped his coffee cup..." Aunt Minnie put a hand up to her mouth. "His head drooped...he was dead. He died right there at the table."

I froze. I stopped breathing... I drew a deep breath and put my hands over my face.

"Pete never needed more than a day of rest, no matter how sick he was...break his hands, drop a log on his foot—no matter! Errrrrr," she growled, and her whole body shook again. "So! So we went back to work, and we worked until we dropped. Thought we could work away our pain. Even little Paul, pulling weeds, hauling water. I was six. I tended the livestock. We had three cows and five pigs...and chickens. And a team of horses: Cab and Holly... Poor Andrew," Aunt Minnie shook her head. "After supper he'd go back out and work under the light of the moon and the stars... Then they'd sit by the fire, and my mother would soothe him, she said, his head on her lap...until he fell asleep." Aunt Minnie drew a deep breath and sighed. "Two years passed that way."

"But they were happily married, weren't they?"

"They weren't married. Pete was still there, his memory. It was like a wall between them. Spring came, and it started raining and wouldn't stop. Andrew got us up and out of the house just in time. A wall of water came down the creek like a runaway train, and it took the house, took the big pine tree, and Pete's grave with it... And then everything was gone, and we were happy."

"How could you be?"

"The flood washed Pete out of our lives, William! He was finally gone! It was a new beginning... We built a new house—back from the water this time—a nice house, a little bigger..."

I was waiting for her to go on, and what did she do but curl her lower lip again, like before.

"Aaaaand," I screeched, "they got married and lived happily ever after!"

Aunt Minnie held up her finger and shook it at me. "I told you, Andrew was shy. So winter came, and it was cooold." Aunt Minnie shivered. "Brrrr. Oh, it was cold. And one night we're waiting for Andrew, and it was snowing hard, like a blizzard. And it was suppertime, and we were very worried when, all at once, the door flies open! And there's Andrew standing in the doorway with his arms up in the air."

Aunt Minnie shot her arms up. "And he's got a big knife in one hand. And he screams, 'Annaaaaa.'" Aunt Minnie shook her hands above her head. "'Annaaaa! I can't stand it another day!'" she screamed. "'Say you'll marry me, or I'll kill myself, here and now! Say it, Anna... Yes or NO!'"

And then all at once, Aunt Minnie started laughing. And then she was laughing so hard she was bent over laughing, and I was thinking, "She's gone nuts."

So I screamed out, "What's so funny?"

She dialed down the laughter. "Ohhhhhh yes, I've heard her tell it many times."

"WHAAAAT?"

"Anna went up to Andrew, smiled, and said very sweetly, 'Of course, I'll marry you, Andrew. Now sit down and eat your supper.'"

57

The Saint and the Sinner
(Tuesday—Dawn)

A hushed, rich voice brought me out of dreamland. Peeking an eye open in the dim light of early morning, I made out the huge frame of Uncle Frank standing next to Aunt Minnie at the foot of my bed. It wasn't that Uncle Fred was that big, really, but he was big enough to be a gang foreman—which he was—of an iron crew that built skyscrapers and bridges. And he sure looked like he could hold a sledgehammer in one hand and a rivet in the other and drive it through iron. And his body was heavy, but not fat—thick, you might call it, so that hanging high in the air wind didn't whistle through him but around him. And his head with its coppery color and hooked nose like an Indian penny, and a forehead with its widow's peak looked like the prow of a ship that could cut through any storm God could muster. But his best feature was his voice. I could listen to it forever; it was full of notes and made every word sound like an orchestra.

Ironworkers—what a trade. They walked on steel beams hanging in the clouds, rivet them together, higher and higher they go, ever closer to God. And I wondered if those that fell off—those whose luck ran out—if their souls went straight up to heaven, since they were so close, or did they have to splatter first, then go way back up? Or down, for that matter, like Uncle Fred, who'd been doomed to hell ever since he brought home a smell of perfume that wasn't Aunt

Minnie's. And that was all I knew about that, because it was one of those things nobody talked about—and that you didn't ask about. Other than that, Uncle Fred had never missed a day at work, and the money was good, very good. Good enough, in fact, to loan my dad a little bundle for the shop at 5 percent interest. Oh, one more thing, Uncle Fred always fell asleep when he played chess with my dad. And one last bit—Peter, before he joined up, never talked to him, not a word. He wouldn't even ask him to pass the salt and pepper at the supper table. And that was another thing you didn't ask about.

Oh, oh, sensing, I guess, that they might wake me up, they'd backed off over to the side window. I couldn't make out what they were saying—probably trying to figure out how many bananas to stuff me with, so I'd gain a few pounds before they shipped me home. I swear Uncle Fred always looked at me like I was the "Eighth Wonder of the World." I think the only time I'd ever impressed him was when I was seven. That was when my mom and I dared to go on the 9-G Rocket Ride that he built and operated at Riverview for a while. It had a big steel arm, like a spoke of a wheel, with a cockpit at the end for four people and would swing up and back in an arc, going higher and higher, getting scarier and scarier, until at the very top—at twelve o'clock—you'd be upside down screaming your lungs out before you'd come looping down with a force of 9-Gs—that was nine times the pull of gravity, like in a dive bomber. My dad wouldn't go near it, wouldn't even watch it. He'd take my sister over to the merry-go-round. Mom and I never kidded him about it, but we'd bring it up once in a while between ourselves when we were treating ourselves to some graham crackers and milk; it was always good for a laugh.

All in all, I think Uncle Fred was paying much too high a price for this perfume thing. But hey, what did I know. But I did think it must be hard to live with a saint. It was like you were always on guard. I knew I was. Like I didn't dare do the "bad thing" because if Aunt Minnie walked in, I'd die. Right then and there. I would! Really! And there was absolutely no doubt I'd go straight to hell with no stops in between. And who knew what my gravestone would read— not to mention the small print. Geeez! I mean, I really liked my

Aunt Minnie, but I wouldn't want her living at our house. Uh-uh. I mean—heeeeey, wait a minute! What's going on by the window? Uncle Fred put his arm around Aunt Minnie, and she ducked away; but then he grabbed her from behind, and now he was talking in her ear. Heeey, watch the hands, Fredddy. Oops, he was twisting her. He was kissing her! Heeey, stop that! Oh…oh, Aunt Minnie was reaching back. She was…she was holding his head, and she was kissing him?

How could that be? She was a saint! Oh look, that was nice; now they were hugging. Oh, Freeedddddy, the hands, the hands! What's with the hands? Oh my god! Now she was biting his ear off! Nooooo. No, she was whispering… What the heck? Uncle Fred just swept her up and carried her out of the room! Holy, holy! And I mean, hoooly mooooly!

Oh my god, Uncle Fred was going to fall off a beam today and go straight to hell. Ugh, I didn't even want to think about it. And Aunt Minnie, they're probably going to burn at the stake like Joan of Arc. *Ugh!*

I'm too young for this stuff. I told you this house was weird.

58

Virginia Belongs to God
(Tuesday—Late Morning)

I slept late and lousy. Had to be almost noon because the sunlight was just starting to draw a bright rectangle on the polished floor. I'd been trying to get up all morning. I'd wake up, roll over, and pass out. After all, I missed a big chunk of sleep with that dream about King Kong and Aunt Minnie. I think it was a dream. Had to be. Anyway, I was filing it way back in my brain, under "Forget it!" I bounced out of bed and raised the other window—the one that faced the shaded porch—and a cool breeze washed over me.

"Aaaaagh!" screeched a voice from the doorway.

I whirled around. Nobody.

"Where's your pajamas?" came Virginia's voice from outside the room.

"It's too hot."

"Put them on so I can come in."

"Okay, okay. Wait." I pulled Georgie's bottoms over my shorts, folded the legs up about a foot, threw on my T-shirt, jumped back in bed, and sang out, "Come iiiiin."

Virginia came in with a breakfast tray. "I made you some farina, sleepy head." (Farina was like oatmeal; only the lumps were smaller.) She set the tray on my lap. I could smell her freshly washed hair. "Where's your pajama top?"

"C'mooon, the shoulders come down to my elbows."

Virginia giggled as she wiggled into the armchair. "Eat your cereal while it's hot," she said and went about braiding her long, dark hair.

I didn't mention Virginia earlier because thinking about her always took a chunk out of your brain. I certainly didn't forget her. Once you saw Virginia, you never forgot her. Not only because she was a fourteen-year-old copy of her radiant, beautiful mother—the one Aunt Minnie was probably looking for in the mirror—but because she was on a different level. One you could never reach. Virginia, you see, belonged to God. And it was perfectly okay. It had to be because there wasn't anything you could do about it. And you knew that the instant she walked into a room. All you could really do was like let her fill you up, and then as soon as she was gone, you punched a hole in your head to let her out, like air in a tire. Otherwise, you'd go crazy thinking about her.

"Eat, Billy," she said, her fingers flying as she twirled her hair into braids.

Girls like Virginia were extremely dangerous. It was just a darn good thing they were as rare as shooting stars. Like the only other one I knew was Mary Ann Podraza. She was a year ahead of me at school, and it was a good thing because otherwise I'd have a head full of holes. I mean it—you'd kill for a chance to kiss her. So it was a good thing you knew that these two belonged to God, because it saved a lot of blood. Of course, with Virginia and me being cousins, it was a lot easier. Then again, maybe I just thought it was, so I wouldn't have to punch a hole my head. Then again, since we're just itty-bitty cousins, I was going to have to rethink this whole damn thing. Hey, if all this isn't too clear, it's because this cousin—itty-bitty or not—this fair maiden with the flashing eyes and luscious lips just plain dazzled the heck out of me. So there! So ten Hail Mary's and forget about it already.

"Billy, eat your farina! It's getting cold."

"Huh?" was all I said, because I was "filling up," naturally.

"Eat! And drink your milk."

"How do you do that? That braid thing."

"It's easy," she said, leaning forward. "You keep crossing them over the middle one, cross, cross—"

"Let me try."

"No, eat!" she said, leaning back, her hands flying.

"I hate to tell you this, but I'm allergic to farina."

"Oh! Oh no." She stopped with the braiding and covered my hand with one of hers. "Oh, I'm sorry, Billy. I didn't know."

"That's okay. Just throw it out."

"Drink your milk. It's good for your bones." She patted my hand and went back to her hair.

"I got bones. I need something to put on 'em. A sweet roll and a cup of coffee does the trick."

"You're too young for coffee. It's not good for you."

"Not good for you maybe. But for me, it's doctor's orders. It's the caffeine, the doctor said. Caffeine's a chemical, see. It mixes in with something in the sweet roll and makes you fat. Uh-huh," I nodded to Virginia's shaking head and flying hands. "It does, Virginia! The doctor said so. He said the best thing for me in the morning is a sweet roll and a cup of coffee."

"It's not morning, it's almost noon." She smiled as she twirled, then stopped. "Oh, I know! I can make you a salad!"

"Salad? On an empty stomach? That can kill you! It forms nitratrichloric acid and eats right through your guts!"

"Drink your milk!" she said, standing up and stamping her foot.

I gripped the heavy stein with both hands and gulped a couple of mouthfuls. "Yum, yum." I licked my lips. Virginia smiled, slipped back on the chair, and went on with her hair-weaving.

"You want some? I mean, I'm not contagious or anything. Well, maybe I am. I have pleurisy, you know."

"Pleurisy? What's that?"

"It's bad. It travels in your blood up to your brain, and then it... It makes you do bad things."

Virginia's hands hung still on her rope. "Bad things?"

I nodded.

"Like what?"

"Well...you won't tell anyone?" Virginia shook her head.

"Well, the thing is, if I don't do what my brain tells me to do, a piece of it—just a little piece—it dies. Yeah," I said nodding. "But it's such a small piece, I hardly even notice the difference. I just black out a little... From the pain I mean... A stabbing pain right here." I stabbed my forehead with my middle finger. "It's nothing really. I mean, I can take it. It's just that... Well, for the rest of the day, my ears ring. And it gets so loud that... Well...it makes them bleed a little. Just a little. But then they hurt like mad. More than my forehead, I mean. I mean they really hurt."

"Oh, blessed God," said Virginia."

"Don't say that... Ohhhhh," I groaned and pressed my fist to my forehead. "Aggh!"

"What?" Virginia reached over and shook my arm. "What, Billy? What's the matter?"

"No, no, I won't do that! Stop it! I won't! I won't, I tell ya. Not in a million years!"

"Won't do what?" She started shaking my arm, her braid unraveling. "What's it telling you?"

"I can't tell you."

"Yes, you can! Tell me!" she said, ripping my arm out of its socket.

"It...it...it wants me to kiss you!"

Virginia let go, drew back, her jaw dropped. (She had great pearls.)

"You're like the stars in the sky, Virginia. Dazzling but unreachable!"

"We're cousins, Billlllly."

"Half cousins, actually."

"What if—" Virginia moved closer. "What if—" Virginia stared into my eyes... Then she dropped her lips on mine... Then, just as I was getting to get the feel of them, she tore them away and ran out of the room.

Ohh boooy! Just wait till she comes back for the farina. I'm gonna...gonna end up in hell, that's what. Ha! Ha! Ha! Ha! Haaaaaa!

59

The Big Lie (Tuesday Afternoon)

For the rest of my life, I will never be able to eat farina. So, who needs it? I don't even know what happened; it was beyond trying to figure out. So go ahead and laugh. Boy, it was just like my Uncle George always said, "You can't figure them. You just never know." Nope. It was not like math. You couldn't add it up, subtract it, multiply it, or divide it. And the worst thing was, you couldn't erase it. It's stuck there in your brain like a coo-coo clock, popping out, going, "Told you so! Told you so!" Anyway, they were gone now, and it was quiet. I heard them earlier messin' around in the kitchen: Aunt Minnie, Aunt Polly, Virginia, and yes, Archie…runnin' around shrieking and laughing, opening and closing cabinet doors, and then the back door slammed, and it was quiet.

"Dazzling but unreachable…like stars in the sky." Hmmmm, not bad. Where did I get this stuff? Boy, I tell you, I got two strikes against me already. If I didn't watch out, it was going to be me and Uncle Fred shaking hands on the elevator down."

The rectangle on the floor hadn't grown much, so it was still early. I swung my feet down on the floor, and all of a sudden, I was dizzy.

"Stop!" I yelled, and it stopped. "Damn! Always somethin'." I went over to the closet next to the dresser and swung open the split doors. All my stuff was on the left side in a space made by pushing all of Georgie's stuff over to the right. I grabbed a flashy red shirt from

357

Georgie's side and held it up. "Geez, am I that small, or is he that big?" I hung the shirt back up, grabbed my sandals, buckled them up, and pushed the doors shut.

I was moving now, getting ready to take on the world. I grabbed the *Herr Frankenstein* book I spotted earlier on the dresser, next to three other hardcover books, all by Joseph Conrad—a terrific writer—but I chose ol' stiff arms, Boris Karloff, because I didn't know the movie came from a book.

And on top of that, it was written by a woman, Mary Shelley. Now what kind of a woman's got such a weird brain? Wow! I checked the window for the grandfolks. Yep, there they were, breaking their backs in the garden. What did they do for exercise in the wintertime? Lift weights at the gym? On my way out, I looked behind the door… Yep, there she flew, the Piper Cub, dipping her wings, slipping through the air as smooth as silk. What a beauty.

The living room was cool and shady, mostly, because the only windows were the three facing the shaded front porch. I passed through the arch and into the warm bright dining room, made that way by the three lacy curtained windows on the sunny side of the house. On the far end of the dining room table was a model airplane kit with a picture of a P-39 Pursuit Plane on it. Wow! Ray said he was going to buy an airplane kit that we could build together, and this must be it, the P-39.

Boy, I tell you Ray was some kind of guy. He was always showing me stuff. Not like Richard. But that was okay. Richard was just different—like the other side of the moon. No, that was not right either. I didn't know what he was, really. Except I thought it had a lot to do with him being an orphan, his all-for-Richard thing. Cousin Ray, on the other hand, was the type would die for you—throw himself on a grenade for you. That type. I wasn't like that. I was the "have to think about it" type. Hey, I have a tough-enough time trying to stay alive; I wasn't going to be throwing myself on no grenade. Uh-uh.

And then I blinked, and the bloody head of Ah-lex was sticking out of the water. A shot of fear flashed through me… It wasn't the first time, and I knew it wouldn't be the last time.

I went through the second arch and into a hallway. On left was a small table with a telephone and a lamp and a chair next to it. Downright led to two bedrooms and a big bathroom. I did the bathroom thing then went back and passed through the arch that led into the kitchen. I dove into a chair at the table and buried my nose in *Frankenstein*:

> Listen to me, Frankenstein. You accuse me of murder; and yet you would, with a satis-fied conscience, destroy your own creature. Oh, praise the eternal justice of man! Yet I ask you not to spare me: and then, if you can, and if you will, destroy the work of your hands."

I said the last line aloud several times, then turned the page and began chapter 11:

> It is with considerable difficulty that I remember the original era of my being: etc., etc., etc.

I read on for a good bit, the language kind of strange, "classy." I liked it. It carried me into a different world. I skimmed forward and saw that there were quite a few pages left to the chapter, so I reached out for the *Chicago Sun-Times*. The headline read, "Tojo, Hitler of Asia." I ripped off the corner that read, "August 13, 1944," and marked the page in my book with it.

The coffee pot on the stove was cold, but there was coffee in it. I turned on the gas and rinsed out one of the cups in the sink. A soft breeze blew in from the window, branches with leaves fanned the wind; rather, the wind fanned the branches. The phone rang. I jumped, then dashed through the archway, and picked it up before the third ring.

"Hello? Helloooo The Obrycki resi—" A clicking sound stopped me. "Hello? Anyone there?" The thing was dead.

I placed the receiver back in the cradle and stared at the black numbers on the white dial... I picked up the receiver and carefully dialed BE (for *Berkshire*) 7-9541. I spun into the little chair next to the table and heard the first ring...then the second...and the third... then hung up before the fourth and flung a hand over my mouth. Breathing through my nose, the smell of coffee registered. I scooted back into the kitchen, grabbed the cup, and filled it with smoking hot coffee. Placing it on the table, I noticed a note under the salt-shaker. It read:

William.

      Aunt Polly, Virginia, and I are going to work at the Red Cross.
      Virginia made you a sandwich for lunch. It's in the refrigerator. There are some Joseph Conrad books on your dresser, so don't go outside until tomorrow. We will be back at dinnertime.

                                Aunt Minnie

The phone rang. I stiffened. It rang again. I dashed into the hallway.

"Hello! Don't hang up! Who is it?"

"William?"

Boy, did I know that voice. "Mom! Did you just call a little while ago?"

"How are you feeling?"

"Good, Mom! Good! I'm all cured! How are you?"

"How did you get so sick?"

"I'm not sick. Not anymore. I'm fine, Mom. Honest. I'll tell you all about it when you pick me up. When are you—"

"Aunt Minnie said you just got out of the hospital. She said—"

"Mom! Mom, listen! I'm cured! I'm all healthy!"

"But you have to see the doctor Friday, Aunt Minnie said."

"I can see a doctor at home, Mom! Just come and get me! Okay?" I wanted to say "please" but didn't. "Today, okay? Mom?"

"We just got home, and your father has to go to the shop. Melvin needs—"

"I know, I know. Okay. Just forget it."

"William!" she said, with that hard edge in her voice now. "We've had some difficulties. And plans have been made. And...ohh, your father will explain. You don't know—"

"I know, I know! Responsibilities! I know!"

"No, you don't! You don't! Things are different now! Oh, William," she said, and I knew this voice too. "The weekend will be here before you know it. And then—"

"Mom! Mom, listen! I was just kidding! Really! I didn't want to bring it up right off, but Ray and I have plans too." And suddenly my mouth was off and running... "We're going up to Uncle Tom's farm to help out. You know, with the flood and all, they need us, see? So we're going up on the Soo Line. On Friday. After I see the doctor. So see, Mom? I was just kidding you! Ha-ha! So don't worry one bit, Mom. Everything will—"

"Stop it, William! What kind of talk is that?"

"But, Mom, they need us. It'll be good. What's a couple more weeks?"

"Nick!" I heard my mother call out, away from the mouthpiece.

"Plans are plans, Mom. And Ray's already got word out to Uncle Tom, see? So everything's set. So I'll say goodbye now, Mom. Oh, and tell Dad I'm eating and getting fat. Okay?"

"Nick. Nick, huuurry."

Geez, my mom sounded like she was about to have a heart attack. So I quickly asked God not to let anything happen to my mom, because it would just kill me.

"Hello, son! How are you?" rang my dad's voice, strong and cheery but with an edge to it. I choked up. "William? Hello?"

"Yeah, Dad, I'm here."

"You okay?"

"Errrrrr," I cleared my throat. "I can't talk now, Dad. Mom will explain everything! Bye!"

I slammed the smoking receiver back on its four-prong holder, then waited for it to leap up and bite me. Waited for the roof to fall in, something. I mean, Jesus, God Almighty! You just don't hang up on your father! Uh-uh! No way! I mean, I was going to hell anyway, but I didn't want to take the express. Geez, I don't know why I said what I said. And then my father was talking to me, and I hung up on him, on top of it. Ohhh, Gooood..."

I dashed into the kitchen and ran around the table a couple of times, then I ran all the way back to the living room and back to the kitchen, and back to the living room, and back to the kitchen, and back to the living room. I don't know how many times up and back, up and back, until I threw myself on the couch and started punching the pillows, punching and punching...

60

The Payoff (Wednesday)

Sounds from the kitchen like yesterday, the same routine, cabinets slamming, feet dashing about, voices with short sentences, including Aunt Polly's—and I imagined Archie sitting there in a corner with his thumb up his... Ahhh, I don't mean that. It just hurts to picture his frightened expression, like he was always waiting for the world to crush him, tear him to pieces, and it was going to do just that. I didn't see any other way. And then the sound of the heavy backdoor slamming shut, and it was quiet...until, suddenly, the same door banged open, someone rushing in—probably Virginia, grabbing something they forgot—then *bang*, and the quiet leaked back in.

Yesterday, hours after I died, when I heard them returning from the Red Cross, I bolted from the couch and ran into the bedroom, but no one came to check on me, because right away they got busy making dinner: pots banging, water running, and the chop-chop of a knife doing its thing on vegetables, and before long cooking smells were sneaking into my bedroom. And then, finally, I heard the humming voice of Virginia approaching, so I quickly opened the Frankenstein book and flopped it on my chest to give the impression that I had dozed off while reading. There was a soft knock on the opened door. I stopped breathing. The second knock was louder,

but not loud. I groaned and moved a little. Frankie hit the floor...
I could smell her; she was that close, onions and parsley. I wanted
to grab her and squeeze her and kiss her and kiss her until our lips
melted together forever. Peeking an eye, I saw her pick up the book
and place it on the table. Then her hand touched my shoulder, and
my heart started thumping. I felt her breath on my cheek, felt her
hair surround me, felt her lips on my cheek. I grabbed her, and...

"No, no, Billy! It's a sin! It's a sin!"

"Whaaaa?"

"It's a sin, Billy! We're cousins!"

"Whaaaaaaa?"

Moments later, I heard the door close. The Piper Cub swayed...
the wings dipped...

A WHILE LATER, there was a rap on the door, and Ray entered
with a big bowl of chicken noodle soup. He'd be back, he said, and
that he had a surprise for me. I figured it couldn't top the one I
just had. The steaming bowl was loaded with every vegetable in the
grandfolks' garden: carrots, celery, loads of parsley, and noodles naturally, and even potatoes, and I don't know what else. I played with
it...ate some...played with it...ate some...and most of all, tried not
to think...

I woke up, and there was a bow at the foot of my bed with a
note. It read: "Tomorrow we'll shoot the bows." Boy, oh boy, oh boy.
I loaded the bow, drew the bowstring back, and the magic began. I
felt the bow come alive, felt the power, felt its heart beat with mine,
and knew it would be a part of me forever.

I spent a chuck of time hunting in Africa, flying over open land
in my Piper Cub, past herds of zebras, and water buffalos, and pink
flamingoes. Yes, there I was, stalking through the jungle looking for
prey...drawing my bow quickly at the sight of a lion or a tiger, but
not letting the bow sing, because always they ran away. Ran away
from me, big hunter Billy Big Bow!

Aunt Minnie came in later, just before all the light left the room through the window. She looked miserable, and that didn't help me any. Her problem was the war; mine was the folks. Lying to them like that. So we did a good half hour on our knees, elbows on my bed, did a whole rosary that way, all the beads, and then she did some asking for Georgie and Peter and some other names, and then her head just hung there, and I thought maybe she had passed out. But no, because all of a sudden, she came on strong with a string of Polish, so strong and full of feeling, in fact, that it left me vibrating like a tuning fork. And that was how yesterday ended.

Oh, but of course, there was the night, which was full of crap. Nightmares ran in quadruple features, and in all of them I'd be running like my feet were in molasses. And then in the last reel I saw my dad staring down at me, and I couldn't move at all. The covers were tight across my chest, holding me down, and they wouldn't budge. I kept pulling at them and pulling at them, and then I was reaching out to my dad, but my arms went weak, like water, and I collapsed and the covers wouldn't loosen, tight across my chest, and I couldn't pull them away...trying and trying...weak, my arms like water. Then I lunged with everything I had, and my hands went right through my dad, and I was grabbing air, grabbing... And then a bouquet of flowers started to grow...bigger and bigger...until it filled the room. And that...that was really the finishing touch to yesterday.

But the hell with yesterday. Today was a new day! It was bright and sunny out there with trees swaying, leaves fluttering, birds singing, everything alive. So like Scarlett O'Hara, I said, "I'll think about it tomorrow." Yeah, babe, what a great line: "Tomorrow." Ha! I swung open the closet doors, climbed into my shorts, buckled on the sandals, threw on my T-shirt, grabbed my bow, and hustled out into the kitchen. Again the note—the Red Cross...the sandwich Joey Conrad, yeah, yeah...and the new thing: "Ray will be home early." I poured me a glass of milk and unwrapped the wax-papered sandwich. Yesterday, delicious egg salad on toast; today, peanut butter on white bread. The garbage can got most of it. Broads, you couldn't trust them.

I grabbed my bow, dashed out the door, ran down the porch steps, and slammed out the screen door. The perfume of fresh cut grass was in the air. I stopped in the middle of the yard, made short by the huge four-car garage. The corner lot was the big yard, running from the street all the way back to the small one-car garage—which, by the way, now housed the big motorboat that Georgie built with over ten thousand screws when he was fourteen. With bow in hand, arms spread, and head back, I started spinning around and around, the puffy white clouds spinning in the blue, blue sky. *Thump.* something hit me in the back. I stopped spinning and sank to my knees; the world was still spinning in front of my eyes. So was Grandpa Andrew... More *thump*'s were hitting around me, and I realized Grandpa was throwing lumps of dried mud at me.

"Hey! *Cho to yest?*" (My Polish surprised me.) I dodged a muddy lump. "Hey! *Cha cleft holeta!*" Grandpa picked up his shovel and shook a fist at me.

I picked up my bow and shook it at him in return. He pointed to his shovel and indicated that he wanted me to dig in the garden. Ho-ho, break my back, that sort of thing, eh?

"*Nie! Nie!*" I shook my head. "Me sick, Grandpa!" I pointed to myself. "Sick! Me!" I stuck a finger down my throat and gaged. "Sick, see? Sorry, no worka me! Sick, get it?" So what did he do? He came at me with his shovel like he was going to crown me. So I drew back the empty bow and aimed it at him, and he stopped. Then, I guess, seeing no arrow in the notch, he started forward again; but then, just in time, Grandma came up and waved him off with her red babushka—like you do a bull—and then she marched him off to the garden with his head hanging down like a bad little boy. Personally, I think he's a little nuts.

Actually, this was the first time we ever talked—if you could call it that. The truth was, nobody could talk to him except Grandma. Oh, you could talk to him, of course, but they meant get him to do something. Grandma was the only one. My mom said he'd get her the moon if she wanted it.

I went back into the house and down into the basement to see if I could find some arrows in Georgie's workshop. The front part of the basement was closed off by a wall and had a door in the middle of it that opened into my grandparents' living quarters. A big furnace on the left side and big coal bin filled the rest of that side. Up on the right side was the clothes washing area with a long table acting as a divider. The rest of that side—most of it—was closed off by a long wall containing Georgie's workshop. The wall was made of plywood on the bottom, topped off by about two feet of chicken wire. There was a padlock on the makeshift door. I stacked a couple of boxes up against the Plywood wall and looked in through the chicken wire. A long workbench with equipment for making arrows was against the cement wall under the three windows. Vertical racks at both ends were filled with brilliantly colored arrows. But the real eye-catcher was the animal skin mounted on the left sidewall. Painted on it was an Indian riding a white horse, his brilliant feathered headgear almost touching the shallow water he was crossing. On the wall itself—all around the painted skin—were hunting arrows with vicious looking tips, and on the top and bottom were two bows with curled ends, like question marks.

"A work of art," I whispered.

Resigning myself to the fact that I'd have to wait until Ray came home, I started out, but at the door spied an arrow tucked between some two-by-fours. The tip was broken off, but otherwise it was perfect, with perfect circles of red, gold, and green painted on it.

I hustled outside, checked on the grandfolks: Grandma's red babushka was at the far end of a row of corn, with Grandpa just ahead of her. Standing in the middle of the big yard, I notched the arrow, drew it back, aimed it straight up, and let 'er rip. Up and up the arrow zoomed through the blue sky...higher and higher until it stopped in midair...hung there for a second then falling backward... turning slowly around...then wagging until it straightened out... then slicing the air...and *thump*. It stabbed the earth, the ring of colors vibrating.

Shooting an arrow wasn't anything like shooting a gun. Anybody could line up the sights and pull a trigger. My sister could do it. Heck,

Archie could do it. And it was all noise. But the bow, it changed everything, my whole mood, even changed the way I walked; there was music to it—if you can understand that. I can't really explain it any better than that.

The porch door slammed. Ray was at the railing.

"Billy! Your dad wants you!"

"Where's he calling from?"

"He's not calling! He's here!"

61

Going Home

We were driving back, and Dad hadn't said a word, not one little itty-bitty word. Oh, and before that, when Ray called me into the house, you'll never guess what happened, never in a million years... Nothing happened. Absolutely nothing. I mean about the lie I told. Nothing! Can you believe? I couldn't. Nobody even mentioned it. Not Ray, not Aunt Minnie, and not my dad. And I certainly didn't bring it up. Unbelievable! But the real kicker, besides the lying, was that I hung up on my own father. Boooy, that was beyond belief; that was about as bad as you can get, like I said before. But the thing was, I just couldn't tell him that when I heard their voices, all I wanted was to be with them. Not tomorrow, or the day after, but that very instant, right then and there. So was that so much to want? Wasn't it worth a lie and the hanging up? I guess not. Not if it came with a wall. Not if it came with your father sitting right next to you and you couldn't even feel his closeness. Not if he didn't even want to touch you, not even look at you. And that was when I realized it wasn't over. That at some point we were still going to get into it. So I sat there sweating bullets, dying a slow death... And then Dad pulled the old Plymouth off the highway and parked where we usually parked to watch the airplanes come in, and I thought, 'This is it. Here it comes."

But we sat there and nothing. Then Dad got out, closed the door, and leaned against it. I just sat there, dying some more... A big silver bird flew over the highway low and loud. I got out of the car and crept around to my dad's side. I was shaking. Dad was smoking a cigarette. I never saw him smoke before.

"You okay now? You not…you're not sick?"

"No, Dad, I'm fine," I rattled off. "Aunt Minnie took real good care of me."

"She that way. It her…it's her nature." Dad flicked ash from his cigarette.

"Talk, William. Keep talking," I said to myself.

"Aunt Minnie said that you lived by her when you came from the farm."

"Hmm," nodded Dad. "Was hour and half on streetcar to see your mother." We watched a twin-engine Delta glide in, cross the road, and touchdown—smoke corning from its wheels.

"Talk William, talk," again to myself.

"So how was Detroit, Dad?"

"Hah-hah," came with a smile, a cough, and a glob of spit. "Detroit." The smile grew as Dad dragged deep on his cigarette and exhaled… "Detroit," he said again, but by this time the smile had turned sour. "We go to lunch with two Ford people. One old man, all gray hair. And nice-looking, tall, young man. From purchasing department, so important men, huh?"

"Yeah, Dad," I said nodding.

"Biiig sign," Dad swept the air with a hand, "BARNEY's. Is famous place, but not fancy. Big steaks, like this." Dad held a finger and thumb two inches apart, "Mushrooms and onions like this." Dad held his hand high over an imaginary steak. "Is veeery good. Mmmm." Dad flipped the short butt away and blew on his fingers as if burned a little. "We talk… Bernie Frazin, supervisor at Zenith— your mother's boss. And his uncle, Julian—big, strong man. Julian make us laugh. Very funny man. And smart." Dad tapped his temple with a finger and nodded. "Yeah… So we finish eating da big steaks, and da waiter, he bring us five bowls. Wooden bowls. Small." Dad cupped his hands. "Is hot water and slice a lemon in bowls. So…" Dad suddenly burst out laughing. I mean, he laughed so loud he kind of scared me. I mean, you can't even hear the airplanes! Then he stopped dead and started talking, fast.

"The young man, the Ford man. Takes lemon, squeezes in da juice, and drinks. He drinks the water. Heh-heh-heh! Ya! So...so Julian, he squeezes in da lemon, and he drinks. So..." nodding, Dad went on, "we all drink the hot water! Ha-ha-ha-ha! Ha-ha-ha-ha... Yah."

I was puzzled, and my look, I knew, showed it.

"Da bowl, William, was for washing fingers. Is fingerbowl." Dad went back to laughing.

"Ohhh, ohhhh, wooow! So everybody drank so the young Ford man wouldn't be embarrassed. Wooooow!" I joined Dad laughing. "Ohh boy. That's something, Dad."

And then suddenly, somehow, Dad's face told me that he was the one to drink the water first.

We watched a silver bullet float in, its four engines screeching as it crossed the highway.

Dad said, "TWA, Boeing Stratoliner. One hundred seven feet, wing tip to wing tip. Body seventy-four feet long. Four, Wright-GR radial engines, 38 passengers, top speed 241 miles per hour, range 1,750 miles."

"Geeeez, Dad, how did you know that?"

"Some things I know...some things I don't." Dad pulled a pack of Lucky's out of his shirt pocket. "Die-making, I know. Is my world." He lit up...shook the flame out of the match, and exhaled. "Your world, school. You smart, William?"

"Yeah, Dad. Pretty smart."

"Not number 1?"

"Nooo. Adrian Franchikoska...and Joan Mindykoska. They're real smart. They're like 1 and 2. They always know the answer to everything."

"And the boys?"

"Hmm, Henry Jachecz is pretty smart. Thomas Kleczes is smart. But his dad's a principal at a school. So I think Jachecz is smarter... Larry Niemerowich is kinda smart. But he's going to be a priest, so he gets away with a lot... And then there's like three of us guys about the same... I was real smart, up to third grade, Dad. I got all As. All As in everything.'

"So then what?"

I shrugged. "I don't know... I started playing baseball. And then I got the paper route, so—"

"Hmpt! Okay, get in da car."

Dad finished his cigarette, got in the car, and nosed the old Plymouth back onto the highway.

I was feeling great. I couldn't even begin to tell you how great I felt. Dad didn't bring up the lie and nothing about me hanging up on him either. Boy, that was what I called getting away with murder... Unless, maybe he was waiting until we got home. But I didn't think so... Could be though, with Mom and all... Yeah, the more I thought about it...could be. So I couldn't let go of it. Uh-uh. Not yet... But one good thing, Dad really talked to me. I mean, we really talked... Boy, I can't tell ya. But now, not a word. Not even a look... Thinkin' about the factory, I bet.

"How's everything at the factory, Dad? With Melvin and everything?"

"Hmmm... Tomorrow."

Traffic was heavy now. It was rush hour, and the sun was really cookin' us, especially my dad, seeing as it was coming in on his side, at a good slant now, and no breeze. I didn't recognize any landmarks, but I could tell from the stockyard smell and the yellow industrial smoke that we were still on the South side. We had a long way to go.

"Can I turn on the radio, Dad?"

He didn't answer. Sweat was running down his face and drippin' off his chin, and he didn't even seem to know it.

"Dad?

Dad swerved, tooted his horn, and growled, all at the same time. Then he blotted his face with his sleeve, gave me a glance, and was gone again.

Oh, hey, listen, I forgot to tell you that before we left the Obryckis', we visited Grandma and the mudslinger, Grandpa, in their garden. Seeing us coming, Grandpa Andrew took off.

"Iggnaaaatz," said my Grandmother Anna, the corn stalks taller than her. "Igganaaaaatz," she said again as they embraced.

Boy, I'm telling you, she had a way of saying his name so that it sounded like a song. I don't know how she got so many notes into it. It really sounded nice. She put a few notes into my name too, but nothing like the trick she did with Ignatz. And then, as their Polish talk continued, my dad changed right before my eyes. A tone came into his voice that I had never heard before. He sounded like a young boy. He even looked different. It was a little odd, but nice...really nice. If it's happened to you, you know what I mean.

Grandpa came through the corn loaded with vegetables. Grandma grabbed some, passed some to me, and we went off to the front porch. Right away, Polish words started exploding behind us. During visits before, my dad and his father barked a few words at each other, and that was that. But not this time. This time, their stormy outbursts rolled on and on, shaking the cornfield with their thunder.

Grandma grabbed a carrot, wiped the mud off it with her apron, and handed it to me. She did the same for herself. Then she bit off a piece, and I watched her jaw move like a squirrel munching on a nut. It struck me so funny I almost choked laughing at her, but all she did was give me the warmest smile you ever saw. It just opened you right up, like the sun does to the morning glory. I hardly knew her, but I really, really liked her. There was just something about her that went right through you and made you feel good. And of course—like everybody said—even scary Grandpa acted like a puppy around her. That wasn't hard to believe. Not one bit.

The storm in the garden finally rumbled down until all was quiet. Then moments later, an explosion of laughter burst from in there but died quickly, and again it was quiet. Grandma shooed her arm at me, indicating, I gathered, that I should go take a look. So I got up off the porch steps and made my way through the corn stalks. Peeking in, I saw them talking. The Polish between them now was low and smooth. And then, my dad took Grandpa's hand and kissed it. I picked up my jaw and snuck back to the porch.

We loaded the trunk with vegetables and left. Through the back window, I saw Grandma standing there, giving us a little wave, her face shining like an angel... I knew I would see that picture in my mind's eye for the rest of my life. That, and my dad kissing his father's hand.

I TURNED ON THE RADIO. Dad didn't seem to notice. His sweaty hands just kept working on the steering wheel, gripping and regripping. The static was so bad I clicked it off. Dad didn't give me a glance, just kept his eyes glued on the road, and his hands on the wheel, gripping and regripping.

And then I started talking and couldn't stop. And although Dad didn't say a word, I could tell he was listening by the way he'd cock his head or give me a sneaky glance—like when I told him about the Garaaab farm—the rich delta, that all you had to do was piss on it and jump aside so you wouldn't get knocked over by whatever sprung up—that one got me more than a glance. And about what Jake said about immigrants buying bad land from a map, sight unseen, like Grandpa. But I didn't bring up what Aunt Minnie told me about Andrew, Anna, and Pete. I went on a lot about the Garaaaab farm: about swimming in the creek and about fishing with Grandma and how she talked to the fish. And about the relatives corning up, the cookout every night in the yard, and the keg of beer, the bonfire, and the dancing. And Uncle John lifting the car. And about Uncle George and the bloodsuckers. And sleeping out by the pump with Richard, under a sky with a million stars. And of course, I talked about the haying and just a little bit about how I wanted to tear my eyes out from the itching. I didn't say too much about the big dance at the Mile-A-Way—nothing about the girl, of course—just that everybody was there, having a great time. Then about the rain: how it rained and rained without stopping for three days and three nights, how the water kept coming up until the creek was as big as a lake—just like the ones we went to on Sundays with the relatives. And about how the poor cows were trapped on the other side.

And then I blurted, "Ah-lex is dead, you know... Dad?" I leaned forward to try and catch his eye, added a waving hand...and that was when I realized that somewhere along the way, I had lost him, that I was mostly talking to myself. And right away, I felt real bad. Bad because the things I said didn't matter to him. And they were all I had to give. Things about me, what I had done, how I felt… I mean, heck, he could have said something about when he was a kid on the farm or about the shop or even about Melvin-Melvin. But no, his jaws stayed clamped—not even a blink about Ah-lex.

I lay back, closed my eyes, and pretended to doze… And then, all of a sudden, I popped up and blurted, "How come Mr. Frazin was in Detroit?"

Dad stared at me wide-eyed. The front wheel on my side ran off the road. I threw my hands on the dash. Dad whipped the bouncing Plymouth back onto the road. I gave him a wide-eyed look. He gave me a smirk in return. Then, just as we started to relax, white smoke started streaming out of the radiator.

"Agh! Overheat."

I think we both spied the Shell Gas Station just ahead of us, off to the right, at the same time.

We pulled in and parked under some trees on the right side of the station. I jumped out and was fishing for the hood latch when Dad waved me off with a red shop rag.

"Get back." Dad popped the hood, opened it wide, and braced it with the rod. The radiator was gurgling white smoke. Dad bunched the rag on the cap, turned it carefully, and jumped back as steam shot up like a geyser, then quickly gurgled down until only white smoke crawled out of the opening. Dad picked up the radiator cap with his rag.

"I'll get some water, Dad."

There was a big Buick parked at a pump with its hood up. A man in a white shirt and tie was pouring water from a pail into the car's radiator.

"Sir? Can I use that pail when you're done?"

"Sure enough, son." When the radiator stopped gulping water and ran over, the man passed me the galvanized pail. "There's a sink in the garage."

I thanked the man, took the pail into the garage, filled it, and headed back to the car. Dad was sitting on one of the wooden crates in the shade of some maple trees. Wisps of smoke were now belching out of the radiator.

"Leave it there," Dad called out.

I put the pail down and joined him in the shade. He handed me a cold bottle of Coke.

"Oh, thanks, Dad." I gulped from the bottle. "Hmmm, nice and cold." I held the bottle against my cheek.

Dad finished his Coke and lit up a cigarette. "See da man on da chair leaning back against the wall?" Dad nodded toward the garage.

"Yeah... What about him?"

"People see da man, I see da chair. How big a man sits there breaks chair, breaks the skinny legs... Everybody think about the man. Tool-and-die maker sees chair."

"If there was a pretty girl on the chair, I wouldn't even see the chair."

Dad smiled, said with a nod, "Ya. Your mother..." He let it hang there, took a deep drag on his cigarette, and flicked it away. He held up the radiator cap. "How you make this? How this made?" He handed it to me.

I turned the metal radiator cap upside down and around. "You make a die and put it in a punch press. Stamp 'em out."

Dad nodded, took the cap back. "Draw die. Not hard, dis one, but not easy. Draw die never easy. Metal tears, cracks, not easy... I make draw die for antenna for CB Radio. Small cups," Dad made a circle with his finger and his thumb. "Like this. Blueprint show dimensions, angles, radius, but not how to make." Dad held his hand out as if he was holding something in it. "I look at block of steel. Look where to start, where to cut... See in my mind like...like Michelangelo see da marble. But not that great. No! No!" Dad traced lines with a finger on an imaginary block of steel in his hand. "I cut angles, curves, thousandths of an inch at a time. And then make da mating part, make fit perfect. Lock together like...like lovers." Dad laced his fingers together. "And then put in da punch press, make da first sample. Press comes down." *Boom.* Dad pounded a fist into his hand.

"I look at piece...here metal too thin, here too thick, hear tear, cracked. I see in my mind how to fix. Day after day, I'm adding, subtracting...getting closer, closer, ten thousandths of an inch here, a little d'ere...better now, shining now, coming alive. D'ere! Now! D'ay come together, and dis time, dis time, it is born. Perfect. Da way I know. Da way I see in my mind…clean and shiny…perfect, like a diamond. A shiny new diamond…" Dad drew a deep breath and exhaled.

I was stunned. I saw a man I never saw before. I don't think anybody ever saw this man before… Did my mom? I don't think so. I don't think he ever showed this man before. But he did, to me! With tears in my eyes and lumps in my throat, I jumped into his arms and hugged him tight.

"What? What, William?" His voice was puzzled.

"I see the chair, Dad. I see the chair!"

"Hal-ha! Is okay. Is okay you see da girl. Is your world now… Your mother…your mother, she see new world…new world in Detroit… Connie too! See dancing, ballet!" Dad struck a ballet pose (hand overhead)… "See plays, with actors! And opera! Opera! Singing! Great voices. I…"

"Geez, Dad…" It was all I could say.

"Hmm… New world, William."

"You saw them too, didn't you?"

"I see, but I not see… I look at da chairs."

We laughed, and we couldn't stop laughing. When we finally did, we filled the radiator and got back on the road. We were going nowhere fast. It was hot, and the traffic was tied up. And so was I, tied in a knot that was getting tighter and tighter, and I didn't know why; it was just a feeling.

Dad snapped on the radio. News blared through the static about the heat, about the Cubs, about the White Sox, and about the war. Dad, I could tell, was paying close attention to the war news, which was about the Allied Forces battling the German Armies on all fronts. Dad clicked off the radio on the commercial that followed.

"Georgie's flying a B-29, in England. That's what Ray said."

Dad nodded. "Sixteen missions."

"Yeah… Peter is in a hospital, you know… Ray said, it's a mental hospital."

Dad laid on the horn. The light had changed, and nobody was moving. Then everybody started beeping, and we started moving… We were struggling due west now on Division Street, and the glaring sun was bouncing off the cars and making it hard to see. I kept glancing at the hood, hoping it wouldn't start smoking again.

"We need a new car, Dad."

"Dino can fix."

Dino was the mad Russian married to my Aunt Stephie in Elmwood Park. He was a small, bouncy guy who always told jokes—the dirty kind. But he was good at fixing cars, and that was what he did, fix cars in his garage. Dad, of course, kept him busy pounding out the fenders on our Plymouth. Dad, you see, wasn't a very good driver. And on top of that, he liked to speed, so that wasn't a good combination... Finally, we turned right onto Central Avenue. It was blacktopped and smooth and had buses running on it, not streetcars. The next stoplight would be North Avenue, where just around the corner was the Manor Theatre. My sister took tap dancing and ballet lessons in the building next to it. Yeah, Tuesdays, Thursdays, and Saturdays, rain or shine, snowstorms even, my mom—or Aunt Jean, if my mom was working—would make the trip after school with my sister in tow because brat sister Connie was going to be a star someday. Ho-hum.

"Remember, Dad, we used to go to the Manor Theatre every Monday night for Plate Night? They'd give you a cup or a plate, and we kept going until we had the whole set. Remember?"

Dad chuckled. "You remember?"

"*Natrulanie* (naturally).

"Oh-hooo." Dad gave me a wide-eyed look.

"Mom used to pack sandwiches, and we'd meet you before the six-o'clock price change. Remember, Dad? And Saturday night was *Rattle Night*. and I used to run up on stage to draw the winning ticket. And the winner always gave you a 'tip.' And once I got a dollar! And you took it and gave me back a dime."

"Dime! Should give you nickel."

"You did. But Mom made you give me a dime."

"And she take da dollar! And I have to buy more popcorn!"

We laughed.

"Remember, they had that giant pipe organ with the red velvet hanging behind it, and the guy playing it used to bounce up and down on the seat with the music? He's probably in the army now… probably dead."

We were stuck at the stoplight now… Yeah, the Manor's a pretty classy place, all right. The ceiling lights were like a giant bull's-eye with glowing circles of gold and black, and the sidewalls have big golden arches with paintings inside them. And before the movie started, the guy would be all lit up, playin', bouncin' up and down… the golden pipes shining—very classy. It was my favorite theatre. Besides the Montclair, that is—which was even classier—probably because it was newer. It was way out by Harlem Avenue. It's got a thick red carpet with black designs in it and a lot of white columns with statues of angels. But the best thing was the goldfish. They were in a pool shaped like a huge shell, and they got an angel hanging over them pouring water out of a pitcher. It was really neat. And the goldfish were huge. I never saw such big goldfish. And some were partly white, and one was completely white—an albino, must be… I could watch them swim forever.

Dad blasted the horn because the light changed and nobody was moving. Then everybody started beeping, and we started moving. As we crossed North Avenue, I turned and looked out the back window.

"The Manor's still there, Dad," I announced and right away thought, that was a dumb thing to say. You'd think I was gone for years. And just like that, a hot flash shot through me, and my eyes got blurry.

"See any good movies lately, Dad?"

Dad hit the brakes hard. A guy jumped back on the curb. "Watch you going, stupid!"

"That's tellin' 'im, Dad! Crazy guy."

Dad mumbled some Polish and wiped sweat from his brow.

I wiped at mine too and made a big show of it. "Phew, sure is hot." I fanned a hand at myself. "Hey, Dad, was Grandpa born with that hump on his back?"

Dad turned to look at me and seemed to forget he was driving. Car horns started blaring, and he swerved a bit before regaining control. We were on the long, narrow Central Avenue Bridge that passed over the railroad yards, and we both concentrated now on getting over it—me, with my nails stuck in the dash, and Dad, with an iron grip on the wheel. We got across, and suddenly I felt sick to my stomach. I leaned over in case I threw up.

"William, sit up! You okay?"

I nodded and swallowed. "Yeah, Dad." I took a couple of deep breaths. The sick feeling started to pass.

We caught another red light at Fullerton Avenue, which was where the streetcar line started and went east all the way to Lincoln Park on Lake Michigan and where, to the right, downtown Chicago started. "City of Big Shoulders"—just in case you forgot. But of course, we were going to go west, out to the sticks, out to Mango Avenue—just three blocks away.

The hot sun was pouring in through Dad's window, but he was shaking as if he was cold.

"Daaad?" I had trouble speaking. "Daaad, you...you all right?"

Dad brushed a hand over his face. "Ya!" he snapped.

The line of cars started moving. We made the turn into the sun onto Fullerton Avenue. There weren't any stores lining the wide concrete street that was now glistening with sunlight, but it did have sidewalks on both sides of the street, in front of some empty lots loaded with weeds, and then the houses started and ran down the block. First was Parkside Ave. My heart started to pound.

More empty lots, more weeds, then Major Avenue with brick bungalows again running down the street. And from there, dead ahead on the right, the American flag was waving from the top of the flagpole at the corner of our street, Mango Avenue. Father Phybilski had the pole put in when the war started. Also coming into view was the big World War I cannon that poked out over the white wooden fence that surrounded the apple orchard—which was where the janitor chased us with his sawed-off bat. And then to my surprise, a Ferris wheel came into view behind the apple orchard.

"Dad!" I shouted. "The carnival is up!"

"Eee-yah! Tomorrow opens. Beer Garden already open."

"Ohhh boy! I forgot all about it!"

Visions of me and my guys riding the Tilt-a-Whirl and the Swings and rocking the Ferris wheel, scaring the girls, filled my mind. And lying in bed and listening to the polka music every night. Boy! My heart was pounding so hard I thought blood was going to squirt out of my ears.

We made the right turn onto Mango Avenue, and there it was: Saint James Parrish. It stretched down the whole left side of the block. The right side was lined with brick bungalows like ours. We moved past the rectory—a three-story, dark redbrick mansion. Only two people lived there: Pastor Phybilski and Father Michael. Next was the reception hall: used for weddings and monthly movies that cost us twelve cents a head. A courtyard of flowers and trees followed with the nuns' brick sanctuary hidden behind it. The last brick building was Alcatraz—our schoolhouse with the sunken church.

Our house was the second house on the next block, across Altgeldt Avenue, on the left. The first house was the Lewandowskis', and before them were two empty lots, with no weeds, because the Lewandowskis always cut them down. Did I tell you earlier that the Lewandowskis resembled Laurel and Hardy? She was the stick, and he was the barrel. They had a blue star in the window for their son, Joe—kind of a sourpuss type of guy. They also had an older daughter, Merriam; she was like invisible. She only came out when there was a full moon. But they were good neighbors, and every year they put up a great Christmas tree. Would you believe they put every silver icicle on one at a time? Uh-huh. It took them a whole weekend to put up their tree. It took us about an hour.

At Altgeldt Avenue, Dad turned left. I glanced at him and wondered why we hadn't crossed the street and parked in front of our house. And then we turned right, into the cinder alley, and I wondered why we were parking in the garage. And then I remembered the vegetables in the trunk. Yeah, that's why, I thought to myself. But pieces of doubt bounced around in my mind. We crawled ahead, dodging all the potholes. The garbage men would fill them up with cinders, but they always came back—and in the same spot, which was baffling. I always spread our furnace cinders behind our garage and back into the prairie so our car and the Lewandowskis' black Packard wouldn't get stuck in the mud.

Dad cut the wheel, backed us up in line with our set of doors on the left, then shifted into neutral, which was my cue to hop out and open the doors.

"Thanks for bringing me home, Dad." I jumped out. Passing through the gate, I stared at our back porch with the swing hanging there. "No place like home." I ducked into the garage. And then for some stupid reason, I thought of the time Uncle George gave Dick and I a pretty good licking with Pete's belt.

Dad never hit me. Never. Not even once. But he did my mom, one time. She wouldn't give him a dollar on a Saturday night to play poker with his friends at the corner tavern, so he smacked her one. I was about five or six. I'll never forget it. I was screaming, "Stop! Stop!" It was the scariest thing, you have no idea. It was like the end of the world to me. After he left, my mom said he always gave her his paycheck and that she should have given him the dollar. She ended up with a black eye, and they didn't talk for a couple of days. Then one night, after supper, he tried to touch her hand, but she wouldn't let him. When she finally did, she told him she was wrong. Dad grabbed her and squeezed the hell out of her…and I think he cried. And he said he'd never ever hit her again. And he never did.

I swung open the big garage doors, and Dad pulled in. I shut the doors and barred them with the two-by-four. I took my suitcase out of the back seat. I wanted to run into the house with it, but I put it down on the cinder floor by the garage door and went back to the car where Dad was digging in the trunk. He pulled out a bunch of bright-red radishes, broke off two big ones, and sat on the edge of the opened trunk. I stood there biting my lower lip. He rubbed mud off the radishes, snapped a bite off of one, and handed me the other. I did a little more rubbing, snapped off a big bite, and we chewed along.

"Hot!" I opened my mouth and blew air.

"Good for blood."

"I'll get a bushel." I made a move.

"William!" Dad grabbed my arm. "Wil—" was followed by a coughing fit.

"Want some water, Dad?" I shook his knee.

He shook his head... Finally, he swallowed hard and cleared his throat. "Your mother... She's in da house. Go!"

I straightened up. *I felt the tip of the knife...*

"Go!" he said, sweeping a hand in the air. "She waiting for you."

His voice wasn't right. I watched him dig some cobs of corn out of the trunk.

He started stacking them. "Your mother not live here anymore." A bullet of pain shot through me. "She and Connie stay by Aunt Jean." He peeled an ear of corn down a bit, took a bite, and spit it out. "Your mother come every day make supper...and go back to Jean and George...they go back...everyday. They—"

We stood there, staring at each other... *The knife went deeper...*

I turned around and stumbled out of the garage. Everything was spinning... Even the clouds were spinning...and the ground... and the yard...everything...spinning...around and around...spinning... And my feet weigh a ton... And the porch is spinning... The steps are moving up and down, faster and faster... Swing swinging...flying... The screen door flapping open, shut...open...shut... waaaaving... *Dreaming! Yes!* Yeeeeees... Bad dream... Baaaaaaad... Flooooooating...

"Billy."

The knife spins away...

I'm in her arms... What can I say? She's my mom. After we slobbered all over each other, Mom had me eating apple pie that only a mother could make.

"Hello, Billy!"

It was my sister, Connie, standing in the dining room doorway. "What do you mean, 'hello!' Come here and give me a hug. I'm your big brother. Back from the war!"

"No, you're not." She walked over ladylike.

"Yes, I am." I stood up, grabbed her, and swung her around. Mom opened the basement door, and Queenie came charging out, knocking us down. The three of us rolled around—shrieking, barking, and yelling—our trademark. Mom shooed us out to the porch, and we ended up on the swing: Queenie on my right, her snoot on my leg; and Connie on my left, her hands in her lap. She did all the talking, telling me how wonderful Detroit was, especially the ballet. She was all hands and toes and big eyes, and then suddenly, she quit and huddled next to me. I put my arm around her.

"You're my favorite sister, you know."

"Well, you're not my favorite brother, you know." She peeked at me and started blubbering, then stopped just as suddenly as she had started. Her hankie appeared, and she used it.

"Gezz, kid, I thought you'd never stop."

"Mommy likes Mr. Frazin."

I hit it back. "So does Dad."

"I do, too," she whimpered.

We looked at each other and broke out laughing, but our faces were hurting. *The knife was back.*

"I'm afraid, Billy! Oh, I'm so afraaaaaaid." She snuggled under my arm and cried.

I took a deep breath and dug her out of my armpit. "Look! Look at me!" I shook her by her arms. "I'm not going to let anybody hurt you. Understand? Nobody. Ever!"

WE WERE SITTING at the table like we always did, eating like we always did, but dead quiet like we never did. Beef stew—one of my favorites—the other being cauliflower. Oh, and of course, corn on the cob. And there's probably one or two other things, like ice cream, and—*Stop it! Stop it, Billy! Stooooooop!* Oh, God… Sitting here at the table was probably the hardest thing I ever did in my whole life. Forget the haying. That was *outside* my head; this was *inside* my head, chopping me to pieces… So this is where life ends? At the table with strangers?

"Is good. Beef stew… Huh, William."

"Yeah, Dad." I looked across the table. "Good, Mom."

"Tomorrow, we eat corn on the cob…from garden…*my family*," Dad said, chewing away. "Carrots, onions, beets—*Uhhhh*, sweet corn!" He bowed his head and stopped eating. "Anna," he looked up and licked his lips. "Anna, my mother…one time, one time at wedding… Leo and George grab a man and throw 'im out da door.

Throw 'im!" said my dad with a big sweep of his arms. "He don't touch da steps!" He chuckled and moved the stew around on his plate. "Dis man...from da bride's side, not our side. Ya... So everybody eating...at long table...and this man—" Dad forks in a piece of potato, chews... "Dis man, he wants 'a know bout Andrew. His back. Uh? Uh, William?"

"Uh-huh." I stopped eating.

"Anna!" he said, loud. "Anna, your husband born with dat *hump*?

Everybody watching, Anna—food on da fork. "Hump?" she said. "What hump?" She puts fork in da mouth and *eats*! Dad slapped a hand down on his knee and chuckled.

"And then Uncle Leo and Uncle George threw him out, huh?"

"Yeeeeep!" said my dad, repeating the big sweep with his arms.

"Oh, wow! I bet Grandpa felt good, huh?"

"Proud," he said, nodding, and his gray-green eyes held me in a vise.

So HOW DO I TELL you what happened? How can I when I don't really know? When it's beyond words. When it's all hurt. And the hurt keeps growing and growing... And truth keeps knocking and knocking, and you won't let it in, can't let it in, die before you let it in. So everybody talks, but the talk is all noise; it says nothing. So you pray that the truth will stay buried, or that if it comes alive, you can change it, twist it, bite it...spit it out. "Oh please, God. Pleeeease."

So there was a lot of talking, but nobody was exactly talking to anybody else; they were just talking, and then there was none. So I started talking to fill the emptiness, to stop the quiet—which was worse than the talking.

"Grandma's got good land, you know, Dad. Good delta. If you plant a seed and p—and pee on it, you have jump back so it won't knock you over." I laughed, but nobody else did.

"Is good land," said my dad, wiping his plate clean with a piece of bread.

So I went on talking, couldn't stop. "So first thing every morning I had to swordfight to get some food, you wouldn't believe."

"You what?" Connie said.

"Yeah, right." I forked a green pea into my mouth. "Oh, and then I had to go into the garden and feed the mosquitoes my blood in exchange for some strawberries. And then—" I held up my hand to stop my sister from breaking in. "Then I had to knock thousands of potato bugs into a can, pour kerosene in, and light it. *Pow!*" I popped my hands together. "The flame shoots up, and you can hear them frying like Rice Krispies: poppin' and crackin'."

"Uuuugg..." said Connie through a mouthful of stew.

She ate like a horse, my sister.

"And then there was the milking. Every day, twice a day, forever. Yeah... My job was to shovel the manure down the troughs, all the way down, and into a wheelbarrow, and then dump it... I used to chase the cows out too. Out to the pasture across the creek. They don't have a dog. Queenie would'a been great up there."

"Aunt Sophie said you did good with the haying," said my mom, as she plopped another dipper of stew onto my plate—which I didn't really want. I was stuffed.

I played with the stew with my fork. "Yeah... The haying was hard work." I looked at my dad; he was sipping coffee and eying my plate. "We had a heat wave, you know. Boiling hot sun every day. In the nineties the whole time. Hot, sticky, itchy...sneezing. Hey, this you won't believe. The *haying* is what got me into medical history." I finally got their attention. "Yeah! No kidding! You're looking at the most allergic kid that's ever been. I'm number one. No kidding. They gave me this scratch test. See. How it works, they break these real skinny glass tubes in half, one at a time, hundreds of 'em. Then they scratch you with them. You should've seen my arms and my back."

"Oh my god, William," said my mom.

"Didn't you shoot any bears or anything?" Wise-puss, of course.

"Then in about ten minutes, the scratches start to swell up. See. The ones you're allergic to. They're supposed to swell up just a little, like a pimple. But mine kept growing and growing, and I had like *golf balls*. Yeah! And the doc, he said I had the biggest balls! HA-HA-HA-HA-HA!" I laughed so hard. I almost fell out of my chair.

"What's so funny?" Wise-puss, naturally.

"My god, Billy, we didn't know you were that sick. We—"

"Sick? I almost died! I had this big tent over me—it's an oxygen tent. But how was I supposed to know. I thought they were trying to suffocate me. Boy, I tell'ya, I was so scared. And I felt so alone. I can't tell you. And I was waiting and waiting for you to come, and all I could think—"

"But Aunt Minnie was there. She—"

I slammed my fists down on the table. "Aunt Minnie! Aunt Minnie! Yeeees! And I don't hardly even know her. And Aunt Polly. And Archie! Archie, the idiot!" I laughed like I was crazy!

Now they were looking at the knife.

"And the Fourth of July. Ohhhh, that was…" I shook my head. "That was—" I screamed. "The whole family was there! And it was, it was…*beautiful!* Oh I know, *I knoooow! The shop! The shop! Detroit!*" And I went flat like a balloon. "The hospital… Mom? Dad? I could have diiied. *And you never caaaaaaaaame!*"

Dad's mouth hung open; his eyes blinking… Mom raced around the table.

"*No!* Noooo." I kept slapping out at her. I wouldn't let her touch me.

"Aaaaaaaaagaa." Connie screamed and made for the door, but my dad caught her and wrapped his arms around her.

The knife dug deeper.

And all the while Queenie was barking her head off.

"*Quiet! Queenie!*" I screamed. She went quiet.

Connie went from my dad's arms to my mother's; her sobbing slicing the air.

Polka music from the carnival cut through kitchen door…

Dad hung his head, his fists on the table. "Is my fault… Everything."

"Nick—"

"No!" Dad slammed the table with his fists and stood tall. "I am da head of dis family… and I fail. Is my fault." He turned and left the room.

Mom put a hand over her mouth and turned away.

Connie looked lost. Then slowly and quietly she started stacking dishes in the sink. They started doing the dishes.

My head on an outstretched arm on the table I watched tears run off my nose. "Mom..." She didn't answer. "Mom! Who's Mr. Frazin?" She turned and looked at me, but didn't say anything. "Really, I mean? You know?..."

She dried her hands on he apron, sat at the table, and it poured out. "One day at work I ran a needle through my thumb... right through the nail." Mom flashed me her thumb. It was ugly, the nail all cracked up. "Mr. Frazin insisted on taking me to the doctor. And while we waited he started telling me about himself. How his family in Detroit were all Ford people. Right from the time the company was started. And that his mother was an opera star in her day, and that his sister was a chorus girl on Broadway, and that now she had a dancing school."

"Is that why you went to Detroit?"

"Well... partly. But what it did was... break the ice, you know. And then one day he told me why he left the Ford Company. He said his wife went to the hospital to have their first child and they... they cut the artery and she bled out... She was twenty-five years old." Mom shook her head. "So then he left the baby with his family and came to Chicago.

"Marie," said Connie. "She's six. Boy, can she dance."

"And then... after that... I don't know." Mom locked eyes with me. "*I don't know... I... I made a mistake.* I didn't know that a glimpse of another life could grab me and swallow me up so... Crying now, my Mom grabbed my sister, tried to kiss me on the cheek, and left the house.

Dad took me to the shop every day after that. The new location was at Mr. Mantel's place on Lake Street and Damen. We'd zoom up Fullerton Avenue, the brick road, making our teeth rattle. Then at Long Avenue, Dad would cut over past St. Stanislaus to Palmer Avenue, a smooth black-topped street that had dips at every block, which Dad didn't slow down for so I had another breakfast. My job was to paint the machines. It took me two days just to clean the grease out of an old broken down 100 Ton punch press that Melvyn bought at auction.

Nights I went to the carnival. I was very popular; I was the one with money in the pocket. We did our thing with the girls and the rides and stuff and you'd never know I was hurting.

The worst part of the day was coming home. We'd walk into the back door, and Mom and Connie would walk out the front door. It was a heck of a way to end the day, the food always salty with tears. And that's the way it went day after day until Labor Day. Mom was making Dad's favorite: roast duck. Connie and I were helping. Dad kept coming into the kitchen looking for this, looking for that, getting a glass of water, going through old newspapers, mumbling and grumbling. At last, Mom took the stuffed duck out of the oven, placed it on the stove, and took off the cover.

"Mmmmmm." If it smelled good before it now smelled supreme. My mouth was watering.

From out of nowhere, a fork stabbed the duck, and the hand that did the deed was quickly smacked with a dipper.

"Owwwwww!" yelled my Dad, rubbing his hand.

"Oh, Nick, I'm—"

They locked eyes. Nobody moved. I don't think anybody even took a breath. Then my Mom turned back to the stove, but my Dad caught her by the shoulders. "Stella."

She whirled around and fell into his arms, crying, crying hard.

"Stella…," Dad kept saying, hugging her, rocking her.

I dragged Connie out to the porch. We stood at the railing and watched the sun go down. She punched me playfully. Polka music shot out like a canon. Connie started whirling around the porch. Queenie and I sat on the swing and watched the sky cool down. I felt happy, but it was a sad kind of happy—it cost too much.

THE END

About the Author

Leonard D. Hodera served in US Army's missile program, wrote space rocket manuals, led to reporting for base newspaper. He was awarded acting scholarship while in service to the AADA in NYC, subsequently represented by William Morris Agency. He wrote scenes for the Actors Studio, which led to playwriting. *Stepping Stones* won the John Gassner Memorial Award in a national contest. It led to a series of produced plays at regional theaters. His latest play was the acclaimed *It's The Family, Stupid!* He sold screenplay *Alley 16* to Am-Euro Productions and had several screenplays optioned by Hollywood. Also, he did screen treatments for Sydney Pollack's films, *Tootsie* and *Presumed Innocent*. His latest work appeared in David Mamet's films: *Things Change* and *Homicide*. He has over two dozen short stories and articles published.